Joy, as dark and bright as hellfire, seared through the Crinti warriors' eyes. "It is time to fight?" Xibryl demanded eagerly.

Shanair shook her head. "Soon. We continue as planned. We loot and raid. We await Kiva. In time, the Crinti will emerge from the shadows, and all of Halruaa will be washed into a blood sea!"

Novels by
Elaine Cunningham

Songs and Swords

Elfshadow
Elfsong
Silver Shadows
Thornhold
The Dream Spheres

Starlight and Shadows

Daughter of the Drow
Tangled Webs

Counselors and Kings

The Magehound
The Floodgate
The Wizardwar
(March 2002)

Evermeet: Island of Elves

The Floodgate

Counselors and Kings • Book II

Elaine Cunningham

THE FLOODGATE

Distributed in the United States by St. Martin's Press. Distributed in Canada by Fenn Ltd.

Distributed to the hobby, toy, and comic trade in the United States and Canada by regional distributors.

Distributed worldwide by Wizards of the Coast, Inc. and regional distributors.

FORGOTTEN REALMS, D&D, and the Wizards of the Coast logo are registered trademarks owned by Wizards of the Coast, Inc.

All Wizards of the Coast characters, character names, and the distinctive likenesses thereof are trademarks owned by Wizards of the Coast, Inc.

Made in the U.S.A.

The sale of this book without its cover has not been authorized by the publisher. If you purchased this book without a cover, you should be aware that neither the author nor the publisher has received payment for this "stripped book."

Cover art by John Foster
First Printing: April 2001
Library of Congress Catalog Card Number: 00-190769

9 8 7 6 5 4 3 2 1

UK ISBN: 0-7869-2609-0
US ISBN: 0-7869-1818-7
620-T21818

U.S., CANADA,
ASIA, PACIFIC, & LATIN AMERICA
Wizards of the Coast, Inc.
P.O. Box 707
Renton, WA 98057-0707
+1-800-324-6496

EUROPEAN HEADQUARTERS
Wizards of the Coast, Belgium
P.B. 2031
2600 Berchem
Belgium
+32-70-23-32-77

Visit our web site at www.wizards.com

Dedication

To Mary Kirchoff, who shipped me off to Halruaa

Acknowledgments

This story owes a debt to Andrew, Sean, Brandon, Tycho, and Tyler: a party of adventurers whose first foray into role-playing reminded me what it was like to discover the worlds of D&D®.

Thanks are also due to editor Peter Archer, a man of considerable tact and patience, who, no doubt as proof that virtue never goes unpunished, got stuck with me once again. The Elizabethan Gardens on Roanoke Island, which combine semi-tropical decadence with imposed order, provided the seed that grew and mutated into the Halruaan landscape. In the art of M.C. Escher, everything transmutes into something else and nothing is as it seems—a perfect model for Halruaan architecture and, for that matter, Halruaan culture. The original and ongoing inspiration for any story set in the Realms is, of course, Ed "The Man Who Needs No Introduction" Greenwood, who built this sandbox in which we all play. Thanks to the collective Wizards of the Coast, who provide a place where tales can be told and adventures begun.

And finally, thanks to Andrew for that truly twisted spell combination in the necromancer's battle. Your mother is very proud.

halruaa

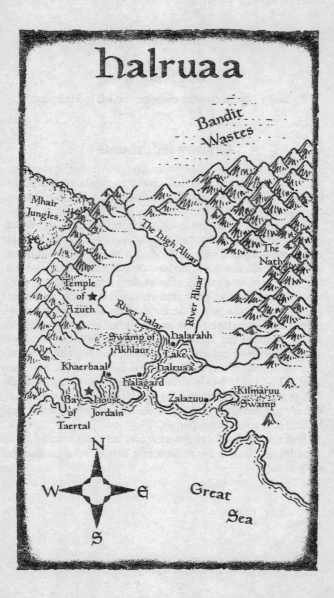

Bandit
Wastes

Mhair
Jungles

The high Aluar

The
Nath

River Aluar

Temple
of
Azuth

River halar

Swamp of
Akhlaur

halarahh

Lake
halaruaa

Khaerbaal

halagard

Kilmaruu
Swamp

Bay
of
Taertal

house of
Jordain

Zalazuu

N

W   E

S

Great

Sea

PRELUDE

The battle had turned against the laraken. The monster knew this, its enemies did not. They continued to fight with the frenzy peculiar to brave men who wish to die well.

Men had come into the Swamp of Akhlaur before, but these warriors were armed not with enchantments but with wicked swords and pikes and arrows. With them was a strangely familiar elf woman who was neither food nor foe.

The laraken advanced, shrieking like the demon it resembled and paying little heed to the arrows and spears that bristled its hide. Its taloned feet crushed the fallen humans. A casual kick tossed aside the body of the wemic—the mighty lion-centaur who had died protecting the elf woman. The battered corpse thumped and skidded along the sodden ground, splattering the surviving warriors with fetid water before coming to rest amid the lurching roots of a bilboa tree.

Still the laraken came, charging into the humans' ranks—and away from its source of life-giving magic. The monster's shrieks had less to do with battle lust than with mind-numbing hunger. Greenish ichor leaked from countless wounds, but starvation, not the humans' weapons, would be the laraken's death.

Its only nourishment was the elf woman's

spells and the tiny draught of life-magic offered by the tall, red-haired warrior. The laraken greedily drained this scant sustenance, leaving the human as translucent as a dewdrop. Yet the man lived, and fought on!

So did his comrades, and none fought more fiercely than the dark-hawk human who clung to the laraken's back like a tick, slashing until the monster screamed with rage and pain.

The laraken's most formidable foe was the small female, a human whose eyes were dark pools of magic and whose voice could not be ignored. Her song lured the laraken onward, when every instinct urged it to flee back to the trickle of liquid magic that was its main sustenance.

She Who Called perched in a tall tree, far above the battle. The magical song pouring from her filled the laraken with exquisite longing, both courting and mocking its hunger. Frustration slowly gave way to fear: the laraken remembered the long-ago wizard whose magic could not be eaten.

A flash of silver darted toward the laraken's eye and exploded into a burst of liquid agony. The laraken screamed and clamped its upper pair of hands against its ruined eye. Its lower arms flailed wildly as it raked at the warrior who had blinded it. Talons found human flesh. At last the man released his hold and rolled down the laraken's back.

Gripped by a desperate, mindless rush for survival, the laraken broke free of the singer's grip and hurtled toward the pool. The elf woman shouted a strange word and tossed something into the bubbling spill of magic. In an instant, the bubbles grew into iridescent, man-sized domes, which burst into sprays of life-giving droplets. As instinctively as a creature aflame, the laraken threw itself at the water.

Immediately the monster was seized by a liquid storm that dwarfed the fury of battle. The laraken fell—or perhaps flew—through the whirling white terror. Its battered senses registered the bruising tumble, the roar of the water, and the thunderous, hollow thud of the magical gate slamming shut.

And then, silence.

Dazed and disoriented, the laraken gave itself over to the water. It drifted, vaguely aware of the tingle of energy that whispered against its scaled hide and sank deep into bone and sinew.

After a time the laraken began to take note of its new surroundings. Water was everywhere, but not like the water in its home swamp. This was liquid magic—less dense than mundane water, more alive than air. The laraken could breathe this water, and each breath brought renewed strength.

The monster moved forward cautiously, speeding its way with swimming motions of its four webbed hands. It did not marvel at the beauty of the coral palaces or undulating sea forests as lush and colorful as a jungle. It paid no heed to the intricately carved arch framing the place where the magical gate lurked, just beyond sight and sense. The eel-like appendages that surrounded the laraken's demon face stirred. Reptilian eyes snapped open and took focus, jaws yawned wide, and fangs extended like unsheathed claws. The eels began to writhe about, snapping at a passing school of tiny, jewel-colored fish.

An overwhelming stench of magic engulfed the laraken, an acrid, gut-clenching odor that the monster instinctively recognized as danger. The laraken spun, snarling, to face the unknown threat.

A white blur swept in with preternatural speed. The laraken's first perception was vast size, and the yawn of a huge, hideous gate. In a heartbeat the laraken recognized that the "gate" was actually the jaws of a gigantic shark, easily wide enough to engulf its twelve-foot prey. Wedge-shaped teeth lined the jaws in multiple rows. Beyond was bone, and nothing more.

Instinct prompted the laraken to flee, but it sensed the futility of this course. Instead, the laraken leaped directly *into* the tooth-and-bone gate, diving powerfully for the open water beyond those empty white ribs.

The skeletal shark's bones folded around its prey. Cartilage creaked as the ribs clattered together and laced like tightly entwined fingers. The laraken's head slammed into the narrow end of the basket weave of bones, abruptly cutting off its dive to safety. Two interlocking ribs sheered off one of the laraken's eel appendages. The disembodied head tumbled free through the roiling waters. A passing fish snapped it up and darted triumphantly away.

The laraken hooked its foot talons on the shark's spine and swung upside down to grasp a pair of locked ribs with all four hands. Bracing its feet, the laraken threw its strength into wrenching the bars of its cage apart. The shark's flexible cartilage buckled, but would neither break nor give way. Frantic now, the laraken flung itself from one side of its prison to another until it was battered and bleeding. The skeletal shark merely kept swimming, long past the lure of blood.

The laraken threw back its hideous head and shrieked like a demon new to damnation. Its cries sent bubbles jetting out to mingle with the thrashing currents.

Through the sound of churning water and its own roaring protests, a new note began to play at the edges of the monster's consciousness, a magic more focused and pungent than that of the water. Instinctively the laraken reached for it but found no sustenance. The elusive magic smelled a bit like the elf woman's life-force, only stronger.

Stronger, and suddenly familiar.

Abject terror seized the laraken. Abandoning any hope of escape, it cowered into the farthest depths of its skeletal cage and began to shriek mindlessly, like a baby monkey that clings to a tree limb and awaits the jaws of a jungle cat.

The laraken saw the wizard, and its scream choked off into a strangled whimper. In profound silence the monster waited—and hoped—for death.

Akhlaur stalked toward the skeletal shark, moving as easily through the magical water as he had once walked beneath Halruaa's sky. The necromancer's magic had sustained his life through his long exile, yet two hundred years in the Elemental Plane of Water had profoundly changed him. He was still a powerful man, tall and lank, with fine black eyes and strong, well-formed features. Now tiny scales covered his skin, and gills shaped like twin lightning bolts slashed the sides of his neck. The fingers holding the wizard's staff were long and webbed, the skin faintly green in hue.

The wizard had not just survived but prospered. His servants supplied him with robes of fine green sea linen, embroidered with runes made with black seed pearls. His necromantic artistry was much in evidence. The staff he carried was not wood, but a living eel locked into a fierce, rigid pose. Small spats of lightning sizzled from the creature's fixed snarl and sent light shimmering across the wizard's bald green head.

Akhlaur reached out with his eel staff and stroked the shark's skull between its empty, glowing eyes.

"What have you brought me, my pet?" he inquired in a whispery tone.

Blue lightning sizzled from the eel into the undead shark. The bony cage flared with sudden light, prompting a thunderous, agonized shriek from the shark's latest captive. An explosion of bubbles and a long, wavering cry spiraled out into the water.

Akhlaur, intrigued but not impressed, leaned in for a better look. His eyes widened in sudden recognition. "By curse and current! I know this beast!"

The wizard's gills flared with excitement as he considered the implications of this latest capture. This was the laraken, the spawn of water demons and elven magic! It was his own creation, and a link to his homeland. If the laraken had found a way into the Elemental Plane of Water, then perhaps at long last he, Akhlaur, could find a way *out!*

"How did you come to be here?" the wizard demanded, "and what have you brought me this time?" He leaned his staff against a coral obelisk and began to gesture with both hands, easily tracing a spell he had not cast in two centuries.

In response, magic seeped from the monster like blood from a killing wound. The laraken clutched its bony cage for support as the wizard drained it to some minutely defined point just short of death.

Akhlaur savored the stolen spells as a gourmand might consider a sip of wine. "Interesting. Most interesting," he mused. "A blend of all the magical schools, with some Azuthan overtones. Definitely these are Halruaan spells, but the chant inflections are slightly off, as if the wizard were not a native speaker. The accent is that of . . . an elf?"

The wizard considered. Yes, the laraken's prey had definitely been an elf, probably female. The influence of Azuthan training flavored the spells—to Akhlaur's particular palate, the taint of clerical magic was as cloyingly unpleasant as sugar in a stew.

He snorted, sending a rift of bubbles rising. "Halruaa is in a sorry state indeed. Elf wenches and Azuthan priests!"

Yet the prospect did not displease him. He had slain hundreds of elves, outwitted and overpowered scores of priests. He could easily overcome such foes.

Or so he could, if only he could win free of this place!

By some odd quirk of fate, Akhlaur, the greatest necromancer of his time, had been exiled from the land he was destined to rule. For over two hundred years his every attempt to wrest free of this prison had fallen short. How, then, had some lesser wizard opened the gate wide enough to admit the laraken?

This should have been impossible. Any wizard who came near the laraken should have been destroyed, his magic and then his life drained away by the monster's voracious need. Akhlaur was invulnerable, of course, but he had created the monster, painstakingly fashioning the channels that made the laraken a conduit through which stolen magic flowed. This was one of Akhlaur's finest achievements, the very height of the necromantic arts. Creating the laraken had taken many years. Several attempts had ended in failure when the growing spawn destroyed its female host. Not until Akhlaur had thought to forge a death-bond with the green elf wench he'd nicknamed Kiva—

His thought pattern broke off abruptly, stumbling over a startling notion.

"No," he muttered. "It is not possible!"

But it *was* possible. Kiva had witnessed many of his most carefully guarded experiments. She had clung to life when thousands of others had yielded to pain and despair. She had even survived the laraken's birth—barely, but she had survived. Akhlaur hadn't wasted much thought on her. Who would have foreseen that a scrawny elf wench could not only survive but learn?

"It would seem," Akhlaur mused, "that I have acquired an unexpected apprentice."

He nodded, accepting this explanation. Apparently Kiva's resistance to the laraken had outlived the punishing birth. She was able to venture near enough to open the gate and let the monster through, even though that meant losing her wizardly spells to the monster's hunger.

Why would she do this?

Akhlaur studied the creature huddled within the undead shark. What had prompted Kiva to risk herself to send the laraken here? Not maternal warmth, surely! Elves could barely abide the notion of mixing their blood with humans, much less water demons. The only possible motive Akhlaur could fathom was vengeance.

Yet surely Kiva understood the laraken could not kill its creator. Perhaps she sent the monster not as an assassin but as her herald.

Yes, Akhlaur decided. This was the answer. His little Kiva had sent him a message.

The wizard glanced at the coral obelisk, where neat

runes marked the passing of each moon tide. The lunar rhythm echoed through the miniscule opening that mocked his captivity, and the obelisk pointed the way home like the very finger of the goddess. Soon, when the moon was full and the path between the worlds shortest and surest, a vengeful and astonishingly powerful Kiva would come to repay him with his own coin.

"Come, then, little elf," he crooned, gazing past to the obelisk toward the invisible gate. "Come, and learn the full truth of the death-bond we forged."

To Lady Mystra

Great Lady, we have not spoken before—at least, not in any words I have fashioned or perceived. I am Matteo, counselor to Queen Beatrix of Halruaa. This summer marks my second year as a jordain in the service of truth, Halruaa, and the wizard-lords who rule. I have always known that you watch over this land. It seems strange, now that I think on it, that this is the first prayer I have ever offered.

You see, we jordaini are taught to revere the Lady of Magic, and to respect Azuth, the Patron of Wizards—but always from a respectful distance. We are untouched by your Art, and possess a strong resistance to its power. We are trained to stand apart from the flow of Halruaan life, observing and advising.

But never doing!

Please, forgive this outburst. It was not only unseemly but also inaccurate. I have done many things since last spring and in the doing have wandered far from my first vision of jordaini service. What I am, what I should be, is no longer as clear to me as it once was.

It is that very uncertainty that brings me to you. I have vowed to serve no master above truth, but how is one man to measure truth? Once I trusted in the wizard-lords, the jordaini order, the clerics and magehounds, the laws of Halruaa, the lore and sciences I have committed to memory. These are all fine things, but I cannot blindly follow any or all of them. And yet, what single mortal is wise enough to fashion his own path? What pattern should I see in the strange turns my life has taken?

Since leaving the Jordaini College, I have been counselor to Procopio Septus, the Lord Mayor of Halarahh, and now to Queen Beatrix. I have learned that great wizards are flawed and fallible. I have mourned the "death" of Andris, my oldest friend, then reunited only to watch helplessly as he was stripped of all but the shadow of life. I expected to counsel wizards on battle strategy but not to test skill and courage in actual combat. Yet I have fought alongside my jordaini brothers, many of whom who were stolen from their lives by the false magehound Kiva. We defeated a dark and ancient evil, and we delivered Kiva to the stern judgment of Azuth's clergy. Yet perhaps the most profound change has been wrought by my friendship with the street waif known as Tzigone.

I suspect that Tzigone, like me, has not been lavish in her prayers. Life has given her little reason to bless the wizards of Halruaa or—forgive me—their goddess. Yet Tzigone is like a gypsy lark, blithe and merry and full of song, despite an inner darkness profound enough to shroud her early memories. She seeks answers to the mysteries of her past and the truth of a mother she barely remembers. I suppose that Tzigone, like me, seeks to know who she truly is.

Her truth, my truth—I suspect that they are somehow linked. This belief defies logic and cannot be explained by my jordaini learning. Yet I know this to be so. My own heart is a stranger to me, but I perceive that it has its own logic and its own wisdom.

This vision, however, is young and far from clear. For the first time, great Lady, I recognize my need of you. Help me honor my oaths yet not betray my heart. Teach me to recognize truth when I see it, to know when to speak and when to honorably keep silent. These are not easy requests, and as I voice them, I suspect that you do not regret overmuch my previous silence! Nor am I fully at ease with the notion that a man can find his own way, guided only by the truth in his heart and the voice of a goddess.

Perhaps we will become more reconciled to each other as the days go by.

CHAPTER ONE

Sunlight beat down upon the hard-packed ground of the Jordaini College training field. A light breeze blew off the Bay of Taertal, bearing the tang of salt but no relief from the summer sun. Heat rose from the ground in shimmering waves, and sweat glistened on the bared chests of the two fighters who faced each other with drawn swords and fierce grins.

Matteo lunged suddenly, his blade diving low—an attack that, if successful, could hamstring a man and end a fight quickly. Andris easily blocked, then spun away. He came back with a flurry of short jabs, feinting high and low in a pattern too complex to predict. Matteo met each attack, enjoying the sharp clattering ring of steel upon steel as a sage might relish good conversation. It was all so familiar that for a few moments he could almost forget the changes this year had brought.

Yet, how could he?

Once Andris's hair had been a rich auburn, his eyes hazel green, and his fair skin speckled by the sun. He used to jest that he'd be a fine hue, if only his freckles would have the courtesy to blend one into another. Now all these odd colors were but ghostly shadows. Even the sword in his hand was more like glass than metal. Andris was no more substantial than a man-shaped rainbow.

As if to disprove Matteo's dismal thoughts, Andris pressed the attack. He came on hard, delivering a series of blows with real weight and power behind them. The two men moved together in a circle, exchanging blows in a rapid, ringing dialogue. As they fell into the new rhythm, Matteo noted that the morning was nearly spent—the sun was edging toward the dome that crowned the Disputation Hall. Both building and sunlight were clearly visible through the filter of Andris's translucent form.

Matteo jerked his wandering thoughts back into line and spun away from a high, down-slashing blow. Holding his sword over his shoulder at a declining angle, he caught the attack in a deflecting parry. As Andris's blade scraped along the length of the sword, Matteo shifted onto his forward foot to remove himself beyond reach of a possible counter. He whirled back, twisting his forearm as he went to position his weapon for a lunging attack.

A sudden burst of light assailed him. Instantly Matteo realized what Andris had done. He'd presented Matteo with a classic opportunity for a deflecting parry. In the moment while Matteo was turned aside, Andris had used his translucent sword like a prism to catch the morning sun and dart it directly into his opponent's face.

Matteo danced back a few steps, blinking to dispel the dark spots dancing before his eyes. He was not quite quick enough. The flat of Andris's blade smacked his hip. Matteo lowered his sword and backed away, rubbing at the offended spot.

"A good trick," he admitted.

"I've a better one," Andris said slyly.

The ghostly jordain came in again with fast, feinting attacks. While his sword kept Matteo fully engaged, Andris pulled a companion dagger from his belt. This he held high, adjusting his movements so that whatever the rest of his body might be doing, the dagger stayed at the same angle relative to the sun. Sunlight poured through the sheer metal of Andris's dagger and concentrated into a thin beam. The thread of light seared the packed ground. Smoke began to rise from a blackened, spreading circle.

Such a weapon in any other hands could be death. Matteo had no fear of his friend, but he fought fiercely to solve the puzzle Andris presented. For many moments they battled toe to toe. It was all Matteo could do to meet each of his opponent's attacks. There was no chance to counter, much less to maneuver Andris out of position and break the dagger's focus.

Suddenly Andris shifted the dagger slightly. The line of red light split into two beams, one of which leaped up to nip keenly at Matteo's arm.

Matteo yelped with surprise and jumped back. He quickly recovered and came in hard, catching the tall jordain's lunging sword under his and bearing it down to the ground. He leaned forward, using his weight to drive the point of his sword into the dirt, pinning Andris's weapon beneath it. With his free hand he seized the wrist of Andris's dagger hand. Andris might be nearly a head taller, but Matteo outmatched him in mass and muscle. With a quick twist, he relieved the taller man of his dagger. Another twist brought Andris stumbling to one knee.

"You're mine," Matteo said triumphantly.

"I think not." The tall jordain gazed pointedly at Matteo's arm.

Matteo glanced down, and his lips twisted in a wry smile. The dagger-captured sunlight had burned a rune onto his skin—the rune for Andris's name.

"It would appear that I am branded," he admitted. He slid his sword into its scabbard and then tugged Andris to his feet, congratulating him with a hearty slap on the back. "And since the rothé cow is butchered and not the farmer, my claim to victory rings false! You have grown devious."

The comment was meant in sincere admiration, but Andris's sly grin dropped off his face so abruptly that Matteo expected to hear it shatter on the hard-packed ground.

"Better a devious mind than arrogant certainty," he said.

"We jordaini wish to believe that everything is simple and nothing is beyond grasp."

The bleak expression in Andris's translucent hazel eyes surprised Matteo. "Many strange events have happened of late," he agreed, "but at the heart of things, our goals are much as they ever were."

The tall jordain shrugged. "Perhaps."

Matteo's sense of unease deepened. Hearing his own doubts spoken in another man's voice lent them shape and substance. On the other hand, why should they not speak openly? Perhaps between the two of them, they might find some resolution.

"Tell me what has changed," Matteo invited.

Andris tossed his sun-heated dagger into a trough of water and watched the steam rise and dissipate before he spoke his mind.

"You know that I have elf blood."

Matteo blinked, surprised by this unexpected turn. "Yes. So?"

"So that changes everything. I don't mean the obvious thing," Andris clarified, gesturing toward his crystalline form. "My life's path would be different even if my appearance had not changed in the Swamp of Akhlaur."

They fell silent, remembering that terrible place.

Matteo spoke first. "Why should a distant elf heritage define your path?"

"Heritage is a powerful thing. Have you never wondered why jordaini are forbidden to seek the knowledge of our parents?"

A disturbing image flashed into Matteo's thoughts: the memory of a small, forlorn woman trapped in the prison of her mind. If Tzigone had—for once—told the unadorned truth, this sad woman was his birthmother. By some odd twist of fate, Tzigone had found Matteo's mother during a desperate search for her own. Matteo did not understand her passionate need for family, but he recognized the same emotion in Andris's ghostly eyes.

"The jordaini order has its reasons," Matteo said, trying not to dwell on Tzigone's hints concerning the identity of his *other* parent. "So you have elf blood. Now that you know this, are you a different man than you were before?"

Andris spun away and strode to the neat pile of gear he'd left at the edge of the field. He stooped over a leather bag and took from it a small, sparkling object.

"Knowledge brings responsibility," he said as he held out his open hand.

In it lay an exquisite statue, a tiny winged sprite no longer than his palm. It appeared to be fashioned from crystal and was as perfect in every detail as a living creature— as indeed it once had been. Matteo marveled that Andris could hold it. In the Swamp of Akhlaur Matteo had accidentally bumped a crystalline elf, and found that it was not solid glass, but an elf-shaped void far colder than ice.

He placed a hand on his friend's translucent shoulder. "The elves in Akhlaur's Swamp and the sprite whose image you carry were freed by death, long before your birth. There is nothing more to be done. It is you who concern me, my friend. After the Azuthan priests do what they can, you must put this behind you and take up your duties as a jordain."

Andris shrugged and turned away, but not before Matteo glimpsed a world of turmoil in his eyes.

"You are dreading this inquisition," he observed.

"Wouldn't you?" his friend retorted. He was silent for several moments as he tucked the tiny crystalline sprite away, then he stood and faced Matteo. "You know clerics. They will test and talk and poke and pray until even Mystra herself tires of it all. They might eventually add to their understanding of magic, but they won't answer the important questions: Why did I survive? Why did Kiva? She's an elf. Why wasn't she swallowed in a crystal void like all the others?"

"Perhaps Kiva could answer that."

Andris's eyes lit up. "She has revived?"

"Not at last word," Matteo said. "The magehounds who tested her say that much of her strength was lost along with her magical spells. It seems that life and magic are more intrinsically bound in elves than in humans. They say it's a marvel she survived."

An impatient sigh hissed from between Andris's teeth. "The temple hosts more clerics than a bugbear has ticks. None of them could heal her?"

"I asked the same question." Matteo shook his head in disgust. "Kiva holds knowledge vital to all of Halruaa. Yet the clerics maintain that praying for healing spells to benefit a traitor would be sacrilege."

Andris muttered something unintelligible. He strode over to retrieve his white tunic, which he slid over his head. The fine linen turned translucent as it settled over his torso. The jordain stooped again to pick up a water gourd. He uncorked it and drank deeply. Matteo half expected to see the passage of water down his friend's insubstantial throat, but the water disappeared as soon as it touched the jordain's lips.

Andris caught him watching and lowered the gourd self-consciously. Instantly Matteo averted his eyes.

"Forgive me. I did not mean to stare."

"No magic, no penalty," he said flippantly, dismissing Matteo's apology with a catchphrase common to jordaini lads. "So what will you do now? Return to the queen's palace?"

Matteo shook his head. "It seems to me that Queen Beatrix has less need of my counsel than Halruaa does of my active service. Kiva did not close the gate to the Plane of Water but merely moved it. This new location must be found. I have also pledged to help Tzigone find her mother, or at least to learn of her fate."

"I don't envy you your first task, but the second should be easy enough. Kiva described Keturah as a master of evocation magic. Such wizards are well known. All you need do is ask."

"It's more complicated than that," Matteo admitted. "Questions could draw unwanted, even dangerous attention to Tzigone. No one else can know that she is Keturah's daughter. I must have your word that you will never speak of it."

Light broke on Andris's face, swiftly replaced by horror. "Lord and lady! Matteo, you don't mean to tell me that Tzigone is a wizard's bastard?"

"No, I didn't mean to tell you," Matteo retorted, "but there it is."

Andris raked a hand through his faintly auburn hair and blew out a long breath. "You keep interesting company, my friend. Does anyone else know?"

"Other than Kiva, I think not." He told Andris about the note Kiva had forged, a letter purporting to be from Cassia, the king's jordain counselor, asking all jordaini in the city of Halarahh to aid in the search for Keturah's daughter. "At first I thought this news was widespread, but Kiva meant it only for Tzigone's eyes and mine. She meant to lure us both to Cassia's chamber, and from there to the Swamp of Akhlaur, by dangling Tzigone's heritage before her like a carrot hung before a hungry mule."

"What carrot did *you* follow?" Andris asked, his ghostly hazel eyes suddenly shrewd and concerned. "The girl herself?"

The question was not unreasonable, and Matteo considered it carefully before answering. Yet he could find no words to explain his friendship with Tzigone. "I suppose so," he admitted.

Andris scowled. "You know, of course, that jordaini are forbidden to marry."

The image of Tzigone, her urchin's grin replaced by a prim smile and her eyes demure under a maiden's veil, was so ludicrous that Matteo burst out laughing.

"That has never entered my mind, and I would wager a queen's dowry that it never entered hers! Tzigone is a friend, nothing more."

Andris looked unaccountably relieved. "She will be a wizard one day. The jordaini are supposed to serve Halruaa's wizards, not befriend them."

A young student jogged toward them, saving Matteo from acknowledging this disturbing truth. The boy's gaze touched upon Andris and slid away.

"Andris has permission to depart the college," he announced, "and the headmaster wishes to see Matteo."

"I'll come directly," Matteo assured the boy. He waited until the messenger was beyond earshot before continuing. "It's unfortunate the college's wizards couldn't test you, and save you the trip north."

Andris grimaced. "One of the hazards of being a jordain. Only the magehounds' magic has much effect on us. An important safeguard, of course."

Matteo did not comment on the obvious irony: Andris had been condemned as a rogue jordain—falsely condemned—by a magehound from the Azuthan order. Once again, his life was in their hands.

He could not leave his friend to face this ordeal alone. "When do you leave?"

Andris turned away and began to collect his gear. "Tomorrow morning will be soon enough."

"I'll ride with you." When Andris glanced back inquiringly, Matteo added, "When Kiva revives, I have questions for her that I'd rather not entrust to a magehound."

"A compelling argument." Andris rose and placed a translucent hand on Matteo's shoulder. "You'd better see what the headmaster wants. The rest will wait patiently until tomorrow; Ferris Grail will not."

Matteo snickered at his friend's all-too-apt jest, then set a brisk pace for the headmaster's tower.

The ghostly jordain watched him go. With a sigh, he shouldered his gear and walked across the blazing soil to the guest quarters. It seemed odd to be a guest in the only home he'd ever known. On the other hand, after just a few months away, his life at the Jordaini College seemed like a distant dream.

Andris was not looking forward to the coming inquisition, but despite his experience with Kiva, he did not believe all magehounds were false and corrupt. No doubt the Azuthans had vigorously scoured their ranks in the aftermath of Kiva's treachery. The inquisition would not be pleasant, but it would end. And then what? A return to the jordaini order? Service to a wizard too insignificant to sneer at the jordain's translucent form and dubious fame?

An image came unbidden to mind: Kiva's rapt and joyous face as she shattered the crystal globe retrieved from the Kilmaru Swamp, freeing the spirits of long-dead elves trapped by the evil Akhlaur.

That image, Andris decided, *mattered*.

He had followed Kiva at first because he had believed she spoke for King Zalathorm. That fancy swiftly faded, but other reasons followed, reasons powerful enough to keep him at the elf woman's side.

According to everything Andris knew and believed, according to the laws of the land and the decree of the Council of Elders, Kiva was a traitor to Halruaa. Was it possible that she followed some deeper, hidden truth? Was her cause worthy, even if the pathways she took toward it were sometimes twisted and dark?

Deep in thought, Andris pushed open the door to the guest chamber. He was greeted by a raucous little squawk and the flutter of bright wings.

His lips curved as he noted the parrot perched on the windowsill. No bigger than Andris's fist, it was feathered in an almost floral pattern of pink and yellow. The bird stood tamely as the jordain edged forward. Its bright head tipped to one side, lending it a curious mien.

"Greetings, little fellow," Andris said. "I suppose you're a wandering pet. Congratulations on your escape. Never will I understand the impulse to cage birds for the sake of their songs!"

"I quite agree," the bird said in a clear, approving tone. "Fortunately, this enlightened opinion seems to be common hereabouts. I come and go as I like."

Andris fell back a step. Many of Halruaa's birds could chatter like small, feathered echoes. Even sentient birds were not all that rare. He'd just never expected anyone at the Jordaini College might keep such a retainer.

"This is an unexpected pleasure, my small friend. Might I ask what brings you here?"

The bird sidled several steps closer. Its head craned this way and that, as if to reassure itself that no one might overhear. "A message."

"A message? From whom?"

"Just read the books."

"The books?" Andris said blankly.

Pink and yellow wings rustled impatiently. "Hidden under the mattress. Read them, put them back."

The bird was gone. It didn't fly away; it was simply . . . gone.

Consternation filled Andris. This was a wizard's work, and serious work at that! Stern laws forbade the jordaini to use magic, or to have any magic used on their behalf. A blink bird might be either a natural beast or a conjured image, but both were forbidden.

That knowledge didn't stop him from looking under the mattress. He picked up an ancient tome bound in thin, yellowed leather. The pages within were fine parchments aged to pale sepia and covered with faded writing. Andris took the book over to the window and began to read.

With each page he turned, he crept farther from the window, as if he could distance himself from the horrors revealed. He held in his hands the journal of Akhlaur! The deathwizard's own hand had written these runes, turned these pages.

Andris's skin crawled. His sick feeling intensified as he considered the book's bindings. No animal yielded leather so thin and delicate. The skin had once been human, or more likely, elf.

Suspicion passed into certainty as he read on. Precise

little runes and neat, detailed drawings related with matter-of-fact detachment atrocities beyond Andris's darkest dreams. Elves had been the necromancer's favorite test subjects, and none had endured so much as the girl-child Akivaria, more conveniently known as Kiva.

Andris felt like a man gripped by the mosquito fever—burning with wrath, yet racked with numbing indecision. This book held secrets that could destroy the jordaini order if they became known. Now, he knew.

As he had told Matteo, with knowledge comes responsibility.

With shaking hands, Andris took up the second book, which proved to be a detailed genealogy of the early jordaini order. As he read, he prayed that Matteo's friend Tzigone did not know the details of his elf heritage, or realize that one of his forebears was still alive and currently a "guest" of the Azuthan temple.

He exploded into motion, snatching up his few belongings and stuffing them into his travel bag. After a moment's hesitation, he added the books to his gear.

His eyes stung with unshed tears as he slipped away, using the route that his friend Themo employed for clandestine trips to the port of Khaerbaal. No one noticed the shadowy figure leave. For the first time, Andris was grateful the jordaini had become so adept at averting their eyes. He could move among them as if he were indeed a ghost.

So he was, by any measure that mattered. His future was gone, snatched away by the lingering madness of the wizard Akhlaur and by the jordaini masters who had first suppressed this knowledge, then spilled it over him in one scalding enlightenment. The only life Andris knew was that of a jordain. His future was gone.

On swift and silent feet, Andris went to claim his past.

CHAPTER TWO

Matteo followed the jordaini lad who headed for the headmaster's tower like a hunting hound hard on a trail.

"I know the way," he pointed out. "If you've other duties to attend, don't let me keep you from them."

The boy shot an incredulous look over his shoulder. "Headmaster said to bring you." And that, as far as he was concerned, was the beginning and end of the matter.

Matteo sighed, envying the lad his certainty. Life had been simpler when the credo of jordaini service—truth, Halruaa, and the wizard-lords—were three seamless aspects of a sacred whole.

The headmaster's tower rose in a stately curve of white marble, resembling a slender stalk crowned by a budding lotus flower. The immense scale did not distort the sense of grace and serenity this blossom exuded. A lush garden surrounded the tower, and servants clad in simple green garments went about their tasks.

Despite the prohibitions on magic use, the wizard's tower did not look out of place. The jordaini were taught to know magic nearly as well as any wizard. Matteo could recognize hundreds of spells just from the gesture of a wizard's hand or from the combined scent of the spell components.

Having wizards for masters had always seemed normal and natural to him.

"Normal and natural," Matteo muttered, with more bitterness than he'd realized he harbored. But there was nothing natural about the image that haunted him daily—an aging woman with a wan face and vacant eyes. He did not know her name. He knew nothing about her, except that she had given him life.

Oddly enough, if Tzigone's hints proved true, his father's name was well known to him. Most likely he had heard it his whole life without knowing its significance.

Since his return to the Jordaini College, Matteo often found himself searching his former masters' faces in search of his own reflection. Of all the masters, Ferris Grail was most like him in appearance. This added an unsettling edge to the coming interview.

A green-robed servant admitted Matteo and led him to a small antechamber to await the headmaster's summons. Here Matteo sat, and when he could no longer sit, he paced. He had ample time for both, for the sun rose to its zenith and sank a distance more than three times its diameter before the servant appeared again. By then Matteo was quietly seething. Why would Ferris Grail call him to the tower and then keep him waiting?

He schooled his face to calm and entered the headmaster's study. Two wizards awaited him. Ferris Grail was a tall man in late middle life, thickly muscled and clad in the simple white garments of a jordain. He might have been mistaken for one of the warrior-scholars but for his neatly trimmed black beard and the gold talisman bearing his wizard's sigil. Had he been jordaini he would have gone clean-shaven, and worn a medallion enameled with the jordaini emblem: semicircles of green and yellow, divided by a lightning bolt of cobalt blue. The second wizard was older, wizened by the passage of time and the casting of powerful magic. Vishna, Matteo's favorite master, had been a battle wizard before he'd retired to teach at the Jordaini College.

Ferris Grail waved Matteo in. "There is a message for you," he said without preamble, gesturing to a moonstone globe mounted on a pedestal.

Matteo glanced at it, and his brow furrowed in consternation. Reflected in the globe was a woman's face, pale as porcelain and preternaturally serene. Her dark eyes were expressionless, skillfully painted with kohl, and enormous in her unnaturally white face. It was a beautiful face, framed by an elaborate wig of white and silver curls, upon which rested a silver crown.

"Queen Beatrix is waiting," urged the headmaster.

The young jordain shot him an incredulous look. Ferris Grail cleared his throat. "The queen knows the restriction upon her jordaini counselors. She would not summon you through magic if the need were not great. Service to Halruaa's wizards is the first rule you must follow."

Matteo was not certain of that, but upon reflection he decided there was no real harm in the scrying globe. Just that morning, he and Andris had practiced with swords rather than matched daggers, the traditional jordaini weapons. Truth was not flexible. The length of weapons and the means of communicating with one's patron were.

His conscience accepted this reasoning, yet Matteo's feet felt leaden as he moved before the globe and into his patron's line of vision.

Nothing in the queen's expression indicated recognition, but after a moment she said his name in an even, almost toneless voice. "I am ready for my walk upon the Promenade. You may come for me."

Matteo suppressed a sigh. "Your Majesty, you gave me leave to attend urgent business. I have been absent from the palace for a moon-cycle and more."

The queen's expression did not alter in the slightest. She did not appear chagrined to have forgotten, or peeved by Matteo's absence. "Is this business finished?"

The expansion of the Swamp of Akhlaur had been halted, the laraken driven away. Kiva was in the hands of the

Azuthan priests. The jordaini falsely condemned by Kiva and conscripted to fight in her personal army had been cleared of all wrongdoing. By any measure but his own, Matteo had met and surpassed his obligations as a counselor.

"It is not, my queen," he said at last. "There are matters yet to attend."

"Very well." She spoke as if his answer, or indeed his presence, was of no consequence to her. Her image winked out of the globe, leaving nothing but faintly glowing moonstone.

"Matters to attend?" demanded Ferris Grail. "What might these be?"

Matteo gave the older man a respectful bow. "Personal matters, my lord. If you have questions, please address them to my patron."

This was as close to falsehood as Matteo had ever come. He did not actually claim that he did the queen's business, but his words could be interpreted as such. Ferris Grail raised one black eyebrow into a skeptical arch.

Vishna leaped from his chair and seized Matteo's arm. "Well, then, you'd best be off," he said heartily. "You've lazed about here long enough."

Matteo allowed the old wizard to hustle him out of the tower. When they reached the courtyard, he disengaged himself from Vishna's grasp and inclined his head in a grateful bow. "That was kind of you. I had no wish to prolong that meeting."

Vishna sent him a wistful smile. "First listen to some advice, my son, then decide whether to thank me or not. You've many gifts, but lying isn't among them! If you're set upon learning this art, I'd suggest you'd practice before a mirror until you can school the guilt from your face!"

The wizard's tone was light and teasing, but Matteo could think of no response. What did one say when a trusted master spoke of competent falsehood as if it were a good and worthy goal?

As the silence stretched, Vishna studied the young

man's face with growing concern. "This unfinished business must be grave indeed."

"No more than that before any jordain," Matteo said shortly. "I seek truth."

"Ah." The old man's wry smile acknowledged the reproof. "The search for truth can take unexpected paths. Yours has put distance between you and the jordaini order."

The man's insight startled Matteo. "Why do you say that?"

"I have known you since you left the nursery to begin your studies. Never have I known you to give evasive answers. That speaks of faltering trust."

Matteo could not disagree. "If I offend, Master Vishna, I beg pardon."

"No need." The wizard patted his shoulder. "The wise man does not trust easily or speak freely."

"True, but suspicion wears at the soul, and so does silence. I miss the days when we could speak our minds plainly, without subtlety or hidden layers."

"A child's privilege, Matteo. You are no longer a child." Vishna's smile took any possible sting from the words. "But let us indulge each other. What wears away at my former student?"

This time, Matteo chose his words more carefully. "We jordaini are considered the guardians of Halruaan lore, yet there is much we haven't learned."

"Ah. I suppose you have something specific in mind."

"Several things. Why did we not learn the history of Halruaa's elves?"

"There are no elves to speak of," Vishna pointed out.

"Precisely. Yet there were once many elves in the Swamp of Akhlaur and in the Kilmaruu Swamp. It seems odd that two such places—neither of which are ancient swamplands—should develop on the graves of elf settlements."

Vishna gave him an indulgent smile and repeated the jordaini proverb about the Kilmaruu Swamp existing to keep the number of Halruaan fools down to manageable levels.

"Andris is no fool," Matteo stated, "and for that, Halruaa should bless Mystra. Haven't you noticed that Kilmaruu's undead rest easier?"

"Now that you mention it," the wizard said thoughtfully, "the farms and the coastlands bordering the swamp have been quiet of late. And this is Andris's doing, you say?"

"He prepared a battle strategy to rid the swamp of undead, and he presented it as his fifth-form thesis. I'm surprised you hadn't heard."

"Hmmm." The wizard considered this, his wrinkled face deeply troubled.

"The Jordaini College is less forthcoming with information than its reputation suggests," Matteo continued. "I have seen with my own eyes evidence that many elves once lived in Akhlaur's swamp. Why were we not taught this?"

Vishna spread his hands, palms up. "Such things are difficult to study. Where elves are concerned, there is always more legend than fact. You might as well to try to fathom the truth of the Cabal!"

His tone was light and teasing, as if he named the ultimate example of futility, but Matteo was in no mood to be humored or indulged. He folded his arms and returned the wizard's smile with a level gaze.

"Perhaps both studies have merit."

Vishna's smile faltered, and his eyes took on a shuttered expression.

"You do not agree," Matteo persisted.

"No. The elves are gone, but for a few here and there. That is the way of nature. Before their time, dragons ruled. Their numbers are greatly diminished, yet they would not take it kindly if you attempted to harvest their eggs with the purpose of tending them until they hatched. Likewise, the elves would not thank you for interfering in their lives, and they would not welcome you if you tried to inquire into their history."

"What of the Cabal? I've heard *of* it all my life, but we never learned anything *about* it."

"With good reason. The Cabal is a particular kind of legend," Vishna said slowly. "The sort that take shape over time, fashioned from whispers repeated so often that they begin to seem true."

"Some say it is a deeply hidden conspiracy."

Vishna snorted. "Conspiracies are useful things. They distract shallow, lazy minds from the labor of true thought. Such people see dire warnings as proof of wisdom. We've both met Halruaans who would regard a cheerful sage as a blasphemer, or at best, a charlatan."

"As the saying goes, never confuse a sour disposition with deep thought."

"Just so, lad." The wizard looked relieved by this return to familiar ground. "So when are you off on the queen's business?"

"Tomorrow morning, at first light," Matteo said. "I will ride with Andris to Azuth's temple."

The old wizard gave him a quizzical look. "But Andris has left already."

"*What?*"

His sharp tone startled Vishna. "It's true," he asserted, as if Matteo had challenged his veracity. "The headmaster's window commands a clear view of the back kitchen gate. I saw Andris slip away while I was in conference with the headmaster. Why is this so strange? He has permission to leave, and the Temple of Azuth is expecting him."

Matteo could not answer. He felt as if his throat was gripped in an iron golem's fist. He could accept that some of Halruaa's wizards kept dark secrets. He could fathom, just barely, that his beloved jordaini order might have had a part in keeping these secrets. That Andris, his dearest friend, could have told him a direct lie—this was beyond comprehension.

He spun on his heel. Vishna seized his arm. "Don't, Matteo," he said quietly. "For the sake of your friend, pause and reflect. I can't tell you why Andris went off alone, but this I know: You don't always need to understand your friends' choices, but you should honor them. Go back to Halarahh, and leave him to follow whatever destiny the goddess has given him."

Matteo gently pulled free. "Thank you for the lesson, Master Vishna," he said, speaking the traditional words between jordaini student and teacher. "Your words hold great wisdom, as usual."

Relief flooded the wizard's face. "Then you will return to court?"

"That is not the conclusion I drew from the lesson," the young man said softly. "What I heard you say was that it is not necessary to understand a man's choice but to honor it." With a quick bow, Matteo turned and sprinted for the stables.

He snatched up tack and travel kit at the door. "I'm taking Cyric," he announced to the startled groom. "I'll saddle him myself."

The lad's sigh of relief was almost comic. Cyric, a black stallion of uncommon speed and vile temper, had been named for an evil and insane god. The horse was nearly impossible to ride, but his temperament precisely suited Matteo's mood and purpose.

He set to work saddling and bridling the horse. Cyric must have sensed the jordain's urgency and found it to his liking. For once the stallion stood docile, and even opened his mouth to accept the bit and bridle. Matteo had barely settled into the saddle when Cyric shot out of the stable like a ballista bolt, thundering toward the gate and whatever misadventure waited beyond.

CHAPTER THREE

In his watery lair, Akhlaur bent over his table, scrawling with feverish haste as he etched runes into delicate, faintly blue parchment. After much experimentation, he'd found that a triton's hide yielded the finest parchment for his current purposes—long lasting and water resistant, not to mention its pleasing azure hue.

A trio of magic-dazed tritons, for the moment still wearing their blue skins, huddled in one of the cages that lined the vast coral chamber. Akhlaur favored these creatures and considered them nearly the equivalent of elves in terms of usefulness. Except for their coloring, their astonishing beauty, and their seal-like flippers, they resembled humans and were thus excellent test subjects. Their innate magic, however, provided some unexpected and interesting possibilities.

Akhlaur did not limit his studies to tritons. Each cage housed creatures whose lives and deaths contributed to the necromancer's art. Their moans and cries provided a counterpoint to Akhlaur's frenzied thoughts.

"An interesting spell, this," he muttered as he scrawled. "Wouldn't have thought an elf could manage it. Can't be necromancers, elves. Bah! Whoever said *that* obviously hadn't met my little Kiva."

A note of pride had crept into the wizard's musings concerning the elf woman. He shrugged aside Kiva's years of captivity and torment, choosing to regard her as his "apprentice."

"Apprentices challenge their masters. That is the way of things. You've done well, little elf—" he broke off to concentrate on shaping a particularly clever and lethal rune— "but you're not ready to face Akhlaur in battle."

The wizard finished the spell with a flourish. He rose and stroked his scaled chin as he stalked past a row of cages.

He paused before the bone and coral dungeon that housed the laraken. The monster instinctively lunged toward the life-giving magic surrounding Akhlaur, then cringed away when it realized the source.

Akhlaur considered his pet for a long moment. He needed a subject upon which to test the difficult spell he'd just transcribed. The laraken had survived this spell once, but Akhlaur could not be entirely certain that it would do so again. Most of the wizardly enchantments drained from Kiva passed through the laraken whole and with full detail; this one came to Akhlaur as the mere shadow of a spell. The laraken had absorbed the general shape and form during the casting, and passed this imperfect report along to its necromancer master. Akhlaur had filled in some gaps. Most likely he had improved the spell, but with elven magic, who knew?

"Too risky," he decided. "Let us send another beast first, and see how it fares."

The necromancer strolled past his collection of monsters. One, a fierce, four-armed fishman that reminded him of a mutant sahuagin, caught his eye. These creatures were common enough in the Elemental Plane. Should the experiment fail, it would be a simple matter to acquire another.

With a nod, Akhlaur shook out the parchment roll and began to read aloud. The spell he'd taken from the laraken—which in turn the laraken had taken from Kiva— rang through the living water. Bubbles rifted from the necromancer's lips and drifted off to encircle the caged beast. They spun and dipped and glowed, bringing to mind elves dancing beneath a starlit sky. Akhlaur ignored the elven flavor of Kiva's spell and concentrated on the sheer ingenuity of it.

As the chant continued, the bubbles began to merge, growing in size as they united. When Akhlaur pronounced the final, keening word of power, the bubbles converged into a single sphere that surrounded the monster.

For a moment the necromancer merely stood and watched as the creature threw itself from one side of its prison to the other, gasping in the thin and unfamiliar air. The scent of its terror was as intoxicating as a greenwitch's herb garden. Akhlaur drew in long draughts, taking time to savor its pungency. When at last he felt pleasantly sated, he took a small coral circlet from a spell bag and placed it between him and the entrapped monster. It hung like a round, empty frame on an invisible wall, or perhaps a peephole such as the powerless and suspicious often carved into their doors.

Again Akhlaur began to chant. A wall of power began to leech from the edges of the coral circle, gleaming with weird greenish light. When the wall spanned the vast chamber, the wizard took a tiny metal token and hurled it at the coral frame, shouting a single word.

The token disappeared with a burst of light and sound. The bubble lurched toward the coral circlet. It clung, and the air it contained rushed through the hole in a whirling spill of bubbles. The monster, too, was sucked toward the opening. Its form elongated weirdly and flowed through the opening like a genie emerging from a narrow-necked bottle.

In moments the giant bubble was gone, and the monster stood but three paces from Akhlaur. The wizard dispelled the wall of force with a single gesture and smiled into his captive's hideous face. The monster bared its fangs and snarled like a cornered wolf.

"Attack me," Akhlaur invited. "This day has been lacking in diversion."

For a moment instinct warred against instinct as the

creature weighed certain death against continued captivity. A tormented roar ripped from its throat.

Akhlaur shrugged. "Indecision is its own choice," he observed. He nodded, and the bone gate of the monster's cage yawned open. A flick of the necromancer's fingers created a miniature vortex that sucked the beast back into its prison and slammed the door behind it.

Not giving the monster another thought, the necromancer set to work affixing the coral frame to one of the cage's bars, securing it with wards and trigger spells.

"A gift for you, little Kiva," he said, gazing toward another tiny opening—the imperfect gate, a leak that spilled water and magic into Halruaa. "You sent me the laraken. When you touch the waters of the spring, I shall respond with a messenger of my own. Given the trouble you've taken on my behalf, it would be rude to ignore you. The proprieties, after all, must be observed."

The necromancer chuckled, envisioning the elf woman's surprise when the four-armed beast leaped from the gate. It was a small ploy, a mere feint in the opening moments of battle. But oh, how marvelous was the prospect of a worthy opponent!

Akhlaur let himself drift into pleasant dreams of vengeance. His thoughts dwelt not upon the little elf woman, but on his oldest friends—his most hated foes.

The Nath, the northeastern corner of Halruaa, was among the wildest and most desolate places in all the land. A few trade roads transversed it, but they were narrow and lightly traveled. Barren, rock-strewn valleys twisted among foothills honeycombed with caves, and often covered with dense forest. Monsters and bandits laired in these hidden places, but more dangerous still were the slim gray figures that moved like shadows through the smoking ruins of a trade caravan.

All were female Crinti, an elf-descended race who were gray of hair and skin and soul. Their leader kept over to the side, mounted on a dusky horse and directing the activity with an occasional gesture of her slim, gray hands. More infrequently, she snarled out a command in a language that once, long ago, had been that of the drow. Shanair, a chieftain among the Crinti raiders, took much pride in her dark heritage.

The Halruaans called her kind "shadow amazons." Thanks to the human barbarians in her ancestry, Shanair was tall for an elfblood, and powerfully built. Her limbs were long and lean, her curves generous over a tightly muscled frame. A mass of iron-colored hair tumbled over her shoulders like a mountain stream, framing a face that was all planes and sharp angles. Although her ears were only slightly pointed, she emphasized her elf heritage with silver ear cuffs that extended up into exaggerated, barbed points. Her boots and leathers and cloak were all gray. Other than her eyes, which were an unexpectedly vivid shade of blue, the only slash of color about her was the jagged red tattoo encircling her upper arm and the red paint that turned her fingernails into bloody talons.

A distant scream floated over the hills. Shanair's head came up in sharp recognition.

"Rekatra!"

She slapped her heels into her horse's sides.

Two of Shanair's aids leaped onto their steeds and fell in behind as she thundered toward the doomed scout—doomed by her own voice, for no true Crinti cried out in fear or pain.

They found Rekatra sprawled beside a swift little creek, clutching at the four deep, widely spaced wounds that sheared through leather armor to plow deep furrows through belly and bowels. The Crinti scout was drained nearly dry. The eyes she lifted to Shanair's face were already glazed and dull.

"Mother," she said faintly. Her voice held hope and supplication, the plea of a wounded child.

Shanair leaped from her horse and stalked over to the fallen scout. She drew two curved swords in a single, fluid sweep. They flashed down, crossed over the young warrior's throat, and came back blooded.

The Crinti chieftain sheathed the stained blades and stooped over the carrion that had been her scout and her daughter. The other two women dismounted and drew near. Their faces held no hint of revulsion at their leader's actions and no surprise.

"Look at these marks." Shanair trailed her fingers along the edge of one deep gash.

The others crouched down to look. The cuts alone were deep enough to kill, but within each slash was another tear, slanting up at a sharp angle to the main cut.

"Whatever cut her was not only sharp, but barbed," observed Whizzra, Shanair's second in command.

"And big," put in the third Crinti. Xibryl, a fleshy warrior nearly Shanair's height and strength, placed her hand on the dead scout's belly and spread her thick fingers as wide as they would go. Her hands were long-fingered and strong, and like Shanair she wore her nails in blood-red talons. "If these marks came from claws, the hand was four times the size of mine. What creature in these hills could have done this?"

Shanair rocked back on her heels and rose in a smooth, swift motion. "Something new. Something we've not seen before."

Her gaze swept the dismal terrain, searching for clues. No tracks were visible to her keen eyes, no trail sign. Rekatra's attacker had fled through the stream.

Shanair's blue eyes narrowed as she considered the bubbling stream. Snow still crowned the highest peaks of the mountain ranges encircling Halruaa, but the spring thaw had come and gone. Summer was upon them, but the heavy rains of the monsoon season were still two or three moons away. The water should not be running so swiftly.

"We follow the stream to its source," she announced.

She vaulted onto her horse's back and set a brisk pace north, sparing no glance or thought for the dead girl.

The terrain grew steeper and more inhospitable with each step. Soon the rocky pass gave way to forest, which thinned to scrub pine as they climbed higher into the mountains. With each step, the song of the stream grew stronger and more urgent.

The Crinti warriors rode until the sun had set, and they pressed on through the lengthening shadows of twilight. The sounds of gathering night echoed through the trees—the screech of raptors, the snarl of wild cats, the sharp sudden squeal of prey. When it grew too dark to ride, they dismounted and led their horses, trusting the keen night vision inherited from distant drow ancestors.

Dawn was near when they came to a small clearing. In the center of it, the stream flowed out of a small and apparently shallow pool. There was no sign of the creature that had shredded Rekatra.

Shanair left her horse at the edge of the clearing and crept cautiously nearer. She circled the stream's mouth, peering keenly at the moss-covered ground. "Bring me a stout stick," she ordered.

Xibryl complied at once, dragging a six-foot length of deadfall wood over and hacking off the side limbs with a hand axe. Shanair took the rough staff and jabbed tentatively at the water. Try as she might, she could not find the spring's source. The bed beneath was solid ground.

"Impossible," she muttered. Raising the stick high overhead, she plunged it hard into the water.

The staff dived so deep and so easily that Shanair nearly lost her footing. She leaped back, staring in amazement at the two-foot length of wood in her hands.

An enormous green hand shot out of the spring and fisted over the empty air where Shanair had just been standing. The hand was the size of a small battle shield. Webbing connected the four fingers, each of which was as long as her forearm and tipped with talons as barbed as fishhooks. As suddenly as it came, the hand disappeared, slapping back into the incomprehensible spring.

Shanair quickly conquered her surprise and drew her swords. Steel hissed free of Whizzra's baldric. The creak of whirling chain announced the lethal dance of Xibryl's spiked flail. The three Crinti moved quickly, silently into triangle formation around the spring.

Suddenly the clearing seemed to explode. The monster leaped out of the water like a geyser, and its voice was the roar of a waterfall.

The massive creature was twice Shanair's height. Roughly humanoid in shape, it crouched on two froglike legs. Four arms, thickly muscled and armored with dull green scales, lifted into a wrestler's ready stance. The creature's head was enormous, crested with a barbed standing fin and nearly split in two by a fanged mouth. Dagger-sized teeth clacked with anticipation.

The Crinti warriors eyed their foe, sizing up its potential strengths and weaknesses.

"Sahuagin?" guessed Xibryl.

"Worse," Shanair said with a fierce smile. This monster, she suspected, was no creature known to this world. Battle lust burned wild and hot in the Crinti chieftain as she began an ancient death-dance.

The others moved with her, dodging from side to side, dipping tauntingly forward, then leaping back. There was magic in their movements, a lure as potent as siren song. The Crinti did not weaken their enemies. They enticed them.

The creature came on with a rush, taking a mighty swing at the nearest Crinti. Whizzra nimbly dropped and rolled away, and Shanair dived in before the beast could recover its balance. Her left-hand sword thrust hard at the juncture of arm and chest—and slid harmlessly off the scaly armor.

Shanair ducked as another massive arm whistled over her head. In a lightning-flash decision, she measured the power of that swing and decided she could not absorb the impact.

She relaxed her grip on her sword and allowed the blow to send it flying. She barked out a one-word command, naming a much-practiced battle maneuver.

The other Crinti moved out wide on either side of the creature, their weapons flashing as they kept all four of the monster's arms engaged. In came Shanair, ducking under the flailing arms. She gripped her sword with both hands, and launched herself into a powerful upward lunge. Her scale mail hissed against the massive green torso as she rose.

Her blade dived into the lizardlike folds under the creature's chin. It grated against tooth and jaw, slammed hard into the bony palate that roofed the massive mouth. The creature's shriek was liquid with blood, but Shanair instinctively knew she had not struck a killing blow.

Xibryl's axe slashed in, knocking aside the taloned hand pawing at the imbedded weapon. Shanair let go of her blade to avoid the sweeping axe, whipped her head to one side so that she was not blinded by the shower of sparks as steel hit steel, then seized the hilt again. She leaped up, planted both feet on the creature's chest, and pushed herself off as she tugged the sword free.

The Crinti dropped into a backward roll and came up on her feet. She backed away and whistled for her horse. The battle-trained steed trotted up, seemingly oblivious to the monster and its frenzied attempts to fight free of its tormenters.

Shanair untied a bundle of javelins and thrust them point-down into the mossy ground. She snatched up one, took aim, and let fly.

The weapon streaked toward the creature, tearing through one of Xibryl's flying gray tresses. Trailing a wavy strand of hair like a banner, it dived into one of the creature's black eyes.

Shanair's yell of triumph came to an abrupt stop as her javelin bounced back and fell free. Her aim was true, yet the spear did not pierce the skull!

Still, the creature was half blinded. Shanair threw another javelin and completed the task. The monster fought on, its swings and parries as accurate as before.

The Crinti woman's keen ears caught the faint clicking sound that hummed through the air like distant cicada song. Under water, the sound probably carried for leagues. Shanair figured that the creature's sound-sight, even in air, was probably as keen as a bat's.

Shanair smacked her mare's flank and sent her running. The other horses fell into pace behind their leader. The trio thundered in tight circles around the clearing, leaping over the stream again and again. The echoing hoof beats blended into a reverberating rumble, like the war drums of jungle elves. Even Shanair's battle shriek was swallowed by the sound as she closed in on the confused and wounded beast.

Now truly blinded, the creature tried to bolt, but it could not even hear the spring and took a fatal pace in the wrong direction. The Crinti warriors closed ranks.

They worked their quarry for a long time, and not just for the joy of a slow kill. They played the creature until it was exhausted, then tried prying up several scales, inquiring with sharp, deep jabs as they studied which wounds bled, which ones brought the sharpest pain, and finally, which killed. If this were not the only creature of its kind, such information could decide the next battle.

Finally the Crinti stood over their kill, drenched with exertion and blood, not all of it the monster's. All three wore fierce, sated smiles.

"Take the trophy," commanded Shanair.

Her warriors set to work, wresting off the head and stripping it clean of flesh and hide. Shanair broke off several dagger-shaped teeth and gave them to her warriors. The skull was too awkward for one horse to carry, so they fixed a cloak between two mounts like a sling. That accomplished, they mounted and set off to rejoin their comrades.

"A good kill," Whizzra observed.

Her words were correct, but her tone held hesitation as well as satisfaction. Shanair lifted an inquiring eyebrow.

"This monster, this stream," the warrior continued. "What does it mean?"

"Do you not recognize this clearing?" demanded Shanair. "This is where I come to meet with Kiva. As for this stream, it is a gate to the world of water. That can only mean the elf woman has succeeded."

Joy, as dark and bright as hellfire, seared through the Crinti warriors' eyes. "It is time to fight?" Xibryl demanded eagerly.

Shanair shook her head. "Soon. We continue as planned. We loot and raid. We await Kiva. In time, the Crinti will emerge from the shadows, and all of Halruaa will be washed into a bloody sea!"

CHAPTER FOUR

A young woman sat before a table in a wizard's library, garbed in the pale blue robe that marked her as a conjurer's apprentice. The robe was left open, revealing a trim form clad in a well-worn tunic and leggings that ended several inches shy of her bare feet. Her face was finely featured, with large dark eyes and a wide, expressive mouth currently pulled down into a mutinous scowl. Her short brown hair stood up in spikes, as if raked through by an impatient hand, and her fingers were stained with purple ink. There was a small stack of parchment to her left, three completed scrolls to her right, and a pile of crumpled and discarded parchments scattered around her feet.

Suddenly she tossed aside the quill and rose. A quick, impatient kick sent parchment wads flying.

"Copy the spell scroll, Tzigone," she repeated, in an uncanny imitation of her master's jolly tones. "By highsun, you'll know the spell as well as your own name, and then you can have the evening free.

"Well, guess what, Basel," she said in her own voice as she stalked across the room to glare at a portrait of the wizard. "I don't *know* my real name, the sun is as high as it's ever going to get, and I learned the blasted spell the first time I copied the thrice-bedamned scroll!"

The image of Basel Indoulur continued to beam down at her, unperturbed by her uncharacteristic spate of ill temper.

Tzigone sighed and blew the portrait a kiss by way of apology. She genuinely liked her new master—her *first* master. If she had to learn the art of magic, and apparently she did, there were worse ways of going about it.

Basel Indoulur was a round, jolly man who enjoyed good times and fine things. He was fun loving but hardly frivolous. A master in the art of conjuration, he was also a member of the Council of Elders and mayor of the city of Halar, just south of the king's city. He enjoyed teaching, and was one of many wizards who had courted Tzigone after the Swamp of Akhlaur incident. Many wizards were eager to train an innate gift strong enough to withstand the magic-draining power of a laraken. Tzigone had picked Basel for two reasons, only one of which she would admit: His eyes knew how to laugh.

He was a patient but exacting teacher. Such discipline was new to Tzigone, and an uncomfortable fit for a girl who had seldom slept two nights in the same place. Basel's other apprentices had lived through the boredom of copying spell scrolls, so Tzigone assumed that her chances of survival were fairly good.

She'd kept at it since morning, copying the runes over and over and over. Basel had patiently explained that magic, like the science of numbers, was best learned in a well-defined sequence. An apprentice must train her memory, hone her powers of concentration, practice hundreds of precise and subtle movements with the dedication of a dancer, learn the hidden language in which all Halruaan spells were declaimed, and acquire a core knowledge of basic spells and cantrips. There was far more to spellcasting, it seemed, than tossing a few smelly oddments into a pot and chanting words over it.

Tzigone flexed her cramped fingers, retrieved one of her discarded quills, and dipped it into the ink yet again. On impulse, she whipped the pen toward a portrait of some grim-faced Indoulur ancestor. Ink arced out in a spray of purple droplets. Tzigone made a deft little gesture, and the ink splashed onto the canvas in the shape of a long, curling mustache.

She grinned, pleased with the effect—even though the ancestor in question was female. It added a piquant note to the woman's fussy silks and gems and sweeping peacock feathers.

This success gave birth to an idea. Tzigone snatched up a blank parchment sheet and stuck it up on the wall. She dipped and whipped again, and this time as the ink flew, she chanted the spell she was supposed to copy.

Ink splashed onto the parchment and began to wriggle around. The runes of the simple cantrip took shape on the page, more accurately and neatly than she'd been able to reproduce by hand.

Tzigone let out a little crow of triumph and danced a few steps of a jig. Her joy was short-lived, however, for she remembered that she could cast the spell twice a day.

Unless . . .

"There's got to be something useful in this place," she muttered as she scanned the room. It was brimming with the usual spellbooks, vials, bottles, and small, covered pots, as well as an odd collection of trophies and trinkets.

Her gaze fell on a statue of Mystra. A small, bright rainbow cloaked the goddess. Tzigone's gaze traced the rainbow to its source. Sunlight spilled through the window, filtering through a glass prism resting on a high, wooden pedestal.

On impulse, Tzigone walked over and picked up the prism. It looked like an ordinary crystal paperweight, but she sensed the hum of magic in it and guessed what it might do.

Her face broke out in a grin as a scheme took shape. She arranged a few dozen writing quills around the prism like spokes radiating from a wheel's center. She placed every bottle of ink she could find along the outer edge of the circle, then stuck parchment sheets against the walls with bits of sealing wax. When all was ready, she cast the spell.

As expected, the prism caught and magnified her little spell. All of the quills leaped into the air and dunked themselves smartly into inkbottles. They rose up and whipped toward the parchments, then returned to refill. In short order, the spell was perfectly copied upon all the available parchments.

But the quills showed no signs of abating. They began to toss ink onto the walls, the silken drapes, the mirrors. Upon the ceiling, and across the portrait of the mustachioed Indoulur ancestor. Into the face of the spellcaster herself.

Tzigone spat out a mouthful of ink and lunged for the prism, only to be stabbed by several quills returning to their bottles. She changed tactics, snatching up corks and stuffing them back into the inkbottles.

That proved effective, up to a point. Some of the returning quills dived into the corks and got stuck. They struggled to free themselves with a fervor that had the stoppered bottles rattling and dancing across the table.

Tzigone seized the last bottle and dodged the large, sharp quill that hurtled toward her like a thrown knife. She stuffed home the cork and leaped aside.

To her chagrin, the quill pursued, dipping and twisting with an agility that brought to mind the flight of a twilight bat.

Other quills joined the pursuit. Discarded quills rose from the floor, untrimmed quills leaped out of drawers, feathers tugged free of the enormous stuffed egret in the corner. As Tzigone darted past the portrait of the Indoulur ancestor, peacock feathers leaped from the painting and joined in the chase.

There was nothing for it but to get rid of the ink, even though a bottle of wizard's ink would buy Tzigone's weight in pearls. She hefted the bottle, took aim at the open window, and let fly.

The swarm of quills dived out after the missile. Tzigone came over to the window and leaned out, watching as inkbottle and quills dived into the garden pool far below. The water took on a soft shade of lavender as it bubbled from the fountain.

She drew her head back into the room and turned, muttering oaths learned over the years from various street sharps and traveling performers. Her voice died in the midst of a particularly pungent phrase. Her new master stood in the doorway, his black eyes bulging with astonishment.

Basel Indoulur stood silent and still. Tzigone found this disconcerting. The wizard was ever in motion: his beaded braids swinging about his shoulders, his pair of chins wobbling in counterpoint to his frequent laugh. He was not laughing now.

Tzigone followed his gaze as it swept over the ruined room. The extent of the damage surprised her, now that she had time to consider it. She placed small value on wealth and the fine things it could buy, but she knew few people were of this mind.

Basel walked slowly through the room. He stopped before the defiled portrait. His shoulders went rigid.

Tzigone sighed resignedly. Few things offended Halruaans more than a slight upon their ancestors. "You don't need to say it. I'll get my things together."

The conjurer cleared his throat and turned to face her. "You gave my grandam's sister a mustache."

She conceded with a little shrug.

"Well, that is a shame, considering all the trouble she went through to have the original one removed."

There was a slightly strangled note to the wizard's voice, and suddenly Tzigone suspected that he was repressing not rage but mirth.

"The ink should clean off, and I could probably put the peacock feathers back into the portrait," she suggested.

"By no means! As a boy I was always compelled kiss Great-aunt Aganzard goodnight, though she always wore at least a bird's worth of feathers. My nose itches just from thinking about it. It does my heart good to see the old boot without her fripperies for once. So," he concluded briskly, with the air of one ready to move on. "The scrolls are finished? Seven and twenty copies?"

"At least."

"Fine, fine," he said, beaming. "Since you've completed your day's work, you have time for a bit of a treat."

This bewildered her. Although grateful that the wizard was not angry, she didn't expect to be rewarded for destroying his study.

"We're taking up *Avariel*," he continued, naming the skyship that Tzigone had been admiring since her first day in the conjurer's tower. "I intend to visit Procopio Septus, lord mayor of Halarahh, and present you as my new apprentice. You may wish to bathe and change first. If Procopio thinks we've been stomping grapes, he'll expect his share of wine."

She glanced down. Her robe, tunic, and arms were splattered with purple ink. A glance in the mirror proved that her face hadn't gone unscathed. It was liberally daubed with deep purple—and gone pale as parchment at the prospect of entering Procopio's villa again.

Tzigone couldn't explain her moment of panic. She'd crept through the villa before to visit Matteo during his service there. Nothing bad had happened. She just didn't like the feel of the place.

"I'm to meet Procopio Septus?" she repeated, a question in her voice.

"Presenting one's apprentices is traditional. It demonstrates the respect I hold for my colleague. I've been waiting for the proper moment, and I daresay it's at hand!"

Basel's motivation was starting to come clear to her. "Sometimes you can't tell the punishments from the rewards."

"Just so, my dear," he said with a dagger-sharp grin. He dropped a fatherly arm around her shoulders. "I'm no diviner—bless the Lady's name—but I suspect that bringing you and the good Procopio together will prove a just reward for you both."

Tzigone followed his gaze around the ruined room and found she couldn't argue.

☙

Procopio Septus was not pleased to receive word of Basel Indoulur's visit. As a master of divination, Procopio was among the most esteemed wizards in Halruaa. Conjuration, Basel's specialty, was not as highly regarded, but Basel remained utterly unmoved by Procopio's attempts to impress upon him his inferior status.

These efforts, Procopio suspected, were coming back to haunt him. Surely Basel was coming to gloat over the loss of Zephyr, an ancient elf jordain who had been in Procopio's service until his recent execution as a traitor to Halruaa.

Such a thing could prove ruinous for any ambitious man, but how much more so for a diviner! Procopio should have known what was happening under his own nose, and he did not. Try as he might, he could put no better face on it than that.

Nor could he ignore the tremendous loss of stature such failure brought. He harbored private aspirations to Zalathorm's throne, yet there were murmurs of replacing him as mayor of Halarahh! If he did not restore himself in popular favor soon, all his dreams would die aborning.

One secret bit of knowledge would help him endure Basel's presence. The fool had taken on Keturah's daughter as an apprentice!

Because of his high office, Procopio had heard of the scandals surrounding Keturah, but he had forgotten about it after the runaway wizard and her bastard child had been captured and dealt with according to law. Recently, though, Cassia, the jordain who had served as King Zalathorm's chief counselor, had told him that Keturah's daughter still lived. Since then, Procopio had made it a point to discover the identity of this girl—a task made more difficult by the murder of Cassia. He had lavished money, magic, and influence to ensure that the secret Cassia confided to him remained his alone. This was a risk, but one he counted worth taking. It gave him a hidden blade to use against Basel Indoulur, should the need ever arise.

Procopio, though a prudent man, rather hoped it would.

He walked out onto the parapets of his villa's walls to watch the conjurer's approach. *Avariel* came on fast, her three gaudily colored sails curved tight, her prow thrusting boldly into the winds.

As the ship neared, Procopio made out a small, fourth sail trailing more than a ship's length behind. Puzzled, he picked up a mariner's glass and trained it upon the skyship. A long rope ran from the stern of the skyship to a small figure, and from there to a bright silk sail that caught the wind and held the wind-dancer aloft.

He'd heard of this sport but didn't personally know anyone daft enough to try it. He slipped a thicker lens into the glass, the better to study the small figure. What he saw made his lips thin in a tight smile.

So this was Keturah's daughter. From this distance, the wench looked more like an urchin at play than the off-spring of the beautiful, fallen wizard. The girl's wind-tossed hair was cropped as short as a boy's, and the form beneath the tunic looked nearly as straight and slender.

Procopio trained the glass upon the deck. There stood Basel with one of his ubiquitous apprentices. Both watched the girl with wide, delighted grins. Their admiration was not uncommon—after all, this "urchin" was the hero of Akhlaur's Swamp.

Stories of that battle were spreading like spilled wine. All who heard these tales glowed with pride, from the most magic-dead rothé herder to the mightiest of wizards. *Such is the magic of Halruaa, that even a street waif untrained in the Art can subdue a terrible monster!* Ballads to that effect were sung in the square, in the festhalls, in the palaces. He had even heard this tale intoned in the plainsong of Azuthan clerics!

Procopio wondered how Basel would respond if he knew that his new apprentice was a thief, a vagabond, and, worst of all, a wizard's bastard.

It was a delightful image to contemplate.

The skyship slowed as it neared the docking gate atop Procopio's southernmost wall. The girl pulled herself down the mooring line hand over hand, shortening the rope as she sank so that she would land on the skyship deck. Basel and his apprentice darted forward to catch her. She plowed into them, and all three tumbled onto the deck, laughing like ninnies.

With a disgusted sigh, Procopio put down the glass and went to his courtyard to await his "distinguished guests."

Basel came first, his black eyes still twinkling with fun. "Greetings to you, Lord Procopio. We come in peace and friendship and will work no magic unbidden within these walls." He glanced back at his apprentices.

There were three of them: a stunningly pretty girl from the Noor family, a commoner named for some sweaty trade or other, and Keturah's bastard. The first two repeated the traditional pledge. Basel looked pointedly at the windblown little bastard, who shrugged and offered, "Fine. What they said."

Basel shook his head and lifted his eyes skyward as if in supplication. "Lord Procopio, you have met Farrah Noor and Mason. This is Tzigone, the newest of my apprentices. I pray she will serve Halruaa as faithfully as you yourself have done."

"May Mystra grant it. With such a master to inspire her, how could she do less?" Procopio said, offering the proper response to Basel's traditional words with a straight face, a dry tone, and a great deal of private irony.

For several moments he and Basel managed to exchange formulaic pleasantries without once choking on them. When servants came with goblets of iced wine and chilled fruits, Procopio suggested that the apprentices might wander the garden as they wished. Not surprisingly,

Tzigone seemed most eager to leave his presence. Procopio knew that people who harbored secrets tended to avoid powerful diviners, and with good reason. Within the hour, the darkest corners of the girl's soul would be his to know. Procopio quickly lifted his wine goblet to his lips to hide the smile he could not quite contain.

"I trust your new apprentice is living up to expectations?"

Basel responded with a dry chuckle. "She's coming along nicely, but after her success with the laraken, she'd have to arm-wrestle a red dragon to meet expectations."

"Ah yes, the laraken," Procopio said. "I would like to hear that tale from the girl's own lips, without an audience at hand to tempt her into embroidering it. With your permission, of course."

Basel could hardly refuse his host's request without violating at least a dozen rules of protocol. Of course, Procopio skirted the edges of propriety as well, but Basel could hardly point that out. Instead he placed his fingertips on his temples in a parody of a charlatan fortuneteller. "I see an arm-wrestling match between my apprentice and a red dragon. And—by Mystra!—I see Tzigone wearing a new pair of dragonhide boots!"

"I am forewarned," the diviner said in a bone-dry tone.

He strode over to the trellis where Tzigone stood, arms folded, glaring at the climbing jasmine as if she held a special grudge against it.

He studied her closely, trying to remember Keturah's face and searching the girl's for anything that might jog his memory. She turned to meet his scrutiny. A wary glint flashed in her eyes—the canny, instinctual caution of an animal that scents a predator.

Procopio smiled reassuringly. "I noted your performance on *Avariel*. Quite daring."

She shrugged, eyeing him and waiting for him to get to the point. He came closer, and with one hand he surreptitiously traced the gestures for a simple spell that measured the general shape of a person's magical power and moral inclinations. A simple spell, but an enormous breach of hospitality. A wizard simply did not intrude upon a guest in this manner.

To his astonishment, the spell simply dissipated. Either the girl was powerful enough to resist his Art, or she was as magic-dead as clay.

Intrigued, the diviner called to mind a more powerful spell and probed harder, deeper, employing magic that could thrust aside the mind's resistance and plunder at will. So intrusive was this spell that a Halruaan woman would be less offended if a stranger were to thrust his hand between her thighs. Even this puissant spell proved futile.

Futile, but not unnoticed. The girl's big eyes went molten with fury. "Back off," she said in a low, dangerous voice. "Poke at me again, and I'll take your hand off at the elbow and shove it up your . . . spell bag."

Despite his own misdeeds, Procopio was not about to accept such disrespect. He drew himself up. "You overspeak yourself, wench! I never expected to see the day when a green apprentice dared to address a master wizard in such fashion!"

"Is that so?" she inquired through gritted teeth. "Then *this* is going to come as a real surprise!"

Before Procopio could react, she clenched a small, ink-stained hand and drove it into his face.

His magical shields were in place. He was certain of that. Then why was he lying on his back, his head throbbing from sharp contact with the cobblestone and his entire face throbbing like a giant toothache?

No answer to this mystery emerged from the blurring whirl that his thoughts had become. After a moment Procopio hauled himself into a sitting position. He lifted one hand to his jaw and worked it experimentally.

Basel bustled over, his plump face twitching with emotion. "I am shocked, my friend! Astounded! Most thoroughly disconcerted! By wind and word, I swear that I shall deal with my apprentice swiftly and appropriately."

The diviner waved away the pudgy, beringed hand that Basel offered and rose unaided, clinging to the jasmine-cloaked trellis for support. When the garden stopped spinning, he turned to regard his unlikely attacker.

The girl stood as taut and ready as a drawn bow, her weight balanced on the balls of her feet, her fisted hands held low but ready. Despite the gravity of her situation, she looked as if she'd like nothing better than to take a second shot at him.

Procopio tamped down his temper and salved his bruised pride. The little bastard would pay in time, after she'd been dealt as a card in his long-running game with Basel Indoulur. Meanwhile, Basel was bound by wizard-word to deal harshly with her. Since attacking a wizard was among the most serious crimes in the land, Basel would be hard pressed to come up with a punishment short of death or dismemberment.

Procopio dismissed them all with a wave of his hand. "Take the wench, and deal with her according to her deeds. You are so sworn."

Basel bowed low and took Tzigone by the arm, drawing her out of the courtyard and into the street.

Now you've done it, she thought, her heart sinking into the pit of her stomach. What had possessed her, that she'd thought she could live within the staid confines of a wizard's tower, and the endless rules and niceties expected of a Halruaan wizard? Tzigone was no more suited to this life than was a half-feral griffon kitten. Sooner or later, something like this was destined to happen. Now Basel, despite his indulgent good humor, was obliged to take action. Tzigone considered trying to break and run, but the tip of a rowan wand peeking out of Basel's crimson sleeve convinced her otherwise. For such a lighthearted soul, Basel carried an extraordinary amount of magical weaponry.

They walked in silence down several streets, Mason and Farrah trailing miserably behind. Tzigone did not think it wise to ask why they did not go directly to the skyship.

At last they paused before a row of fine shops. Basel released Tzigone's arm and pointed to the goods in the window before them. "Tell me, do these please you?"

She glanced at the window, then did an astonished double take. Displayed against draping folds of black velvet was a collection of the finest weapons she had ever seen.

The shopkeeper bustled out, beaming. "Just the thing for prudent wizards to carry, lords and ladies! Not a sword, dagger or knife among these will hold a spell. No one can trace them, enspell them, or turn them against you. Of course, you'll have to sharpen them—they won't magically hold an *edge*, either." He chuckled at his little joke. "But we sell whetstones for that purpose," he added, lest there be any hesitation on that account.

Tzigone studied the fine weapons. Why was Basel dangling them before her like this? She didn't have the coins to buy one, and she doubted that he intended for her to demonstrate her thieving skills. If he meant to have her killed or marked—and if her understanding of Halruaan law was correct, he had the right to do either—why have her choose the weapon? He had never struck her as a sadistic man.

"Do any of these please you?" Basel repeated patiently.

Tzigone cleared her throat. "I've never seen better."

"They are quite fine. They're also overpriced, but what can I say? I am bound by my wizard-word oath to act promptly. Choose one."

She sent him an inquiring look. To her vast relief, Basel's disturbingly calm expression gave way to a wide grin.

"You knocked Lord Procopio on his scrawny excuse for an arse. I swore that you would be dealt with appropriately. I'd say an extravagant gift is in order." He turned to his apprentices. "Mason? Farrah?"

"Highly appropriate," Mason agreed with a relieved smile. Farrah Noor laughed delightedly and clapped her jeweled hands.

"There is more to this than you know," Basel said, suddenly serious. "Spells of divination are as common in Halruaa as rain during the monsoon, but there are rules and limits. Lord Procopio skirts them. A hungry urchin risks losing a hand when he cuts a rich man's purse strings, yet the most powerful of wizards can raid another man's mind with impunity. Procopio has intruded upon one of my apprentices before," Basel said, glancing at Farrah Noor, "and I suspected that he could not resist the challenge you present. He was due for a gentle reminder that not everyone will tolerate his arrogance."

The wizard's mood darkened still more. "Forgive me, child, for subjecting you to such indignity. I never suspected that Procopio would go so far. I should have, knowing him as I do."

Tzigone heaved a sigh of profound relief and enfolded Basel in a quick hug. She reached for a length of gleaming silver—a long slim knife, perfectly balanced for fighting or throwing. "I knew I should have followed that punch with a knee to the groin."

"I'm just as glad you didn't," Basel told her, his black eyes twinkling with unholy glee as he counted out the needed coins. "Had you done so, I would have felt compelled to sign *Avariel* over to you."

CHAPTER FIVE

Matteo's pursuit of Andris took much longer than he
had anticipated. His eager stallion ran hard the
first day, and Matteo suspected that Cyric would
have run through the night had not Matteo called
a halt. On the second day, heavy rains slowed his
progress and blurred the trail. Matteo was a
strong tracker, but had he not known Andris so
well, he would have missed the trail entirely. It
was not the trail sign, but the small tricks and
diversions that the jordain left to cover his path
that Matteo found and read.

By the third day, he could no longer doubt
Andris's destination. The jordain was bound for
the Temple of Azuth, as he had been instructed.
That made no sense to Matteo. If Andris intended
to submit himself to the inquisitors, why slip away
without a word?

The sun's last long, golden rays gilded the
high-domed Azuthan cathedral as Cyric thundered up to the temple gate. Matteo gave his
name and purpose to the gatekeeper and waited
while the man went to fetch a priest.

An elderly man came to the gate, wearing the
gray vestments of Azuth. Matteo's eye dropped to
the holy symbol over his heart: a man's hand,
index finger pointed upward, surrounded by
flame. The flames that surrounded the needlework

hand were not fashioned from silken threads but from magic flumes that leaped and danced, giving off a deep red light. The flame's color denoted rank. Matteo's host was a high priest. Given Matteo's part in returning the traitorous Kiva, he supposed it fitting that so august a person should come to greet him.

The priest made short work of the usual courtesies, not even offering his name. He ushered Matteo into a private study and closed the door firmly. Matteo waited with growing puzzlement as the priest fell into prayer, chanting Azuth-given spells to ward the room from magical intrusion.

At last Matteo could not contain his curiosity. "You fear that some wizard might intrude into this sacred place? That is forbidden!"

"Forbidden or not, it has been known to happen." The priest sank into a chair and waved Matteo toward another. "The man you seek, the jordain Andris. He did not present himself to the temple."

"He assured me he would come here."

"You mentioned that to the gatekeeper. You also said that Andris promised he would not leave the Jordaini College until the following morning," the priest pointed out.

Matteo had no answer for this. "I must admit that my friend's actions are a complete mystery to me. I would be grateful for whatever enlightenment you could offer."

The priest hesitated for a long moment. "You must treat what I am about to tell you with the same discretion a jordain grants his patron."

Matteo nodded cautious agreement. "Insofar as I may, without betraying the interests of my patron the queen, or the service of truth."

"That will have to do." The priest sighed heavily. "Andris did not present himself at our gates, that much is true, but he was here. It is my opinion that he was looking for Kiva."

This was the strangest news Matteo had learned yet. "Did he find her?"

"When you learn the answer to that question, let me know. Me, and no other."

As the man's meaning became clear, Matteo slumped back into his chair. "Kiva has escaped? But how?"

The priest shifted. "I could fashion an explanation, but why waste breath on something that will not change the situation?"

Matteo silently accessed "the situation." Kiva was gone, and with her the secret of the gate to the Plane of Water. A smaller concern, but no less urgent to Matteo, was what part Andris might have played in this. Andris believed his destiny was bound to the elven people, and Kiva was the only elf he knew. It seemed incredible that Andris would have anything more to do with the treacherous elf woman, but Matteo could not be certain.

After a long moment, he put words to his fears. "Do you suspect that Andris might have aided Kiva's escape?"

The priest shook his head. "Kiva was long gone before the jordain came. After she regained her senses, she was examined immediately, if briefly, by one of our inquisitors. She named an accomplice, who was duly executed."

"Zephyr," Matteo murmured, bringing to mind the kind, worn face of the elderly elf—the only jordain who had made him welcome during his service to Procopio Septus. "What evidence was brought against him?"

"The sentence was just," the priest assured him. "Kiva told the truth about him, if little else. The inquisitor deemed her too weak to continue, yet she fled within the hour. I wouldn't have believed it possible, but there you have it."

This pronouncement mingled good news and bad. Andris was not culpable, but on the other hand, Kiva had been running free for quite some time. Zephyr had been executed by the light of a gibbous moon, as was Halruaan custom. Since then moondark had come and gone, and a plump crescent overlooked the temple like a lazy, heavy-lidded eye.

Matteo swallowed his frustration. "What efforts have been made to recover her?"

"Officially, none," the priest told him. "You see, Kiva has disappeared into the forested pass that leads through the mountains into the Mhair Jungle. By treaty with the Mhair elves, Azuth's priests cannot enter that pass. Wizards, swordsmen and commoners among Azuth's followers are not bound by this prohibition, but none have found the elf's trail."

"Nor will they. Following an elf in a forest is like tracking a falcon's flight in a cloudy sky."

"Just so. You understand why we were hesitant to ask for assistance elsewhere."

Matteo understood perfectly. As long as Kiva's disappearance brought no additional harm to Halruaa, the Azuthans would seek her quietly, hoping to retrieve her before her escape became general knowledge.

He studied the priest. "You wouldn't have told me any of this without good reason."

The priest raised his eyebrows at this blunt speech, but he did not offer a disclaimer. "Do you know this Andris well?"

Matteo repeated words he had spoken many times before. "As well as one man can know another."

His host smiled thinly. "Is that an expression of brotherhood or cynicism?"

"Both, I suppose."

"A wise balance. Tell me: in your opinion, did Andris go after Kiva? For vengeance, perhaps?"

"Were he so inclined, he would have ample reason."

"Interesting," the priest murmured. He looked keenly at Matteo. "You tracked this jordain to the temple. Could you follow him into the forest?"

"I would fare better with some assistance. There are two men at the Jordaini College who are excellent trackers, and good fighters. Will you send for them?"

The priest nodded. "If you think their expertise will balance the additional delay, yes. You trust these men?"

Matteo's answering smile was both sharp and sad. "As much as I trust anyone."

Three days passed as Matteo awaited the arrival of his jordaini brothers. He spent much of the time in the temple's library, studying maps and lore of the Mhair Jungle. The rest he devoted to learning to ride the huge, tame lizards the priests kept in their stables—just as a precaution, or so the stable hands assured him at every opportunity. These were the only mounts that could traverse the jungle. While no one from the temple actually rode into the jungle, they stressed, if need arose the proper mounts were available.

Finally the tolling of temple bells announced the approach of visitors. Matteo hastened to the gate to meet his friends.

Themo was a mountain of a man with the bluff, cheery face of a mischievous boy, and a temperament to match. Although he was Matteo's age, repeated infractions of jordaini rules forced Themo to repeat the fifth form before he could become a full-fledged counselor. Matteo suspected that Themo would not be heartbroken if this honor was never his to claim, for he was more suited to the battlefield than the council chamber. Iago was a slight, dark man with a sage's introspective eyes. He was also among the best battlemasters the Jordaini College had produced, as well as a master of horse.

Iago had also been one of Kiva's captives and had nearly as much reason for vengeance as did Andris. He listened to Matteo's story and readily agreed that Andris had gone in pursuit of Kiva. Themo, on the other hand, was eager to pursue this quest, or any other.

The high priest himself accompanied them to the side gate, wishing them success and admonishing them to secrecy.

"Success," muttered Themo later that day, climbing back onto his lizard mount for at least the fifth time. "If I fall off this slimy excuse for a horse only twice more before sunset, I'll call it a good day's work."

"Wishing you were back at the college?" Iago asked.

Themo looked genuinely surprised. "Nine Hells! A man can't complain for love of hearing his own voice?"

"A man can. A jordain shouldn't. The measure of a man's spirit is the distance between ordeal and adventure," Iago pointed out, quoting a familiar proverb.

"The *college* is an ordeal," Themo grumbled. "As for adventure, I wish I'd been with you two in Akhlaur's Swamp."

"No, you don't," Iago said with quiet certainty. "Consider what happened to Andris."

The big man conceded this with a shrug. "Poor bastard. Going through life looking like a glass sculpture isn't my idea of fun. Makes people hesitate before taking a swing at you."

"Hold your sympathy until we find Andris and Kiva," Matteo advised, giving voice for the first time to his reluctant suspicions.

Iago sent him a considering stare, but Themo responded with an out-thrust tongue and a rude, moistly vibrating buzz.

"You sound like the logic and rhetoric master, Matteo. *Before that, therefore because of this,*" Themo quoted in a derisive singsong. "One thing doesn't always follow another, lined up like swimming ducklings. The elf is gone, and so is Andris, and what of it? Doesn't mean Andris has thrown in with Kiva. Maybe he just didn't want the Azuthans poking at him. Can't say I blame him."

"Nor I." A stab of guilt pricked at Matteo. Yes, Andris had misled him, but he had to assume that his friend had a good reason for doing so.

They rode on, stopping frequently to search for the faint, subtle marks of Andris's passing. The lizards moved soundlessly, finding passages through the thick vines and dense underbrush that none of the men could see.

"We're following Andris, but what the Nine bloody Hells is *he* following?" demanded Themo as he picked a leaf from his hair. "Besides the sun, that is."

"According to the temple lore, there is an elf village due west of the temple. Kiva was badly weakened by the laraken. She will need help. It is logical to assume that she would seek out others of her kind."

"I'm not sure which idea I like less," the big man grumbled. "More jordaini logic, or the notion that there could be more at home like Kiva." He suddenly brightened and pointed to a long, narrow clearing up ahead. "There's a path. Going due west, too!"

The "path" was an odd, cone-shaped swath cut into the jungle. No, Matteo noted suddenly, the path had not been cut but burned. The foliage had wilted away, matting the jungle floor with a thick, blackened mass.

Matteo dismounted. He studied the passage, then kicked at some of the wilted vines. The smell of rotting plants rose into the air, and with it the distinctive stench of spoiled eggs.

"Chlorine gas—the breath weapon of a green dragon," Matteo said softly. "Some of the jungle plants can absorb poisonous gases, which is no doubt why we can smell it still."

Iago came to stand beside Matteo. "The dragon is long gone, judging from its droppings." He pointed to a pile of fewmet, nearly dry and littered with bones from long-ago meals.

"Might as well take advantage of the dragon's path." Themo gave his lizard a sharp nudge with both heels. The creature took off like a loosed arrow. Themo jerked back in the saddle, swearing as he struggled to keep his seat.

Startled by the impulsive act, Matteo had no time to shout a warning. He lunged for his friend and seized Themo's tunic as he rode past. He dug in his heels and managed to drag the big jordain off the lizard.

Themo fell hard and came up mad. He launched a wild

swing at Matteo, connecting with a blow to the jaw that sent the smaller man reeling.

"I don't need your help to fall off the damn lizard!"

Matteo scrambled to his feet in time to intercept Themo's second swing. He caught the big man's wrist and twisted his arm behind his back. He spun Themo around to face the path. "See those spider webs at the end of the passage?"

The big jordain squinted at the layers of delicate netting spanning the end of the passage. "So?"

Before Matteo could speak, the "web" enfolded the charging lizard and jerked it up into a tree.

"Oh. Not your usual web," Themo observed, glancing sheepishly back at his friend.

But Matteo's attention was on the trees overhead. He abruptly released Themo and reached for his sword.

The jungle suddenly came alive with exited little yips. Golden, catlike eyes blinked from the deeply shadowed underbrush. A small, hunched green figure dived toward them from high overhead, clinging with one hand to a long vine. A wicked bone-headed spear was couched under one arm, giving its flight the appearance of an airborne joust.

The creature passed harmlessly overhead and landed on a high branch behind them. It sat there, chittering and shaking a small fist.

"What the—"

Themo's outburst ended in a sharp *oof!* as another vine, this one bearing three of the creatures, slammed into his back. He pitched forward onto all fours, and more of the creatures dashed out of the underbrush, swarming over him. They clung to him, clawing and squealing, as he struggled to his feet.

More creatures encircled Matteo. They were hideous beasts, green as goblins but emaciated in form and hunched over in a permanent crouch. None of them stood much higher than Matteo's knees. Their gait was awkward, their mien cowardly. Yet they wielded an assortment of weapons crafted by humans and elves, a silent but powerful testament to previous successes.

"Tasloi,"Matteo muttered.

"Lizard grub!" countered Themo. He peeled off one of the creatures and hurled it toward his entrapped and struggling lizard. The tasloi sailed down the passage, wailing pitifully, and landed well short of the trap. Themo shrugged this off and backhanded another of the pests. He drew his dagger and began to cut free of the mob, working his way toward Iago and dragging the tasloi that clung doggedly to one ankle.

Matteo glanced toward Iago. The small jordain was whirling about, slapping at the tasloi that clung to his back. Several more of the creatures tittered excitedly, circling around Iago and his dervish dance. Though all held weapons, they did not strike. Clearly they expected their comrade to bring the jordain down.

Themo caught up a chunk of dried fewmet and hurled it into the midst of the tasloi spectators. Dragon dung splattered, and the tasloi scattered with shrill, startled yips. Iago took advantage of this reprieve to stagger over to a tree. He slammed his back repeatedly into the trunk, trying to dislodge the clinging tasloi.

Matteo's friends seemed to have matters well in hand. That was just as well, for the tasloi pack that encircled him left him in no position to give immediate aid.

He turned this way and that, sword menacing as he kept the creatures at bay.

The tasloi swarmed him suddenly. He lunged low, knocking aside the spear wielded by the creature directly in front of him. At the same time he kicked out with his back foot, connecting hard with one tasloi rushing in from behind. He pulled his sword free, whirled to the left with a fierce yell that sent several of the creatures skittering back. Just as suddenly he reversed and lunged toward the pair of tasloi that came in from his right. One of the creatures panicked and all but threw his comrade onto Matteo's blade in his haste to backpedal. Matteo grimaced and pulled his sword free. He parried a dagger thrust, kicked the attacking creature aside and turned to face a regrouping trio.

By now most of the tasloi had reconsidered their chances. The surviving members of the pack melted into the jungle, leaving behind a score of their dead.

The three men worked together to cut down Themo's mount and tried not to listen as the other two lizards fed noisily upon the fallen tasloi.

"Fine sport," Themo observed happily. "Of course, the green dragon would have been better, but there's something to be said for starting small."

"The tasloi ambush obscured what little trail sign Andris left behind. Any more time spent tracking would be time wasted," Iago said.

Themo looked unwilling to give up this adventure. "But if we keep traveling west, we'll find this village."

Matteo shook his head. "I wish that were true. Our only chance of finding the village was following Andris to Kiva. From what I can ascertain of wild elves, we could walk directly beneath the village, and not see it unless the elves wanted us to."

The three friends fell silent. Themo's lizard scuttled over to the battlefield and nosed aside one of its comrades. Except for a few of the less palatable bits, the feast was over. Cheated, the reptilian mount returned to its rider, dragging its tail and looking as dejected as a kicked cur.

"What now?" Themo asked in a resigned tone as he climbed back onto his disgruntled mount.

"Perhaps the answer lies in Iago's recent past," Matteo said slowly. His eyes were apologetic as he turned to the small jordain. "You were in the service of Procopio Septus. It seems likely that Zephyr, his jordaini counselor, betrayed you to Kiva, but Zephyr did not give you directly into the elf woman's hand."

Iago's olive skin paled. "That is true."

"Perhaps we should trace the path between. It led to Kiva once. It might again."

The small jordain rode in silence for several moments. "Three days I spent in the Crinti camps," Iago said softly. "By the end of that time, I was grateful to be sold as a slave."

Matteo acknowledged this with a somber nod. "Did the Crinti deal directly with Kiva?"

"Yes. They spared me the indignity of a slave market, if nothing else. Understand this, Matteo: the rumors of the shadow amazons fall far short of the reality."

Themo cast him a disgusted look. "If you don't like the plan, just say so."

"I didn't say it wouldn't work," Iago said slowly. "If I could think of a better one, I'd be swift to speak it."

"Dangerous, is it?"

"I would rather leap naked into a pit of molten tar than return to that hell."

Iago spoke with a stillness that chilled Matteo, but Themo nodded as if this pronouncement confirmed a dearly held hope. "There'll be fighting involved?"

"I can almost guarantee it," Iago murmured. As he spoke, his eyes went cold and hard.

Themo noted the change in his friend's expression and hooted with approval. He slapped the reins on the lizard's neck, his good spirits fully restored. "Well then, what are we sitting around here for?"

CHAPTER SIX

A small, bedraggled figure crept through the jungle, staggering from tree to tree, clinging to each as if she took strength from it. Kiva, the once-powerful magehound, walked barefoot, clad only in the plain gray tunic of an Azuthan penitent. Long, jade-green hair hung about her face. The only magic in her hands was that which rippled through the mazganut tree she clutched for support. Kiva sensed the forest's teeming pulse, heard the soft music of the Weave, but faintly, as if from a great distance.

So frail was Kiva that she felt a disturbing kinship to her own shadow. Her strength had been stolen in battle with the laraken, her wizardly magic siphoned away. For days, only pride had kept her going. Now even that was gone. All Kiva could call upon were ancient memories and the vendetta born of them. Whenever her vision began to blur, she closed her eyes and whispered, *"Akhlaur!"*

Hatred focused her, strengthened her. She had not trained and plotted and fought for two centuries to die now, her vengeance incomplete!

Kiva pushed away from the tree and stumbled onward. Instinct led her where memory failed, for she had been a child of this forest. No elf, no matter how long away from the trees of her birthplace, no matter what transpired in the years between, ever lost her connection with the land. No living elf was completely devoid of magic.

As twilight came on, insects emerged in stinging clouds. Childhood lore came back to Kiva, and she drew in long breaths of air until she caught the faint, sharp note of an acridia plant. She followed the scent and picked a fat spear, crushing it and smearing the fragrant green gel on her skin. The scent disappeared at once, and so did the hungry insects.

This small success heartened her. She noted a hooded flower, nearly knee high, with a blood-red stamen that resembled a sneering goblin. It was the only truly ugly flower she knew, and it held one of the most lethal poisons of the Mhair. Kiva fell to her knees beside it and began to dig for the treasures it protected.

After a few moments she found them—truffles, big as her fist, fragrant and meaty. She brushed the dirt from a savory fungus and began to eat, dutifully at first in order to regain strength, and then with real hunger.

"Kiva," said a male voice, a human voice, deep and disturbingly familiar.

Startled, she leaped to her feet. The too-sudden movement set her head whirling and her vision dancing with sparks of light. When she focused, it was upon the ghostly form of Andris, the jordain she had condemned, used, and discarded.

For a moment Kiva went cold with horror—she, who thought herself beyond reach of such emotions!

"Is this my fate, then?" she murmured. "Am I to be haunted by all those whom I have killed?"

"If that's so, you will never lack company," Andris responded. "Perhaps the others will be along presently, but I am no ghost."

Even as he spoke, she saw it was true. The tall jordain was translucent, but he retained color, like delicately tinted glass. The jungle grasses bent beneath his feet and parted before him as he came toward her.

Her first response, honed by dozens of years among Halruaa's wizards, was to hurl a spell. None came to her call. She pulled her only remaining weapon—a broken boar's tusk, long as a dagger and nearly as sharp—and slashed at the approaching human.

Andris easily dodged and seized her wrist. The elf tried to twist away, but her captor's grip was surprisingly firm and strong. She quickly realized the futility of struggle and forced herself to meet his eyes. To her relief and puzzlement, her death was not written in them.

"How is this possible?" she demanded, her gaze traveling his translucent form.

"The laraken did this. I carry elf blood, the gift of a distant ancestor. 'Distant' only in terms of time," he added pointedly.

Understanding touched the elf's golden eyes, bringing light but no warmth. Andris felt an illogical stab of disappointment.

At loss for words, he handed Kiva the necromancer's tome. She paged through the ancient book, her face deathly pale and her lips set in a tight line.

"Is this true?" Andris asked gently.

Kiva slammed the book shut. "As far as it goes, yes. There is much left unsaid."

Andris whistled softly. "If that is true, I am glad for the omission. "

"You should be." Her voice was faint, and memories haunted her eyes.

After a few moments, Andris ventured, "This book explained many things. I've wondered how you, a full-blooded elf, could face the laraken and live."

His question jolted her back into the present moment. "Do I?" The elf spat out the words. "The laraken and its *creator*—" she punctuated this by hurling the book back at Andris—"have taken from me everything of value. I breathe, I speak and move. I hate! But do I live? Such things the sages debate!"

Andris recognized the bitterness in her voice and heard

the insanity. Neither changed his chosen path. "You will resolve the question for them if you stay here much longer. You are weak, Kiva. You cannot survive alone."

Her chin lifted. "I have allies."

"You had better find them, and soon."

She was about to respond when they caught the distant sound of underbrush rustling and a faint, grating snuffle. A boar, Andris noted grimly. In her hunger, Kiva had apparently forgotten that the scent of truffles might lure one of the dangerous beasts.

Kiva's eyes darted toward the sound, then to the ghostly sword on the jordain's hip. "I can help you," Andris said softly as he eased his weapon free. "With the boar and with other things."

The elf managed a scornful little laugh. "At what price?"

"Tell me how the Cabal can be destroyed."

This Kiva had clearly not expected. She regarded the jordain with curiosity. "Only idiots and elves believe in the Cabal. You spoke truth when you claimed elf blood?"

Andris noted that she spoke only of race, not of kinship. "Did I speak truth? Lady, I am a jordain," he said, self-mockery sharp in his eyes.

She let this pass. For the first time she looked at him, and there was something approaching kinship in her amber eyes. "You saw the captured elves of Kilmaruu, you read Akhlaur's journal," she said in a soft but steely voice. "You know who we are and what we must do. So be it."

Andris met the elf woman's eyes and saw there a destiny that encompassed them both. He responded with a grim nod.

There was no time for anything more. The underbrush exploded into a sudden fury of sound and motion. Andris whirled to face the charging beast—an enormous black sow, her belly swinging slack from a recent litter and her red eyes gleaming with desperate knowledge of her piglets' hunger. He judged the creature as nearly half the mass of a war-horse, with thrice the fight and fury.

Kiva touched Andris on the back, just below the shoulder blades. "Here," she said tersely. "Strike hard."

He acknowledged this with a curt nod and then pushed her aside, holding his ground as the wild pig charged in, its snout tucked like a charging bull. At the last moment Andris sidestepped, spun, and drove the sword home.

The blade sank into the hump of fat that was the wild pig's most vulnerable spot. Andris felt the sword grate against ribs before it was wrenched from his grasp. Even so, the great sow took several more steps before she stumbled and went down.

"Careful," the elf cautioned as Andris closed in. "The sow could still gut you with a nod of her head."

The wounded pig managed to get her feet beneath her and a tree at her back. At bay, she swung her massive head as if daring Andris to attack. The jordain stood his ground, battle-poised but patient.

It was not the sow's nature to wait tamely for death. She let out a searing bellow and burst into a charge, heading not for Andris but for the weaponless Kiva.

Andris shouted a warning and sprinted directly through the beast's path, slashing at the pig's sloped forehead. Blood poured freely. Blinded, the creature veered wildly aside.

Andris leaped onto the bristly back and groped for the hilt of the embedded sword, but the pig whirled and bucked, its tusks slashing the air. With each movement the upright sword swayed and danced like a palm tree in a monsoon gale. Andris was battered by the flailing movements of his own sword. Try as he might, he could not get a grip on it without slicing his hand on the blade or losing his hold on the pig.

As the sow frantically pitched and spun, the forest colors blurred into a whirling green haze. Andris was dimly aware of Kiva's shouts, barely audible above the creature's furious squeals and roars, and the thunderous pounding of his own heart. He sensed a dark streak sweeping in at him, felt a bruising blow glance off his shoulder and thud heavily into the sow's ribs

The wild pig stopped to consider this new threat. Andris focused his spinning vision on the elf woman, who stood with her feet planted wide and a stout length of deadwood in her hands.

"The sword!" she shrieked as she hauled back the club for another swing.

Andris seized the hilt. Before he could thrust it down for the killing blow, the sow took off toward Kiva in another running charge. The jordain jolted back, certain he would lose his seat and yank the sword free.

He might have done just that, had Kiva been less agile. The elf dived aside, rolling quickly and coming to her feet. From the corner of his eye, Andris saw Kiva throw herself into a spin, bringing the club up and around as she came.

The stout stick caught him across the flat of his back, slamming him forward. Pain radiated through his limbs like molten fire, but he pushed it aside and used the momentum to help him thrust the sword deep between the sow's ribs. Still holding the hilt, he threw himself from his perch, wrenching the sword to one side as he fell. He let go and rolled away from the wounded beast. Coming up in a battle crouch, he pulled his jordaini daggers and waited.

Blood poured from the pig's snout and dripped from its tusks, but it took a few staggering steps toward Andris. It closed in, nearly to arm's length, before its legs finally buckled and gave out. The stubborn beast fell, twitched, and went still.

Andris released his breath on a long, ragged sigh of relief. He cast a wry look at Kiva. Her angular, elven face was drawn and ashen, almost gray beneath its coppery tone. He bit back the sarcastic "thanks" that danced ready on his tongue and set to work butchering. Kiva managed to light a fire. By unspoken agreement, they worked together and with great haste. Night was falling, and scavengers would soon come prowling. They quickly seared and ate several small chunks of meat.

When their hurried meal was over, the elf gestured toward a nearby mazganut tree. Andris helped her climb into its branches. He leaned against the stout trunk, winced with pain, and shifted around until he found a position that didn't hurt his bruised shoulders too badly. They settled down in relative safety to await the dawn.

The silence stretched between them, heavy with unanswered questions. Kiva spoke abruptly. "This is no paladin's quest you undertake. Have you the stomach for it? For me?"

She reached out and touched his throbbing shoulder. "This journey started painfully. Most likely, matters will not improve. I won't mouth regrets I don't feel, and I'll do whatever it takes to avenge the wrongs done to your people and mine. Knowing this, will you follow me still?"

Andris answered as honestly as he could. "I can't pretend to understand all that you have done, but I believe we share a common goal."

"And that will content you, jordain?"

He hadn't expected anything more. Aloud he said, "Where do we start?"

Kiva's smile was suddenly feline. "We meet some of those allies I promised you. I admire your confidence, Andris, but did you really think that we two could take on the whole of Halruaa?"

Andris awoke while the sun still slept. He watched as light slowly filtered through the layers of forest canopy and lit the quiet, ravaged face of the elf woman beside him.

Kiva was in reverie, the uniquely elven state of wakeful dreaming, more restful than sleep. Her feline eyes were open, fixed upon some distant, pleasant sight. A small, innocent smile curved her lips. She looked very young, and not at all like the coldly determined magehound who had shattered his life. For a moment Andris wondered how far back Kiva had to go to find this person, these memories.

Then, suddenly, she was awake, and her eyes were as cold as a hunting cat's. Andris glanced aside, but not before she took note of his scrutiny.

"Well?" she demanded.

"We have much to do. I will ponder the mystery of evil some other day."

She looked puzzled, then astonished. For a moment he thought she would dispute his assessment. But Kiva was no jordain, and apparently she did not share his passion for either disputation or truth.

Or perhaps, he realized, his opinion simply did not matter to her.

Without further speech they unwound the vines that tethered them to the mazganut branch. Kiva quickly braided her hair into two plaits, and they drank some of the dew that collected in the large, almond-scented leaves.

As they scrambled down the tree into the deeply shaded clearing beneath, Andris noted that the elf seemed stronger. She seemed to be absorbing strength from the teeming life of the forest. An image flashed into Andris's mind—the hideous laraken gaining flesh as it drained magic and life. Like mother, like child. The analogy sent a shudder of revulsion through Andris. He dropped the last few feet onto the thick carpet of moss, suddenly eager to put some distance between himself and the elf woman.

As Kiva's foot touched the forest floor, an arrow flashed into the clearing. It pierced one of her jade-colored braids and pinned it securely to the tree.

The elf woman's eyes went wide, but she did not struggle. She called out in a language that was more akin to wind and birdsong than to human speech.

Five elves stepped into the mazganut clearing, soundless as shadows. All were male, and none stood taller than Andris's shoulder. Their sharp-featured faces were beautiful, their skin ranging in hue from copper to polished sandalwood, their hair rich shades of brown or green. These were not primitive folk, as Andris had always heard, but people who possessed artistry, even riches. They wore finely woven linen, and the arrowhead that pinned Kiva to the tree was carved from a gemstone.

These thoughts flicked into Andris's mind and were gone, chased by a growing sense of awe as the elves stalked in. They moved with the taut, deadly grace of jungle cats. Never had Andris beheld warriors who filled him with more admiration or more foreboding. And these wondrous people were his kin!

Of course, that didn't mean they wouldn't kill him where he stood.

With great reluctance, he reached for his sword.

"Put away your weapon, *karasanzor*," one of the elves said in heavily accented Halruaan. "We mean no harm."

A moment passed before Andris realized the elf was speaking to him, not Kiva. The former magehound was weaponless, yet the elf fixed his gaze upon her as he spoke.

Because he wanted to believe them, and because he really had no choice, Andris accepted the elf's pledge. He slid his sword away and lifted both hands in a gesture of peace. Still no one met his eyes.

"You are of the People," the elf said to Kiva, "and your voice knows the song of the jungle. Yet you wear human clothes and travel with a human . . . companion."

Kiva started to speak in Elvish, but the male cut her off with a few sharp words. She went pale, but her chin lifted. "Very well, I will speak the human tongue until I have earned the right in your eyes to speak as one of the People.

"I have lived among the humans of Halruaa for many years, but once my name was sung in these forests as Akivaria, a daughter of the Crimson Tree."

The elves exchanged glances. "Yes, I am *that* Akivaria," Kiva said tartly. "A survivor of the village you patrol—the only living survivor. My kinsman Zephyr was slain by the humans."

A moment of profound silence met this news. Tears burned in one elf's eyes and ran down his face, unchecked and unashamed. Andris felt the elf's grief as if it were his own, yet mingled with it was a strange sense of joy. Zephyr was Kiva's kin, and this warrior wept a kinsman's tears over the old jordain. Perhaps these elves were his family in fact, and not just through distant bonds of shared race.

Family—it was a word he had never thought to employ in his own service. He turned it over in his mind, trying to fit what he knew of such things to the watchful, wary elves with their alien eyes and ready weapons.

"Why have you come back now?" There was no kinsman's welcome in the elf's copper face. Andris would not have noticed Kiva flinch had he not felt an identical pain.

"Is it not enough that I want to come home?" asked Kiva.

"If that were true, you would have come sooner." The elf tipped his head toward Andris. "You would have come alone."

Kiva let that pass. "We are still several days' walk from the Crimson Tree. You found us quickly."

"Our scouts brought word of humans in the forest pass," offered another, younger elf. "Several hunting parties. The latest had only three men, but unlike the others, they found and followed the *karasanzor's* path."

A deep foreboding came over Andris. "Were they dressed in white, and did they wear medallions like mine?"

The elf leader and Kiva shot identical quelling glares at their companions. But Andris took his answer from the glint of surprise in the young elf's eyes.

So Matteo had come looking for him. That was not completely unexpected, but it was distressing nonetheless. There was no friend whom Andris valued more and no enemy he would rather avoid.

"We remember Akhlaur," the elf spokesman said. "We remember the raid on your village. Later, many of us lost friends and kin to Akhlaur's swamp monster. We want nothing to do with Halruaa or with People who love the humans enough to live among them and their foul magic."

"Do you love the boar, the river eels, the swamp dragons?" demanded Kiva. "If you intend to hunt a creature, you must first stalk it and observe its habits. I know Halruaa better than she knows herself."

The elf folded his arms. "So?"

"Knowledge is a deadly sword. I offer it to the People of Mhair."

"We're to hunt wizards, are we?" demanded the elf leader with knife-edged sarcasm. "With what? The weapons of the jungle?"

"With their own weapons," Kiva countered. "We will fight with wizardly magic."

The elf sniffed derisively. "You might as well offer to bring sea-going ships into the jungle! What value are weapons we cannot use?"

"I can use them. I am a wizard," Kiva said. She grimaced, then amended, "Or so I was, until the laraken drained away my spells."

A moment of profound and respectful silence fell over the elves. "You have faced the laraken? And it took no more from you than your human spells?" demanded the speaker.

"I am weakened," Kiva admitted, "but I still live."

"How is this possible, when the monster ripped so many elves from life so swiftly that they left holes in the very fabric of the Weave?"

"My wizardly magic was strong," Kiva said. "The laraken drank and was satisfied. What was taken from me can be restored."

The elf leader glanced at the ghostly jordain. "And the *karasanzor*?"

"He is called Andris. He also survived the laraken. He is a jordain, a name humans of Halruaa give to their loremasters. He is also a battlemaster, resistant to wizardly magic and skilled at fighting against it."

The elf looked puzzled. "He *is* these things, you say?"

"Yes. *Is*."

Andris was not sure what this cryptic exchange meant, but he noted that Kiva had neglected to mention his elf blood. He ached to claim what kinship he could. Before he could speak, Kiva stabbed him with a glare, eloquently and unmistakably warning him to silence.

The elf spokesman was not yet done with his questions. "Let us say that you have these weapons of magic. Let's assume that we could prevail against the humans. Why would we want to fight them again, when peace was so hard-earned and long in coming?"

"Because if we don't, Akhlaur could return."

Stunned silence met her words. Andris felt as shocked and skeptical as the elves looked.

"All these many years," Kiva went on, "the laraken's source of strength was a trickle of water from another world, a world full of magic—an endless supply of magic. The laraken escaped into that world. So did Akhlaur."

Horror startled Andris into speaking out of turn. "Why did you help it escape?"

The elf woman's glance flicked over to him. "Why would I lead an army of magic-dead warriors against the laraken, except to destroy it? It was my intention to enter the Plane of Water once the laraken was destroyed, to face Akhlaur. But Tzigone did not hold the laraken, choosing instead to waste her spells attacking me."

Andris thought back upon the confusion and chaos of battle. The laraken had broken free of Tzigone and rushed back to the spring just as Kiva conjured a large, bubbling gate. When Kiva fell, it was within arm's reach of this gate. Perhaps the larakan's escape truly had been accidental, but the notion of her "facing Akhlaur" was too much for his mind to absorb.

"Kiva, the necromancer disappeared over two hundred years ago. No doubt he is long dead."

"Since when was a necromancer inconvenienced by death?" Kiva spoke as if quelling a child who interrupted his elders' conversation. "Do you think him incapable of transforming himself into a lich?"

Andris had no answer. The specter of an undead Akhlaur dwarfed any possible response into insignificance.

"There is more," the elf woman went on. "It was Akhlaur who created the laraken, fashioning it so that whatever magic the monster absorbed would pass to its master. Now the laraken is again within Akhlaur's grasp. That can only speed his return to power and to Halruaa. When he emerges—and eventually he will—alive or dead, it matters not—it will be as the most powerful deathwizard Halruaa has ever known. If he is to be stopped, it must be now."

Andris nodded slowly, seeing a thread of logic in Kiva's complicated tapestry. How could she avenge herself and her people if the wizard responsible for so much suffering was beyond her grasp? Given what he knew of Kiva, her plan involved more than a simple spellbattle confrontation. He did not exactly trust Kiva, but if at the end Akhlaur was vanquished once and for all, wasn't that worth the risk?

The elves seemed equally conflicted. "I am called Nadage," the elf spokesman said at last. "I am a scout and warrior. What you suggest is a matter for the elders."

"There is little time," Kiva protested. "Such a trip would take days."

"Not so. When humans were first spotted in the forest pass, battle preparations began. We can reach our camp by nightfall. You will come and speak before the People."

Without further discussion, the elves turned and headed westward. Kiva gave Andris a little shove, and they fell into step behind.

"Perhaps it was a mistake for me to come with you," Andris observed softly. "They seem reluctant to speak their minds before strangers."

"It is not the elven way. I was born in this jungle, but I have been gone for many years. You'll notice that they did not welcome me with joy or offer to gossip about all that has happened since I left."

"They disapprove of mixed blood?"

Kiva gave a derisive sniff. "You jordaini have a talent for understatement."

Andris found this painful, but logical. "Reasonable

enough, given the dwindling numbers of elves. I assume they perceive elfbloods as a threat?"

She sent him a small, hard smile. "If they considered you a threat, you'd be dead. Did you notice that they did not look at you?"

"Yes, but I was too busy being glad they didn't *shoot* at me to worry about it overmuch," Andris responded. After a moment's consideration he added, "Perhaps I owe my life to the fact that they thought me already dead."

"That's very close. They called you *karasanzor.* That means 'crystal one,' and it is a term of respect. They did not look at you because we do not gaze upon the crystal ghosts of our elf kin."

Andris gestured toward his translucent form. "So looking like this is a good thing, according to the forest elves?"

"It puts you in a unique position," Kiva agreed. "You're clearly human—you should pardon the expression—but you appear to share the *karasanzor's* fate. Furthermore, you faced the laraken and lived. They don't know what to make of you."

"They are not alone," Andris muttered.

They did not speak again until the elves stopped for the evening. The scouts showed them to a small house built high into the forest canopy, well away from the camp itself.

Andris and Kiva ate the fruit that the scouts left for them and settled down for the night. Deeper in the jungle, the unseen elves began to sing. The melody was slow and languorous, with a gently pulsing rhythm.

Andris had never known a mother, but he suspected that this song was a lullaby. Never had he heard anything so moving. It comforted and saddened him at the same time.

Kiva stopped brushing her hair and turned to him. "What do you know of the Lady's Mirror?"

The sudden question shattered the music's spell. Andris frowned. "It is a pool sacred to Mystra, Lady of Magic, tended by wizards who worship her servant Azuth, the Lord of Wizards. Some say that on a full moon the face of the goddess can be seen in the still waters. This sight is considered to be a sign of great blessing."

"There is a small temple near the shore of the Mirror. A repository of spellbooks and artifacts, and not a particularly well-guarded one." Her glance slid over, held his puzzled stare, and waited for him to catch up.

Comprehension came over him slowly. A score of Azuthan priests served the temple, and at any given time there might be perhaps another twenty visitors who came for pilgrimage or study. There was no fortified keep, just a few small buildings, little more than traveler's huts, scattered throughout the nearby grove. Yet none of the magical books or items had ever gone missing. Such an act would be tantamount to ripping tapestries off the walls of King Zalathorm's festhall.

"You cannot mean to desecrate the Lady's Mirror!" he protested

"No," she said with dark amusement. "I plan to *raid* it. Upon the morrow, you will tell me how."

She smiled at his dumbfounded expression and patted his cheek as if he were a slow but promising child. "Get some sleep. We rise with the dawn."

Andris settled down, certain that he would never find slumber with such a task before him, but the evensong of elves spoke to him as wizardly magic could not. It stole into his blood, into his soul, soothing and calming him in a manner he had never dreamed possible.

Andris wondered about elven reverie and wistfully coveted the vivid, waking dreams that were said to be more refreshing than sleep. Perhaps here, in this place, he might share some of that fey peace.

When he slept, though, his dreams were not of peace. And when the morning came, the plan he lay before Kiva made her eyes burn with golden fire.

CHAPTER SEVEN

The distant spires of Azuth's Temple rose against
the sunset clouds as Matteo and his friends
emerged from the forested pass.

"A little dove's flying this way," Themo
observed, nodding toward the small gray figure
that ran toward the jordaini, arms and legs pump-
ing steadily. "Making good time, too."

"Must be important if it couldn't wait a few
more hours," added Iago.

Matteo nodded and shook the reins over
his lizard mount. The others followed suit. They
hurried to meet the runner—a barefoot and
barelegged girl, clad in a short tunic of Azuthan
gray. She dipped into a bow and then handed
Matteo a scroll. "I am to wait for your reply,
my lord."

"Just Matteo," he corrected absently as he
broke the seal. "The jordaini claim no titles."

"As you wish," the girl murmured politely.

"It's not as *I* wish," Themo put in, only half in jest.
"What do you say, Iago? What title would suit me?
Themo the war baron? Themo the king's general?"

"Themo the horse's arse," Iago suggested.

Themo snorted and reached out to punch
Matteo's shoulder. "Well, are you going to tell us
what's worth wearing out this lass's pretty feet, or
do you want us to guess?"

Matteo glanced up at his two friends. "A message from the queen's steward. He is concerned about Queen Beatrix and requires my presence at once."

"Your response?" the acolyte prompted.

"There can be only one. I will leave for Halarahh at first light."

"I will accompany you," suggested Iago.

"And I!" put in Themo stoutly. He slapped the reins against his lizard's neck, as if he would ride all the way. The great creature's shoulders rose and fell in an astonishingly human gesture of resignation.

Matteo reached out and dropped a hand on the big jordain's shoulder. "I would have you, and gladly, but your training is not yet complete."

"Training!" grumbled Themo. "My head holds all the information that's ever likely to fit. Every now and then a man's got to stop thinking and start doing. By Mystra, what this country needs is a good war!"

Dark memories of the recent swamp battles flooded into Iago's eyes. For a moment Matteo thought that Iago would draw a weapon on Themo and wash the big man's theory away with his own blood. The small jordain regained his composure quickly.

"War usually results from a cessation of thought," Iago observed. "So I suppose your argument has some basis in logic."

"Logic," Themo sneered. "I liked it better when you called me a horse's arse."

Iago smiled. "Fortunate is the man who is content with what and who he is." Though he spoke to Themo, he sent a long, somber stare in Matteo's direction.

Themo, whose enjoyment of a good insult surpassed his subtlety, heard the jest and missed the warning. Matteo marked it and would think of it often in the days to come.

☙

The journey to Halarahh was swift and uneventful. The River Halar ran deep and fast, and the Azuthans' shallow keeled boat sped along the water like a low-flying swan. At the delta harbor, Matteo and Iago changed to a sea-going vessel. Their captain hugged the coast, for far out over the lake sullen gray clouds grumbled and clashed like titanic dwarves roused too soon from slumber. By day's end the docks of Halarahh lay within sight.

The two jordaini leaned against the ship's rail and watched the gap between ship and city narrow.

"We have not spoken of your plans, Iago. Will you return to Procopio Septus?"

The small jordain shrugged. "No doubt Lord Procopio will release me to the first minor wizard who requests my service."

Matteo shook his head. "You are a noted battlemaster, and Lord Procopio is an ambitious man. He will not lightly let you go."

"He is ambitious," Iago agreed, "and because of his ambitions he cannot afford to be tainted by failure. Zephyr was Kiva's ally. I fought for her. Although the Jordaini Council declared me innocent of wrongdoing, in the eyes of many observers it may appear that both of Procopio's errant jordaini were hit by the contents of the same chamber pot."

"You fought the laraken and won," Matteo reminded him. "Your success may go far toward canceling out Zephyr's treason. Certainly it proves your battle prowess, something Lord Procopio values greatly. He's too ambitious to see such skills as yours wasted on a midwife or an apothecary."

Iago snorted. "In truth, I would rather serve a potion peddler than a warlord."

Warlord. The title hung heavy in the silence that followed its naming. Matteo nodded grimly. "So you see it, too. Procopio prepares to wear that mantle."

"Lord Procopio is ambitious," Iago repeated cautiously.

"War is often the path to power. Stay with Procopio if you can," Matteo urged. "He should be watched."

The jordain gave him an incredulous look. "What are you suggesting?"

Matteo considered his next words carefully, for he was picking his way through new and dangerous territory. "We jordaini swear many oaths, binding us to our patrons, to Halruaa, and to truth. What happens when these pledges conflict?"

"But—"

"Hear me out. What is our primary concern? Do we serve the ambitions of a single man? The good of the land? Truth? And what defines this 'good,' this 'truth?' Our own perceptions or those of our patron? Do we listen to the voice of conscience or the demands of ambition?"

Iago was silent for a long time. "You should be careful about speaking such thoughts, my friend. Some might call it treason."

"Others might call it honor," Matteo pointed out. "If we jordaini abandon honor, what good can we possibly do? Can we be Halruaa's guardians with no moral compass other than the whim of the wizard-lords? You know history. You know what wizardly ambition can do."

"We serve the wizard-lords," began Iago.

"Yes, and so do the message boys that carry word from the wizard's kitchen to the butcher. If we do everything we are bid, without thought, how are we any different?"

The small man fell silent. "I will consider your words, Matteo. Since you are a friend, I will not repeat them."

Iago spoke with great finality. Matteo was surprised, therefore, when Iago picked up the awkward threads of their conversation.

"You have spoken plainly. Will you hear some blunt words?"

"Of course!"

"You're quick to trust," the jordain observed, "and far too impulsive. You seem willing to do whatever a friend requires of you. Perhaps you care too deeply about your friends."

Matteo's brow furrowed. "How is that a fault?"

"I didn't say it was a fault, exactly, but it is a danger. What will you do, Matteo, if you must make a choice between your jordaini duties and your friends? You puzzle over the conflicts of truth, the good of the land, and the will of the wizard-lords. How much more difficult would you find it to weigh the good of Halruaa against the life of a friend? And what of truth? Would you lie for Andris?" His steady black gaze narrowed and sharpened. "Or perhaps for Tzigone? It seems to me there is little you would not do for that girl."

Matteo felt his cheeks flame. "As I keep repeating, she is a friend and nothing more."

"As I am trying to tell *you*, perhaps you care too deeply for your friends. You've already fought a magehound's wemic for Tzigone. You went to prison rather than name her as a thief, even though she stole the sword that led to your arrest and didn't bother to tell you she'd hidden it among your possessions. To protect her, you killed a wizard. A *wizard*, Matteo! The Disputation Table absolved you of legal wrongdoing, but have you any idea how the wizard-lords regard a jordain who kills? In the eyes of many, you're as dangerous and unpredictable as a half-feral dog."

"I know this," Matteo said quietly.

"You know a great deal, and yet knowledge does not give you wisdom! Whenever that beguiling little witch shows up, you cease thinking and merely act."

Matteo was silent for a long moment. His words, when he spoke, surprised him. "You find her beguiling?"

The older man sighed heavily. "It does not matter what I think. I am not the one who missed the purification ritual."

Matteo was unlikely to forget this particular disgrace, though he wasn't certain why Iago brought it up in the current context. "I will remember," he promised.

Iago was not yet finished. "We've all learned the tales of

impossible quests and tragic passions. Only heroes can afford such things, Matteo. We are not heroes. We are counselors."

The young man shook his head in bewilderment. "I know what I am."

"I hope so, Matteo," he said softly, his black eyes fixed upon the rapidly approaching docks.

They did not speak again, except for a strained recitation of ritual parting words as they left the ship and went their own ways.

Night enfolded the city as Matteo worked his way through the teeming dock area and out onto the broad, tree-lined streets of Halarahh. Magical lanterns winked alight as he set a brisk pace toward the palace.

His thoughts turned to Queen Beatrix. He did not know the exact nature of the steward's concern, but he could think of several possibilities. He owed his position to the death of his predecessor. The queen's former counselor had been slain by one of her clockwork devices.

This had long puzzled Matteo. No one at the palace ever spoke of this accident. Nor had the jordain's death been discussed at the College. Matteo had still been a student at the time, and certainly would have heard the stories. Was it possible that a man's death could be held in such strict secrecy and without consequence to those at fault? Halruaa was a land of law. Surely even the queen was not above its rule!

Yet as far as Matteo could tell, no steps had been taken to curb the queen's strange and dangerous pastime.

Many things about his royal patron troubled him, not the least of which was the strange song he had overheard her sing at their last meeting. For a brief moment, the queen had reminded him of Tzigone.

Yet the voice was not the same, nor was there any physical resemblance between the queen and his friend. Surely he was seeing ghosts in a house not haunted! He had promised Tzigone to help her find her mother, and of course he would search for Tzigone's face in that of every woman he met. It didn't help matters that Tzigone, with her uncanny knack for imitation and her mobile, expressive features, could change herself at will. No doubt she could resemble half the women in Halruaa!

He absently dodged a pair of giggling lovers who staggered out of an alehouse, supporting each other as they wove down the street. As Matteo passed the narrow alley that ran behind the tavern, a small figure stirred amid the shadows, and a very grubby face turned to watch him pass.

The jordain walked on, aware of the soft pad of footsteps behind him. He was not entirely surprised to sense a furtive touch on the hilt of his silver dagger.

Matteo reached back and seized the fragile wrist. He spun toward the thief, twisting the lad's arm and spinning him about so that his back was to Matteo and his captured wrist held high behind his back. Matteo pushed his captive back toward the privacy of the alley. All this he did quickly, with as little sound and movement as possible. The laws of the land dealt harshly with thieves.

The lad seemed to realize this. He went along quietly, no doubt hoping to escape once they were well away from prying eyes.

Matteo marched the boy behind a pile of crates. "You've nothing to fear from me," he said softly. "Thievery suggests great need. If this is so, speak plainly. I will keep your confidence, and do what I can to help you."

"Well, since you offered, there's an itch between my shoulder blades that I just can't seem to reach," suggested a familiar voice, a rich alto that bubbled with suppressed mirth.

A familiar jangle of emotion sang through Matteo—amusement, affection, exasperation, and the mingled chagrin and delight he'd felt as a lad when he fell victim to one of Andris's pranks.

"Tzigone," Matteo muttered. He released the "urchin," who whirled to face him.

Even now that he knew her, Matteo had difficulty seeing his friend under her disguise. She'd smeared dark ointment on her face for a sun-browned appearance, and one swollen cheek bore the yellowing remnant of a huge bruise. She spat out a small, wadded rag, and her face took on a more familiar shape.

Tzigone fisted both of her grubby hands in his hair and pulled him down to her level. She planted a resounding kiss on the bridge of his nose, then matter-of-factly wiped away a smudge of greasepaint she'd left behind.

Feeling strangely discomfited, Matteo stepped back and drew his jordaini dignity around himself like a cloak. "Is this how Basel Indoulur dresses his apprentices?"

"I dress myself, thanks," Tzigone retorted, her eyes dancing with glee. "Same goes for the *un*dressing. Don't think that I don't get offers, though, glamorous wench that I am."

"No doubt," Matteo murmured. "So. How are your studies progressing?"

Her smile faded and reshaped itself into a lopsided grin. "I expect to be elevated to the Council of Elders within the tenday."

"Have you learned more of your mother?"

The light faded from her eyes. "I thought it would be easy to find a lost wizard once I was inside the tower, so to speak. Wizards hoard information like heirloom spell books. Since we're being blunt and serious, I might as well take a turn. What news of Kiva?"

"She has escaped." Matteo placed a hand over Tzigone's mouth to cut off her outburst, then promptly released her. "I gave my word to the Azuthan priests that I would keep this in confidence, subject only to previous vows. The pledge of friendship between us is one such vow. Since Kiva has been pursuing you your entire life, I felt that you must be forewarned."

"Thanks," Tzigone muttered absently. "So you've got the same problem I have—you have to find someone without letting anyone know you're looking. Is there anyone you can trust? What about that old elf who was nice to you when you both worked for Procopio Septus? Maybe his friends know something useful."

"I'm afraid that path ends against a solid wall. Zephyr died a traitor's death. All who knew him are scrambling for as much distance as they can get."

Tzigone regarded him appraisingly. "Cynical. That's a new color for you."

Matteo sighed. "Can we be serious for a moment?"

"One of us can, that's for damn sure," she murmured.

He ignored the good-natured insult. "As a jordain, I am pledged to serve the queen, my patron. As a friend, I have promised to help you learn what became of your mother. Both of these things are important, but Kiva must be found, and soon."

"Agreed," Tzigone said readily, "but why are you looking for Kiva in Halarahh?"

"I'm not. I was ordered back to the palace. I will continue my search as soon as I can obtain leave."

She considered this. "What happens to a jordain who just picks up and goes?"

"I don't know," he said in surprise. "As far as I know, it has never happened."

"Hmm." Tzigone sent him a sidelong glance from beneath lowered lashes, but did not press the matter.

They spoke for a few moments of other things, and in that time Matteo laughed more than he had under the light of the past two moons. After Tzigone slipped away, Matteo continued to the palace with a lighter heart.

He made his way directly to the queen's chambers. As he had expected, the workshop hummed with activity. He found the queen working at a table in a far corner of the chamber and drew near to pay his respects. He might as well have tried to discuss philosophy with a cat. She never once looked up from the half-finished device, oblivious to everything but the winged metal creature taking shape under her hands.

After several unsuccessful attempts, Matteo left in search of the queen's steward. He found Timonk in the wine cellar, taking a long pull from a bottle of haerlu gold.

He entered quietly and seized the man's wrist. Startled in mid swallow, Timonk jerked away with a gurgling protest. Fragrant liquid spilled over the steward's tunic.

Matteo pulled the coughing, sputtering man to his feet. "I will apologize after you explain why you called me back."

A measure of sobriety crept back into the man's fuzzy gaze. "She's getting worse," he said darkly. He lifted a bandaged hand. With drink-addled fingers, he fumbled off the bandage.

Matteo's eyes widened. Only two fingers and a thumb remained on the steward's hand. The others had been sheared cleanly away.

"One of the clockwork creatures?" Matteo asked quietly.

The man nodded. "Since you left, all she has done is build."

"Why didn't you tell the king?"

Timonk's only response was a loud snort, drunken but derisive.

Matteo rested one hand on the man's shoulder, then turned and sprinted up the stairs that led into the queen's palace. He strode through the triple doors that kept her toys from disturbing the rest of the court, past the clockwork ice dragons that stood guard, and down the hall toward the king's council chamber.

A plump, sweet-faced woman wearing the blue of a royal herald stopped him at the door. Her face turned grim as she listened to the jordain's tale, and she asked him to wait.

The herald returned in moments. "The king is holding open court, but he will speak with you as soon as he might."

Matteo nodded his thanks and worked his way through the throng that gathered in the high-vaulted hall. He waited quietly in an alcove until the last of the supplicants had been given audience. At last the king dismissed his courtiers and guards and motioned for Matteo to approach.

With a grateful sigh, King Zalathorm removed his crown and set it on the empty table to his right. The left-hand table was still piled with parchment, mute testament to the multitude of mundane matters that absorbed the great wizard's attention.

Halruaa's king was a mild-looking man of average height, with a soft brown beard and a thoughtful, almost dreamy expression. He looked to be in midlife, yet he had ruled the kingdom for all of Matteo's life, as throughout the lifetimes of Matteo's unknown parents, and theirs before them.

"Your face is troubled, Matteo," the king said. "Since you are a jordain, your concerns are beyond divination. Speak freely."

"The queen's steward summoned me back to Halarahh, expressing concern for her well-being." Matteo said carefully. "There is much about the queen that I do not understand. If I am to serve her, I must know how she came to be as she is. Can you tell me of her life before she came to Halarahh?"

Matteo doubted there was a safe door into so dangerous a room, but this was the most tactful approach he could fathom. Once before the king had confided in him. Perhaps if Zalathorm started talking about his queen's dark past, they might find a way to discuss her present troubles.

A shadow passed over Zalathorm's face. He lifted one hand and rubbed distractedly at his jaw. "Beatrix was born into a family of wizards, raised in a quiet settlement in the northeastern hills," he recited wearily. "All of Halruaa knows her history. The Crinti attacked and brutally slew every living thing in that settlement. Beatrix was the sole survivor."

"She was gravely wounded," Matteo prompted.

"That and more. She was horribly disfigured." The king fell silent for a long moment. "A simple spell gives her a fairer face, but that is not sufficient for Beatrix. Her porcelain façade is more than a queen's pride or a woman's vanity. It is a shield she places between herself and the assault of memory."

"She remembers nothing?"

"No. Perhaps that is for the best."

"When the queen came to the city years ago, she was examined by the magehound Kiva, now condemned as a murderer and a traitor to Halruaa. What significance might that hold?"

Zalathorm waved this away. "None that I know of. Obviously the elf woman kept her secrets for a very long time. She could not have done so unless she carefully avoided scrutiny. I can only assume that for years Kiva did her work correctly and well. She got the story of the Crinti raid from Beatrix, using the prescribed spells and artifacts. I have no reason to doubt it."

"Yet Kiva claimed she murdered Cassia at the command of Queen Beatrix. She claimed the queen was concerned about the purity of the jordaini order, and the quality of counsel you were receiving. The queen called in Kiva, who examined Cassia, then passed sentence."

The king lifted one eyebrow. "Tell me, Matteo, in your opinion is Beatrix consumed by concern for jordaini purity?"

"No," he admitted.

"The Elders agreed with you. Kiva's story was repeated and considered. Most find it ludicrous. Beatrix is not capable of treachery." The wizard king's shoulders rose and fell as if under a great burden. "I almost wish she were."

Zalathorm's eyes took on the unfocused look of one who looks deep into the past. "When Beatrix first came to Halarahh, she was like a blossoming flower. She remembered nothing, so everything was new to her. I have lived too long," he concluded with a wistful smile. "I had forgotten how bright was the world when it was new. For several years, Beatrix was my eyes. Indeed, she was every gem in my crown. Magic lent her beauty, but all Halruaa admired her grace, her charm, her vivacity, and most of all, her courage. The people loved her then. I love her still."

In Matteo's opinion, the king was getting sidetracked by his memories. "So in these early years, it is possible that more of her background might have been uncovered."

The light in Zalathorm's eyes disappeared. "I suppose so, yes, but what purpose would it serve if she remembered the family she had lost and the monsters who slaughtered them?"

"What if there was someone she had left behind? Someone whom she wished to remember?" Matteo persisted.

A shuttered expression fell over the king's face. "There are some things that lie beyond a king's decree and a wizard's power. Beatrix is what she is. Try to live with that, as I have."

Matteo bowed to show his acceptance of this advice. "There is one thing more, your majesty. I am curious about my predecessor, a jordain named Quertus."

"Ah, yes," the king recalled. "A wise man, I suppose, but a quiet one. Anyone in the palace could tell you this much and more."

"No one in the palace speaks of Quertus," Matteo said bluntly, "but I have heard that he was slain by one of the queen's clockwork creatures."

Storm clouds began to gather on Zalathorm's brow. "Who spoke this lie?"

"Someone sworn to truth, your majesty. Your former high counselor, the jordain Cassia."

"Ah." Zalathorm flicked one hand in a gesture of dismissal. "You would do well to disregard Cassia's words. There is much about her you do not know."

"I know of her grudge against the queen, and the one-sided rivalry that embittered her," Matteo responded.

Zalathorm leaned back and regarded the young man astonishment. "Well, I see that you believe in speaking unadorned truth."

Matteo bowed. "If I offend, I beg pardon."

"You surprise me. It has been many years since I heard plain speech from a member of your order." He rested his elbows on the arms of his throne and settled in. "Please, say on."

"Cassia had a hand in my promotion to the queen's service. She caught me in some foolishness and thought it amusing to foist an inept counselor upon the queen."

"That sounds like Cassia," Zalathorm noted. "Now let's have some of that much-vaunted jordaini truth." The king leaned forward, his eyes searching Matteo's face. "What would you do, jordain, if serving Halruaa conflicted with your duty to your patron? Where do your deepest loyalties lie?"

For a moment the shock of hearing his dilemma given voice by Halruaa's king stole Matteo's wits and voice. He recovered and gave a diplomatic response. "The jordaini serve truth, your majesty. I trust that truth will serve both Halruaa and Queen Beatrix."

Zalathorm's face crinkled with disgust. "If I wanted meaningless sophistry, I'd talk to a politician! Just once I'd like to hear an answer rather than an evasion. If forced to chose, which would you serve: your patron or your homeland?"

The question was impossible to answer. Nevertheless, Matteo spoke without hesitation. "I pray that one choice will always favor both, Your Majesty, but should there be a conflict, I would serve Halruaa."

The king nodded slowly, not giving any indication of how he received this announcement.

"In fact," Matteo went on, "this very dilemma prompted me to seek this audience. Timonk, the queen's steward, summoned me back to the palace. His concern is not for the queen's health so much as her safety. He showed me his hand. He lost two fingers to one of the queen's clockwork devices."

"I see," Zalathorm said slowly. "No wonder you asked about Quertus. The truth is that Quertus was not killed by clockwork but condemned for harboring magic."

A sudden suspicion stabbed at Matteo. "Condemned,

my lord? By any chance, was Kiva that magehound who passed sentence?"

There was a long moment of silence, then Zalathorm said, "It is possible."

"It would not be the first time Kiva condemned an innocent man to serve her own purposes. Nor would it be the first time Kiva's path crossed that of Queen Beatrix. This matter requires closer attention."

Zalathorm let out a single burst of unamused laughter. "I have heard the jordaini proverb that cobblers' children go barefoot. Are you suggesting that the diviner should tend his own household?"

"Respectfully, my lord."

The king's eyes frosted. "That is enough candor for one day, jordain. You may return to my queen and serve her as well as you can."

CHAPTER EIGHT

After leaving Matteo, Tzigone found a barrel of rain-water and washed the greasepaint from her face. She took a tightly rolled robe of sky blue silk from her bag, shook out the wrinkles, and shrugged it on over her ragged street clothes. Properly attired, she made her way back to the villa that Basel Indoulur kept in Halarahh for his frequents visits to the king's city.

A lone figure waited near the gate, seated in the lamp-lit alcove that offered shelter to passersby. Tzigone took one glance at the elegantly clad woman and spun on her heel, ready for a fast retreat.

"Don't go," Sinestra Belajoon called out. "I'll only find you again. Who's to say our next meeting won't be less private, and far less convenient?"

Tzigone considered. If this confrontation was not to be avoided, this was as good a time as any. The sky was velvet black, and the position of the stars proclaimed that midnight was near. Few people had reason to walk this quiet street, and most were already in for the night.

Reluctantly Tzigone turned back to her visitor. Not long ago, she'd pretended to be a wizard and a lady, slipping into Sinestra Belajoon's confidence so that the woman would introduce her to a certain snooty behir merchant. She had liked Sinestra, and didn't feel very good about deceiving her.

But Sinestra seemed to have taken this in stride. Her gaze swept over Tzigone's blue robe, and her painted lips curved in a half smile. "A conjurer's apprentice. Last time we met you were a full-fledged illusionist. Come down in the world, have you?"

"Depends. You should have seen me an hour ago."

Sinestra's eyes lit up. "I wish I had. I'm sure it would have been quite instructive."

Tzigone folded her arms. "Excuse me?"

The wizard handed her a bit of parchment. "This is a note from Cassia, the king's jordain. She wrote to me shortly before she was killed, naming you as a thief. Is there any truth to that?"

"She's dead. That's true enough."

Sinestra hissed with exasperation. "Do you see a squadron of the city militia cooling themselves in my shadow? If you admit to being a thief, I'll not only be discrete, I'll be thrilled!"

This strange encounter was beginning to make sense to Tzigone. "You want to hire a thief to retrieve something for you."

"In a manner of speaking. I want to hire a thief to teach me the trade."

Tzigone's gaze slid over the woman. Her hair was dressed in elaborate black ringlets. A fortune in blue topaz draped her bosom and matched the watered blue silk of her gown and slippers. "You don't need to steal. You already have more than you know what to do with."

"That's precisely the point! I have everything I could possibly want, and I'm bored out of my wits," the woman announced. She rose abruptly. "Walk with me."

They fell into step, walking in silence down the tree-lined street. After a few moments Tzigone got down to business. "What do you want to retrieve?"

"My sanity," Sinestra said bluntly. "I am afflicted with ennui—gravely afflicted, a mere heartbeat away from running screaming through the streets!"

"So do what other over-pampered noblewomen do. Take a lover."

Sinestra lifted one ebony brow. "I said I'm bored, not stupid. Might I remind you that I'm married to a diviner? Not a particularly powerful one, but he's got enought talent to indulge his suspicions."

"Short leash?" Tzigone commiserated.

The wizard hooked one finger under her necklace and tugged at it in a parody of a chokehold. "My lord Belajoon has encircled me with spells warding against such sport."

"So what makes you think you could make a thief?"

"Because old Belajoon doesn't expect it of me," Sinestra retorted. She sighed heavily. "By wind and word, I have to get away with *something*, or I'll go mad!"

Since Tzigone had spent the better part of the day as a street urchin, avoiding her wizardly studies in favor of one bit of mischief after another, this was a sentiment she understood. She gnawed her lower lip for a moment. "How serious are you about this?"

"How serious is a necromancer about death?" Sinestra shot back. "Teach me, and I'll do whatever you say."

Tzigone lifted one hand to her head and ruffled her shorn locks. "Would you cut your hair like this?"

The wizard paled. She stopped walking and squeezed her eyes shut. But after a moment she focused a resolute gaze upon her chosen mentor. "Yes," she said stoutly.

Tzigone grinned and patted Sinestra's arm. "Forget it. A thief needs to use every advantage she has. You'd be the center of attention in the midst of a wizardwar, just by showing up. We'll figure out a way to make that pay."

The older woman grimaced. "I thought I had. I hope you can come up with something more interesting."

In response, Tzigone handed her a small book. "As I recall, you enjoy gossip. These things always contain a few priceless nuggets."

Sinestra's eyes bulged when she recognized her own grimoire, a spellbook that contained a wizard's most personal spells and secrets. After a moment, she burst out laughing. "Oh, this is going to be great fun!"

"That's what I keep telling a friend of mine," Tzigone observed with a grin. "You're much easier to convince than he is."

Sinestra's brows lifted. "So there's a 'he,' is there?"

"Lots of them," Tzigone said, dismissing Matteo with a sweeping wave.

"Smart girl. If I'd thought that way, I wouldn't be having these problems." The wizard linked her arm through Tzigone's.

The gesture was friendly, casual, but a spark of magic jolted through Tzigone. That puzzled her. Few spells could touch the wall around her. Conversely, she could sense nearly any spell, except that which her mother had cast long ago to block away her daughter's dangerous early memories—

Mother.

Tzigone stopped dead. Her mother's touch—that's what Sinestra's magic felt like!

Her heartbeat thundered in her ears, and the quiet street swirled around her like a kaleidoscope gone mad. After all these years of searching for her mother, could success come from a chance meeting?

Part of her wanted to believe it. She had liked Sinestra at once, had felt an immediate kinship between them. However, the woman was far too young—probably still south of her thirtieth summer.

She realized that Sinestra had also stopped and was looking at her strangely. "Are you ill, Margot?"

Tzigone seized on the word. "Margot! Is that my real name?"

The wizard's puzzlement deepened. "It's the name you used when we met. You also claimed to be an illusionist, though, so how should I know?"

Disappointment surged, then quickly receded. Tzigone had survived by being cautious; if this woman had once been Keturah, she would be equally wary. Their reunion, if such this was, would of necessity proceed one small step at a time.

She slanted a look at the beautiful wizard and saw nothing that reminded her of her own face. "I wonder what I'd look like with your hair."

A horrified expression crossed Sinestra's face, and she clamped both hands to her raven-hued curls. "Forget it! You already said I could I keep it!"

Tzigone chuckled. "I wasn't thinking of clipping it for a wig. I was just admiring it. Maybe I'll go to an illusionist and have him drop a spell over me."

A flicker of emotion flashed in Sinestra's dark eyes, quickly replaced by her usual expression of slightly amused boredom. She patted her gleaming tresses. "This is all mine. It reaches my knees when I take it down."

A distant memory assailed Tzigone, an image of her mother at play, running after elusive globes of light. Her unbound hair flowed behind her like a silken shadow.

"Yes," Tzigone said in a slightly strangled voice. "I imagine it does."

For several days, Matteo tried to honor the king's request and serve his patron as best he could. Beatrix did not require his counsel. She turned aside his requests for audience.

Yet a steady stream of artisans and craftsmen and wizards flowed through the queen's laboratory. Matteo's frustration grew with every passing hour.

One morning he could take no more. He left the palace before dawn by way of the kitchen gates, weaving his way through the merchants who kept the palace tables supplied. He dodged a small flock of geese and nodded a courtly but absent response to the goose girl's greeting.

A glance at the rising sun prompted him to increase his pace. Procopio Septus usually left his villa early. The wizard would not welcome Matteo's inquiries in his home or at the city palace, but perhaps he would speak more freely in the moments between.

During his service with Procopio, Matteo had often walked this route. He caught sight of the wizard a few streets away from the city's pink marble palace.

"Lord Procopio!"

The wizard glanced up. His smile was slow and studied, his black eyes unreadable. "So the hero of Akhlaur has returned at last! A rogue magehound unveiled, a laraken vanquished, a nation of wizard-lords saved. Gods above, Matteo! You left my employ three moons past, and *this* is how you account for your time? I thought I'd trained you to do better."

Matteo chuckled. "Had I stayed in your service longer, I might have woven a tighter tapestry. The edges of this tale are sadly frayed."

The wizard lifted one snowy brow. "Flattery, subtlety. A neat segue from jest to compliment to the matter at hand. You are learning quickly, young jordain. What are these loose threads you think I might help you bind?"

"You know that Kiva, the elf inquisatrix, was taken to the Temple of Azuth." Matteo chose his words carefully to avoid betraying his oaths of secrecy. "I assume you know the issues involved."

Procopio's jaw tightened, and he took a moment before responding. "As the sages have long known, the secret of the swamp's expansion was a leak from a gate into the Plane of Water. The presence of the laraken made it difficult to deal with this leak. Any magic used against the monster simply made it stronger. Conversely, were the gate closed, the laraken would be forced to seek magical sustenance elsewhere. Eventually the creature would have been destroyed, but the blow dealt to Halruaa's wizards would be considerable. The Council of Elders believes that this was Kiva's intent. Now the laraken has been dealt with and the gate closed, thanks to you and your friends."

"Not closed," Matteo stated. "Moved."

Shock flared in the wizard's eyes, quickly extinguished by a wave of doubt. "That is an extraordinary claim. I assume you can defend it?"

With a few terse words, Matteo described the final moments of battle in Akhlaur's Swamp. The laraken disappeared into a shallow spring. Kiva tossed an enormous square of black silk over the water.

"Both spring and silk disappeared," Matteo concluded. "Closing a magical gate requires great strength—more, I would think, than Kiva possessed at that moment. A powerful artifact might have done the job, but very few magical items could have survived the laraken's hunger."

"A portable hole would," Procopio said grimly. "Since the magic is focused upon the escape site rather than the silken portal, the laraken would find less nourishment in Kiva's silken scarf than it might in a lady's gown. I agree with your assessment: The gate was moved. Why is this not known among the council?"

"As to that, I cannot say," Matteo answered carefully. "I gave full report of these details to the Jordaini College and to the priests of Azuth. There is related matter, a very delicate one." When the wizard nodded in encouragement, Matteo added, "The jordain Zephyr was Kiva's ally."

Procopio's face went cold and still.

"I know that Zephyr died a traitor, and understand that speaking his name and deeds is an egregious error of protocol," Matteo hastened to add.

"Then why speak?" The wizard's voice was curt, his eyes fixed straight ahead. A red flush stained his face, and he quickened his step as if to outdistance this distasteful subject.

Matteo matched the man's pace. "Perhaps Zephyr left behind some small threads that might lead to the gate's new hiding place. For the good of Halruaa—"

Procopio stopped dead. He turned and impaled Matteo with a glare that stopped the young jordain's words as surely as a lance through the throat.

"You presume to tell me what that 'good' might be? The wizard-lords decide such things! A jordain provides information and advice—judiciously, it may be hoped, and with proper discretion."

Matteo heard the accusation in Procopio's voice. "I served you faithfully," he replied. "The queen has no reason to complain of my counsel or my discretion. Never have I betrayed a confidence."

"Yet you come to me with winks and nudges, if not words!"

This was neither fair nor accurate, but Matteo did not protest.

"Zephyr did what he did," Procopio continued. "I cannot explain or excuse it. I *will* not, despite those who wish me to run about shouting undignified disclaimers. You are young and far too idealistic for your own good or anyone else's, but surely you've observed that ambition is Halruaa's ruling star. Every ambitious wizard in this city—*every* wizard—will remember my jordain's disgrace and use it as a weapon against me. Do not add arrows to their quivers!"

"That is not my intention."

"Your intention? The jordaini have a dozen proverbs about the worth of good intentions!" snapped Procopio. "Forget your *intentions* and remember your oath. You may speak of nothing you saw or heard while in my employ, not with direct words, not even by innuendo. If you do, I swear by wind and word that you will come to envy the old elf's fate!"

The wizard gained height and power with every word, and by the time he finished his rant he towered over the much-taller jordain. It was a simple spell, a glamour that some wizards evoked almost unthinkingly when angered or challenged.

"You need not remind me of my jordaini vows," Matteo said with quiet dignity. "If you wish, I will swear anew that all I learned and saw while in your employ will stay within the walls of memory."

"As long as it does," Procopio growled, "I will have no reason to speak to the Jordaini Council. But know this: If I charge you with betraying confidence, your exploits in Akhlaur's Swamp will not save you!"

The wizard disappeared in a flash of azure fire. Matteo was still blinking stars from his eyes when he felt a light touch on his back, tracing a lightning bolt surrounded by a circle. The symbol of the jordain.

He turned to face a small woman who wore an apprentice's blue robe and an insouciant grin. She leaned against a garden wall and casually twirled a jordaini pennant from one finger. Matteo glanced down. His medallion was missing. He, a highly trained warrior, had neither heard Tzigone's approach nor sensed the theft.

Chagrin sharpened his voice. "Have you no duties, no responsibilities?"

Some of the high spirits faded from Tzigone's face. "Basel sent me shopping," she said glumly. She held aloft a string of small, pungent mushrooms. "You wouldn't believe what he intends to do with these."

Matteo answered automatically. "The spores are used as a spell component. Strewn upon a battlefield before rain, they conjure an instant army. In times of peace, the spell can be altered to guard against intruders. The mushrooms are also used as an ingredient in cockatrice stuffing, a natural antidote to any poison that remains in the fowl's flesh."

Tzigone regarded him with a sour expression. "You must be very popular at parties. What did old Snow Hawk say?"

Since he was becoming accustomed to the girl's lighting-quick turns of mind, Matteo made the necessary shift. Actually, "Snow Hawk" was an apt name for the lord mayor.

"Nothing of value, I'm afraid. Lord Procopio did not wish to discuss Zephyr and warned me against making further inquiries. It appears that yet another door is closed to me. I'm sorry, Tzigone."

She shrugged away his apology. "Has Procopio found a jordain to replace Zephyr?"

"I don't think so."

"Good. Then the elf's quarters are probably undisturbed."

Matteo blew out a long breath. "I don't like where this is going."

"Don't worry," she said with a blithe wave of one hand. "I've been to Snow Hawk's villa recently, and I'm not eager to return."

"Oh?" said Matteo warily.

Her gaze slid away. "I'd sooner be stripped naked, smeared with honey, and staked out where bugs could crawl over me than face that man again. How's that for a deterrent?"

"It will serve." A rumble of thunder rolled in from the lake. Matteo gestured to the mushrooms. "You'd better get those to your master before the rain starts."

Tzigone blew him a kiss and sauntered off. She sang as she went to keep from screaming in frustration. If Matteo couldn't bypass the barriers they encountered around every turn, what possible hope had she of success?

She went directly to Basel's study. He looked up, a smile of genuine affection on his plump face. On impulse, Tzigone decided that Basel was probably her best hope of learning about her mother. He was patient with her questions and did not plague her overmuch with his own. Basel had a dark secret or two—she'd gone to considerable trouble to ferret them out—but who didn't?

"Lord Basel, can you tell me of a wizard named Keturah?"

His face went rigid with some incomprehensible emotion. His eyes dropped, and he cleared his throat. When he lifted his gaze to her again, he was composed and faintly smiling. Tzigone marked the effort this had cost him, and wondered.

"Where did you hear that name, child?"

"Akhlaur's Swamp. They said that Keturah was skilled in evocation. They compared me to her." That was true, as far as it went. Tzigone elbowed her protesting conscience into silence and kept her gaze steady on Basel's shrewd face.

"Who was this 'they' you speak of?"

She responded with a shrug and a vague, milling gesture of her hands. "You know. *Them.*"

"Tzigone." His voice was uncharacteristically stern.

"Kiva, the elf magehound."

"Ah." Basel exhaled the word on a sigh. "Well, that follows. What else did this Kiva tell you?"

"Not a thing. Unless tossing fireballs counts as conversation, we didn't exactly chat."

"I see. So from whom did you hear this name?"

The wizard's persistence puzzled her. "Andris, the jordain who has lived through the laraken's magic drain."

"Ah, yes. That tale created quite a stir." Basel propped his elbows on the table and laced his plump fingers together. "Fascinating story. A jordain shows no sign of latent magical talent, yet magic—echoes of some distant elf ancestor—lies dormant within. The Jordaini Council debated whether Andris possessed magic or not, was a false jordain or true. Nor are they alone. A wizard cannot leave his own privy without encountering a philosophical debate on the nature of magic and life. The Azuthans won't solve *that* puzzle, but I'm eager to read their reports concerning this Andris.

"Back to the subject at hand," Basel concluded. "If I may ask, what is your interest in Keturah?"

Tzigone gestured to the portraits that ringed the room, an ever-present circle of Indoulur ancestors. "You come from a long line of conjurers. I have no family. No one can say, 'Don't worry, your sister had a hard time with that spell, too.' You've said yourself that my magical talents are puzzling. Maybe talking to someone who's even a little bit like me will help."

Basel leaned back and gazed at some distant point, as if he were studying one of the portraits on the far wall and measuring the worth of kith and lineage. "A reasonable argument," he said at last, "but wouldn't it make more sense to seek out your own family, rather than a wizard with a similar talent?"

"Of course it would," she answered quickly, understanding that a disclaimer would be too blatant and obvious a lie. "Don't think I haven't tried. I even tended behir hatchlings for a while so I could learn how to read genealogy records. With all the tinkering breeders do, the records are almost as complex as the wizard-gift charts."

"Very ingenious," he murmured, "but unless your forebears were eight-legged crocodilians, such efforts will only get you so far."

Tzigone hesitated, considering how much more she could safely tell even her kindly master. "I tried to get at the Queen's Registry."

The wizard stiffened. "What did you learn there?" he asked, a bit too casually.

His reaction put her into swift retreat. "Before I could find much of anything, Cassia, the king's jordain, interrupted and tossed me into a locked room."

"To which the door mysteriously opened, I suppose."

"Life is full of mystery," Tzigone agreed.

"And Cassia was murdered before she could chase you down," he added.

That was not something she liked to contemplate. Kiva used Cassia to lure Tzigone to Ahkluar's Swamp. Tzigone lived with this as best she could. Was there more to this? Did Cassia know some secret that prompted Kiva to kill her?

Basel shook off his introspection first. "Keturah simply disappeared one day. No one learned with certainty what became of her. Since no Halruaan likes to speak of his failures, your quest will be considered an enormous breach of protocol, and a challenge to those wizards who tried and failed. You must understand that any question you ask will be answered with a hundred more. Forgive me, child, but can your past bear such scrutiny?"

This was no casual question in a land where traveling entertainers were viewed as frauds and pickpockets, and thievery was punished by dismemberment. "So there's nothing I can do," she said in a dull tone.

Basel studied her for a moment. "If you are determined to pursue this, perhaps Dhamari Exchelsor can help you. He was married to the lady in question."

This knocked Tzigone back on her heels. Sudden, vivid memories assailed her of long-ago nights when she was dragged from sleep to flee "her mother's husband." So great was her antipathy toward the man that she never once thought of seeking him out or even learning his name. It was a simple solution, a straight, short path. Yet the thought of facing down this man touched ancient depths of fear and anger and loss. Tzigone bore down hard, pushing the memories back into place.

"So I should just stop by this wizard's tower for a chat?"

Basel spread his hands in a gesture of uncertainty. "Dhamari Exchelsor is a very private person. He is not a member of the Council of Elders, and he keeps to himself. I can tell you little about his thinking on this matter. After Keturah left, he petitioned the Council for a legal divorce. Even so, he sent a number of wizards and mercenaries in search of her. I stopped hearing reports of these activities after five years or so. Perhaps he accepted that Keturah was gone for good."

This tallied with Tzigone's memories. "Why did she leave?"

"That, I cannot tell you," Basel said with a shrug. "Dhamari Exchelsor might. Or even better, send someone else to talk to him, someone who can present a plausible reason for asking these questions."

Matteo could go. Any wizard would open his door to the queen's jordain. The battle of Akhlaur's Swamp would come into conversation—it always seemed to. Kiva had been behind that battle, and Kiva had also been one of the agents sent to find Keturah. Matteo could surely find a way to move the conversation from Kiva to the runaway wizard.

"That seems reasonable," she said at last.

"Which no doubt means that you will do the opposite."

This droll observation surprised a grin from her, and

then a frown. "Being contrary is almost like being predictable, isn't it?"

"Yes, but only if you're *consistently* contrary. Do what is right from time to time," he advised. "It will astonish most people and mystify the rest."

Her laugh rang out, rich and delighted. "Good advice. I may even take it."

Basel smiled and bid her goodbye with a wave of his hand. He held his smile until the door shut behind her, then he buried his face in his hands. He thanked Lady Mystra, and then he cursed her, for the bittersweet memories the girl evoked.

"Keturah," he murmured in a voice filled with a longing that neither faded nor forgot. "I never thought to hear your name again, much less your song! But by wind and word, it echoes through your daughter's laughter!"

Tzigone shut the door to Basel Indoulur's study and leaned wearily against it. She lifted her hands, palms up. "Procopio Septus," she muttered, lowering her left hand as if she'd just placed a heavy weight in it. She spoke the name of her mother's husband, and her right hand dropped even lower. For a moment, she stood with her hands see-sawing back and forth like an indecisive scale.

Suddenly she pushed herself off the wall and hurried to Basel's scrying chamber, employing the gliding, silent gait she'd perfected in a hundred forbidden corridors. It never hurt to keep *all* of her skills honed to a fighting edge.

The chamber was an odd bit of whimsy. The room was round, and the domed ceiling and mirrored floor made it appear spherical. A mural covered the walls with an underseascape depicting waving seaweed, fantastic coral buildings, and schools of bright fish. A pair of painted mermaids were fiercely entwined, frozen in an undignified but entertaining catfight. Light filled the room with a deep blue, softly undulating haze. Scrying globes bobbed gently through the air like oversized bubbles. Tzigone seized a passing globe and settled down on a mock coral settee.

Basel had tutored her in the basics of magical communication, but Tzigone had picked up some interesting skills on her own. Contacting Sinestra Belajoon was a simple matter—she attuned the globe using the ring she'd taken from the woman's hand last time they'd met.

Clouds roiled within the crystal sphere, parting to reveal Sinestra's lovely face. The wizard looked curious but composed, an appropriate reaction when answering an unknown summons. But when Tzigone held the ring up, Sinestra threw back her head in a decidedly unladylike whoop of laughter.

"Keep the ring," Sinestra offered, still grinning broadly. "Consider it advance payment for teaching me that trick!"

"First things first," Tzigone advised. "Learn to walk in my shadows, and then I'll teach you how to make your own."

Excitement lit the wizard's face. "When? Where?"

"You know Procopio Septus?"

Sinestra's jaw dropped. "*Know* him? He's one of the most powerful diviners in all the land! *His* is the villa you've chosen to raid?"

"Why not?"

"Why *not?*" The wizard threw up her hands. "Where should I start? Have you gone completely moon-mad?"

"I've gotten in before. It's not as difficult as you might think."

"Since I think it's impossible, you're probably right. Lord and Lady, girl! Don't you have a better plan?"

"I have other options. None of them are good. This is the best and easiest way to get the treasure I have in mind."

Speculation crept into Sinestra's eyes. "What might that be?"

"You're a diviner. What sort of treasure do you go after?"

The wizard's hand went instinctively to the fortune in

black pearls at her throat, but her eyes lit up in understanding. "Information can be more precious than rubies, and more difficult to trace than stolen gems. Let's do it!"

Tzigone had been expecting a longer argument. "You're putting a lot of faith in a thief you hardly know. This could be risky."

"Not really. I wear a ring of teleportation, and you can count on me deserting you on the first sign of danger. My dear Lord Belajoon gave it to me, so I could appear at his side whenever he bellows."

"Nice gift."

"A last resort, I assure you."

Tzigone instinctively traced a gesture of warding over her heart—a habit she'd picked up from the superstitious street performers she'd traveled with for years. In their world, there was no such thing as a "last resort." There were many possibilities, and the hope a better one around the corner. That was the reasoning that guided her now. Going to Dhamari Exchelsor sounded too much like a last resort. First she needed to explore the link between Sinestra's magic and her own memories of her mother. Of course, if the improbable proved true, and it turned out that Sinestra and Keturah were one, Tzigone wouldn't have to bother with Dhamari at all.

"Lesson one," Tzigone said firmly. "If you're serious about becoming a thief, you should never call anything a 'last resort.' It's like daring the gods to prove you wrong. No matter how bad things get, they can generally manage to come up with something worse."

Sinestra's face turned both sympathetic and speculative. "How can you possibly be so cynical when you've never been married? Someday, I would like to hear your story."

Tzigone suppressed a wince and managed a wink. "Someday, so would I."

CHAPTER NINE

A band of elves crept through the forested pass leading from the Mhair Jungle through the mountains of Halruaa's western wall. The trees ended abruptly, giving way to a swath of open field as suddenly as a cliff might drop into the sea. The elves stopped and looked to the ghostly human who had led them here.

Andris crouched low and surveyed the borderland. Several days' rain had allowed the grasses to grow knee high. Heavy mist shrouded the night sky, and the only illumination came from a monument at the end of the field—the likeness of a man's left hand, index finger pointing upward. Arcane fire surrounded the stone hand in a dancing nimbus, sending a soft glow through the surrounding mist.

"The symbol of Azuth." Andris spoke softly because this was a holy place, not for fear of being overheard. A distant cacophony of laughter and music drifted toward them, a bacchanal strangely at odds with this serene setting. "Be alert for manifestations of the Lord or Lady."

Kiva pointed to the sleek gray dogs that paced the edge of the temple complex in apparent agitation. Azuth's favor was often signified by the appearance of gray animals. "What of those?"

A tiny elf woman wearing the elaborately

beaded braids of a shaman crept to Andris's side. She took a handful of polished black stones from her bag. Clenching her fist, she gazed at, and far past, the agitated dogs.

"The pattern of the Weave lies smooth around those beasts," the shaman announced. "They are troubled—puzzled by their masters' behavior perhaps, or by the wild magic, but they are natural creatures."

Kiva nodded with satisfaction and gestured to four archers who crouched behind her. They fitted darts into small crossbows, letting fly in two quick volleys. Startled dogs leaped, pawing wildly at the air. In moments they sagged to the ground in deep, herb-induced slumber.

Andris began to crawl through the tall, sodden grass. He sensed, rather than heard, the elves moving behind him. A thick grove of trees surrounded the temple, giving promise of shadows and shelter ahead.

The wild celebration grew steadily louder. As they moved past the monument, Kiva pointed to the Azuthan creed carved into the base. "*Calm and caution,*" she murmured derisively.

"They love magic for its own sake," Andris pointed out. "From time to time they unleash wild magic and dance amid the chaos, just to experience it."

The battle leader Nadage crept to Andris's side. "How did you know the wild dance would be this night?"

"There is no pattern, no set time." Andris glanced at the elves that crept near to listen. "When I was at Azuth's Temple, I overheard two priests speak of a new Magistrati—a special sort of priest. Many gathered here have also been elevated in rank. They wish to celebrate before the moon is full, on a night when there is no rain, but a thick veil of mist."

"They wish to veil their foolishness with darkness," reasoned Nadage.

"They wish to use their magical devices and light spells to best effect," Andris corrected. "The light within the circle will be dazzling. All the better for us, for it will blind them to our approach."

Cibrone, the shaman, squinted into the grove that lay between them and the revelers. "I hope you are right, *karasanzor.* We are breaking treaty to enter these lands, and risking the wrath of Halruaa's wizards. Many of us bear scars from their last war against the People."

Andris put a translucent hand on the elf woman's shoulder and was grateful that she didn't flinch. "Your spells are ready?"

The shaman patted the bag at her belt and looked to Nadage for the signal to proceed.

"We go," the leader said simply.

The elves rose and glided toward the trees. Nimble as lemurs, they climbed into the branches and disappeared. Andris stayed on the ground, trusting his translucent form to provide cover. He crept in, alert for signs of Azuth's displeasure. He paused near the edge of the grove and studied the scene in the clearing beyond.

A glowing circle had been drawn in the soft moss, a large circle that enclosed the Lady's Mirror and most of the clearing surrounding the pool. An enormous, translucent dome enclosed the whole. Within its confines, wild magic raged. Magical sparks leaped and flashed, lending ever-shifting color to swirling mists. Fleet, fanciful illusions darted through the air and reflected on the surface of the pond. The sounds of surf and storm and song rolled like waves over the people who frolicked within the circle. All were dressed in the gray vestments of Azuth and wore the god's symbol over their hearts. Colored fire danced around each embroidered hand, marking the rank of the celebrants. The Azuthans whirled like giddy children or wandered about dazedly, letting the brilliant mists sift through their outstretched hands. Their songs and laughter rose with the maelstrom, magnified and distorted by the wards that contained it.

Nadage padded quietly to Andris's side. "Calm and cautious," he repeated in a derisive murmur.

A few people stood outside the magical circle. Andris pointed to two women who carried swords and wore practical gray tunics and trews. Red flames danced around their Azuthan symbols. "That color denotes experience and strength. Those women are not clergy, but fighters, possibly battle wizards. Subdue them first. Next deal with those bearing yellow auras."

"And the white?" The elf pointed to a tall man whose holy symbol flamed like a small star.

"The new Magistrati," Kiva said as she came toward the two males. "Remember what to expect from him."

Nadage glanced up into the trees and let out a soft call, like that of a drowsy, contentedly nesting bird. In response an arrow rustled through the foliage and rose high into the sky. It slowed as it traced a downward arch, then picked up speed as it dived into the midst of the revelers. It hit the dome and exploded. Sheets of light flowed over the clearing like a protective shield.

As Andris suspected, the arrow triggered a spell that would keep attackers out until the revelers could shake off the effects of the wild magic. Just as effectively, it kept them safely *in*.

Caught up in the wild magic, the revelers were slow to take note of this latest burst of magical light. All the watchers went on instant alert. One of the warrior women pulled a slender pipe from her belt and blew lustily into it. Andris heard nothing, but the elves cringed.

"They're calling the dogs," Kiva explained through gritted teeth. "Much good may it do them!"

The guard quickly came to the same conclusion. She tossed away the pipe and pulled her sword. Her partner began the gestures of a spell. The crimson flames around the spellcaster's holy symbol climbed higher with gathering power. Holy fire leaped out and licked down the length of the warrior's sword.

Andris sucked air in a sharp hiss. At his side, Nadage shot a concerned glance in the jordain's direction. "Not good?"

"A glowing sword seldom is, unless you happen to be the one wielding it."

A sharp *twang* resounded, and suddenly an arrow sprouted from the warrior woman's throat. Her blood flowed, first mingling with and then quenching the crimson flames of Azuth. She dropped her sword and fell to her knees, both hands clenched around the killing shaft.

"No!" shouted Andris as he whirled on Kiva, who stood calmly, bow in her hands.

The word burst from him before he could consider the consequences. Nadage looked as deeply shocked as Andris felt.

"This was not what we agreed!" Nadage hissed. "We were to subdue the humans, not kill them." He met Andris's eyes for the first time. "We must withdraw at once."

Kiva shook her head and pointed to the Magistrati. "Too late! Drop and hide!"

The new priest had turned toward Andris's shout. He lifted one hand high, like a child about to throw a ball. A glowing sphere appeared in his hand.

Before the wizard could hurl the magic missile, the elves disappeared into the trees like shadows, and Andris shrank behind a thick cypress. He held very still, hardly daring to breathe.

From the corner of his eye he watched the light speed past him into the trees. It separated as it flew, reforming into five seeking balls of flame. The lights darted here and there among the trees. They faltered, faded, and then flickered out like fireflies at dawn.

Andris let out his breath on a sigh of relief. The ability to hurl this particular spell was granted to all Magistrati, but this man had not wielded the power long enough to remember its limitations: He could not hit a target he could neither see nor name.

He peeked around the tree as an old woman struggled from her chair, her sparse white hair glowing like the moon in the reflected light of her holy symbol. She lifted both hands, beginning the gestures of a spell.

"The old Magistrati," Andris muttered, shielding his

eyes with one hand as he squinted into the brilliant white light that surrounded the aging priestess. He lifted his voice to shout, "Get ready, Cibrone! The wizard is casting a protective spell. A wall."

The shaman dropped from the trees. She dug both hands into her bag and brought them out full of seeds. "Get me in closer, *karasanzor*."

Andris began to run toward the clearing, zigzagging through the trees with the elf woman following closely at his heels. Several Azuthans hurled gouts of magic at the shadowy attackers. A meteor storm of tiny fireballs arced toward them, but all fizzled away just short of Andris—his jordaini resistance to magic repelled such weapons.

Andris searched for the first sign of the wall. He smiled with grim satisfaction as an expanse of stone began to rise out of the ground, just beyond the grove. Azuthans were a devout lot—a wall of fire would have been harder to breach, but their first impulse was to surround themselves with Azuthan gray.

The shaman hurled her seeds at the base of the wall and began a high, ululating chant. Tendrils of green rose from the soil, clinging to the rising wall and matching its soaring growth.

As soon as the wall had grown high enough to obscure their attack, the rest of the elves dropped from the trees and came running. Timing was crucial, for they had to breach the wall before the wild magic died and the celebrants joined in the defense. They seized the vines and hauled themselves up the rapidly growing wall. As they reached the top, Andris seized Kiva's arm.

"Subdue them," he reminded her. "Only that."

The elf woman shook him off. Dropping to one knee, she took her bow from her shoulder, nocked an arrow, and let fly—all in a single, fluid movement.

Her bolt took the new Magistrati through the heart, sending him staggering back several paces. For a moment he stood, staring at the shaft that protruded from his chest.

"Too stupid to know he's dead," Kiva said as she reached over her shoulder for another arrow.

Andris seized her wrist. "Stop this!"

"Too late." She hurled herself over the edge, bringing Andris with her.

He rolled wildly down the steep incline and hit the ground hard. The sounds of battle thundered in his ears as he got his feet under him and pulled his sword.

The wizard woman he'd noted earlier advanced on one of the elves. Her dead partner's sword glowed in her hands, and wrath burned on her face. She chanted a spell as she stalked in, and the sword's light began to pulse with gathering power. Andris threw himself between the wizard and the elf—just in time to catch a lighting flash of crimson energy squarely in the chest.

Waves of power swept over him, sending his hair dancing around his face and making his flesh tingle and twitch. He recovered quickly and snapped into position for a high, slashing attack.

The woman's eyes widened in shock as she noted her new opponent. Reflexively she swung upward to parry Andris's descending strike.

Her glowing sword met his translucent blade with a ringing clash. She had not anticipated the ghostly jordain's strength—Andris knew this from the way her sword dipped under his. Before she could adjust her grip, he twisted his sword in a quick circle, spinning the enjoined weapons and wrenching the sword from her too-slack hand.

The wizard pulled two long daggers from her belt. Andris thrust aside his sword and matched her weapons. They circled each other, slashing and testing. The woman came on quickly in a wild flurry of blows, slashing at him like a caged wildcat. Andris met each blow, and the clattering daggers all but drowned out the fading cacophony of the wild dance, and the sound of a deadly battle.

Suddenly the woman pitched forward. Andris leaped aside as she fell facedown, and stared with astonishment into Kiva's stony face. An arrow shaft protruded from the warrior's back. The elf already had another arrow ready.

"She was an honorable warrior," Andris said with quiet fury. "You will answer for this!"

"Not now, and never to you." The elf snapped her bow up into firing position, letting fly as she shouted, "Behind you!"

Andris whirled as the arrow whizzed past him, instinctively lifting his daggers into a defensive **X**. A thick staff slammed into the crux of his weapons. His attacker was a black-bearded man with clerical vestments, a warrior's fierce scowl, and arms as sinewy as a sailor's.

With all his strength Andris pushed up, thrusting the captured staff higher. Pivoting on his left foot, Andris kicked out hard with his right. His boot connected hard with the man's gut. The priest folded with a grunt, and Andris brought the hilt of one dagger down sharply on his neck. The man fell, stunned but alive.

The jordain glanced around. All of the guardians were dead or subdued. Several small fires flickered here and there, remnants of their defensive magic. The dome of light surrounding the Azuthan revelers was fading fast.

One of the elves hurried toward Kiva. A sack stuffed with spellbooks and artifacts hung heavy over his shoulder, and he cradled a pair of small dark spheres in one hand. Kiva seized the spheres and hurled them at the protective dome. Delicate crystal shattered on impact, and a viscous black substance began to slide over the rounded surface. The elf woman nocked another arrow and dipped the head into one of the small fires. The arrow caught and blazed. She swept her bow up high and loosed the flaming missile at the dome.

The arrow struck in an explosion of light and power. Fire flowed down like lava, swiftly engulfing the protective dome with a curving wall of flame.

Rage blazed through Andris, matching the heat from the burning dome. He followed the elves' retreat, stopping only to hoist a wounded elf over his shoulder. Two of the elves took their wounded comrade from Andris and disappeared into the trees.

Andris sprinted over to Kiva, who stood studying the blaze. "You will kill them all!"

She regarded him with a supercilious smile. "Efficiently and quickly. Your plan was excellent, as far as it went, but I required more."

"Why?" he demanded, gesturing toward the fiery dome. "We could have subdued the guards, raided the library, and fled before the protective barrier could be dropped. No one needed to die!"

The elf woman did not respond. Andris was not even sure she heard him, so intense was her scrutiny of the dying flames. Reluctantly, he turned to see what had so captured Kiva's attention.

The fire faded almost as quickly as it had flared. The protective sphere disappeared as well, revealing the carnage within. Revelers lay in twisted, tormented postures, their festive garments blackened and smoking.

Andris walked forward as if in a dream. He crouched beside a fallen priest. A glance was enough to know that nothing more could be done for him.

A soft whimper caught his ear. He rose and whirled toward the pool. On the banks lay a young woman. Light from the scattered fires danced over her pale, naked form, and bedraggled wings hung limply from her shoulders. Her face was twisted with pain and bewilderment. Instinctively Andris shrugged off his cloak and moved toward her.

Kiva darted to the girl's side, speaking soothingly in Elvish, calling for the shaman. The two elf women bent over the confused girl. Kiva poured a potion into her mouth while the shaman chanted a prayer of healing. At last the shaman helped the girl to her feet and led her gently away. Andris seized Kiva before she could follow.

"An undine," she explained. "The pool was no doubt her home, and hers the face that pilgrims saw in the water. The

Azuthans were either fools or charlatans, blessing Mystra for these signs of her 'great favor!' "

"You knew!" Andris said with suddenly certainty. "You knew that an undine lived in the Lady's Mirror. Why else would you set that fire but to draw her out of the heated water and into the air?"

Kiva's gaze swept pointedly over the grim battlefield. "Scores lie dead—wizards, magehounds, priests of Azuth. By my measure, this was a good night's work, even without the spellbooks. Which of course I also intend to take. Our friends should have finished emptying the library by now."

The spellbooks kept at the Lady's Mirror were beyond price. Andris understood their worth and knew Kiva needed such things to restore her wizardly magic. "Why the undine?"

The elf woman's gaze turned mocking. "I warned you that this would be no paladin's quest. You wish to upset the order of Halruaa, to tear the veil away from her ancient secrets. Surely you didn't think this could be done without fire and blood!"

"I am not quite so naïve as that," Andris retorted. "To see the Cabal destroyed, I am willing to fight and to die if needs be. But in honest and honorable battle, Kiva, and not in senseless slaughter."

For a moment the elf woman looked surprised, and then her laughter rang out over the ravaged clearing like mocking bells. "My dear Andris, I thought you were a student of warfare! Haven't you learned when all is said and done, the difference between victory and slaughter depends upon who tells the tale?"

CHAPTER TEN

After the raid upon the Lady's Mirror, Andris and Kiva headed north, following rough, barely discernable paths rather than trade routes. They traveled alone, for none of the Mhair's elves would have anything more to do with Kiva.

One elf had been badly burned and would always bear scars. Several more sustained wounds from sword or spell. None had died, though, and they carried a rich treasure back into the Mhair. Kiva had assured them that this magical treasure would restore her wizardly power and prepare her to defeat Akhlaur.

Even so, the elf leader had bidden them farewell that very night, firmly and in a manner than left no room for argument. Kiva did not seem unduly troubled by this rejection, though she did secure the elves' promise to care for the wounded and displaced undine. To Andris's eyes, they were offended that she thought it necessary to ask.

They'd walked until they found a remote farm village. A few coins from the temple's treasury had purchased them horses and travel supplies. As they rode, Kiva studied the spellbooks constantly and frantically, her lips moving as she practiced one spell after another. Each night when they stopped to rest the horses, she would test small cantrips: summoning lights, igniting small fires— things Halruaan children could do.

Never had Andris seen such fierce, absolute focus. He knew wizards and their ways, but had no idea that magic could be acquired so fast. The effort was costly. Kiva aged swiftly and visibly, as if she were trading her life-force for another sort of magic. Step by hurried step, like an infant determined to compress an entire childhood into a single day, she pressed through the books and scrolls.

For several days they skirted the mountains, moving steadily north and then east. The way became rougher and more dangerous as they went. Each day Andris pressed Kiva for answers about their destination and their purpose. She ignored him until finally his importuning ignited her temper. Raising furious golden eyes from the page, she flung out one hand. Gouts of flame flashed toward him.

Instinctively Andris ducked—not away from the flame, but *toward* it. He lunged between the flame and the horse's neck, barely clinging to the saddle as he protected his vulnerable steed.

The arcane missile caught his shoulder and sizzled off, dissipated into smoke. Andris felt the impact but not the heat. The jolt knocked him from his uncertain perch. He hit the rock-strewn ground and rolled away from his unnerved horse. Andris rose and glared at the elf. "What was that for?"

"Practice," she responded with a cool smile.

He captured the horse's reins, then hauled himself into the saddle. He was reaching into his bag for a salve when a sudden movement caught his eye. He looked up, and reached for his sword instead.

A steep cliff rose along the path. Up ahead, not more than a dozen paces, was a shallow cave. Shadows collected there like rainwater in a ditch, but the shadows breathed, and moved, and came forward to claim substance. The battle-trained jordain's mouth went dry.

Three warriors, deadly females armed with curved swords and spiked flails, paced steadily toward them. All were tall, beautifully formed, and formidably muscled. All wore leather armor, all had wild mops of curly gray hair and large almond-shaped eyes in angular faces the color of smoke.

"Crinti!" he shouted as he drew his sword. He reached out to slap the flat of it against the flank of Kiva's steed, hoping the horse would run and carry the elf to safety.

The horse merely snuffled indignantly. Kiva glanced at the shadowy trio, then back at Andris. "So they are. Greetings, Shanair," she called out.

To Andris's astonishment, all three warriors dropped to one knee before Kiva. The tallest elf balled her right fist and pounded it once against her left shoulder.

"Shanair reports," she said in a curiously harsh, sibilant voice. "The foothills are ours, the treasure is great."

"What of the gate?" Kiva said anxiously.

In response, Shanair removed a leather thong from around her neck and held it up for inspection. A dozen bone-colored objects hung from it, long and curved and as barbed as fishhooks. After a moment Andris realized that they were talons.

"When the Crinti guard," Shanair said with fierce pride, "nothing passes."

Kiva slid down from her mount and accepted the gruesome tribute. For a long moment she studied it with an unreadable face. Andris watched as the ghost of a smile touched her lips, and the unmistakable light of battle lit her amber eyes. What that meant, he could not begin to say.

She gestured for the three Crinti to rise. "Nothing passes," she echoed, then she smiled and added, "Nothing we elves cannot handle."

The Crinti leader threw back her head and laughed with wild joy. She threw her arms around Kiva, nearly crushing the delicate elf in her strong embrace.

"Come, elf-sister," she said when they fell apart. "My warriors and I will take you to the floodgate."

Throughout that morning, Procopio Septus received supplicants, read reports—many of which brought disturbing news from diverse corners of the land—and presided over meetings. However, his recent conversation with Matteo insistently played through his mind.

When the sunsleep hours put a halt to city business, Procopio returned to his tower to send a message to Ymani Gold, a priest of Azuth.

The diviner locked and warded the door of his most private room and settled into a comfortable chair. He began the chant that would put him deep into a wizard's trance and send his sentient image to the priest's study.

Procopio's vision went black, then slowly brightened into swirling gray mist. The scene took on shape and substance, if not color, and settled into an austere chamber suitable to an Azuthan priest.

The entire room was a study in gray. Cedar paneled the walls, aged to a silvery sheen. The writing table was carved from somber marble, the chairs padded with smoke-colored silk. Even the carpet was patterned in shades of gray. Procopio noted, however, that it was a fine Calimshan carpet, a work of art that would cost most men a year's wages.

Ymani Gold sat behind his table, absently decimating a pile of sugared figs as he read a messenger's scroll. His plump hand moved steadily between plate and mouth, and the plodding movements of his jaw brought to Procopio's mind the image of a cud-chewing rothé cow. The priest was not yet in midlife, but his bulbous nose was a map of broken veins, and deeply shadowed skin sagged in tired crescents beneath his eyes. He wore beautifully embroidered gray silk, cut in flowing layers to conceal his bulk. In short, Ymani Gold was visibly fond of fine things. Procopio knew of other, less readily apparent indulgences. Since a priest's wages could hardly begin to satisfy Ymani's various appetites, Procopio found that Ymani was quite willing to serve the lord mayor of Halarahh—for a price.

Procopio quickly cast a spell of divination, hoping to lift the scroll's message from Ymani's mind before the priest discerned his presence. The pilfered news startled an involuntary gasp from him, which he covered by pointedly clearing his throat.

Ymani Gold leaped to his feet, noisily upending his chair. The befuddlement on his face would have cheered Procopio considerably, had not the stolen information been so grim.

"Greetings, priest, and peace to this house. I pledge not to work any magic within these walls unbidden." Any *further* magic, he added silently.

Ymani gathered his composure and settled back in his chair. "Lord Procopio," he said in a fluting, nasal tenor. "What brings so great an honor to my door?"

Procopio arranged himself in room's best chair before speaking. "We have a mutual problem. Kiva the mage-hound has escaped."

The priest blinked in surprise. A flicker of suspicion crossed his face. "You are well informed. I just learned of this myself."

Procopio reasoned that the best way to cover one misdeed was to focus upon another. "It is difficult to hide such matters from a diviner, although the church of Azuth has certainly tried."

"Apparently we have not done well enough, if you learned of it." A sour expression crossed his face. "Don't bother telling me what a powerful diviner you are, how nothing is hidden from you. The truth, now! How did you come by this knowledge?"

"I had a visit from a jordain who was once in my service, a youth known as Matteo."

Ymani's eyes took on a malicious gleam. "I have heard that name. His masters call him a shining example of everything his breed purports to be. They claimed that since he was instructed to keep his counsel on this matter, he would never speak of it. It is gratifying to know that such a paragon is capable of indiscretion and that the so-called jordaini masters are as fallible as other men."

"The jordaini masters were more right about this than they know," the wizard grumbled. "Matteo is persistent, dedicated, and honorable."

The priest narrowed his eyes. "Am I to conclude that you have some power over this jordain that enabled you to divine this news from him?"

Procopio saw where this was going. "An unsound conclusion."

Undaunted, the priest continued. "Only the inquisitors of Azuth have the ability to enter a jordaini mind. You may have promise. If you'd like to apply as a temple acolyte, I would sponsor your petition."

The diviner let Ymani have his fun but noted the price of it for later reckoning. "The question remains: What's to be done about Kiva?"

The priest's smirk faded. He helped himself to another fig. "This is a grave matter but not the usual province of Halarahh's lord mayor."

"I have a personal stake in this," the wizard said bluntly. "An elf jordain in my employ was in league with the traitor. I do not appreciate any stain upon my name, however small. I intend to see that the elf woman does nothing that might cause this stain to spread."

"Most understandable. What would you have me do?"

"I want the magehound who examined Kiva before her escape. Bring him to Halarahh on some pretext, and I will take from his mind the details of his findings. Perhaps some small bit of information might be a trail marker."

"If such existed, surely my fellow Azuthans would have found and followed it," Ymani protested. "Partisanship aside, such spells are hideously illegal. I cannot be part of this!"

The wizard sniffed. "The Azuthans let a traitor to king and country slip between their fingers. Worse, you kept silent, valuing your reputation over the security of the land. You and

I stand aboard the same skyship, my friend. We fly or fall together. Find a way to bring this man to me, and soon."

"You are most persuasive. Of course, I will do what I can." Ymani lifted one hand and formed the Azuthan blessing.

Usually Procopio would be insulted by so blatant a dismissal, but he had already spent too much time on the fat priest. He eased himself away from his projected image, pulling back along the threads of magic to his tower.

Procopio returned to his spell chamber to a body grown painfully stiff and chilled. Cursing himself for tarrying too long, he struggled from his chair and shuffled over to the hearth like a toothless old peasant. A quick spell conjured a blaze, and he chafed his icy hands as he considered the problem before him.

Kiva's disappearance cast a grim light upon other, recent events. Just this morning he'd received word of the raid on the Lady's Mirror. There were no survivors, but magical inquiry revealed that the attackers were wild elves. The Mhair savages had kept to their forests for over five human generations. Penalties for breaking the treaty would be harsh. Something unusual—or someone powerful and persuasive—must have urged the elves into this suicidal course. Elves scorned other races, so most likely their leader was one of their own kind. Yet who but a Halruaan-trained wizard knew the value of the stolen books and scrolls? The best use the elves could make of them would be to rip them up for privy conveniences, and Mystra knew they had leaves aplenty for that purpose! By Procopio's reckoning, the person behind the raid was a wild elf and a wizard, someone who had an urgent need of magic, someone with very little to lose.

In short, Kiva. The thought that a former magehound possessed the treasures of the Lady's Mirror and the possible uses she could make of this magic made Procopio's mind spin.

He considered the reports of raids upon isolated monasteries and towers and caravans. The hills were always plagued by bandits, and it was generally accepted that these were random events, but what if they were not? Kiva had spent years quietly building an army of magic-resistant warriors for her assault on Akhlaur's Swamp. What if she had also been stockpiling magical treasure? The result would be a staggering fortune, as well as more magical fire-power than most northern mages might see throughout a lifetime and a lichdom. What could one malevolent and undoubtedly insane elf wench do with such power?

It was a chilling thought.

It was also purest speculation, but Procopio was a diviner, and he felt the familiar prickle of premonition. Even if he were not correct in all the particulars, he was certain something dire was afoot.

He hurried up to Zephyr's spartan room and flashed through the gestures of a seek-magic spell. No telltale azure glow resulted. Irritated, he doubled the power of his casting with no more success.

The wizard spun to stalk from the bedchamber. He was almost to the door when he saw threads of blue light out-lining a portion of the wooden floor.

Excited now, he dropped to his knees and took a fine-bladed knife from his belt. He slipped it into the glowing crack and pried up a trapdoor. In a compartment beneath was a small crystal globe.

"Blessed be Mystra," he breathed as he lifted the sphere. It was a scrying globe, of a sort used for private communication. Even a commoner or a magic-dead jordain could use such globes, which were attuned to one person and required no more magic than a touch. Surely this was Zephyr's link to Kiva!

Procopio cupped the globe in his hands. He cleared his mind and quieted his heart. Few diviners had achieved his level of skill, but men such as he could perceive the magic that clung to certain objects like scent to a flower. He listened for the faint echoes of the attunement spell with wizard-trained senses as keen as a hunting hound's nose.

A triumphant smile curved his lips when the spell was his. He quickly chanted the words and gazed deeply, expectantly, into the globe.

Clouds gathered deep within the crystal and swirled about like wheeling gulls, but they did not part to reveal an elf face. The magic was there, of that Procopio had no doubt, and the message sent, but there was no magic on the other end to complete the link.

Bitter disappointment assailed the wizard. Of course Kiva would not answer! If she had brought the twin to Zephyr's globe into the swamp, the magic would have gone to feed the laraken. By all reports, she had been stripped of wizardly spells. She possessed no more power than a human toddler. Procopio considered the magical items taken from the Lady's Mirror and the use that Kiva might make of them. The elf would learn quickly. Meanwhile, he had other inquiries to make, even riskier than speech with a treacherous elf.

Returning to his study, Procopio unlocked a hidden cabinet and took from it an exquisite bottle of transparent green glass. Within it was a luxurious room, and a tiny woman in the garb of a Calimshan harem girl.

The wizard took a bit of parchment and scratched a few runes. He rolled it into a small scroll, uncorked the bottle, and dropped it in. As it fell, it shrank to the scale of the room.

The tiny woman picked up the scroll and unrolled it. Her head went back in a burst of delighted laughter, and she disappeared in a burst of glowing smoke.

Procopio removed a golden ring from the neck of the bottle, which he firmly re-corked. He slipped the ring onto his finger and closed his eyes.

The scent of anise and sandalwood and roses filled the air. Procopio opened his eyes to find himself in a world filled with green light. The bottle was not the abode of a genie servant but a window into another dimension, one Procopio had spent long years creating. The "genie" was actually a courtesan with a small talent for magic and a powerful hunger for adventure. She relished the challenge of luring men into this world at Procopio's behest.

He poured himself a goblet of fruit nectar and settled down to await his guest. Perhaps an hour passed before mist began to rise like steam from the silk cushions heaped in a curtained alcove. The mist intensified, taking the form of a portly, black-bearded man entwined with Procopio's servant.

The wizard cleared his throat. His "guest" sat up abruptly, eyes wide as he took in his new surroundings. The woman disentangled herself, adjusted her veils, and glided out into the garden.

"Greetings, Ameer Tukephremo," Procopio said. "This is indeed an occasion. I seldom have occasion to entertain a wizard of Mulhorand."

The wizard gathered himself and brushed aside the curtain, adjusting the belt of his robe as he stood. "What is this place?"

Procopio nodded his approval. "Not *where*, but *what*. This is a dimensional portal, my good man, a plane unknown to all but the greatest masters of the Art."

"Ah." The bearded wizard smiled thinly. "By the accent and the modesty of your speech, I know you as a Halruaan. May I also know your name?"

"It is better you do not. Would you care for a refreshment?"

"Most gracious of you."

Procopio gestured, and porcelain cups appeared, suspended in the air. Fragrant steam rose in delicate wisps.

The Mulhorandi took a sip. "Green tea with honey and ginger, and something more. . . . "

"Haerlu brandy. A fine Halruaan spirit."

"Exceptional."

They sipped and exchanged pleasantries for several moments before Ameer got down to business. "You did not invite me into your home. In my land, this would be considered an insult."

"In my land, it would be considered a crime," the Halruaan countered. "My fellow wizard-lords frown upon the idea of consorting with a Mulhorandi wizard."

Ameer let loose a burst of belly-shaking laughter. "Frown on it? They would cut you down like a rabid dog! You take large risks to deal with me. You must expect a large reward."

Not from you, Procopio noted silently, carefully masking his distaste at the Mulhorandi's smug expression. The man was clearly delighted that a Halruaan wizard would come to him for anything. Procopio's countrymen scorned the magic of their eastern neighbors as hardly worthy of notice.

That attitude was precisely what Procopio was counting on.

"You Mulhorandi have spells of cloaking to keep others from prying into your affairs. Some of these spells require materials not available in Halruaa."

The man blinked and set his cup down with a sharp click. "If you know so much, these cloaking spells are not as good as yours."

"We know *of* them. There is a difference."

Understanding began to dawn in Ameer's eyes, and a sly smile curved his lips. "You wish to hide some of your activities from your fellow wizards. A spell cast with materials unique to Mulhorand, a family spell treasured from one generation to the next, would accomplish this. Do you know what is needed for such a spell?"

"The finely ground remains of a mummified Mulhorandi wizard. Preferably an ancestor."

Ameer nodded solemnly. He placed his hand, fingers splayed, over his heart in a dramatic gesture. "You ask much of me, Halruaan. What price should a man put upon his heritage? Upon the sacred honor of his ancestors?"

"What price would you pay for a Halruaan spellbook?" Procopio countered.

The wizard's hand unconsciously fisted, crushing the embroidered silk of his robe. "You would sell me Halruaan secrets? That would be death to you!"

"I do not intend to *sell* you Halruaan magic. What I will do is enhance the meager spell you give me. I will alter it, give it the weight and power and authority of Halruaan cloaking magic and use it to place a second, secret ward upon Halruaa's eastern boundaries."

Since his guest still looked dubious, Procopio led the way to a curtained alcove. He pulled back the silk draperies to reveal a large, oval window. On the other side was a bedchamber resembling a rose garden in full bloom. Pink silks swathed the windows and covered the vast bed, upon which sprawled a raven-haired woman. A large wine bottle lay on its side on the low table nearby, as well as a pair of goblets.

Procopio clicked his tongue reprovingly. "It would appear that Miohari had yet another late night. Even so, it is time she awoke." He tapped sharply on the glass.

The woman stirred and sat up, looking around muzzily. After a moment she shrugged and rose. She came over to the window and sat in a small chair that faced it. Picking up a pot of tinted ointment from the small table before her, she leaned forward and began to daub at her face. There was no sign that she saw the two men, though to all appearances she was but a hand's breadth from them.

"A former mistress," Procopio said negligently. "Beautiful but not gifted in the Art. To her the portal is but a gilded mirror. She sees only what she expects to see. But you and I perceive both the magic and the reality beyond."

"Fascinating," Ameer murmured. His black eyes shifted from the lovely woman to his host. "You make your point well, my lord Halruaan."

"The wizards of Halruaa will see what they expect to see. What actually goes on beyond the Eastern Wall is entirely up to you. I will be aware of it, of course, but I will keep my own counsel until I see fit."

"You would compromise the security of your own borders?" the Mulhorandi said wonderingly.

Procopio's laughter was tinged with scorn. "Oh, I think we will survive whatever you may bring against us!"

"Then why do this thing?"

"It is quite simple. Our king, Zalathorm, rose to power as a battle wizard, and he kept his throne these many years because he foresaw and averted every major threat since that day."

"Ah! Who knows what might happen if he should miss a threat and another wizard does not?" Ameer said shrewdly.

The diviner spread his hands, palms up, in a parody of modest disclaimer. "Who am I to say what will be? History has seasons that fade and then return."

The Mulhorandi nodded and lifted one hand in an absentminded gesture. A smoking pipe appeared in the air beside him. He took it up and sucked thoughtfully for a moment, then blew several rings of smoke—rings that encircled elaborate, rune-marked designs. No doubt they were minor spells of some sort, probably to veil his thoughts and intentions. The technique was interesting, the diversion subtle, but Procopio had little inclination to learn the trick. He could blow smoke in a rival's face without blackening his own teeth or shortening his breath.

"I am not completely unfamiliar with your history," Ameer said at last. "I know that all who have attacked Halruaa have been defeated."

"Victory and defeat are not absolute terms. Come."

Procopio led his guest to a side room, which held a gaming table similar to those housed in his villa, a detailed landscape in miniature with jagged mountains and rock-strewn passes. He drew a wand from his sleeve and tapped the edge of the table. Drawers flew open along all four sides. Out leaped hundreds of tiny, magically animated toys: foot soldiers, cavalry, griffon riders, and even a trio of tiny wizards buzzing about upon flying carpets. Ameer grinned like a lad beholding a wondrous new toy.

"This is a reenactment of the battle of Starsnake Pass," Procopio said. "Watch and learn."

The tiny figures threw themselves into warfare. Sparks danced in the air above the battlefield as spells were hurled, and a miniature river ran red as charging troops went down under a storm of pin-sized arrows.

"Those are Crinti!" Ameer exclaimed, pointing to a wave of tiny, mounted warriors thundering into the valley.

"These as well," the diviner said as he reached over and took the top from a mountain. Inside was a maze of caves and passages. A band of warriors crept through, coming around behind the Halruaan nobles at the rear of the battle. The Crinti burst out from cover suddenly, and the slaughter that followed was swift and brutal. The shadow amazons fled as quickly as they came, carrying a treasure hoard of enchanted weapons and spell-filled artifacts.

Ameer smiled and nodded. "A clever move. They will win this game, I think."

"Yes, but not in the manner you might suppose. Watch."

The Crinti raiders ran back through the passages and emerged on the far side of the mountain, far from the battle. They mounted the horses tethered there and thundered off toward the grasslands of their barbarian homeland. Behind them, trapped in the steep-sided pass as they waited for reinforcements that would never come, their gray-skinned sisters died by the score at the hands of the Halruaan battle wizards.

When at last the scene was played out, Procopio tapped the table again. The still-moving figures melted away, leaving the battlefield eerily silent and littered with tiny corpses.

"Who remembers the foot soldiers who molder where they fall? It is the wizards, their spells, their legacy—these are the tales that fill the lorebooks."

An avaricious light began to dawn in the Mulhorandi's eyes. Encouraged, Procopio went on. "A single Halruaan spellbook would ensure your fame. Halruaan bards will sing of an invasion repelled. The Mulhorandi might sing of a daring raid. Amazing, how the same tale can be sung to many a tune."

Ameer took another long pull at his pipe before answering. "You think that I might stumble upon such a book?"

"Who can say?" Procopio said with a shrug. "The fortunes of war take curious turns."

It was all the confirmation the Mulhorandi expected to get. "I will get you the spell and the dust of my ancestors," he said. "You to your betrayal, me to mine. May Lady Mystra judge between us."

"Oh, come now," Procopio chided. "We are neither of us priests or paladins! Magic is not right or wrong: It simply *is*. We need not think of judgment, only of skill."

Ameer Tukephremo smiled grimly. "A comforting thought, I'm sure. For both our sakes, lord Halruaan, I hope you are right."

CHAPTER ELEVEN

Dawn was still hours away as Tzigone walked carefully through a hallway in Procopio Septus's villa, trying not to slop the contents of a brimming chamber pot upon the gleaming marble floor. One pace behind her trudged Sinestra Belajoon, similarly armed. The beautiful wizard was clad in a servant's smock and kerchief, but her expression—a blend of distaste and disbelief—was hardly that of an experienced chambermaid. Fortunately, the few people they passed quickly caught their breath, averted their eyes, and hurried past.

"Why are there no wards? No magical guardians?" hissed Sinestra.

"There are." Magic filled the air, thicker and fouler than the stench rising from the pot Tzigone carried. It skittered over her until her skin crawled. "It took me days to find a way through them. There might still be thought-thieving spells wandering around. Remember that we're servants, duly hired, performing our duties. Keep your mind on that, and we may just get out of here with our skins still attached. And stop wrinkling your nose! Anyone would think you never touched a chamber pot before."

Sinestra grumbled and then subsided. They traversed several back corridors, then tossed their chamber pots down a laundry chute and slipped through a paneled door. This led into an antechamber of the wizard's library, a room off the luxurious study. Tzigone pulled down several books before she found what she needed.

"Here it is—notes on all of Procopio's jordaini counselors." She paged through quickly, and let out a long, low whistle. "He's had more than his share of them. Wonder why."

"Forget the others. We came about this Zephyr," reminded Sinestra. She shifted uneasily, her eyes darting nervously from door to door.

"Here it is." Tzigone slid her finger down the page, scanning the neat runes. "Zephyr once worked for Queen Fiordella. Very impressive."

"What does that mean?"

Tzigone shrugged. "Damned if I know. Write this down: After Fiordella died, Zephyr went to Cyclominia the necromancer, and from there to Rondati Denister, and finally to Procopio."

The wizard scribbled furiously on a scrap of parchment. "Any before the queen?"

Tzigone read the names of his patrons, which Sinestra transcribed. "That goes back nearly two hundred years, but he was a very old elf. This doesn't say what he did before." She sighed in frustration and closed the book. "Let's check his room."

Sinestra looked dubious, but she handed the parchment to Tzigone and followed as the young thief paced the library, tapping softly on the bookshelves and wall panels.

"Here it is," she said at last. She leaned against one of the shelves, which turned as easily as a weather vane in a stiff breeze. Small lamps flickered on to reveal a long, narrow hall.

Sinestra peered in. "Magical lighting. No dust. Not my idea of a hidden passage."

"If you want cobwebs and ghosts, there are more interesting tunnels in the lower levels," Tzigone told her, only half in jest. She prodded the woman into motion. Sinestra moaned but started down the passage.

They hurried to the end of the corridor and up a narrow spiral staircase. "Wizard-lords don't like to be kept waiting," Tzigone explained, "and they like to keep secrets. After you've gone through a few villas, you see a pattern: back corridors for the servants, private entrances for the counselors and mistresses. I'll bet you coins against crumbs that this leads to his chief counselor's room."

Tzigone was almost right—the passage led to a richly appointed bedchamber. Two servant girls were busily stripping the crumpled silk covering from the wide bed. They looked up, startled, at the new arrivals.

"Take off your scarf," Tzigone whispered.

Sinestra complied. Her hair fell in long, gleaming dark waves about her face.

"Start undressing."

The wizard's lips curved as she caught Tzigone's ploy. She began to peel off the servant's smock to reveal the daring gown beneath.

Tzigone turned to the servants. "Is there a bath prepared?"

The girls exchanged glances. "No," one of them ventured.

"Well, go to the kitchens and fetch heated water! See that you steep it well with jasmine and hyssop. Lord Procopio specifically asked for a sunrise tryst, so there is little time to waste!"

The servants bustled from the room to tend this apparently routine task. Sinestra chuckled and tied her scarf back into place. "Quick thinking! We return to the library and try again?"

"Unless you'd rather await Procopio here."

They tried twice more before they found their way to Zephyr's chamber. The room was sparse and somber: a cot, a table with an inkpot and a candle, a small hanging mirror, and three narrow windows. A few jordaini garments in pristine white linen still hung on the wall pegs.

Still, Tzigone checked the room methodically. She found a small empty cupboard hidden behind the mirror, a trapdoor in the floor, but nothing more.

"Nothing here links Zephyr to Kiva," she said at last. "I was sure he'd leave at least one small thread. People generally do."

"Maybe he was careful."

"Maybe someone else got here before us," Tzigone countered. "Procopio probably wants to find that link between Zephyr and Kiva as badly as I do!"

"Surely Procopio Septus would have nothing to do with an elf rogue!" protested Sinestra.

"My point exactly. He'd want to get rid of anything that might appear to link them." Tzigone sighed and rolled her shoulders to ease the tension-knotted muscles. "I'm finished. Do you want to take something before we go?"

The wizard surveyed the austere room, tapping her chin thoughtfully with her forefinger. "Not much here to take. A jordain's lot seems rather bleak."

"True, but there's always something." Tzigone went to work again, checking again for hidden compartments, patting down the garments for pockets. She found a tiny pocket sewn into the seam of a tunic. In it was a scrap of paper wrapped around fine, brown dust. She held it out to the wizard. "Does this look interesting?"

Sinestra licked the tip of one finger and dipped in, then touched it to her tongue. She made a face.

"Unspeakably nasty, which almost guarantees that it's an important spell component. I'll take it."

"Not all of it," Tzigone cautioned. "It's the greedy thieves who get caught. If you just take a pinch, Procopio isn't likely to come looking for you."

The wizard looked puzzled. "Why would he? I doubt he knows it's here. Wizards have well-warded rooms for their spell components."

"If they came under suspicion for any reason, the first place to be searched would be those well-warded rooms,"

Tzigone pointed out. "Besides, someone has been in here recently. The trapdoor was pried up with a knife—you can see the fresh scrapings on the wood and the marks from someone's fingers in the dust beside it. I'm betting on Procopio. His servants wouldn't venture in here."

"Why not? The wizard trusts his servants entirely too much. Look how easily we walk anywhere we please!"

Tzigone didn't try to explain. She had no idea why she sensed magic so keenly while remaining invisible to it. Magical wards protected nearly every doorway of this villa, every corridor. She had sensed them all, but not they her. Sinestra, walking always a half pace behind, stayed in her shadow. Tzigone had learned by hard experience the boundaries of her peculiar sphere of protection. She knew it, she used it—but she did not understand it.

"Let's go," she said shortly.

Sinestra's eyes were glowing with excitement, though her "treasure" was scant and of uncertain value. In her elation, she forgot to keep the half-pace distance to the young thief. Tzigone did not remind her. As they passed a large oval mirror, she glanced at their combined reflections. Tzigone appeared as she would in any other mirror. Sinestra did not.

The young thief darted a look up and down the hall to make sure they were alone. She seized the wizard's arm, yanked off her concealing scarf, and dragged her before the mirror.

Sinestra's reflected eyes widened with horror, then dulled with resignation—and with the passing of years hidden beneath her magical disguise.

The wizard's reflection was not just older but less comely. Her hair was still long and thick, but instead of a gleaming black, it was an ashy brown dulled by time and streaked with gray. She was still slender, but her curves were not as lush. Her face was pointed rather than heart-shaped, her mouth wider. A few lines gathered in the corners of her painted eyes. The smooth, dark honey silk of

Sinestra's skin was replaced by a sallow complexion marked with sunspots. It was not the face of a pampered noblewoman, but a commoner who'd led a hard life—or perhaps a wizard who had lived for many years on the run.

"Look at us," Tzigone whispered, intently studying their reflections. "We could be kin."

Sinestra's unfamiliar mouth curved in a little smile. "Sisters, perhaps."

"Not likely. You're old enough to be my mother," Tzigone said bluntly.

"Ouch! Why not just stab me and be done with it?"

Tzigone ignored her and took a deep breath. "*Are you?*"

For a long moment Sinestra did not answer. Tzigone studied the reflected face for any signs of hope, guilt, regret, dishonesty. Anything!

After a while the wizard shrugged and looked away from their joined reflections. "I suppose it's possible."

"*Possible?*"

The sharp scent of camphor intruded. Tzigone whirled to see one of the wizard-lord's physicians approaching. His interested gaze traveled down Sinestra's ebony tresses and rounded curves. Tzigone quickly stepped between the wizard and her telltale reflection.

"Hello, pretty thing," the physician crooned to Sinestra as he closed in on the two women. "You're new here. Has anyone welcomed you properly yet?"

He reached for her. Sinestra shied away, but the man's fingers brushed her arm. Lord Belajoon's "gift" responded to the touch of another man, and Sinestra disappeared in mid curse.

The dumbfounded physician turned his gaze toward Tzigone. She smiled sweetly. "Lord Procopio is getting possessive, is he not? Imagine wasting so powerful a spell, just to ensure that none of the servants get into the cooking wine. So to speak."

"An accident. I tripped. I never intended to touch the wench," the man babbled. Tzigone patted him on the cheek and went her way, quite certain that he would not carry tales about a chambermaid's sudden disappearance.

Tzigone left the villa without further incident. An unfamiliar darkness clung to her spirit as she trudged away. In all the years she'd sought her mother, it had never once occurred to her that Keturah might not know or care what became of her child. Even if Sinestra and Keturah were not the same person, Sinestra's response raised disturbing questions.

Perhaps it was time to consider last resorts.

Within the hour Tzigone had exchanged her smock for a skimpy gown she found drying on a bush behind a brothel, smudged her eyes and lips with some of the face paint she'd borrowed from Sinestra's bag, and made her way to the palace. She waited by the gate Matteo usually took. He was an early riser, so she hadn't long to wait. She all but pounced on him, seizing his arm and dragging him away from the early morning bustle.

Matteo sent her a sidelong glance as they hurried away from the palace gate. "Anyone who sees us will click their tongues and complain that the city's doxies have become far too aggressive! If you've no thought for your own reputation, Tzigone, have you considered mine?"

"You're a jordain," she retorted. "Being seen with a courtesan could only improve matters. Never mind that right now. I need you to find someone for me."

"You found someone willing to speak of Keturah?"

"Well, sort of. I came straight out and asked Basel Indoulur if he knew anything about Keturah. He suggested someone who might be able to help me."

Matteo's eyes widened with alarm. "Did you tell him she was your mother?"

"How stupid do I look?" His eyes dropped briefly to her tawdry gown. "You know what I mean."

"Indeed. Tell me about this person you wish me to find."

"Dhamari Exchelsor. He's a generalist wizard, a potion stirrer. You'll find him in the green marble tower at the corner of Sylph Street and South Market Road."

Matteo regarded her thoughtfully. "No doubt I can manage that, but if you know so much already, what do you need me to do? Why not go yourself?"

"He was Keturah's husband."

"Ah. You want me to meet him under some pretense, take his measure," Matteo mused.

"He's very quick," Tzigone announced to no one in particular. Her tart expression melted, and she turned a look of appeal to Matteo. "This could be my best hope of finding the truth about my mother. Perhaps my only hope. I know you jordaini are sworn to truth," she added in a rush, "and I'm not exactly asking you to lie for me. Just sort of . . . fish around. You know—trim the bait into bite-sized bits but hide the hook. . . ." Her voice trailed off uncertainly.

Matteo considered her for a long moment. "You took a risk asking about Keturah so openly. Do you trust Basel Indoulur?"

"Sort of."

His smile was faint and devoid of humor. "A common sentiment these days. Very well, I will see this wizard and learn what I can."

Acting on impulse, Tzigone threw her arms around Matteo's neck. From the corner of her eye, she noted two white-clad men coming from the palace gate. Mischief seized her, and she let herself drop. Matteo's arms went instinctively around her to keep her from falling. After a moment she released him and stepped back, her eyes twinkling and her lips curved in a lazy, replete smile.

"Oh *no*, my lord," she protested breathlessly as she handed him back his own coin bag. "Who could put a price on such mastery?"

She heaved a deep sigh and smoothed her hair. Then, turning, she sauntered off with a doxie's undulating swish.

She glanced back and grinned when she noted the respectful stares the other jordaini sent Matteo. One of the men clapped him on the shoulder in comradely fashion as he passed.

Matteo glowered at her and closed the distance between them with a few quick strides. "You were worried about your reputation," Tzigone said innocently, backing up to keep her distance. "It seems to have risen a trifle."

His stern expression wavered, and his lips twitched in a reluctant smile. Quickly he reclaimed his scowl and snatched up a melon from a passing cart. He tossed a coin to the protesting merchant, and then hefted the melon and aimed it at Tzigone.

She fled with a startled squeal, scurrying into an alcove in the thick wall of the palace. When no missile hurtled by, she chanced a glimpse out.

Matteo stood a few paces away. He held out a neatly carved slice. "Breakfast?"

Tzigone took the offered fruit and patted the bench beside her. Matteo settled down. In companionable silence, the queen's counselor and the painted street waif shared the fruit and split the loaf that Tzigone produced from her bag. For once, Matteo didn't ask her how she'd come by it. Nor did he comment upon the strange looks that passersby sent the mismatched pair.

They did not speak of the differences that separated them or the troubles that bound them. Nonetheless, by the time the sun edged over the eastern wall of the city, the darkness had likewise lifted from Tzigone's heart.

CHAPTER TWELVE

Matteo went directly to Dhamari Exchelsor's tower, confident that he would be received. No one refused the queen's jordain, though the reasons for this hospitality varied. Matteo was well accustomed to receptions that ranged from extreme wariness to blatant ambition, depending upon which sort of news was anticipated.

To do away with this, Matteo explained to the gatekeeper that he came not on the queen's business but inquiring about a personal matter. He noted with interest the servant's reaction to this announcement: there was despair in his eyes, as if this news had shattered a dear hope. Some people knew no limits to their ambition!

The gatekeeper returned quickly and brought Matteo into the tower. The receiving room was not overly large, but it was appointed with comfortable chairs and small, scattered tables. A fountain played in one corner, spilling over the bottles of wine immersed in what Matteo assumed was a magically cooled pool. Silver goblets stood ready on the table nearby, and sugared fruits were arranged under a glass dome. Books lay on tables placed between the chairs, and candles to aid reading. Bell pulls hung at intervals on every wall, suggesting that servants would come promptly to tend a guest's needs. In all, an extremely comfortable and welcoming room.

Matteo had just barely taken a seat when his host appeared. He rose at once and gave the wizard the proscribed courtesies. Though jordaini were not required by law to lower their eyes while bowing to a wizard, Matteo did so to cover his surprise. He could not imagine how the woman who'd given birth to Tzigone would find herself wed to such a man!

Dhamari Exchelsor was mild looking, soft-bodied, and pale of complexion. His balding head came level with Matteo's shoulder, and his eyes had the myopic squint of a man who spends little time out of doors. His dark brown beard was neatly trimmed, his clothes simple and well made. Like his reception chamber, the wizard lacked ostentation or pretense. He looked like a man comfortable with the circumstances of his life and too content to strive for much of anything more. The word that came most strongly to mind when Matteo sought to describe him was "inoffensive."

"Please! You do me too much honor," Dhamari protested mildly. "I hope you will allow me to return the courtesy. If there is any way that I might serve you, speak freely."

Matteo lifted his eyes to his host's curious gaze. "You are most gracious, but you may regret your offer when you hear the story that brought me here."

"We will judge the tale once the telling is done. Will you have wine?" Dhamari gestured toward the cooling pool. "It is an Exchelsor pink, a fine companion to long and thirsty tales."

The jordain politely declined and took the chair Dhamari offered him. He told him a brief version of the story of Akhlaur's Swamp, describing the injury that sent Kiva into a long and sleeplike trance but omitting the fact of her escape.

"So you see," he concluded, "it is vital that we learn what became of this gate—if not from Kiva, then perhaps from those who had dealings with her."

Dhamari leaned back in his chair. "You have come well

prepared. I had almost forgotten the time I spent with Kiva in this very tower."

This was news indeed! "How long ago?"

"I should say a good six and twenty years," the wizard reminisced. "We were both apprentices under the same mistress, a very talented wizard of the evocation school. It seems impossible that it could be so long ago!"

Matteo had intended to mention Kiva and work his way back to the elf's capture of Keturah. This was an unexpected shortcut! "Might this wizard, your former mistress, have knowledge of Kiva's life beyond this time of apprenticeship?"

"Would she? Oh yes, to her sorrow and mine!" The wizard took a long breath and sent Matteo an apologetic smile. "Forgive me. I speak so seldom of my lady Keturah. It is a great joy to do so and a great sorrow. Perhaps you know the name?"

"I heard it spoken in the Swamp of Akhlaur."

"I can see why." Dhamari leaned forward eagerly. "This girl, this untrained commoner whose voice held the laraken—tell me about her."

Matteo spread his hands in a negligent gesture. "There is little I can say. She is a street performer, a girl with a merry heart and a clever mind. She can imitate any voice she hears. Untrained in Art she certainly is, but she picked up a stray spell here and there. She possesses a strong wild talent, such as is seldom seen in these civilized times, but she is training now."

"Yes, with Basel Indoulur. I have heard," Dhamari said. "I was one of many wizards who offered to teach her, but both the council and the girl herself inclined toward Basel. He has had much experience as a teacher, you know."

Matteo didn't know, but he nodded politely. "Lord Basel is fond of apprentices," Dhamari went on. "He trains three at a time. He has done so ever since he left the Jordaini College."

This information hit Matteo like a barbarian's warhammer. "He was a master at the college?"

"Oh, yes. Before your time, I should think. Not much before, though. Eighteen, perhaps twenty years."

That was before his training, but certainly not before his time! Matteo remembered Tzigone's claim that one of his jordaini masters was also his father. He had looked to the masters still at the school, never considering other possibilities. Apparently, Tzigone had.

It would be like her, Matteo mused. Tzigone had a strong if unconventional sense of honor. When he agreed to help Tzigone find her family, perhaps she decided to repay him in kind. She had found his mother for him. Perhaps she had taken an apprenticeship with Basel Indoulur to learn about his father.

Matteo realized that his host was regarding him with concern. He managed a smile that apparently looked as unconvincing as it felt. Dhamari poured a glass of wine and handed it to him, gesturing for him to drink. Matteo took an obliging sip and felt his composure begin to return.

"The day is unseasonably hot, and one must drink frequently to keep from growing lightheaded," the wizard said.

It was a gracious and convenient observation. Matteo nodded his thanks. "You mentioned a tale that concerns Keturah. I have not heard it."

After a long moment, Dhamari Exchelsor nodded. "I am not sure this tale will help you, but you can make of it whatever you will.

"Keturah, who was once my mistress in the art of evocation, became my wife," he began slowly. "We lived together but a short time, in this place, the very tower in which I trained. At first we were well content, but Keturah was ambitious, and she grew ever more daring in testing the limits of her power. She could bring the most powerful creatures to her side as easily as a shepherd might whistle up his dog. As time passed, she turned to creatures from dark places, monsters far beyond her strength. They strained her magic. They stained her soul," he concluded in a barely audible voice.

After a moment he cleared his throat and continued. "I sensed that not all was well with Keturah. She was often away, sometimes for days at a time. Even when she stayed at the tower, oftentimes she slept half the day away with terrible headaches, which came on swiftly and without warning. She became tempestuous, sharp-tongued, quick to anger. I turned a blind eye to her moods. Had I acted sooner," he said with deep and painful regret, "this tale might be very different. The last day I saw Keturah was the day a greenmage died, attacked in her tower by three starsnakes."

"That is impossible!" Matteo protested. "Such creatures avoid wizards and shun each other."

"Under normal circumstances, yes. It appears that these creatures were summoned."

The implication was disturbing but unmistakable. A greenmage was a midwife skilled in the herbal and healing arts, usually with a bit of the diviner's gift and always trained by the Azuthan inquisitors. Not quite a wizard, not quite a cleric, not quite a magehound, not quite a witch, but definitely more than a physician, a greenmage saw to the health of Halruaa's wizards. Since a wizard's magic and health were so entwined, such complex training was necessary.

"You said Keturah was feeling unwell. She visited this greenmage for treatment?"

"Yes. By the word of the greenmage's servants, Keturah was the last to see the woman alive." Dhamari heaved a ragged sigh. "Perhaps she summoned the starsnakes. Perhaps not. I will never know, for on that day she was lost to me."

Murder through magic was a grave crime, one that would certainly warrant Keturah's death. That alone would explain her flight. Nevertheless, Matteo suspected that there was more and said so.

"Yes," the wizard agreed sadly. "There always seems to be, doesn't there?"

The jordain nodded, returning his host's faint, rueful smile.

"Keturah eluded pursuit for several years. In Halruaa, that is an astonishing feat! Many sought her, and from time to time some word of her came to me." The wizard glanced at Matteo. "She bore a child. No one can name the father. You understand the seriousness of this."

"Yes."

In Halruaa the children of wizardly lineage were not born to random couplings, as in the uncivilized lands to the north. Wizards were paired through divination and carefully kept records, matched to ensure that the lines would remain strong. Dangerous magical gifts, instability of mind or weakness of body—to the wizardborn, such things could be deadly. So entrenched was this custom that few Halruaan children were born out of wedlock. Bastards carried a lifelong stigma. A wizard's bastard, if no father could be named, was killed at birth.

"Keturah knew the law, too," the wizard continued. "She ran, she hid, she protected her child. With her very life she protected her child!"

Dhamari rose and walked with quick, jerky movements over to a table. He took up a carved box and removed from it a small object wrapped in silk. Smoothing back the coverings, he returned to Matteo's side and showed him a simple medallion.

"This belonged to Keturah. Kiva ran her to ground, then brought me this talisman like a trophy. She told me how my wife died, and laughed." The eyes he turned upon Matteo were bright with unshed tears. "Since Kiva found Keturah, I assume she captured the girl, as well."

"I have heard it said," Matteo said carefully. He did not add that somehow a young Tzigone had also managed to escape.

The wizard looked away and cleared his throat several times before speaking. "You are a jordain. The hidden lore of the land is open to you. Things that no man can speak are entrusted to your keeping." He glanced up, and Matteo nodded encouragingly. "If the child survived, a man such as you could learn what became of her. Perhaps you could take this trinket just in case. If you should find her, give it to her and speak to her of her mother. Tell her as little or as much as you think she can bear to hear. A jordain must speak truth, but sift the grain from it and let the chaff blow away."

Matteo was uncertain how to respond, but he knew that Tzigone would cherish her mother's medallion. "I will make inquiries, if you like," he said. "If Keturah's daughter lives, I shall see that she gets this—and I will speak to her of her mother."

Profound gratitude swept the wizard's face. "You are very kind. I hesitate to ask for yet another kindness, but . . ." He stopped and cleared his throat. "If the girl lives, would you tell her that I wish to meet her? Keturah was my beloved wife. I was forced to divorce her, but I would gladly—proudly!—call her child my own. The girl would know of her mother, but she could also claim a father's name and lineage, and this tower and everything in it would be hers when I am gone."

Matteo's head swam with the enormity of this offer: a family, a name, an inheritance, an end to Tzigone's sentence of bastardy and her lifelong flight. Though she was acclaimed for her part in the battle of Akhlaur's Swamp, all silver tarnished in time. Matteo knew enough of human nature to understand that the only thing many people enjoyed more than raising a hero to the skies was to see them come crashing to the ground. Tzigone was a wizard's bastard. In time, that would out.

"I will do what I can," he promised.

Dhamari smiled. "I am content. But you—you came to speak of grave matters, and stayed to listen to an old man's stories. What can I tell you that might help you find Kiva?"

"Kiva hunted down Keturah and came gloating to you. I understand the first—she was a magehound doing her duty—but not the second. Why would she boast of the deed? Was there enmity between you three that would prompt the elf's vengeance?"

The wizard paused for a moment, then nodded grimly. "Kiva summoned an imp and could not dismiss it. The creature did considerable damage before Keturah arrived and contained it. She banished Kiva from this tower."

"So there was a grudge between them?"

"Not on Keturah's part. She banished Kiva because it was the right and responsible thing to do. I stand before you as proof that Keturah's heart, though large, held no room for grudges. You see," he said with obvious reluctance, "I helped Kiva cast that spell. Keturah not only forgave me but consented to wed."

The wizard's expression darkened. "Still, it is hard to believe that Kiva took joy in killing Keturah years later, just to avenge that one slight. Who could be capable of such evil?"

Because Dhamari's question was rhetorical, Matteo did not respond. He exchanged the final formalities and went his ways. As he left the green tower behind, Matteo sifted through all he had heard. Grain and chaff, indeed! Keturah was a fallen wizard, a murderer, and an adulteress. How could he tell Tzigone these things?

How could he not? Keeping important truths from a friend was no better than open falsehood.

Yet wasn't that precisely what Tzigone was doing? Surely she knew about Basel Indoulur's background—she was as cautious and canny as anyone Matteo had ever met. Perhaps she was doing exactly what she had asked of him, and taking the man's measure. He was not sure whether to be angry with her or grateful. He was not sure how to feel about any of this.

Matteo took the medallion from his pocket and studied it. The design was simple, the craftsmanship unremarkable. Yet Keturah had been a wizard, one successful enough to attract apprentices and claim a fine, green-marble tower as her home. She was not likely to wear so paltry a trinket unless it was powerfully enchanted. If this were so, he might be endangering Tzigone by putting it in her hands. He did not know Dhamari well enough to trust him.

Prudence demanded that he have the piece examined by a wizard, but whom could he trust? Not the queen, certainly. Since the medallion had no gears and whistles, she would have no interest in it. Not Procopio Septus. Not any of the wizards from the Jordaini College.

An impulse came to him, one that he refused to examine too closely for fear that it might not hold up to jordaini logic.

Matteo turned on his heel and strode quickly to the closest boulevard. He let several magical conveyances pass by, waiting for the rumble of a mundane coach and four. Matteo told the driver to take him to Basel Indoulur's tower.

The wizard's home in Halarahh was a modest, comfortable villa on a quiet side street, hardly the usual abode of an ambitious wizard-lord. Matteo reminded himself that Lord Basel was mayor of another city, where he no doubt indulged in the usual displays of pride and wealth. He asked the driver to wait, then gave his name and that of his patron to the gatekeeper, requesting a private audience with the lord wizard.

A servant led Matteo into the garden and to a small building covered with flowering vines. Once Matteo was inside, large windows, not visible from the outside, let the sun pour in. Lord Basel, it seemed, was well prepared for clandestine meetings.

As Basel entered, Matteo's first thought was that Dhamari must have been mistaken about this wizard's past. Jordaini masters usually mirrored the simplicity and discipline that marked their students' lives. Basel's clothes were purple and crimson silk, colors echoed in the beads that decked dozens of tiny braids. His face was round and his belly far from flat. Matteo could not envision this man among the warriors and scholars who shaped jordaini life.

He searched for some physical resemblance between them and found none. Basel's hair was black as soot, his nose straight and small, his skin a light olive tone. Like most jordaini, Matteo was as fit and strong as a warrior, and at six feet he was tall for a Halruaan. His hair was a deep chestnut with red highlights that flashed in the sunlight like sudden temper. His features were stronger than the wizard's, with a firmer chin and a decided arch to his nose. If this man was indeed his sire, the evidence could not be read in their faces.

"How may I serve the queen's counselor?" Basel asked, breaking a silence that had grown too long.

Matteo produced the medallion. "A jordain is forbidden to carry magical items. Can you tell me if this holds any enchantment and if so, what manner?"

The wizard took the charm and turned it over in his pudgy hands. His jeweled rings flashed with each movement. "A simple piece."

"But does it hold magic?"

Basel handed it back. "A diviner could give you a more subtle reading. You served Lord Procopio. Why not go to him?"

Matteo picked his words carefully. "Recently I attempted to speak with Lord Procopio concerning Zephyr, a jordain in league with the magehound Kiva. I am attempting to learn more about Kiva and thought this a reasonable path of inquiry."

"Ah." Basel lifted a hand to his lips, but not before Matteo noted the quick, sardonic smile. "Knowing Lord Procopio, I assume he had scant interest in pursuing this topic."

"None that I could perceive."

"He will be keenly attuned to anything that hints of further inquiry. If you came to him with a talisman, he would immediately assume it was part of your search."

In an odd way, perhaps it was. A protective talisman would explain why Keturah had managed to escape capture for so long. "Can it be magically traced?"

Basel gave him a quick, lopsided smile. "If so, it would be very poor protection."

"Indeed." Matteo rose, intending to thank the wizard and go.

His host halted him with an upraised hand. "Your eyes say that you're unsure whether to trust me or not. That shows caution. You didn't go to Procopio. That shows wisdom. If my old friend is angry with you—and I don't need a diviner's gift to know how likely *that* is—he might report you for carrying a magical item or demand that you turn it over to him at once. It would be within his rights and power to do so."

"As it is in yours."

"True enough," Basel admitted. "You have little reason to trust me. Yet here you are. If you believe nothing else I've said, believe this: If there were any danger in that medallion, if there was any possibility that it would bring harm to Tzigone in any way, it would never leave this room."

Matteo could not keep the surprise from his face. The wizard nodded confirmation. "Yes, I know that Tzigone is Keturah's daughter. I knew Keturah, and I recognize her talisman. It served her well for far longer than I thought possible."

The jordain's mind raced. "Will others recognize it? Could it establish a connection between Tzigone and Keturah?"

"Unlikely. Keturah acquired the talisman just before she flew Halarahh. We were childhood friends. She came to me in need a few times after her escape."

The enormity of this revelation stunned Matteo. If all that Dhamari Exchelsor said of Keturah was true, then Basel had defied Halruaa's laws and risked death to help her.

"Does Tzigone know any of this?"

"No," Basel said emphatically. "Since she is so determined to find out about her mother, I decided to guide her steps. She would have found her way to Dhamari Exchelsor in time. When I suggested that she send a trusted friend, I rather thought she would ask you."

"Did you expect me to come here?" As he spoke, Matteo half wished that this would prove true.

The wizard considered, then shook his head. "No, but I am glad you did. Having met Tzigone's friend, I feel easier for her."

Matteo could not miss the sincere affection in the wizard's eyes. "You care for her."

"Like a daughter," Basel agreed. "To ease your mind in turn, I tell you in confidence that I'll do whatever is necessary to protect her from the stigma of her birth. If she is discovered, I will claim paternity."

For the second time that day, the world shifted under Matteo's feet. For Basel to claim paternity would mean admitting that he'd seen Keturah after her escape. This was against the law, as was siring a child of two wizard lines outside the boundaries of Halruaa's carefully controlled lineage. Either offense meant certain disgrace. Yet Basel Indoulur was prepared to do this for Tzigone's sake. For a moment, Matteo actually wished that this good man truly was his father.

But would a good man stand by while his wife destroyed her mind and magic to ensure that she bore a jordaini babe? Matteo's training taught him that service to Halruaa came first. Perhaps Basel had once believed this and learned that other vows lay deepest in his heart.

Another thought hit him, an aftershock no less jarring than the quake that proceeded. What if Basel's claim was actual truth? What if the wizard was Tzigone's father? If that were so, perhaps Matteo's friend was also his sister! As Matteo considered this complex marvel, he found that he did not want to reject these possibilities out of hand. If he were able to do so, he would claim this unlikely family with pride. He searched the wizard's face for a similar epiphany and found none.

"I've seen lightning-struck men who looked less stunned than you," Basel said with a faint smile. "Yet we are not so different. I suspect that one of your reasons for seeking Kiva so diligently is that she obviously knows of Tzigone's heritage. You don't want her hurting Tzigone any more than she has."

Matteo blinked. "I had not thought of it in those terms."

"Sometimes the hardest truth to see is the one within." The wizard spoke the jordaini proverb with the air of long familiarity.

They spoke for a few minutes more, and Matteo took his leave. On impulse, he gave the driver the name of a place he had visited but once. The horses trotted swiftly to the west, through rows of fashionable houses magically grown from coral, on through neighborhoods of dwindling wealth and prestige. Finally they stopped at a tall, stonewalled garden.

He passed through the gate and walked swiftly to the cottage he and Tzigone had visited. The door was ajar. He tapped lightly and eased it open.

A woman stood by the window, gazing out at the small garden beyond, her arms wrapped tightly around her meager form.

"Mystra's blessing upon you, mother." It was merely the polite address for women of her age, but the word felt unexpectedly sweet on his lips.

The woman turned listlessly toward him. Matteo fell back a step, his breath catching in an astonished gasp.

She was not the same person.

"What did you expect?" demanded a soft, furious voice behind him.

Matteo turned to face a woman dressed in a servant's smock. Her face was round and soft, and it would have been pretty but for the grim set of her mouth.

She nodded at his jordaini medallion. "If one of you comes around asking questions, any woman he meets is moved to another place. Don't you think these women have suffered enough, without losing their homes? Now this woman, too, will be moved. Moved again, if need be, until you and yours finally leave her be."

Guilt and grief struck him like a tidal surge. "I did not know."

"Well, now you do. Get out before you do more damage.

There are some things, *jordain*, that are more important than your right to all the knowledge of Halruaa!"

She spat out his title as if it were a curse. Matteo was not entirely certain she was wrong. He made a deep bow of apology and pressed his coin bag into the servant's hands.

"To ease her journey," he said, then turned and fled.

He walked back to the palace, though it took the rest of the day and brought him to the gates when the last echo of the palace curfew horn rang over the city. It had been a deeply disturbing day, one that had brought more questions than answers. One path, however, was clear. He would tell Tzigone all, though the tale would be difficult to hear. The accusations against Keturah were both dire and plausible, but he understood now what drove Tzigone toward these answers for so many years. As painful as it might be to hear of her mother's fate, Matteo now understood there was something far worse:

Not knowing.

CHAPTER THIRTEEN

Andris sat alone beyond the light of the campfires, watching in disbelief as Kiva gleefully received the treasure the Crinti bandits had gathered for her. She lifted a moonstone globe in both hands, cooing over it like a fond young mother admiring her babe.

Sternly Andris reminded himself of the importance of their quest. The Cabal was a rot at the very heart of Halruaa. He had to destroy it, not only because of his elf heritage but because he was still a jordain, sworn to serve Halruaa. Kiva was his only ally, his only chance to right this wrong.

All this he told himself. The phrases were as well practiced as a priest's sunrise chants. Unlike the Azuthan prayers, though, his silent words seemed hollow and false.

He watched the Crinti shower the elf woman with pilfered wealth and grisly trophies. They were particularly proud of a huge skull that looked a bit like a giant sahuagin. Their demeanor was oddly like that of children who courted a parent's approval but did not expect to get it.

Andris understood all too well that elves shunned and disdained those of mixed blood. Kiva exploited this fact. The simple gift of her presence made her a queen among the Crinti, and her feigned acceptance they embraced as a longed-for sister-hood. They were deceived by Kiva because they wanted to believe.

How well, he wondered, did that also describe him?

Kiva, enthroned on a fur-draped rock near the campfire, was vaguely aware of Andris's unease, but she was too absorbed in her new treasure to spare much concern. The scrying globe particularly pleased her. She stroked the moonstone, attuning it to her personal power.

Shanair watched with a proud smile. "It is enough?"

"It's a wonderful treasure," Kiva assured her. "I will require some time to explore it."

The Crinti gestured toward the massive skull. "This was fine sport. Will more of these come through the floodgate?"

Andris sat up abruptly, startled by the implication of Shanair's words. His gaze shot toward the trophy. Firelight danced along the ridges and hollows, making the fanged jaws gleam like a demon's snarl. It was not a sahuagin nor any creature known to his world!

"The gate will open in time," Kiva assured her. "This monster is just a taste of what will come."

Andris leaped to his feet and strode forward. Five Crinti blades halted his progress. Five gray-faced warriors regarded him with searing blue eyes, like small flames amid the ash.

"Kiva has not called for you," one of them said, eyeing Andris as if he were something she had just scraped off her boot. "Know your place, and return to it."

"Let him speak," Kiva decreed.

Andris brushed his way past the warriors and crouched at Kiva's side. Leaning in close so that the watchful Crinti could not hear his words, he said urgently, "You cannot mean to open the gate. The Cabal must be destroyed, but not all Halruaa with it!"

The elf's golden eyes narrowed and burned. "Need I remind you of the eif city in the Kilmaruu Swamp, drowned by the wizard Akhlaur and two of his cohorts? If Halarahh sank beneath sea and swampland, would you call that an injustice?"

"Is that your intent?"

Kiva was silent for a moment. "No," she said softly. "Justice demands that the wizards pay for what they have done. It does not demand that I destroy more of my ancestors' lands."

"Your friends seem to think otherwise."

She rose to her feet. "My friends honor their elf ancestors and destroy those who do not." Her voice rang out clear and strong, and her gaze included not just Andris but the battle-ready Crinti warriors.

Shanair caught the implication, and she looked at Andris with a bit more respect. "The male is elfblooded?"

"Would I deal with him if he were not?" Kiva retorted.

The bandit turned to her band and issued a sharp, guttural order. They put away their blades with obvious reluctance and returned to the campfire.

It occurred to Andris that Kiva was telling the Crinti what they expected to hear—as she had the forest elves and the jordaini who had fought for her in the swamps of Kilmaruu and Akhlaur. As, no doubt, she was doing with him. Andris was surprised at how painful this realization was. He thought himself well beyond the sting of betrayal and half-truths.

With difficulty he brought his attention back to the discussion of the floodgate. "When the time is right, we will unleash creatures that might even challenge Shanair," Kiva went on.

The Crinti's laugh rang with scorn at this notion, and anticipation lit her strange blue eyes. "May that day come soon, elf-sister! Tell us how to prepare."

"To begin with, you might want to improve your swimming skills."

The females shared a dark chuckle, and neither of them noticed that the ghostly human in their midst did not share their amusement.

Andris woke the next morning to the splashing of water and the thud and clash of weapons. He belted on his sword and followed the sound to a stream not far from the Crinti encampment.

Several of the elfbloods were training in water past their waists. He had perceived Kiva's comment about swimming as a jest, but apparently the Crinti were more literal of mind.

For a long time Andris stood on the banks watching the Crinti warriors. They were good—among the finest fighters he had ever seen—but weighted down by their leather armor and heavy weapons. The water stole their strength and halved their speed. In light of last night's revelation, that presented a serious problem.

The creature whose skull Shanair took would not be hampered by water or weapons. Andris had seen such a creature etched in a lore book detailing creatures from the Plane of Water. He had seen the laraken slip through the crack in the floodgate. He suspected that the slaughtered monster had been a response in kind. Last night, for the first time, Andris had begun to believe that Akhlaur was still alive. He doubted that the wizard's minions were limited to a single monster.

Perhaps the Crinti's precautions were not so far-fetched, after all.

Andris unbuckled his sword belt and hung it on a tree limb. He stripped off his tunic and trews, leaving only his linen undergarment. He would fight better in water if he were completely naked, but given the Crinti attitude toward males, he saw little wisdom in presenting them with a convenient and obvious target.

He waded into the stream, armed with his jordaini daggers. One of the Crinti took note of him and elbowed a sister warrior, a well-fleshed woman who was by far the biggest of the lot. This woman snorted and called out an incomprehensible but clearly derisive comment.

Andris decided she would provide as good an example as any.

When he was yet a few paces away, he took a deep breath and dived toward the big Crinti and her sparring partner. His translucent form all but disappeared. The water began to roil frantically as the two women stabbed at their unseen foe. He held back out of reach until the right moment, then seized the gray hands that drove a sword into the water. He worked with the Crinti's movement, adding his strength to push the blade deep into the stream bed. The extra "help" threw the elf off balance. Andris kicked out hard, catching her leg just above the knee. He burst out of the water, dancing away in time to see the woman flop facedown into the water, her ample, leather-clad rump followed by her flailing boots.

"A breaching whale," Andris mocked. He turned to the downed woman's companion, who held her sword above the water in lunge position. "Next, I suppose, comes the narwhal."

The Crinti woman came on hard but did not anticipate the full impact of the water's resistance. Andris ducked under the water. He caught the woman by her hips, just under her center of balance, and pushed up hard as he rose. The precisely timed movement sent the Crinti into brief and impromptu flight. She splashed down and skimmed the water, like a leaping swordfish.

Andris spoke into ominous silence. "The whale and the narwhal are creatures I know. For the wise warrior, knowing comes before fighting."

The light broke over the big Crinti's wet, gray face. "You know the creatures of this water world?"

Andris gave a succinct description of the mantinarg, the creature whose skull Shanair had displayed with such pride.

The big Crinti nodded. "Yes, that is the beast we fought. Tell us of others."

The warriors gathered around as Andris told them what he knew. He started with tritons, powerful blue-skinned warriors with fins for feet. The Crinti scoffed at the idea of fighting against tridents, equating these pronged weapons with the pitiful defense mounted by human farmers. Andris fashioned a crude trident from a tree limb to prove them wrong. After he dropped three Crinti on their muscled backsides, the others were willing to take him seriously.

Andris slipped once again into the role of battle leader—showing the Crinti new attacks, offering suggestions to pairs of sparring warriors, keenly observing the strengths and limitations of his troops and building a battle strategy. After the intense inner conflict of the past few days, it was an enormous relief to be engaged in something he understood.

From a distance, Kiva watched with an approving smile. Andris, like the laraken, was proving useful beyond his original purpose. His elf heritage had nearly killed him in Akhlaur's swamp, yet it had welded him to her cause. He obviously struggled with the grim realities of his chosen path, but he would not turn back. Andris was hers. She had read this knowledge in his eyes when he realized his kinship to the Mhair elves.

The power of kinship was strong, even in the humans. Family was destiny—Kiva believed this to the depths of her soul. Perhaps that was why she stumbled over the three direct descendants of Akhlaur and his conspirators at nearly every turn. Perhaps they, too, had a destiny.

The globe in Kiva's lap began to glow. Puzzled, she placed one hand on the cool moonstone. The magic that hummed from the globe was Zephyr's signature enchantment: familiar, but subtly changed.

She carefully opened the magical pathway. A face appeared in the globe—a misty face, gray as a Crinti's and without form or feature. The wizard could have been old or young, male or female, elf or orc. But Kiva had spent long years collecting scrying devices and researching their properties. She cast a counterspell and watched as the mist peeled back to discern the true form of her "visitor." Reflected in the glove was the face of a human male with sharp black eyes and a scimitar nose.

Her throat tightened with dread as she recognized Procopio Septus, the wizard who had employed Zephyr. If the man knew enough to bring him here, she had better take the full measure of his knowledge.

She greeted him by name.

The wizard blinked, momentarily nonplused. He promptly returned the courtesy, even giving Kiva her lost title of inquisatrix, and then started in with the usual string of meaningless formalities that Halruaans thought necessary to every occasion.

Kiva sharply cuffed the globe, startling the wizard into silence. "State your purpose."

"Perhaps I simply wish to gloat," Procopio's image suggested "You took Zephyr from me, but I managed to recover another misplaced jordain. You recall Iago, my master of horse? He is quite the hero after the battle of Akhlaur's Swamp. His fame adds luster to my household. So perhaps I also wish to thank you."

Perhaps, Kiva noted grimly, the wizard was a flatulent bag of wind. She responded with an innocuous remark. "Iago is an able man."

"Very able," Procopio agreed. "He is an excellent tracker and possesses a fine memory. The maps he has made of his travels are quite remarkable. He was riding the Nath when the Crinti raiders took him. Terrible experience, I would imagine. I hear that few sounds can curdle the blood like a Crinti battle yell." He tipped his head to one side, as if he were listening to the shouts and curses coming from the nearby stream.

Not a bag of wind, Kiva realized, but a dangerous man. Nevertheless, she would not be toyed with in such fashion. "What do you want?" she demanded bluntly.

The wizard smiled. "Tell me, Inquisatrix, what news of the far northlands?"

"What makes you think I would know?"

Procopio's white brows rose. "I am willing to share information, even if you are not. I recently had a visit from Matteo. He is looking for you."

"How frightening," Kiva observed blandly. "Perhaps later today, I'll faint."

"He is a persistent young man," Procopio continued as if he hadn't heard her. "He is trying to persuade Queen Beatrix to request Iago's hire. Since Zalathorm's moon-mad queen has no more use for another jordain than a cat has for a second tail, we can assume that Matteo has a task in mind for my jordain—and for his maps and memories."

"You seem to have trouble keeping your counselors," Kiva observed coolly, giving away nothing of the unease building within.

"Indeed. You have been raiding my henhouse quite regularly, Kiva. I would like to know why."

"I am a wizard," she reminded him. "I would not be the first wizard to find a use for magic-resistant servants."

"If you're thinking to use Matteo, perhaps you should reconsider. I never found him a particularly docile tool."

"Neither is his father, but I find him useful all the same."

A silence fell as Procopio considered this truth disguised as falsehood. The jordaini were the offspring of wizards, and no Halruaan would believe that any of their wizards could be subject to an elf woman. "On whose behalf do you act?" asked Procopio, predictably enough.

Kiva laughed scornfully. "No wizard holds my leash. I command myself."

To her surprise, relief flickered in Procopio's eyes—not the patronizing incredulity that she anticipated.

"How much can you expect to gain from any wizard weak enough to yield to your control? A partnership between near equals, however, could be of great benefit to both."

"What could you possibly give me?" Her tone was scornful but not so scathing that it couldn't be interpreted as genuine inquiry.

Procopio caught the nuance. "A spell that would enable you to scry the lands beyond the eastern outposts."

"Such riches," she scoffed. "I have such spells. What wizard does not?"

"Use them, and tell me what you see."

After a moment's hesitation, she did as Procopio suggested. Instantly the scene in the globe changed, showing in detailed miniature the sweeping mountains to the east and the livid sunset colors gathering over the vast and empty plains of Dambrath.

Kiva dismissed the image with an impatient flick of her fingers and glared into Procopio's smug face. "I see nothing."

"Which is what every other wizard in Halruaa sees. Look deeper, and not with magic. We will speak again."

The wizard's visage disappeared from the globe. Puzzled, Kiva called over Shanair and asked what the Crinti knew about Halruaa's eastern frontier.

"Warriors come," she said with satisfaction. "Mulhorandi foot soldiers, cavalry, and wizards, marching toward Halruaa. A good army, even if they are males."

Kiva hissed with rage. This she had not expected! Not that she was averse to bringing another weapon against Halruaa, but only if it was part of a coordinated attack!

"These humans march over Dambrath lands. Why have your people not stopped them?"

Shanair looked astonished. "We believed it part of your invasion. If it were not, would we let their feet soil our land?" Suddenly she spat and then swore. "By the legs of Lolth! We kept our weapons dry for no reason?"

"They will soon be wet with Halruaan blood," Kiva assured her.

Too soon, the elf woman added grimly. The battle was approaching, spurred by events she did not control. She saw little choice but to work with Procopio Septus. Later, he would pay for forcing her to act before a time of her choosing. A pivotal part of her plan was not yet in place. Before the battle could begin, she had to return to Akhlaur.

Not just to the swamp but to Akhlaur himself.

CHAPTER FOURTEEN

Tzigone took a slow sip of the wine Matteo had chosen. It was marvelous—the best she had ever tasted, bought, or stolen. Who would have thought the man had taste?

In fact, everything about this lovely inn spoke of taste, elegance, and privilege. The tables were draped with white damask. Flowers graced each place setting. The dishes matched. The servants were polite, and they didn't count the silverware after they removed each course. Any one of these things would have constituted a new level of luxury and respect. Put together, this meal was a treat Tzigone would remember with pleasure for a very long time.

More importantly, it was the first time Matteo had actually sought her out. Usually their meetings were irregular and entirely at her instigation— more of a friendly ambush, really, than a meeting. Her pleasure at this invitation was so great that it could not be marred by the sidelong glances and whispered gossip their presence elicited. In well-mannered Halarahh—or anywhere else in Halruaa, for that matter—jordaini simply did not consort with apprentice wizards.

For once, Matteo did not seem concerned with such niceties. As he spoke his mind, her bright mood dimmed, but she heard him out without interrupting, cursing, or dumping the kumquat trifle on his head—though she dearly wished to do all of these things.

"I don't know about this," Tzigone said dubiously when at last he paused for breath.

Matteo leaned forward. "Dhamari Exchelsor made a generous offer, one that could change your life—one that could *save* your life. You should at least consider it."

The girl shrugged. "I'll think about it. Did you get any information for yourself?"

For a moment he looked startled. "Oh. You mean information about Kiva."

Tzigone cast her eyes skyward and moved the wine decanter closer to her side of the table. "Obviously you've had enough of this. Remember Kiva? Yellow eyes, green hair, black heart?"

"It seems there is little to be learned in all this city," he said with deep frustration. "The Temple of Azuth refuses to deal with me. Zephyr and Cassia are dead. I've sought out the few elves in the city, but none have knowledge of or dealings with Kiva."

"Maybe you're just asking the wrong questions." Tzigone tipped the decanter into her glass. A single golden drop fell. With a sigh of resignation, she reached for her table knife and tucked it back into her belt, leaving, with no small regret, the house silver still on the table. Matteo rose and came around the table to pull out her chair for her—a proper courtesy for a jordain to show a lady wizard. A shudder went through Tzigone at the thought.

"What is wrong?" he asked softly.

"Lady," she muttered. "Wizard."

Matteo did not require an explanation—he knew how uneasy Tzigone was with the role she'd taken on. "Patron," he countered, bowing to her with a pantomimed expression of abject horror.

They burst out laughing, drawing stares from the more sedate diners. Chuckling still, they left the cool luxury of the inn for the glare of the street.

Tzigone suddenly remembered something. She stopped dead and seized his arm. "We forgot to pay! Run!"

He looked incredulously at her for a moment, then let out a whoop of incomprehensible laughter. Tzigone folded her arms and glared as she waited for his mirth to subside.

Matteo wiped a tear from one eye and reached down to touch his jordain medallion. A familiar pedantic expression settled over his face, but the rumble of an approaching ice wagon drowned out the ensuing lecture.

As the wagon pulled level with them, the heavy canvas curtain at the rear jerked open. Two men leaned out and seized Tzigone, jerking her up into the covered cart.

The attack was sudden, and completely unexpected. One moment Matteo was preparing to explain to Tzigone that jordaini seldom handled money, on the theory that they were less likely to be corrupted by its lure. Of course, the same reasoning kept the jordaini from forming close friendships, for fear that these might cloud their judgment and shape their counsel.

For one heart-stopping instant, Matteo understood how this could be so. The only thing that mattered to him at this moment was the small, fiercely struggling girl and the two thugs who laid hands on her. He kicked into a run.

The curtain twitched aside to reveal a leering, bearded face. A third man, big and hairy as one of the northland's barbarians, hurled a pale blue robe—identical to the one Tzigone wore—into the street. Though all this happened within the span of two heartbeats, Matteo noted that the robe was soaked with ominous red.

The message was clear.

Matteo ran full out, wishing for the first time that he had some magic in him, some way to slow the ice wagon. As if to mock him, the driver shook the reins over the horses' neck, and the cart leaped forward in a sudden spurt.

Desperate, Matteo put all his strength into a final, leaping lunge. He fell just short of the ice wagon, but his fingers closed on the dragging end of a rope meant to bind the rear canvas shut. Only faintly aware of his passage over bruising cobblestone, Matteo hauled himself hand over hand up the rope and onto the cart. He found a toehold on the back axle and hung on as the ice wagon careened through the streets.

As they thundered along, children pointed at him and passersby smirked, but no one raised an alarm. The cart moved fast, but not more so than was custom in a land so hot that ice disappeared quicker than a wizard's fireball.

Matteo took a calming breath and began to plan the battle ahead. There were at least four men—the two who snatched Tzigone, the leering thug, and the driver. The cart was a good size, though, and there could be many more inside. And Tzigone was alone with them.

He tried not to dwell on this. Every instinct prompted him to fight his way to his friend's side. Logic and training prevailed. He had no possibility of making a surprise attack, and he could not expect the thugs to stand patiently by as he hauled himself up into the ice wagon. His best chance of aiding Tzigone was to wait until the cart reached its destination. Paradoxically, the bloody robe gave him hope that she would be unharmed. Her abduction was meant as a warning and perhaps a lure.

Very well, he would give them opportunity to deliver that message directly, and sooner than expected. With a grim smile, Matteo vowed to make the coming "conversation" as interesting as possible.

Finally he saw the huge bulk of an icehouse up ahead. The cart veered around the small streets that surrounded the vast building and approached the rear. Wide, double doors swung open to admit them, then slammed shut behind. The ice wagon slowed, and the rumble died into silence.

Matteo dropped quietly to the ground and swept the icehouse with a quick measuring gaze. Everything seemed to be in good order. The metal hooks and tools were free of rust. Fresh straw had been strewn on the packed dirt floor, and the high beams were free of cobwebs. The spells that opened and closed the doors for the cart were obviously well maintained. In short, this was no long-deserted building. Yet no one was working, even though highsun had come and gone and the sunsleep hours past. Matteo also noticed that the walls were thick to keep the ice cool and, not coincidentally, to muffle sound.

The momentary silence exploded into a fury of thuds and curses—most of the latter coming from Tzigone, though a few muffled and pained exclamations from her captors suggested that she was making a good accounting for herself. Tzigone's voice abruptly dwindled to a furious mumbling. The cart's back gate fell open with a crash, and three men stumbled out from behind the curtain and down the ramp, carrying their uncooperative captive. They'd managed to stuff a rag into her mouth and bind it with a gag. She writhed and kicked and, presumably, swore, but to no avail. The men pinioned her so that her hands were stilled, leaving no chance that she might cast a spell.

Another man followed them—a wizard holding a long wand in one hand. When he saw Matteo, he quickly touched the wand to each of the three men. Matteo noted the soft click as the wand touched the men, as if the wizard were tapping against granite.

Stoneskin, he thought grimly. These men had expected him to follow, and they were well prepared. Quickly he calculated his chances against fighters wearing this magical protection. Four men against one was challenge enough—five men, if he counted the man climbing down from the driver's seat. Now he would have to strike several solid blows on each man to dispel the stoneskin charm, and figure in the permutations presented by four such opponents.

"Seven hundred and eighty-five to one, give or take," he murmured. He shrugged, drew his daggers, and charged.

"Get him," shouted the thug holding Tzigone's ankles.

The wizard leveled his wand at Matteo and spat out a trigger word.

The jordain dropped and rolled as a golden streak burst from the wand. The bolt missed him, but it did not disappear. The stream of light slowed, broke up, and began to reform. A swarm of bees traced a collective arc and buzzed unerringly toward their intended target.

They swarmed over Matteo in a dark, whirring cloud. He felt a stinging jab at the back of his neck and schooled himself not to slap at the insect. Instead, he veered aside, heading directly toward the smirking wizard—bringing the bees with him.

The wizard's eyes widened, and he lifted the wand for another attack. Matteo dropped, using the leg sweep move that Andris had taught him just a few moons past to bring the wizard down. He seized a rock-hard ankle and thrust a dagger into the soft leather of the boot sole—the only unprotected place on a wizard wearing a stoneskin spell.

The blade slipped through leather and past bone. Matteo leaned hard on the blade, scraping between the twin bones of the wizard's lower leg and reaching for the tendon behind. With a quick wrench, he severed the cord.

Ignoring the bees that still swarmed and stung, Matteo rolled to his feet and charged the men holding Tzigone's hands. One of them trusted the wizard's magic to hold firm, but the other released the girl and dragged a knife from his belt.

Matteo's bloodied dagger struck the man's weapon hand before the blade could clear its sheath. The jolt of steel against stoneskin vibrated through his arm. He struck again and again. Through it all, the bees followed his movements like a treacherous shadow.

The thug defended himself as best he could and managed to parry some of Matteo's strokes, but with each hit Matteo landed, the efficacy of the stoneskin spell faded away. Within moments the jordain's dagger struck normal flesh—then, bone.

Matteo's opponent stumbled back, shrieking in shock and pain as he stared at the gash that opened his arm and at the white bone beneath.

The jordain spun and drove his one foot into the man's gut. Reversing direction with stunning speed, he whirled and landed a high roundhouse kick to the man's chin. His head snapped back, and he went over like a felled tree, arms falling wide and limp at his sides.

Matteo spun toward Tzigone, who was down to one captor. She was standing now, her hands firmly pinioned behind her back. The big, bearded man who'd held her feet slumped against the wagon, spitting teeth into his cupped palm. Blood poured from a garishly broken nose. One of his eyes was already swelling shut, and the other was starting to lose focus. Tzigone continued to writhe and kick and stomp, wearing down the stoneskin spell on her final opponent with a barrage of blows and kicks. For a moment Matteo wondered if she had really needed his help at all.

Suddenly Tzigone slumped as if in defeat. Matteo was not fooled, but the thug who held Tzigone let out a relieved sigh. The sound ended in a gasp, and the man's eyes opened wide and glazed with pain.

Apparently Tzigone had managed to seize something her captor held in great personal regard. She twisted free. Ripping off her gag, she kicked the man in the already offended area, then kicked him once more after he fell. She swatted at a circling bee and began the gestures of a spell.

Fragrant smoke rose from the hard-packed ground, a scent reminiscent of poppies and summer sun. The bees swarming Matteo stopped their stinging attack. Their flight slowed, and they drifted off to settle on the wooden beams.

Free of that hindrance, Matteo looked around for the final thug—the driver, who had not yet entered the battle. The back door flew open, and the man came on in a rush, followed closely by the reinforcements he'd apparently gone to summon. As the men rushed Matteo, they snatched up ice hooks long as swords, with wicked curved tips.

Tzigone began another spell—a simple cantrip to heat metal. Yet the men's ice picks showed no red glow. Puzzled, Matteo followed Tzigone's gaze toward the ceiling. There, suspended from ropes as thick as his arm, was an enormous set of iron tongs that lifted ice to the loft above. The metal tongs were red as a sunrise, and mist rose from the block of ice in their grip.

Ice shrieked against metal as the massive chunk slipped loose. Matteo grabbed for Tzigone, but she was quicker than he and was already running toward a sheet of heavy canvas on the far side of the room. She held it up so that Matteo could dive for cover, then rolled in with him and buried her face against his chest.

The impact was thunderous, and the shattering ice splintered off again and again like a brittle echo. Shards rained over the two friends, but no ice penetrated the thick, oiled cloth.

When all was still, Matteo and Tzigone crawled out from under the tarp and somberly regarded the scene around them. The icehouse resembled a battlefield. The wagon lay on its side, one wheel shattered and the other three spinning wildly. The horses, amazingly enough, had escaped serious injury. They had broken free of their traces, and now blew and stomped in the far corner of the room. Chunks of ice were strewn across the floor, some of them tinted with crimson. At least two of the thugs were thoroughly, messily dead. Several more lay still. One pile of ice shimmered with movement as an injured man fought his way free. A faint groan came from under the upturned wagon.

Tzigone stared at the carnage, her face pale and still.

Matteo slipped a steadying arm around her shoulders. "This must be reported to the officials."

She started to protest, then sighed. "I never thought the day would come when I went looking for the law instead of the other way around."

"I will see to it," he promised.

Tzigone's first response was a quick, grateful smile, quickly chased by a frown as her nimble mind danced ahead. "Someone might have seen them grab me. You'll have to tell the militia something."

"These thugs seized a young woman. I followed and fought them. She escaped."

She snorted. "Is that the best you can do? It's not very interesting."

"One of the benefits of telling simple truth," he said dryly, "is that you don't have to remember interesting details. That said, I've learned one very interesting detail this night: I'm making more progress than I thought."

Tzigone looked at him incredulously, then her eyes cleared and she nodded. "Someone doesn't like the questions you're asking, which means that you're probably doing something right."

He walked with her toward the back door. "The next question will be who owns this building. A working ice-house does not lie empty and idle during the afternoon. This attack might not have been instigated by the owner, but he or she would know who had the authority to send the workers away."

"Why don't we just get someone to ask him?" She pointed to one of the dead men.

Matteo's first instinct was to protest. Powerful clerical magic was required to speak with the dead. The jordaini were not to have any magic worked on their behalf.

He never got the chance to remind her of this. Before he could speak, the corpses and the injured changed to rapidly fading mist. In an instant, he and Tzigone were alone in the icehouse.

She let out a long, slow whistle. "You've been asking the right questions, all right. I don't think we're going to like the people who've got the answers."

"All the more reason for you to go. I will pursue this matter and tell you all I learn when next we meet."

She nodded and disappeared—not out the door but up a

wall. Climbing nimbly on crossbars and ropes, she melted into the shadows that lurked about the high ceiling.

Matteo went into the street to alert the city militia. He was spared the trouble, for the thunderous crash of falling ice had drawn the notice of a nearby fish market. The vendor stood nearby with a long, curving horn held to his lips, winding a raucous but effective alarm. A small crowd of fisherfolk had already gathered around the building. They parted to allow the city militia to pass through.

Matteo quickly explained what had happened, not identifying Tzigone by name but saying only the abducted girl had escaped. The city guards lifted their eyebrows and exchanged incredulous glances when Matteo told them that their assailants had also disappeared. None of them dared to challenge the veracity of the queen's jordain, but Matteo understood the path their thoughts must be taking. Why would several men flee from a single jordain? If Matteo defined the word "disappeared" in its literal and magical sense, the guards would accept his story with a nod. After all, this was Halruaa, and strange magical occurrences were the norm.

Strange magical occurrences were also closely examined. And as Tzigone had pointed out, it was unlikely that the answers would be reassuring.

An hour later, Matteo strolled into the pink marble palace that housed the city officials. Several of the guards and scribes recognized him, nodding respectfully as he passed. He walked unchallenged into the lord mayor's suite and made his way down the corridors to the domain of Procopio's head scribe.

As he expected, he found the man at a writing table. His duties involved summarizing each of the lord mayor's missives into a single line so that Procopio could scan the day's news and decide how best to order his time.

"Greetings, Shiphor," Matteo called softly.

The scribe glanced up, startled. A pleased smile crossed his face. "Matteo! Please tell me you've been demoted to our level!"

Matteo acknowledged the jest with a chuckle and glanced around Shiphor's small, paper-clogged room. "Your level? This is the heart of the city. Its lifeblood flows through your hands."

"At least one man recognizes my importance," the scribe said dryly. "Because you show such remarkable intelligence, I will save you the necessity of further flattery and simply tell you whatever you wish to know. Not that I'm not enjoying this, mind you."

The jordain grinned, noting that Shiphor's cynical tone was offset by the twinkle in his eyes. "May I see your summary notes for the past several days? As well as today's missives?"

Shiphor promptly drew several sheaves of papers from various stacks, as unerringly as a mother hen might pick her own chick from a barnyard crowded with yellow peepers. Matteo glanced at the summaries and started in on the new messages. He leafed through until he caught a glimpse of Kiva's name. As he read, his already dark mood turned a deeper shade of black.

Kiva had already been declared traitor, but apparently Procopio had not deemed that sufficient. She had been excommunicated by the church of Azuth. Matteo repeated one of the oaths he'd recently heard Tzigone employ.

The scribe looked up sharply. "Problems?"

"Halruaa is full of them, it would seem," Matteo said grimly. "With your permission, I would like to bring a particularly troublesome one directly to Lord Procopio's attention."

Shiphor took the page Matteo handed him and scanned it. His grasp of politics was far better than his employer credited, and he caught the implication at once. "The lord mayor is going to be highly displeased with this news and, no doubt, with the person who brings it." He handed it back with a wry smile. "I won't fight you for the privilege, but perhaps it would be best if Lord Procopio learned this news along with the rest. There is no shortage of ill tidings with which to pad it."

"Why pad it?" Matteo demanded. "Procopio has earned a hit or two."

The scribe sat back and regarded the angry jordain. "You'll get no argument from this quarter. Go with my blessing—though you'd be better off with Mystra's."

Matteo was already gone, too furious to consider either the warning or the possible consequences.

This writ of excommunication meant that contact with Kiva was proscribed. Any questions asked about her would be viewed with an extremely jaundiced eye. Matteo could think of no more effective way to squelch inquiries into the magehound's whereabouts.

He brushed past the guard at Procopio's door and burst into the room. The wizard waved away the guard.

"Your troubles must be great, jordain, to urge you into such imprudent behavior," he observed with measured calm.

"What have you done about Kiva?" demanded Matteo.

"Kiva?" Procopio echoed blandly.

Matteo took a steadying breath. "We are neither of us fools, but treating with me in such fashion casts shadows of doubt upon us both."

Procopio acknowledged Matteo's words with a curt nod, motioning Matteo to a chair. The jordain shook his head and remained standing—yet another lapse of protocol.

"I can see this matter is of some importance to you," began the wizard.

"Kiva," Matteo cut in pointedly, for he knew well the wizard's skill at wandering from the matter at hand.

Procopio smiled faintly. "To the point, then. What have I done about Kiva? In a word, nothing."

He held up a hand to cut off Matteo's indignant response.

"I will admit that my negligence is pure selfishness. Surely you realize that as Zephyr's patron, I was tainted by the elf's treachery."

Matteo nodded.

"There has been talk of need for a new lord mayor," Procopio went on. He gestured around the fine study and the wide window that overlooked the king's city. "As you see, I have much to lose. But when I become more concerned with my own success than with the good of Halruaa, perhaps it is time I stepped down."

This disarmed Matteo. Never had he see the arrogant wizard so humble. It occurred to Matteo that Procopio was merely taking another sidetrack. The manipulation was insulting, but he took the wizard's lead to see where it went. "That would be the city's loss, my lord."

Procopio's answering smile was faint and self-mocking. "You no longer serve me, Matteo. You no longer need trouble yourself to find soft words."

"When did I ever do so?"

The wizard blinked, then burst out laughing. "Well said! You were ever quick to tell me when I was wrong. Perhaps, then, I should trust in your judgment when you tell me I am not."

"I would not go quite that far, my lord," Matteo said coolly. "Forgive me for speaking so bluntly, but I have neither time nor patience for games. Did you persuade the church of Azuth to declare Kiva excommunicate?"

The color vanished from the wizard's face, leaving it slack and gray. This was answer enough for Matteo.

"Are you certain of this?" Procopio demanded.

Matteo handed him the writ. The wizard's face hardened as he read. "This is no doing of mine. I give my wizard-word bond on it," Procopio said grimly.

"That is not necessary." Matteo bowed. "If I have offended, my lord, I beg pardon."

"You have enlightened. Enlightenment, while often annoying, is something I value." The wizard studied him, suddenly speculative. "You are happy in the service of Queen Beatrix?"

"It is an honor I could hardly turn aside when it was offered," Matteo hedged.

"Nor could you turn away from it now, I suppose," Procopio said. "A pity. You are a fine counselor, yet it appears that your most important work is outside your patron's palace. I could support you in these efforts. Be warned, though, not everyone you encounter will be of like mind."

"So I have learned," Matteo said dryly. Claiming the wizard's offer of assistance, he briefly described the attack in the icehouse.

The wizard nodded thoughtfully. "Titles and deeds in this city can be complicated, but it should not be too difficult to trace the owner of that building. I will see to it."

After Matteo left, Procopio Septus sat calmly and listened to the young man's footsteps fade into silence. When he was certain that the troublesome jordain would not return, Procopio leaped to his feet and flung both arms into the air. Brilliant light burst up from the floor like a gout of dragonfire, engulfing the angry wizard. In a blink he traveled across the city and into the opulent gray world of Ymani Gold.

He caught the priest in the midst of one of his favorite indulgences. The young acolyte, startled by the lightning flash of Procopio's entrance, fell away with a squeak. She snatched up her robe and scuttled toward the back door.

Ymani, on the other hand, did not seem put out by the interruption. He adjusted his robes and settled down behind his writing table. "There's no need for such theatrics, Lord Procopio. I told you I would deal with Kiva, and so I have."

"There is an old proverb," Procopio said, black eyes spitting fire, "that those with talent become wizards. Those without talent spend their lives *praying* for it."

The priest's complacent smile vanished at this insult. "Now, see here—"

Bah!" Procopio threw up his hands in disgust. "How

could anyone, even a *cleric*, possibly mishandle anything so badly?"

"If you're speaking of Kiva, there is no need for concern. I ensured that there would be no further queries into her whereabouts," Ymani said stiffly.

"To the contrary. You managed to make a mess so big that no one can help but step in it," Procopio retorted. "It was bad enough when Kiva was accounted a traitor. Now she is an excommunicate. Zephyr, a jordain in my employ, would have been similarly condemned by his association with Kiva. No Halruaan wizard can afford that taint to come so close. You might as well have included me in the general damnation!"

For a moment the priest looked as if he regretted this oversight. His fleshy lower lip thrust forward in a petulant scowl. "You wanted to stop the jordain Matteo from making inquiries. This should do it."

Procopio placed his hands on the table and leaned forward. "You do not 'stop' a man like Matteo by putting roadblocks in his path. If anything, you've hardened his resolve."

"So what, in your inestimable wisdom, should we do?"

The wizard smiled unpleasantly. "Distract him, then discredit him. It has worked before, albeit briefly, and I daresay that this time it might take permanent hold."

CHAPTER FIFTEEN

By the time Matteo left the city palace, his many bee stings were beginning to swell and throb. In search of a soothing salve, he set off for an apothecary shop he had passed many times during his service to Lord Procopio.

The shop was a wattle-and-daub building set in a neat garden full of herbs. Birds skittered about picking at the seeds some softhearted soul had strewn for them. A pert yellow songbird followed Matteo right up to the shop and perched on the sill of the open window, as if to listen in on the conversation.

The apothecary was a minor wizard, with plump cheeks and a near-toothless grin that made him look rather like a wizened, oversized infant. Matteo exchanged courtesies and explained what he needed.

The man scratched a list on a bit of parchment and went to the back room to fetch the supplies. Busy with his work, he did not notice the yellow bird fly in the window and settle on the rush-strewn floor.

Swift as thought, the bird transformed into its true shape: a female wizard with bold, black eyes, wearing a simple chemise and skirt of yellow linen. The bird-turned-woman picked up a crockery urn and brought it down hard on the back of the apothecary's head. He pitched forward onto the bench and slid to the floor. The woman gathered up the supplies and hurried to the front room.

"My father was called away," she told Matteo. "He bade me tend your hurts. Why, it looks as if you were rolling about in a thicket of briars!"

She continued her bright chatter as she led the way to a small room off the shop. Matteo, after an initial moment of surprise, followed her. At her bidding he sat down upon the edge of a narrow cot.

The girl sat beside him, salving the stings on his neck and arms with a deft, practiced touch. "Remove your tunic, and I'll tend to the rest of you," she suggested with a coy smile.

Matteo rose. "Thank you, but I don't think there are any more stings."

"So you say, but I'd like to see for myself."

"Nothing more is necessary. You are a credit to your father, and a fine healer."

Her smile broadened and became feline. "I have other talents."

"No doubt," he murmured, now thoroughly puzzled.

With an exasperated little sigh, the woman pushed her chemise aside to bare her shoulders and struck an unmistakably seductive pose. "Join me," she invited bluntly.

Matteo's cheeks burned with embarrassment. He felt a fool for not reading her meaning sooner.

This seemed to amuse her. "Why so amazed, jordain? I offer a hour's pleasure, no regrets or consequence."

Matteo quickly collected himself. "All actions have consequences, lady. This, perhaps more than most." The girl's puzzlement seemed genuine, so he explained. "The jordaini are forbidden to have families."

She sent him an indulgent smile. "I am not asking you to wed with me. A bit of frolic—what could come of that?"

Matteo studied the girl. She was young and by all appearances pampered and gently raised. Halruaan girls were often sheltered. Despite her bold ways, was it possible that she truly did not know?

"A child could come of it," he said gently.

Dumbfounded, she gazed at him for a long moment. She shook her head and began to chuckle. "Now, *that* would be one of Mystra's better miracles! That 'purification' ritual of yours is one of the best ideas to come out of the Jordaini College. With magical bloodlines so important, no one dares risk a bastard." Her smile turned knowing, and she began to loosen the ties on her chemise. "Stallions might be swift, but geldings run best and longest. Why do you think the jordaini are so popular among the ladies of Halruaa?"

It was Matteo's turn to be stunned beyond speech. He had not undergone the purification ritual, a final trial followed by a time of solitary contemplation. He had never suspected anything like this, but he did not doubt the truth behind the girl's words. It was too logical, and it explained many things.

One part of his mind calmly acknowledged that the purification rite was a prudent precaution. He would not be surprised if unreliable or even dangerous gifts had crept back into the line through jordaini offspring. Precaution was the grandchild of disaster, and a measure so drastic would not be taken unless it was necessary.

Even as he acknowledged this, another part of him burned with white-hot anger. How could such a decision be taken from the young men and women who became jordaini? Did they not deserve to know, and chose?

He gave the girl a curt bow. "Thank you for your kind thoughts, but I must leave."

She shrugged and pulled her chemise back into place. "Your loss." With a grin, she preened a bit at her hair and then ran a hand down the length of her body. "If you doubt that, just ask any other jordain in the city about me."

Her boast troubled him greatly as he hurried toward Procopio Septus's villa. It was wrong to impose this rite upon unwitting young men, but that did not give them license to behave irresponsibly. As he had told the girl, actions had consequences. Even if a child could not result, a man and woman could not lie together and leave their shared bed unchanged. Families could be made in many ways, and no jordain could afford to put anything before his duty to Halruaa and her wizards.

Yet Matteo thought of his friend Themo. He always had time to show the jordaini lads a new game or to practice weaponry with them. He was also known to speak wistfully of a certain barmaid in Khaerbaal—not like the lewd soldiers who lusted after women in general. Matteo could see Themo serving as a battle wizard's jordain, but also taking up the sword to fight once his advice was given. At battle's end, he might return to a merry wife and a family of boisterous children. Such a life would be a better match for Themo than his own shadow, but it would never be his. He would not know this until it was too late.

Why had Matteo been spared this ritual? Delayed in Khaerbaal by his dealings with Kiva, he'd arrived at the college a day late and was hurried away and out of sight. He was left ignorant of this omission, which was nearly as distressing as the rite itself.

The walls of Procopio's villa loomed before Matteo suddenly. He glanced at the sun. He was early—at this time of day, Procopio usually held council with other city Elders. He chatted briefly with the gatekeeper, then hurried to the long, low building that housed the wizard's steeds. There he found Iago grooming a pegasus foal, painstakingly smoothing the pure white coat.

The jordain glanced up when Matteo approached. His face lit up. "The queen has consented?"

"I have not yet had opportunity to ask her," Matteo said slowly. "Queen Beatrix has not granted me an audience for several days now, but it will be no problem to convince her that she needs your services. For the moment, though, you do not look too unhappy in Lord Procopio's service."

Iago glanced up and down the row of stalls, checking for

listening ears. "You were right about Procopio's ambitions. You know, of course, that he intends to be king after Zalathorm."

"Procopio always spoke freely before his counselors," Matteo replied carefully. "The king has not named a successor. This inspires ambition. But ambition can be either the father of achievement, or the mother of treachery. Has Procopio done anything to cross that line?"

"Nothing specific," Iago said slowly, "but he seems unduly interested in reports of troubles from the west and the north. He is the mayor of the king's city. These things lie beyond his authority."

"They also lie beyond your authority and mine," Matteo reminded him. "Yet you cannot wait for Queen Beatrix to request your service so we can ride into those troubled northlands."

Iago acknowledged this with a shrug. "I bear many scars from the time I spent in Kiva's service. Not the least of these is discontent. All our lives we jordaini train for battle, only to watch and advise. It is difficult to stand idly by, yes?"

He waited for Matteo to speak his mind. For many moments the only sounds were the swish of the curry brush and the contented melody hummed by the pegasus foal.

"During our journey to Halarahh, you reminded me that I had missed the purification ritual. How did you know this?"

The brush stilled, prompting the foal to break off her song and stamp her tiny feet imperiously. Iago took up the rhythm again. "I spoke with the guard who admitted you the following day."

Matteo conjured a mental image of the man's face—tan as saddle leather, deeply seamed by lines and framed by thin wisps of graying hair. Though the man had been with the Jordaini College as long as Matteo could remember, he did not recall seeing him during his last visit. "That would be Jinkor. He is well?"

"He is dead," the jordain said bitterly. "The man who killed him stands before you."

Matteo slowly sat down on a bale of meadow grass. "How did this happen?"

"He was fond of haerlu wine. Did you know that?"

"No."

"During my years at the college, I would occasionally bring him a bottle from the storehouse." Iago shrugged. "He would never take more than a single goblet at a time. So I was surprised when he uncorked the bottle and drank as if he intended to see the bottom before he came up for air. I assumed he had troubles to drown and I sat with him in case he needed a friendly ear."

"That was good of you."

"Good intentions," Iago said with dismissive scorn. "Jinkor spoke, all right. When his mind held more wine than good sense, he forgot the pill that Kiva made him swallow."

Matteo jolted. "Kiva?"

"Oh, yes. It seems she has been watching the jordaini order for years. She needed sources of information and found one in Jinkor, who, as it turns out, has more than one expensive habit. Kiva ensured his silence."

Matteo had heard that wizards sometimes gave their servants potions that physically bound them to secrecy, but this method was far too extreme for the matter at hand. "Why would Kiva care about jordaini ritual?"

Iago glanced at Matteo. "You were getting in Kiva's way. She wanted to do away with you."

"She had ample opportunities! Why this?"

"Jinkor asked the same question. Kiva told him that killing you would set off an alarm. She could not destroy you outright, so she arranged for you to destroy yourself."

Matteo considered his previous conversation with Iago. "So this is why you asked me if there was more than friendship between Tzigone and me."

"Kiva knew how much you risked for that girl. She assumed that a human male could have only one interest in a female. Even some of her soldiers behaved in a manner that bolstered this opinion. You know how elf women are regarded."

Matteo nodded. Elves were rare in Halruaa, where being non-human was virtually synonymous with being *sub*-human. A few people of mixed race became wizards, and a few elfblooded wizards had risen to the Council of Elders. The most common profession for half-elf women, however, was that of courtesan. If the soldiers serving Kiva approached her in this manner, how much bolder were the wizards with whom she dealt? He did not like Kiva's assumptions about him, but he understood the path her thoughts must have taken. The jordaini were forbidden to marry, and he'd never heard of one siring a child, but he suspected that course, had he followed it, would indeed have destroyed him.

"Why couldn't Kiva kill me outright? What 'alarm' would this set off?"

Iago set to work with a hoof pick. "What do you know of the Cabal?"

Matteo let out a bark of startled laughter. "Strange context, Iago. Are you suggesting that a secret conspiracy has been formed to ensure my safety?"

The small jordain's face closed. Matteo instantly regretted his sarcasm. "Your pardon, Iago. If there is something I should know, please tell me."

The jordain shrugged. "It's not uncommon for a jordaini student to pursue a personal obsession. With Andris, it was the Kilmaruu Paradox. Mine was the legend of the Cabal. Some of the stories seemed to sing in tune with what Jinkor implied, that's all. It is nothing." His tone left no doubt that the matter was closed.

"Kiva's plan lacks logic," Matteo said, returning to the previous matter. "Had I followed the path she anticipated, it would have been obvious that I had not undergone the ritual. The college records would confirm this. I would not be held blameless, but since I did not know the nature of this rite until today, neither would my actions be deliberate treason."

"The college records would *not* confirm it," Iago countered. "Nor would the records support your innocence. Jinkor told me that a peasant man, one close enough to you in age and build to pass as your double, rode into the college on your horse. This man wrote your mark on the records, and submitted to the ritual. The attending priest never knew the difference. Nor, I suspect, do the jordaini masters. Obviously, I was the first person in whom Jinkor confided."

Matteo rose slowly to his feet, his hands clenched into fists. It was bad enough that a jordain should submit to such a thing! The peasant who'd taken his place had no part in Halruaa's laws of magic and power! "Do you know what became of this man?"

"No, but if you value his life, you should not seek him out," Iago pointed out. "On the other hand, if you value *yours,* perhaps you should. There would be an inquiry if he died while answering questions, and perhaps the spell could be traced back to the spellcaster."

"Are you suggesting that some might suspect me of arranging this travesty?"

"You were released from prison with ample time to ride back to the college, yet you came a day late. Another man rides in on your horse just in time. At whom, logically, will the fingers point?"

"Kiva, of course."

"Therein lies the problem," Iago said grimly. "Kiva is nowhere to be found. If a magehound examined you, he might find you innocent, and he might not."

"That's absurd!"

"Is it? Now that you know the nature of the purification ritual, would you return to the Jordaini College and willingly submit to it?"

"Would you?" Matteo countered.

Iago smiled thinly. "There you have it. A magehound's magic would discover your rejection of jordaini rule. Guilt or innocence is often a matter of tone. The details are like pieces in a strategy game—they can be used by either side, to very different result."

Matteo could not dispute this. "Does anyone else in the college know of this?"

"I don't intend to tell anyone, if that's your concern. Just . . . be careful."

Matteo placed a hand on the jordain's shoulder. "Thank you for telling me this. You are a good friend."

"Just get me out of this stable and onto a horse's back, and we'll call the debt paid," Iago said with a faint smile.

The stable lights flickered on, responding to the approach of twilight. "Lord Procopio will be in shortly," Matteo said. "We'll speak again as soon as I've news."

He hurried to the wizard's tower. Procopio received him at once with a grave face and without the formulaic courtesies demanded by Halruaan protocol. He ushered Matteo into his study and shut the door firmly behind him.

"You're not going to like this," he said bluntly. "I've no idea what to make of it."

Matteo swallowed hard. Never had he heard Procopio make so bald an admission—the wizard prided himself in reading all things clearly. "Go on."

The wizard's hawk-black eyes bore into Matteo's. "The ice building where you and the girl were attacked is owned by Ferris Grail, headmaster of the Jordaini College."

CHAPTER SIXTEEN

Matteo hurried to the queen's palace, his mind a whirl of confusion and anger. He had no reason to doubt Procopio. He fervently wished he did.

His belief in the jordaini order had long been eroding. Now it was crumbling under him. Zephyr had been turned by Kiva. Matteo had tried not to dwell overmuch on Andris's disappearance, but as time passed and Andris did not surface, Matteo had to face the very real possibility that his friend had turned traitor. The *possibility*—he would not accept it as truth unless he saw Andris at Kiva's side. Was it also possible that the headmaster of the Jordaini College might have employed thugs to silence a jordain's search for truth?

He strode toward the heavy doors that separated Beatrix's court from the rest of the palace, determined to receive the queen's permission to leave the city. If she did not grant it, he would do as Tzigone had advised and leave anyway.

Several men and two women, all of them carrying crafters' tools, waited by the outer door while the sentry loosed the magical wards. Judging from the clatter and bustle within Beatrix's rooms, the sentry had been kept busy with the various comings and goings. There were three doors, all of them carefully locked and warded.

Again Matteo recalled a jordaini proverb:

Precaution is the grandchild of disaster. Such careful measures would not be taken to isolate the queen's workshop from the rest of the palace unless the need was real and proven. However, King Zalathorm had dismissed the rumors about Matteo's predecessor, and Matteo could not believe the king had lied.

He fell in with the laborers and nodded to the harried sentry as he passed. The man, recognizing Matteo, raised his fingertips to his forehead in a salute, then rolled his eyes to express his opinion of the goings-on. Matteo nodded in heartfelt agreement.

Inside the queen's workshop, chaos reigned. A smith's forge had been set up in a massive hearth. Hammers clattered as they beat metal into thin, smooth sheets. Metalworkers bent over a long table, shaping heated metal with tiny tools and painstaking care. Stout, hairy-footed halflings from nearby Luiren perched on stools and fitted tiny gears, their clever small hands darting with practiced ease. Off to one side of the room, a trio of artificers argued over a mechanical behir, a twenty-foot crocodilian with twice the number of legs nature usually allotted. As the debate grew more heated, one of the men kicked at the metal beast in frustration, harder than he might have had he not been so distracted by the argument. The ensuing clang rang out loud and long. He howled and limped around in a small circle as his comrades hooted with mirth.

Matteo looked around in growing bewilderment. At least two hundred workers toiled in the vast chamber, and he glimpsed more in the rooms beyond. The results of their labor—clockwork creatures of every size and description—ringed the room like sentinels. They were propped against walls, heaped in piles, stacked on shelves, suspended from the ceiling beams. These mechanical marvels ranged from a life-sized elephant to metallic hawks to monstrous beasts, including fanciful constructs for which there were no living counterparts. Metal renditions of creatures Matteo had never seen and could never begin to imagine stood ready for some unfathomable command.

Matteo went in search of the queen. He found Beatrix in a windowless room lit by a low-hanging chandelier ablaze with candles. The queen stood alone, studying a hideous metal creature with thin, batlike wings and a pointed snout filled with steel fangs. It looked vaguely reptilian but for the bristling mane that ran the length of its spine. Each hair was a metal filament, fine as silken thread.

"It is wondrous, my queen," he said softly, not wishing to startle the woman.

She did not start or turn toward him. "It is a darkenbeast," she said in her flat, toneless voice. "The wizards of Thay fashion them from bits of dead flesh."

Matteo wasn't sure how to respond to this odd pronouncement. "You use steel. This is a better way, Your Majesty."

Beatrix tipped her head negligently. Her elaborate white and silver wig sparkled in the light of the candles. "Flesh or steel. It matters not. They will both be plentiful on the battlefield."

She spoke with a certainty that chilled him. "Battlefield?"

When the queen did not answer, he took her by the forearms and turned her to face him. He captured her vacant stare and gazed intensely into her kohl-rimmed eyes.

"I hear the future in your voice. Diviners reading auguries in the flight of birds speak with less certainty. What battlefield?"

A flicker of life crept into Beatrix's brown orbs. "I do not know," she whispered. "War is coming. War goes wherever it wills."

Matteo did not dismiss her claim. The queen showed little interest in the world around her, but perhaps she heard things, sensed things others did not. At the moment, she seemed almost lucid.

"I must leave the city and learn more of this coming conflict."

She considered him for a long moment, as if weighing

whether or not he might be able to do what he offered. Before she could speak, a loud shriek rose above the clamor in the main room. A fierce clatter followed, then a chorus of screams and a panicked rush for the door.

"By your leave," Matteo said hastily. Though protocol demanded it, he did not await the queen's dismissal. He whirled, drew his weapons, and ran into the main room.

The laborers were pushing toward the exits, trampling anyone who stumbled. One of the halflings lay battered and unmoving. Most of the clockwork creatures stood silent. A few paced unsteadily about, abandoned to their toddling first efforts by their panicked creators.

Matteo heard a metallic creak above him. He glanced up, then dived to one side.

A nightmare creature leaped to the floor from a pile of crates, landing with catlike grace despite the resounding clash of its impact. Its body resembled a suit of plate armor such as a northern warrior might wear. The creature held no weapons and needed none. Each of its four fingers ended in a curving steel talon. Long spikes covered its metal body, and its head suggested the unlikely offspring of an ogre and a shark. A piggish snout bristling with small spikes rose at the end of long, fang-filled jaws. The fangs were even more peculiar—sharp triangles that fit neatly and tightly, like the teeth of a giant piranha.

The clockwork knight snatched a dazed and moaning woman from the floor. It jerked her in close and crushed her to its spiked chest in a deadly embrace. The woman's shriek of agony ended abruptly, and the clockwork monster peeled her corpse away.

There had been no time for Matteo to intervene. He thrust aside a numbing wave of horror and guilt and forced himself to take stock of the battlefield. One thing was immediately apparent: His daggers would be of little use against this foe.

No better weapon lay near at hand. Remembering Tzigone's quick thinking in the icehouse, he glanced up.

A gigantic metal seabird hung from the ceiling, suspended by a pair of thick ropes connected to the tip of each massive wing. The trick Andris had played not long ago lent him inspiration.

Matteo mentally measured the distance from the floor to the avian construct, then noted the angle of the sun streaming through a window high on the walls. He seized the metal fist of an iron centaur and clenched its jointed fingers around one of his daggers. The highly polished metal of the weapon caught the sunlight and reflected it precisely toward one of the ropes.

Now, to stay alive long enough to let the sun do its work!

Matteo lifted his remaining dagger and lunged at the clockwork monster. He struck a ringing, futile blow and then leaped away. The construct dropped the dead woman and swiped at its new foe.

Matteo was gone, running lightly around behind the creature. He kicked its metal backside hard enough to leave a dent. The monster made a ponderous turn and began to stalk Matteo with a slow, heavy tread.

The jordain kept it moving, staying just beyond the reach of the construct's talons and the increasingly frenzied snapping of its piranhalike jaws. All the while, he watched the smoking, fraying rope high above. When the moment was right, he moved into position. Feigning a stumble, he dropped to one knee.

The clockwork beast lumbered in, its hands flexing in anticipation.

The rope snapped overhead, and the giant seabird creaked into motion. The monster's head snapped back, and its glowing red eyes flared suddenly at the sight of the massive wind slashing down toward it.

Matteo dropped flat and rolled aside. The metal bird swung like a pendulum, slamming into the clockwork creature and carrying it along. The enjoined machines crashed heavily into a stack of metal orcs. These came clattering down, rolling like logs off a badly stacked pile of lumber, burying the spiked metal warrior in a steel cairn. The seabird swung free of the mess. Its metal wingtip scraped the ground with a grating screech.

Matteo rose. Before he could take a relieved breath, the pile of metal orcs began to buckle and heave. The spiked warrior fought free and barreled toward Matteo like a gigantic hedgehog berserker.

The jordain looked about for a weapon or an escape. He noted a rope tied nearby to a metal ring on the floor, and his swift gaze followed it up to a metal pulley, then to the indescribable winged creature suspended from the other end of the rope. He seized the secured rope and began to climb it frantically. The clockwork monster leaped at him.

Matteo swung out as far as he could, trying to move beyond the reach of those deadly teeth. The metal jaws clashed shut—not on Matteo's legs but on the rope.

It snapped beneath him, and the winged creature tied to the other end began to plummet to the floor. As it fell, Matteo sailed up toward the ceiling. The bird-thing fell squarely on the clockwork warrior and buried it beneath a pile of crumbling metal.

Matteo clung to the rope until he was certain that the battle was over. He swung back and forth until he could reach the longer part of the rope. Wrapping his arms and legs around the main line, he tied his end securely to it, then slid down to the metal pile and climbed off to survey the damage.

Sheets of the monster's plate armor had broken loose and skidded across the floor. Gears rolled like spilled coins. Pinned beneath an enormous wing, the remains of the clockwork monster twitched like a hound beset by nightmares. Little sizzles and faint grinding noises came from its metallic innards, growing reassuringly fainter. The light in its glowing crimson eyes faded and, finally, flickered out.

Matteo scanned the room. No other clockwork devices stood ready to pick up the banner. A few people huddled at the far wall. He bade them tend the wounded and went to check on the queen. After an hour's search, he found her—not in the candlelit antechamber but in a secure room much deeper into the palace.

Beatrix was seated on a tapestry-covered settee, studying a drawing of yet another clockwork creature and busily employing a stylus.

"The problem is here," she murmured, making several tiny marks on the drawing. "The crystals inside distort the spell of activation. Magnetic stone would serve better, perhaps absorb the energy of the life-spell. Yes, we shall try that. Yes."

Matteo spun on his heel and stalked out, his own task still untended. He could not stay in the queen's presence another moment without letting his anger flow in a treasonous torrent. His oath to the queen still stood, but his sympathy for the woman was sorely shaken. How could anyone, however troubled, treat the results of her deeds with such blithe disregard?

He found the queen's steward standing at the doorway to the workroom, staring with bulging eyes at the mess.

"See to this," Matteo snapped. "I am leaving the city with tomorrow's dawn. The queen did not withhold her permission. I take that as assent."

The steward simply nodded, too overwhelmed by this disaster to pay much heed to the angry jordain. Matteo brushed past him and stormed into the king's council hall, shaking off the restraining hands of the heralds at the door. He strode directly to the throne and dropped to one knee before the king. He did not, however, lower his challenging and furious gaze.

Zalathorm raised a hand to warn off the guards, then directed a silent command at his seneschal. The man promptly began to herd courtiers from the room. The king and the counselor locked stares until the doors firmly shut behind the last man.

"Well?" Zalathorm inquired. The single word echoed ominously through the empty hall.

Matteo took a steadying breath. "Not long ago, you asked me if my ultimate loyalty is to Halruaa or to my patron. I had hoped that this dilemma would never arise. I deeply regret to inform you that one of Queen Beatrix's clockwork creatures has killed a craftswoman."

"That's impossible," the king said flatly.

"I was there. I saw it happen."

Zalathorm's hands gripped the arms of his throne until the knuckles turned white. "You would contradict your king?"

"My king was not there. I was."

The diviner nodded somberly. "Very well, jordain. Rise and tell me what you saw."

Matteo described the spiked warrior, and the other dangerous beasts that Beatrix had constructed. Zalathorm listened without comment until the jordain was finished. Abruptly he rose from his throne and strode toward the queen's palace.

They walked in silence down the long corridor that led to the queen's workshop. Matteo entered, and then stopped short.

The room was almost empty.

A few metal constructs remained, but only the more whimsical and least frightening creations. There was no sign of the spiked warrior or the enormous winged beast whose fall had crushed it. The dead woman and the wounded halfling were gone. A few artisans looked up from their tasks and dipped into surprised bows when they noted the king was among them, but Matteo did not recognize any of them.

"They were here," Matteo whispered. "I swear it, on my life and honor."

Zalathorm took his arm and led him from the room. "I do not doubt you," he said quietly, "but I wanted you to see with your own eyes that your most dire fears were ungrounded. What I am about to tell you must remain in strictest confidence."

Matteo nodded his assent.

"There is a protective shield around the heart of Halruaa. A very old, very powerful ward."

The jordain's brow furrowed. "A spell?"

"Not precisely," the king said carefully. "It is a powerful and mysterious force. I cannot explain it any better than that. When there is a threat against the heart of Halruaa, this power ensures that either the threat or those threatened are removed to a place of safety."

Matteo recalled the men in the icehouse melting away into magical haze. "What is the heart of Halruaa?"

Zalathorm was silent for a moment. "Removing a malfunctioning machine from the palace is the sort of manifestation I have come to expect. You need have no fear for your patron's safety."

"What about the safety of those around her?"

The king sighed. "Very well, I will admit that the queen's clockwork toys have grown too numerous and dangerous. I will see that this building frenzy is curtailed and have priests heal the wounded and restore the slain woman to her life and her loved ones. Will that content you?"

Matteo considered pressing for an answer to the "heart of Halruaa" question and decided to leave this for another time. "Almost, Your Majesty," he said. "Now that I have your assurances that the queen is safe, I request permission to leave Halarahh for an indeterminate period of time. I will need horses and supplies for my journey. I have tried for some time to bring this request to the queen and ask that she retain the jordain Iago, currently serving Procopio Septus. He will accompany me on my journey."

"Is that all?" the king inquired in a dry tone.

"Not quite. There is a jordain yet at the college—Themo, a fifth-form student. The queen has need of his service, as well. We will ride north and meet him at the travelers' rest on the road out of Orphamphal, but he must leave today, though he has not yet completed his training."

Zalathorm studied Matteo's face, then nodded slowly. "I cannot read your mind, jordain, but there is much urgency in your eyes and voice. Coming to me was not an easy thing, but you held service to Halruaa above all else. For this, all will be done as you have asked."

Matteo bowed. "Thank you, Your Majesty."

"Don't thank me," the king said with a grim smile. "Don't the jordaini have a proverb claiming that virtue never goes unpunished?"

"I have never heard that proverb, but most seem to be of jordaini origin."

"Blame it on the jordaini, in other words?"

"Perhaps, sire," said Matteo dryly, "that is our true function."

To his surprise, the king chuckled and clapped him on the back. "Mystra speed you, lad. I look forward to speaking with you again, when your business in the north is completed."

Matteo bowed again, and watched as Zalathorm strode down the hall that separated the king's palace from the queen's. He turned and sprinted to the royal stables and rode quickly to Basel Indoulur's tower. A pretty, dark-eyed apprentice greeted him at the door and went to fetch Tzigone for him.

His friend came to the door wearing her sky-blue robe, liberally dusted with soot. Her face was likewise blackened, and her hair stood up about her head in spikes, lending her the look of a swarthy hedgehog.

"Don't ask," she advised.

"I'm leaving the city by dawn tomorrow. Before I go, there are things I must tell you."

Tzigone took his arm and drew him into the garden. They took refuge in a rose-draped arbor, a retreat that sheltered a tiny pond and a bench piled with bright silk cushions. As soon as they were seated, Matteo reached into his bag and produced the medallion Dhamari Exchelsor had entrusted to him.

Before he could explain its origin, Tzigone's eyes grew enormous. "That was my mother's," she whispered.

Her grubby fingers closed around the token, and she turned it over and over in her hands. "I can't feel any magic in it," she said absently. "I seem to remember there was. Every time we had to flee, my mother would touch it, and her face would become very still, as if she were listening. Sometimes she let me touch it, but all I could feel was *her*. Why is that, do you think?"

"Perhaps children become very attuned to their parents," Matteo suggested. "Magical items sometimes hold something of their possessor's aura. No doubt that is what you perceived."

Tzigone looked down. "I'm holding the talisman now. I can't feel anything."

The silence between them was long and heavy. Finally Tzigone lifted agonized eyes to Matteo's face. He nodded, answering the question she could not ask.

Tzigone squeezed her eyes shut, and her face went very still as she sought some reservoir of strength deep within. Several moments passed before she won command of her emotions.

"How did you come by this?" she said in a small voice.

"Dhamari Exchelsor gave it to me. I meant to give it to you when last we met, but did not have the chance."

"How did *he* get it?"

"Kiva brought it to Dhamari like a trophy and gloated over Keturah's capture. They were apprentices together, you see, and Keturah was their master. They were conspirators in the miscast spell that prompted Keturah to banish Kiva from her tower. Clearly Kiva held a grudge against your mother. Possibly she resented Dhamari because he did not receive the same treatment."

"What was he like?" she asked grudgingly.

"A quiet man, modest in his ways and habits. He spoke of your mother with great pleasure and deep sadness."

The girl sniffed, unimpressed.

"You should meet with him."

Her head came up sharply. "So you said before. Dhamari offers to give a wizard's bastard a home, a name, a wizard's lineage, a tower, and a fortune. Ever wonder why?"

"You are Keturah's daughter. Perhaps that is reason enough."

"That's what worries me. Why would my mother flee from this Dhamari if he is a good man?"

Matteo told her about Keturah's fascination with dark creatures. He told her about the greenmage's fate and the starsnakes that gathered to attack, against their nature. Disbelieving tears spilled unheeded down Tzigone's dirty face as she listened, leaving muddy tracks in the soot. Matteo expected her to reject the notion that her mother could have become so twisted through the practice of dangerous magic, but after a moment she nodded.

"It is . . . possible."

"So you will see Dhamari?"

"Why should this wizard—or any other, for that matter—trouble himself about me?"

Matteo hesitated, wishing he could tell her of Basel Indoulur's vow to claim paternity if need be. But that would not only violate the wizard's confidence, it would also undo the very thing Basel wished to achieve. Tzigone would never accept such a costly gift.

He brushed a sooty tear from her cheek. "Given the options before you, yes, I think you should see Dhamari and give serious consideration to his offer."

"I'll think about it."

They spoke briefly about the clockwork creatures, and Matteo's destination. When they rose to leave, she lifted one hand to trace a brief, graceful farewell dance—a wizard's convention as common as rain in summer. Then she spun and slipped away, like the thief she had been.

This small, familiar rite set Matteo back on his heels. For the first time, he understood that the training Tzigone was undertaking was not a whim but a true path. She was wizard born, wizard blood.

Because of who *he* was—a jordaini bounded about by proverbs and prohibitions—he could not follow where she went.

CHAPTER SEVENTEEN

Tzigone hurried to Basel's tower, oblivious to the young man who watched her departure with bleak eyes. She had much to do and little time. The Council of Elders met that night, and Procopio Septus would certainly be present. This would be the best time to slip back into Procopio's villa. The diviner was indeed powerful, and though her resistance to magic was almost total, she did not relish the thought of creeping about under his very nose.

She considered contacting Sinestra, but quickly abandoned the idea. She wanted nothing more to do with the woman. *"It's possible,"* Tzigone muttered, repeating Sinestra's response when Tzigone had asked if she might be Sinestra's daughter. *Possible!* What the Nine bloody Hells did *that* mean?

But Sinestra was not her mother. Her mother was dead. That was almost easier to comprehend than the beautiful woman's easy dismissal.

Tzigone put Sinestra firmly out of mind. She slipped into shadow-colored garments and made her way over the walls that bordered a public garden. From there it was simply a matter of climbing a bilboa tree and creeping through the treetops toward the home of Procopio Septus. She found a perch with a commanding view and settled down to watch and wait.

When night fell and the wizard-lord left the villa, she slipped in through the kitchen orchard and went to his private study. She found the volume titled *King's Decrees*, issued a year or so before her birth.

In its pages she read the truth of Dhamari Exchelsor's claim. Keturah stood accused of murder through magical means of Whendura, a greenmage of Halarahh. She had fled the city that very day rather than submit to magical inquiry that, had she been innocent, would have cleared her name. By the laws of Halruaa, flight from justice was an admission of guilt.

Tzigone closed the book with shaking hands. By the laws of Halruaa, her mother was a murderer. This knowledge only increased Tzigone's desire to learn the whole truth. By the laws of Halruaa, she herself was not exactly as white as cream. There was a larger story here, and unless she was very mistaken, Kiva was the thread that tied Tzigone's past to events still in play.

She found the most recent book of *King's Decrees*, as well as the hefty tome that contained Lord Procopio's latest notes from the city council. She sat down cross-legged under a table and began to read.

Trouble, it seemed, was everywhere. The increase in piracy was predictable—a seasonal hazard, since the sea vultures were eager to collect as much treasure as possible before the summer monsoons started in earnest. Less understandable was the number of trade caravans that had been disappearing in the Nath. Then there was the totally unexpected attack on the Lady's Mirror by wild elves. As a precaution against further incursions, huge numbers of militia had been moved to the western border. More guards had been moved to the north to guard the electrum mines and the nearby mint. The mountains that formed the eastern wall seemed to be secure and quiet, but there was a great deal of activity in Akhlaur's Swamp.

"Well, that figures," she muttered. As word of the laraken and its defeat spread, the swamp lost much of its terror. It was only a matter of time before packs of wizardly idiots blundered in, chasing rumors of Akhlaur's lost treasure.

Tzigone sniffed derisively. Next she searched the room for a hidden place where Procopio might keep important papers. In a carved wood chair she found a hidden compartment and paged through the neat pile of parchment stacked within. Among the pages was a listing of Zephyr's past patrons.

She fingered the scrap of parchment tucked into a pocket—the notes Sinestra had taken the day they'd searched the elf jordain's chamber. It seemed that this information was important, after all. She just wasn't sure why.

Her eye fell on the first name on the list of Zephyr's patrons:

Akhlaur Reiptael, Necromancer.

Her breath whistled out in a long, slow hiss. So Zephyr had served the infamous Akhlaur, the wizard whose legacy she tripped over every time she turned around!

She'd be willing to bet that the old elf hadn't liked to brag about this particular fact, and she'd double the bet that this record didn't exist anywhere but in Procopio's study. It was the sort of information a powerful diviner might ferret out, but it wasn't something he'd wish to hear sung of in taverns and at the spring fairs.

Zephyr, Kiva, Akhlaur, the laraken, Keturah, and now her. And Matteo, and perhaps even his friend Andris. They were all connected somehow, but Tzigone could not perceive what pattern those intertwined threads might make.

She scrawled a quick copy of Zephyr's history and hurried to the palace, hoping that Matteo could do better. On the way, she "borrowed" some suitable clothing and gear and slipped into the queen's palace.

Despite the late hour, Matteo was not in his room. Tzigone, unnoticed, finally found him at the kitchen storerooms, collecting supplies for his trip. Nor was he alone. The kitchen buildings teamed with activity.

"Gods above," she muttered. "Don't palace servants ever sleep?"

A soft, quickly stifled giggle drew her attention to a nearby goat shed. A pail of fresh milk stood off to one side, not far from the ladder leading up to the loft. Tzigone climbed the ladder and found precisely what she'd anticipated: a pile of fresh hay, two people entirely oblivious to her presence, and some hastily discarded clothing. Tzigone quietly stripped off her chambermaid's gown and tugged the girl's short blue dress over her head.

Thus accoutered, she hurried back down to the abandoned bucket of goat's milk. She picked it up and staggered into Matteo's path, taking care to slop some of the contents of her bucket onto his boots.

He took in Tzigone's pert dairymaid costume without comment and managed not to roll his eyes while she apologized extravagantly in the rolling accents of the northland herders. And he followed her as she babbled and backed away. He deftly accepted the list she handed him during the distraction and tucked it into his belt.

By Mystra, she thought admiringly. There might be hope for him yet!

They worked their way to a quiet spot between the goat shed and the brewery. Matteo took the note from his belt, scanned it, and lifted grim eyes to her face. "Where did you get this?"

"There's a new tavern by the south gate," she began, still in her goat-girl voice. "The cook makes puff pastries that are hollow inside, then slits the crust and slips in a fortune or a small favor. I got an emerald ring, and traded it to the friend I was with for this list."

Matteo glared at her. "If you don't want to tell me, just say so."

"I don't want to tell you," she replied promptly. "What do you make of it?"

He handed back the parchment. "Zephyr was in service to Halruaa's wizards for well over two hundred years. He was one of the first jordaini. Perhaps Akhlaur had a hand in the order's creation."

Tzigone looked doubtful. "Jordaini and Akhlaur. Those two flavors don't belong in the same pot."

"So I would like to think, but Akhlaur was a powerful necromancer. Such wizards do not deal exclusively with death but alter the living to suit their purposes. When you get right down to it, how better to describe the jordaini than men altered to suit the purposes of wizards?"

She took this in. "How does Kiva fit in?"

"Elves live very long lives. Kiva may look no older than you and me, but it is possible that she knew Zephyr, and possibly Akhlaur, two centuries past."

"What does any of this have to do with my mother? With us?"

Matteo sighed. "You and I are much akin, Tzigone. We are both resistant to magic, we were forcibly separated from our families. Perhaps we were both 'made' to suit some wizard's purpose, as they might fashion a golem from iron or clay."

"Well, that's cheery!"

"What would you rather have—a grim truth or a cheerful lie?"

"Hmm. Do you need the answer right now?"

"Yes, and so do you," he said, turning her half-hearted jest back on her. "Talk with Dhamari Exchelsor."

She was silent for a long moment. "You know what, Matteo? I really, really hate it when you're right."

"In that case," he said somberly but with a suspicious glint in his dark eyes, "you should reconcile yourself to constant irritation."

His teasing sent an irrational mixture of exasperation and delight sweeping through Tzigone. "Constant irritation, is it? Well, I suppose I can live with that if you can." Before he could respond, Tzigone upended her bucket of goat's milk over his head. While her friend sputtered and swore, she darted out of the kitchen grinning like a gargoyle.

Yes, she concluded happily, there was definitely hope for Matteo.

⊙

Before leaving the city, Matteo visited Queen Beatrix once again. He did not relish the prospect of facing the royal madwoman, but neither could he leave without trying to make sense of her dire pronouncements.

The queen listened with an impassive face as he spoke of his plans to travel in search of knowledge important to the palace. Whether she cared or even understood, he could not say. It was getting harder and harder to enter the strange landscape of her mind. At last, he abandoned subtlety and reminded her that she'd predicted a coming war.

"Did I?" she said vaguely.

"Yes." He hesitated, then added, "I will be gone for quite some time. The Nath is a wild and dangerous place, and the paths are too rough for swift travel."

The Nath. Matteo felt cruel for mentioning the site of her great tragedy, but he needed to take some measure of her sanity. Perhaps she had spoken of some battle in the past, most likely the raid that had destroyed her family.

Matteo studied her face for the emotion this name might evoke. There was not even a flicker of recognition. The queen's detachment was chilling and nearly absolute.

He silently admitted failure but made one more request. "Before I leave, I must contact the headmaster of the Jordaini College. May I use the device that you employed to seek me out when I was last there?" The queen granted permission with an absent wave of her hand. "But I do not work magic," Matteo added, turning back suddenly. "I cannot use the globe without the aid of a wizard."

"A wizard," Beatrix repeated. It seemed to Matteo that there was an ironic edge in her usually flat voice. "Touch the globe. That is all it requires."

Matteo went to the small scrying chamber and shut the

door. Globes hung from elaborately knotted slings, rested on pedestals, or bobbed in the air with no apparent support. Hesitantly, he reached out to touch the smooth, floating moonstone globe that matched the one in Ferris Grail's study. The device glowed to life. After a few moments, the cloudy surface of the stone cleared to reveal the face of the jordaini headmaster.

The headmaster's jaw fell slack as he discerned the identity of his caller. Matteo wondered if that surprise was due to this infraction of jordaini rules or because Ferris Grail had assumed that he'd fallen to the icehouse thugs.

Matteo put this question squarely on the table. "You didn't expect to see me, Lord Ferris, and not just because of the order's restraints."

The wizard's dark brows pulled down into a stern **V**. "If you've a question, speak it. I haven't leisure for games and puzzles."

"No doubt you are a very busy man, with the demands of landlord added to your duties at the college," Matteo retorted. "Imagine my surprise when I learned that your name is inscribed on the deed to an icehouse in the king's city."

"What of it?" Ferris demanded. "Though I am headmaster of the college, I am a wizard, not a jordain. No laws forbid me to own property."

"That is sophistry."

"That is practicality," the headmaster countered. "Most of Halruaa's wizard-lords amass fortunes. A headmaster's wages are sufficient for my current needs, but what of the future? I make such purchases as I feel will increase in value, so that I may live comfortably once I leave the college. Not that I need explain my business to you."

"Actually, there is one small thing that does require explanation," the jordain shot back. "When thugs attacked me and a companion, why did they take us to your icehouse to dispatch us?"

The surprise on the wizard's face seemed too genuine

for pretense. Perhaps, Matteo admitted, Ferris Grail didn't know about the attack. "Would you like to hear of it?" he asked in a milder voice.

"I think I'd better," the headmaster said grimly.

Matteo told the story in a few words. "You will no doubt receive a notice of my complaint from the city officials."

"If several men died in the icehouse, I will expect more than that! You know that if there is a legal inquiry into your actions, you will have to appear before the Disputation Table. For the third time this year, I might add."

"There will be no inquiry, as there were no bodies." Matteo described how their attackers, slain or injured, had simply faded away.

The headmaster's face turned nearly as pale as the moonstone globe. "The girl you were with—was she the same who fought with you in Akhlaur's Swamp?"

"Yes," Matteo said curtly, anticipating the now-familiar lecture.

Ferris sent him a long, speculative look. "You spend a considerable amount of time with this wench. More than is seemly for a jordain."

"Our paths seem destined to cross," he said shortly. "I should think you would be far more concerned about the magehound Kiva. What do you know of her?"

"The same as you, and no more," the headmaster said. "Yes, the Azuthan temple contacted me with word of her escape. I agreed that for now the jordaini order would hold this information in confidence. These are troubled times. It is important, especially in light of the raid upon the Lady's Mirror, that the Azuthans do not appear unduly vulnerable."

"I would argue that the times are troubled because of Kiva, and that the vulnerability is real."

Ferris scowled. "You give the elf woman too much credit."

"That is worthy of debate, but perhaps another time. I will answer your question about Tzigone. Let the Azuthans concern themselves with their good name, but the jordaini are pledged to serve the land. I accept the aid and friendship of those who are likewise pledged."

"Your duty is to serve your patron," Ferris reminded him, "not to take up personal quests."

"I have royal permission to do as I will and to use what resources I need."

"Yes, I know," the headmaster complained. "Themo left the college yesterday, riding faster than a flea off a firenewt. It is not seemly to send a jordain into service who has not completed his training."

"Perhaps Themo should never complete his training. At heart he is a warrior, not a jordain. I wanted him released now, before receiving the rites and tests that end the final form." Matteo paused meaningfully, then added, "As some others have been."

Ferris Grail's eyes narrowed. "Why would you think one jordain's experience would differ from any other's? The jordaini are sworn to secrecy concerning the nature of these rituals."

"*After* the fact! By Mystra, what man would wish to boast of it!" he said heatedly. "This much I *do* know: This practice is wrong."

The wizard's face darkened. "Do you think to challenge the entire jordaini order? These rules might seem harsh, but they exist for good reason."

"When I know all these reasons, I will judge for myself."

"You are not meant to know everything, young jordain. You were trained as a counselor, not a judge!" snapped Ferris.

"In seeking truth, I am doing no more than I was trained to do. What I was *bred* to do," he added bitterly.

A long moment of silence followed. Matteo marked the guilt and fear on the wizard's face. It occurred to him that Jinkor the gatekeeper might not have been Kiva's sole source of information. Over the years someone had betrayed jordaini students best suited to her purpose. Who could better fill this treacherous office than the headmaster? Or perhaps Ferris Grail, a diviner, knew who the culprit was but kept silent to protect the college from scandal. That would explain his willingness to allow Kiva to remain conveniently lost.

"You may have Themo," the wizard said at last. "He is released from his jordaini vows. In return, I require your word that you will look no closer at these hidden things."

"I cannot give it," Matteo said bluntly.

Ferris Grail's face clouded. For a moment Matteo thought he would renege on his promise to grant Themo his freedom, but the wizard's stern posture wilted, and he passed a hand wearily over his face.

"Go, then, and Mystra's blessing upon you. I ask that when your quest is over, you return to the college. There are things you should know before you proceed much further down this path."

"Such as the fact that the necromancer Akhlaur had a hand in our order's creation?"

It was a shot into the clouds, but it found its mark. The color drained from Ferris Grail's face. "Come to the college," he repeated. "I will do what I can to help you. And may Lady Mystra have mercy upon us both."

CHAPTER EIGHTEEN

Tzigone stared at the green marble tower, trying to imagine her mother living there, doing the things that Dhamari Exchelsor and Halruaan law said she had done. She gave herself a brisk shake, tucked away her troubled thoughts, and marched to the gate. The servant there took her name and her request for audience. When he returned, a slight, balding man came with him.

The unimpressive newcomer did not look like the lord of a tower, but he held out his hands in the traditional greeting of one wizard hosting another.

So this was Dhamari Exchelsor, the monster she had known all her life as her "mother's husband." Before she could say a word, the wizard stopped dead and stared. He quickly regained his composure and inclined his head in the bow that acknowledged a wizard of lesser experience, but greater rank.

Tzigone was not sure what impressed her more: that Dhamari Exchelsor obviously recognized her as Keturah's daughter or that he did not immediately press the matter. An effusive greeting, any sort of claim on her, would have sent her sprinting down the street. Tzigone had learned caution from her mother. Maybe this man understood Keturah well enough to give this meeting real value.

She removed Keturah's talisman from her bag and held it up.

Dhamari studied the medallion in silence for a long moment. When he turned his gaze back to her, his eyes were gentle. "Come to the garden, child. I'm sure you have many questions."

She followed him through fragrant paths, listening as he spoke of the uses of this or that plant. He seemed exceptionally learned in herbal lore and considerate enough to grant her time to adjust herself to his presence. Tzigone was reluctantly impressed.

"I'm ready to talk," she announced abruptly.

"Talk we shall." He gestured toward a bench in a small alcove and sat down beside her. "Ask what you will."

"Keturah left the city the same day a greenmage was eaten by starsnakes."

He nodded sadly. "That is so."

"Do you think she did it? Called the starsnakes?"

"In all honesty, I do not know."

Tzigone's eyes narrowed. "Did you join the search for her?"

Dhamari hesitated. "Understand that in answering freely I put my life in your hands. If you harbor any ill will toward me, you could use what I am about to tell you. Yes, I sought Keturah," he continued, not even waiting a beat to gauge her reaction and thus his own safety. "I employed rangers to comb the wilderness, diviners to cast spells and to read the auguries in the flight of birds. A hundred trusted merchants carried messages to every part of the land announcing a reward for her return. But I acted only for love of her. Had I found her, I would have seen her safely away from Halruaa and into the best care the Exchelsor fortunes could purchase."

"Care?" Tzigone echoed. "She was ill?"

"She was preparing herself to bear a jordaini child," he admitted readily. "We were matched for that purpose, but Keturah was never one to leave things to chance. She took potions to ensure that the child she might bear would be among the most powerful jordaini known."

Tzigone's heart thudded painfully. She, a failed jordain? Well, why the hell not? She'd been a pickpocket, a street entertainer, a behir tender, and half a hundred other odd jobs over the course of her short life. There wasn't much new territory to explore.

It made a horrifying sort of sense. Her resistance to magic, her quick mind and nimble tongue. Unlike the true jordaini, though, she also had a wizard's gift. The result yielded a potential wizard who could use magic and yet was nearly immune to counterspells. No wonder a wizard's bastard was considered dangerous!

"The process was disrupting her magic and stealing her memory," Dhamari continued. "I begged her to stop, but she was determined. A very stubborn woman, my Keturah."

Yes, that also made sense. Tzigone's last memories of her mother included her diminishing and unreliable magic. The potions given a jordain's dam could do that. Even so, Keturah might have lived, had Kiva not intervened.

"You knew Kiva," Tzigone said. "Did you hire her to find my mother?"

Dhamari was silent for a long moment. "Yes, to my eternal shame and regret. She had skills I thought useful. No human knows forest lore like an elf."

"But my mother was captured in a city!"

"That is true, but the search was long." Dhamari did not offer further comment. There was no need, for Tzigone's early life had been defined by that long search. "Kiva betrayed my trust and killed your mother. She told me that she had killed Keturah's child, as well. She taunted me about it and gave me the medallion as proof."

"Did you seek vengeance?"

"No." The admission seemed to shame him. "By then Kiva had become an inquisatrix of Azuth—a magehound. I might have prevailed against someone of her high office, but more likely I would have met failure and disgrace."

Dhamari sighed wearily. "In all candor, I will never be numbered among the great Halruaan wizards. Keturah would have been, had she not died at Kiva's hand. I measured my chances against a better wizard's failure.

"The laws of Halruaa are a powerful safeguard, but sometimes they are also a dark fortress. Occasionally a tyrant such as Kiva hides behind them as she rises to power. The laws supported and aided her, at least for a time."

"Well, that time's done and over with," Tzigone said.

"Thanks in no small part to you. Keturah would be proud." Dhamari gave her a wistful smile.

Tzigone rose abruptly. "I should be going."

The wizard's face furrowed in concern. "Are you happy in Lord Basel's tower? He is a fine man, do not mistake me, but I wonder if a conjurer's path is most suited to your talents. Your mother was a master of the evocation school. You may wish to explore many branches of the Art before you settle upon one."

"Good idea," she said noncommittally, knowing full well what was next to come. More than one wizard had tried to lure her away from Basel's tower.

He shrugged modestly. "I am a generalist wizard of moderate talents, but I learned many spells from your mother. If you wish, I would be happy to teach them to you. Not as a master—I haven't Lord Basel's talent for instruction—but as a gift, in tribute to your mother."

"I'll speak to Basel."

Her agreement surprised both of them. Dhamari blinked, then turned aside to surreptitiously wipe away a tear.

All her life Tzigone had viewed Keturah's loss as her private pain. Never once had she considered that this burden might be shared by her mother's husband.

"Is tomorrow good?" she asked abruptly.

Dhamari's eyes lit up. "If it suits your master."

Something in his tone set off warning bells in her mind. "Why wouldn't it? Does Basel have any cause to object?"

"Not really," he said slowly. "Basel and Keturah were childhood friends. I thought he fancied himself to be something more than that. It is hard to fathom, looking at him now."

"Oh, I don't think so." Actually, Tzigone could see how a young Basel might have been a fine companion and conspirator. "Why did nothing come of it?"

"Wizards do not chose whom they will wed. Lord Basel comes from a long line of conjurers, and it was assumed that he would continue the family tradition with a woman from his school of magic. I heard a rumor that he appealed his assigned match to the council and was denied. If he bears me a grudge, I would not blame him."

Dhamari paused for a wistful smile. "Wizards are rarely as fortunate in marriage as I was. I loved your mother, Tzigone, and it took many long years before I could reconcile to the fact that she was gone. But her daughter lives. That brings me more happiness than I ever expected to know again."

He asked nothing of her and offered nothing but her mother's spells. That pleased her.

"Most of Keturah's spells involved the summoning of creatures," Dhamari went on. "We would do better beyond the city walls, where we don't run the risk of summoning behir guardians and wizards' familiars. It has been quite some time since I left this tower. A short journey would serve the purpose, but I'm not sure how to go about arranging the particulars."

This was something Tzigone knew well. "I'll be back in the morning. Get yourself a good pair of boots and send to Filorgi's Hired Swords for some travel guards. Leave the rest to me."

"You can prepare for a journey by tomorrow morning?" he marveled.

"Sure." Tzigone grinned fleetingly. "Usually I have a lot less notice than that."

The wizard caught the implication, and an ironic smile

touched his lips. "It would seem that I am partly responsible for your resourcefulness. Mystra grant that from now on our association will be an unmixed blessing."

"That'll never happen," she said as she rose to leave. When Dhamari raised an inquiring brow, she added, "I've been called a lot of things over the years. I might as well be honest with you: 'Mixed blessing' is about as good as it's likely to get."

Dhamari's smile spoke of great contentment. "Then you are your mother's daughter indeed."

A golden wedge of sun peeked coyly over the forest canopy, proclaimed that the morning was nearly half spent. In a mountain travel hut perched above the tree line, Matteo and Iago stood at the open door and gazed uncertainly at the road that led from Orphamphal, and into the wilderness known as the Nath.

"Themo should be here by now," Matteo grumbled. "Perhaps we should go out looking for him."

"We should await him here," the smaller jordain said firmly. "If he has met with delay, leaving this agreed-upon place will ensure that we miss each other."

Matteo conceded with a nod. "I'll scout the area. You stay here and await him."

He whistled to his horse—a black stallion he'd named Cyric Three—and mounted before Iago could protest. Slapping his heels against the horse's sides, he headed up a path that wound steeply uphill through scrub pine and rock.

Earlier that day he'd wrapped the horse's hooves, not only to pad them against the shards of dark rock that splintered off the cliff faces, but also to muffle the sound of their passage. This precaution paid well—he rode silently enough to catch the sound of a small-scale battle taking place a league or so ahead.

Matteo rode as close as he dared. He swung down from

his horse, drew his weapons, and quietly walked the rest of the way to a small, level clearing.

Two strange combatants were locked in fierce battle. A gray-skinned female, looking less like a woman than a deadly shadow, bared her teeth in a snarl as she slashed with sword and flail at a male warrior even stranger than she. Sunlight glinted off the man's crystalline daggers. Rivulets of sweat—or perhaps translucent blood—ran down the ghostly face.

"Andris," whispered Matteo.

The moment of surprise passed quickly. Andris was among the best fighters he knew, but the shadow amazons were notorious for ferocious treachery. Despite her pointed ears and the high, sharp bones of her face, there was nothing of an elf's delicacy about the Crinti. Matteo had seen barbarian warriors who carried fewer weapons and less impressive musculature.

Roaring out a challenge, Matteo surged to his feet and charged to his friend's aid. The gray shadow wheeled to face him. Twin scabbards swung out from her hips as she spun. With three quick strides she was upon him, the promise of death in her ice-blue eyes. Her sword flashed down and around in a reverse circle, giving momentum to a stroke that whistled down in a swift, deadly arc toward his neck. Meanwhile her flail—a length of chain ending in a spiked metal ball—swung out wide and whipped in from the other direction in a rising arc. Working together, the Crinti's weapons formed a deadly parenthesis that cut off evasion or retreat.

Retreat was the last thing on Matteo's mind. He leaped in close and slammed his dagger into the curved cross guards of the female's sword. The heavy blow jolted through his arm and sang down his spine, but he did not allow the pain to slow his counterattack. With all his strength he heaved upward, first stopping the sword's momentum and then forcing the enjoined blades up. At the same time he spun his body swiftly under the locked weapons, forcing his opponent to turn with him so that they stood back to back. With his longer reach he heaved the weapons high and broke the woman's grip on her sword as his spin brought him inside the path of the flail.

The Crinti's sword clattered to the rocky ground. Matteo gritted his teeth as the flail's chain wrapped heavily against his thighs, but the real danger—the spiked metal head—slammed into his opponent's leg with a wet, sickening thud.

Matteo quickly brought his dagger hand down and jabbed lightly at the gray hand grasping the flail handle. The Crinti snarled and released her grip. Matteo shoved aside the chain and whirled away, then lashed out behind him with one foot. The kick caught the Crinti just above the back of her knees. She fell heavily to her hands and knees. Recovering quickly, she pushed herself off the ground and leaped to her feet, ignoring the blood that poured from the holes the flail's spikes had punched through her gray leather leggings.

The jordain snatched up her fallen sword, keeping his familiar dagger as a companion weapon. He'd already proven the value of a longer reach, and none of his own weapons matched the second sword the shadow amazon carried on her left hip.

The Crinti drew her sword—twin of the weapon Matteo held—and spun it in a deft circle. Though her gesture held the flavor of ritual, Matteo knew better than to mirror her move. The sword was heavy and strangely balanced: She knew the weapon, he did not.

Matteo stepped back and took several short cuts to get the feel of the weapon. Its weight leaned closer to the point than he was accustomed to—a choice that added power to a thrust or cut and that spoke of great strength and deadly intent. He did not relish the idea of fighting the Crinti warrior with such an unfamiliar weapon.

The elfblood exploded into motion. To Matteo's astonishment, she tossed her sword into the air. It flipped end over end and fell, point down. She caught the sword as it fell, her hands fisted at the midpoint of the blade. Blood seeped from between her white-knuckled fingers as she clenched the weapon. She caught Matteo's eye, sneered, and spat.

Then she raised the sword point to her chest and with both hands drove it into her own heart.

With her last strength she threw herself backward, as if determined not to fall prostrate at his feet. She landed hard, and her arms flew out wide. Her bloody hands spasmed into clenched fists, slowly opened, and fell slack.

For a long, shocked moment Matteo stared at the dead warrior.

"It is their custom," Andris said softly. "A Crinti who feels herself disgraced will chose death over shame. They are a brutal people, but proud."

Matteo slowly turned to his friend. "How did you come by this knowledge?"

Andris swept one hand in a wide circle that encompassed the high, wild country. "This is the Nath. If you wish to survive, you must learn of its dangers."

"That does not mean you must join them!" Matteo protested. "Gods above, Andris, what are you doing?"

The jordain's ghostly jaw firmed. "What I think is right. Go your way, and leave me to it."

"You know that I cannot. Kiva must be found and stopped. The Crinti bandits are my only link to her."

Even as he spoke, he knew his words to be false. The shuttered expression on Andris's ghostly face forced Matteo to admit the full and painful truth.

"You fight with Kiva again," he marveled, "and with the accursed Crinti! Andris, what could possibly justify such an alliance?"

"Halruaa," Andris said shortly. "My vows as a jordain. The wrongs done to my elf forebears."

"Kiva is a traitor to Halruaa. How is it possible to serve the land by following one who betrayed it?"

"Do not judge me, Matteo," Andris warned. "For both our sakes, do not hinder me."

For a moment Matteo stood, torn by his own conflicting loyalties and by the plea in Andris's eyes. Slowly he threw away the Crinti's sword. A smile that was both relieved and sad touched Andris's face, only to die when Matteo drew his jordaini daggers.

"Return with me, Andris," he said quietly.

In response, the ghostly jordain drew a dagger of his own and dropped into a defensive crouch.

Matteo tried one last time. "I don't want to fight you, my friend!"

"Small wonder. You usually lose."

Andris's hand flashed forward. His dagger stopped well short of Matteo's lighting-quick parry, but the jordaini blade was not Andris's true weapon. With his free hand he hurled a fistful of sparkling powder into Matteo's face.

The powder struck him in an explosion of unimaginable pain. It burned him, blinded him. Matteo dropped his daggers and reeled back, both hands clasped to the white-hot agony in his eyes.

With a strange sense of detachment, Matteo registered the sharp blow just below his ribs. The pain was a whisper compared to his screaming eyes, but his body responded by folding over at the waist. Two sharp, precisely placed blows to the back of his neck brought the ground racing up to seize him.

As if from a great distance, Matteo heard Andris's voice speaking with what sounded like regret. "The powder's effect wears off swiftly. Until then, try not to rub your eyes too much. But don't follow me, Matteo. I might not be able to let you go next time."

From a rocky perch high above the clearing, Kiva watched the battle between Andris and Matteo. Her lips curved in a smile as the troublesome jordain fell. As she suspected, Andris was hers. Like the Crinti, he put such value in his elf heritage that all other considerations paled. For Andris to turn against a fellow jordain, his best friend, made that abundantly clear.

This meant more to Kiva than she wished to admit. She had chosen Andris before she knew of his heritage and because he was *not* Matteo. Matteo's heritage she had known for a long time. The fact that Andris and Matteo were friends disturbed her, as did Matteo's incomprehensible friendship with Tzigone. Kiva's nighttime reverie had been haunted more than once by the fear that the three humans were bound by a destiny none of them fully understood.

The elf woman made her way down to the Crinti camp and sought out Shanair. She described Matteo to the chieftain, instructing the elfblood to take a group of warriors and lure him and any companions into the haunted hills. The men were to be kept alive, she stressed, until Shanair received word otherwise.

Once the Crinti chieftain gave grudging assent to these constraints, Kiva took her scrying globe and went off in search of a quiet place and a conversation with a certain wizard. She had not contacted him in years, and finding him among the silver threads of magic's Weave would be no easy task.

Mastering the spell of attunement took Kiva most of the morning. Even then, the wizard took his time in answering. The elf woman's lips curled in disdain when at last the man's face appeared before her. The years had not dealt kindly with the human. He was thin and balding, and the furtive expression on his face made him look disturbingly like a hairless ferret.

"Damn it, Kiva! After all this time, you had to pick this precise moment?" he hissed.

"Trouble, my love?" she said mockingly. "I would have thought you incapable of spawning anything quite so interesting."

"Where have you been? What's going on?"

"No doubt you heard of my capture in Akhlaur's Swamp."

"Yes, and your excommunication from the Fellowship of Azuth. I'm sure that broke your heart."

Kiva laughed scornfully. "Yes, but my faith in the humans' so-called Lord of Magic will sustain me through these trying times. Enough prattle. The battle nears, and we need to unleash all our weapons or fail utterly! You will have to cast the summoning we prepared."

The wizard shook his head. "You know I cannot. After the incident with the imp, Keturah bound me by wizard-word never to summon a creature I did not understand or could not control. Death comes to any wizard who breaks a wizard-word oath!"

The elf lifted one jade-colored brow. "I can live with that."

"Obviously, I cannot. Fortunately, I will not have to."

Kiva's golden eyes lit up. "You have the girl?"

"In the palm of my hand," Dhamari Exchelsor said smugly. In a few words he described the events of the past few days and his new relationship with Tzigone. "We are heading north even now. Keturah's bastard has not yet learned the spell we require, but she will master it by the time we arrive in the Nath."

"You have done well," Kiva said. "Surprisingly so! This Tzigone is a canny little wench, with reason to distrust you. How did you win her over?"

"As a novelty, I tried telling the truth as often as possible. The accusations against Keturah are a matter of public record, so that was easy for her to confirm, but it took some clever magic to convince her and the jordain Matteo of my sterling character and good intentions."

"Now I know you're lying," Kiva said scathingly. "First, you're not terribly clever. Second, you have no character of any kind, and third, your intentions are never good. More to the point, neither Matteo nor Tzigone can be convinced of anything by magical means."

"Ah, but the spell was not on them, but *me*! That talisman of Keturah's? The one that protected the possessor against me and my agents? I had it reproduced. I gave the copy to Matteo to pass along to Tzigone, and I carry Keturah's original for my own protection."

The scorn melted from the elf woman's face. "It protects you from yourself!"

"Just so," Dhamari said smugly. "Since the jordain and the girl are currently the greatest threats to my success, the talisman protects me by ensuring that I do nothing to reveal my true thoughts and purposes." The wizard's smile held great satisfaction. "If you wish to retract your insults, I will listen graciously."

"Just get the girl to the Nath with all haste. See she learns the spell of summoning on the way!"

Kiva passed her hand over the globe, erasing the image of the gloating human ferret. She tucked the scrying device into a bag and began to climb down the steep ravine that led to a small, well-hidden valley.

The ground here was barren except for a covering of silvery lichen, and roughly level except for the single, conical mound that rose some twenty meters toward the slate-blue sky. Jagged rocks lay strewn about in a pattern that suggested a long-ago explosion. There were several places like this in the Nath. This was the least daunting and therefore the best choice for Kiva's current purpose.

She walked over to the mound and gingerly pressed one hand against the mossy side. She felt a faint vibration, a not-quite-audible hum of magic and power and ancient, primal evil. Kiva, despite all that she had endured and all that she had become, shivered with dread.

As tentatively as an urchin whistling in a graveyard, she began to hum an eerie little melody, a song that sometimes echoed through the wild places and passes of Halruaa. It was an act that mingled bravado and desperation, and as she sang the hairs on the back of her neck rose in protest. The evil beneath her hand chilled her like the caress of a malevolent ghost.

Still Kiva sang, preparing for the task that might yet fall

to her. There was always the chance that Keturah's daughter could not accomplish the task she had been born to do.

Kiva sang until her throat was dry and tight, but her efforts brought no change to the humming magic of the mound. She fell silent, unsure whether to be disappointed or relieved. As Keturah had once told her, it was rank foolishness to summon a creature one could neither understand nor control.

No one understood the Unseelie folk, the fey creatures that haunted the mountain passes and wild places of Halruaa. Hidden gates led into the netherworld of the Unseelie Court—a place of evil, a land not quite in this world. Few who entered it returned. Even the Crinti feared the dark fairies and would flee at the sound of their song.

Precisely why Kiva needed this spell.

Accepting the Crinti into her plan was rather like inviting rats into a granary to eat unwanted surplus. The nasty gray creatures—whether two-legged or four—were unlikely to leave once their purpose was fulfilled. The appearance of dark fairies would send Shanair and her muscle-bound sisters scuttling back to Dambrath.

As far as Kiva knew, no one had ever managed to summon the Unseelie folk, much less control them. Decades of study into dark elven magic had given her some insight into the dark fairies, for legend had it that ancestors of the southland's drow had learned their ways during captivity by the dark fairies, to their great sorrow and utter damnation.

Be that as it might. Years of work had yielded a promising spell. Research, however, was one thing, talent quite another. Neither Dhamari nor Kiva had the gift of summoning. Keturah had had it, to a degree that few Halruaans had ever achieved. Unfortunately, the stubborn little wizard-wench would do nothing to promote Kiva's cause. But Kiva, being elven, was able to plot a long path around this obstacle.

She turned to the east, where wild, snow-topped mountains rose like a spiked wall between Halruaa and the wastelands beyond. She could not see the troops gathering on the plains beyond, but then, neither could Halruaa's wizards.

This was an unexpected addition to her assault, but she neatly folded it in. For nearly two centuries Kiva had scripted and adapted and enhanced her plan. A few lingering uncertainties remained, but she had already proven she could push beyond setbacks.

It was time for Halruaa to die. All that remained was the one wizard who could complete the destruction.

It was time for Akhlaur to return.

CHAPTER NINETEEN

Tzigone warmed her hands over the campfire, rubbing them briskly to drive away the morning chill. She had not expected the Dhamari Exchelsor's "little journey" to turn into a wilderness expedition.

She'd been a vagabond all her life, and there were few places in Halruaa unmarked by her footsteps. Unlike most Halruaans, she had even ventured into some of the lands beyond the mountain walls. However, she avoided the Nath, as did every sensible person she knew.

Oddly enough, Dhamari set a straight path for the northern foothills. Despite his protestations of travel inexperience, he had augmented Tzigone's preparations with well-chosen supplies and an unusually large armed band.

Money, she told herself. If you had enough of it, you didn't need expertise. Dhamari apparently had pots of money. He was a first-generation wizard, the pride of two families of wealthy merchants. His inheritance from his mother was a fortune in electrum mining, and his father's people owned lands ideal for growing multicolored grapes for Halruaa's fanciful wines.

Dhamari had told her stories of his family as they rode north. She would need to know such things if she decided to take the Exchelsor name, he told her gently. Tzigone listened, but she preferred the time they spent studying Keturah's spells.

At least, that's how she felt at first.

Tzigone's unease increased with each passing hour. As they rode, Dhamari taught her spell after spell. They summoned wild cats, boars, and even a small band of goblins. The problem was, once the creatures came, they had to be dealt with. Last night a difficult spell had gone awry, and her song had brought an owlbear roaring into camp. Two of their escorts had died fighting the massive bird-thing. Tzigone blamed herself for the men's deaths. To her surprise, their comrades did not.

When she was not learning spells, Tzigone moved freely among the warriors. Some of them had dealt with Dhamari before, and those who knew him best seemed to like him least. No one told tales or gave any direct complaint. Even so, after several days on the road, Tzigone was beginning to wonder if both she and Matteo had been mistaken about the wizard.

She poked at her morning campfire, coaxing the blaze higher. A small iron pot sat among the coals. The scent of herbs and mushrooms and root vegetables rose with the steam. The hired swords gathered around a larger fire a few paces away, using their knives and their teeth to tear strips of meat from the bones of roasted conies, mountain rabbits that were nearly as big as hounds.

The rich, savory smell made Tzigone's stomach lurch. For some reason, she had not been able to eat meat of any kind during this trip. Calling creatures required a strange sort of affinity with them. Tzigone suspected that this would pass, but for the time being she stayed with herbs and greens.

"Can you keep strong on such food?"

Tzigone glanced up into Dhamari's gently concerned face. She stirred the pot and lifted a steaming ladle. "Want some? It's not bad."

"Perhaps later. I have another spell for you." He diffidently handed her a rolled scroll.

Tzigone flattened it out on her lap and studied it. It was a complicated spell, without doubt the most difficult she had ever seen. The incantation required elven intonations that would task her powers of mimicry. There was also an odd tablature that looked a bit like written music, indicating that the spell was to be sung. The melody, however, ranged down into the lowest depths of Tzigone's voice and soared into regions she had never attempted to explore. At first study, the markings that choreographed the hand gestures appeared to be less orderly than the footprints left by the last staggering sprint of a beheaded chicken. At least half the runes were totally unfamiliar to her. She suspected that they were taken from a magical tradition very different from that of Halruaa. As she studied, though, the spell's basic meaning emerged from the tangled mess.

Tzigone stared at the spell scroll in disbelief. Dhamari had just given her a spell to summon and banish the Unseelie folk!

She lifted an astonished gaze to his expectant face. "If you wanted me dead, you could have poisoned me before we left the city and saved us all some wear on our boot leather."

He blinked and then frowned. "I don't understand."

"The hell you don't! I'm just an apprentice. This spell would challenge a graybeard wizard."

"You have exceptional talent—"

"And astonishing beauty," she interrupted, mimicking his tone. "But for argument's sake, let's say I can cast this. What then? Wasn't the owlbear enough excitement for you? For them?" she concluded furiously, waving with one hand toward the surviving members of their guard.

Dhamari lifted a placating hand. "I do not intend for you to summon the dark fairies," he protested mildly. "That is not the point at all. It would not only be foolish but redundant. They are here already. Have you not heard them?"

She hesitated, then nodded. The strange, compelling song, distant and faint, had haunted the edges of night for three days.

"These hills are strange and fey," the wizard went on. "The veils between the worlds are thin in Halruaa—few places in all the world provide more portals into distant places. The Unseelie folk are around us. Knowing that I have brought you into a dangerous area, it would ease my mind tremendously if you could cast the spell of banishment."

"Why is that necessary? Can't you do it?"

He sent her one of his small, wistful smiles. "I do not have Keturah's talent and defer to the wizard whose voice held the laraken."

Tzigone didn't like flattery, but neither could she deny the practicality of Dhamari's words. So she let him tutor her in the preliminary spell, one that would enable her to read the runes. He gave her a ring of translation so she would pronounce the strange elven words properly.

As she murmured the words over and over, the morning breeze seemed to grow colder. Her arms prickled with gooseflesh, and the warm cloak Dhamari had draped around her shoulders didn't help. Tzigone let him build up the campfire, but she didn't expect it to improve matters. She was not chilled by the relatively thin mountain air but by the sound of her own voice.

The spell frightened her, even at this early stage of its casting. Since it was meant as a banishing, this was, as Matteo would say, logical. Tzigone didn't suppose that the Unseelie folk could be cowed by some minor magic. The magic felt twisted, though, and somehow wrong.

Throughout that day and the next she studied the spell, though her vision swam and her head throbbed with the effort of wrapping her mind and her will around the convoluted magic.

By the second night, the flicker of the campfire made the runes dance on the page. Tzigone kept at it, spurred on by the faint, mocking echoes that tossed from hill to hill—the unholy music of the Unseelie folk.

❧

Far to the south, Basel Indoulur paced the garden of his Halarahh home. He'd expected Tzigone back days ago, and he cursed himself for granting her permission to leave the city with Dhamari Exchelsor. Tzigone considered the wizard harmless, and Basel trusted her judgment. Her candor, however, was less than total.

Nor was Basel blameless on this score. He could have spoken to Tzigone of her mother, and he did not. He had not told her of Matteo's visit, or suggested that the young jordain had urged Tzigone to contact Dhamari as a means to save him, Basel, from the follies of fatherly instinct.

The irony—layers and layers of it—was almost overwhelming.

With a sigh, Basel left the garden and made his way up the tower's winding stairs to the apprentices' floor. He had given Mason and Farrah Noor a day's holiday from their studies. There was no one to ask why he felt compelled to stop by Tzigone's room.

He missed the troublesome little wench. He enjoyed her quick mind and impish spirit, and he loved her as he would the daughter he should have had—*might* have had, if the council had not intervened. Instead, he had been turned out like a bull into a pasture containing an idealistic and single-minded heifer. In the eyes of the law, in any way that truly mattered, Basel's wife was dead—destroyed by her own dedication to the good of Halruaa.

The wizard's gaze fell upon the door to Tzigone's room, and the past disappeared from his mind like a windblown candle. The door was slightly ajar.

Basel's eyes narrowed. Tzigone always left the door open. She was accustomed to open spaces and could not sleep unless every door and window was flung wide. The wizard edged closer. The sounds of a furtive search came from within the room, then a gasp of astonishment.

Despite his size, Basel could be quick and silent. He reached into his spell bag for a small iron nail and eased himself into the room. His hand flashed in a quick circle as he spoke a single, arcane word. The nail vanished, and the intruder froze in the act of whirling toward him.

Basel paced into the room for a closer look at the would-be thief. The woman was of medium height and extraordinary beauty. Her hair was a glossy blue-black, her features delicate, her curves lavish. She wore a pale blue robe—an attempt at disguise, no doubt. A startled expression was carved onto her immobile face, and a medallion swung from her still hand.

The wizard's heart quickened as he studied the trinket. That was Keturah's talisman! There was no magic left to it other than the memories it evoked. No doubt Tzigone had left it there for safekeeping rather than risk losing it in her travels.

Basel tugged the chain from the woman's frozen fingers. Her trapped eyes followed his movements and glazed with despair.

He recognized the woman as Sinestra, a minor wizard married to one of the Belajoon brothers. The family was a well-established wizard line, and they held considerable wealth and respect in the king's city. What would prompt a pampered young wife to thievery?

More curious than angry, Basel released the holding spell with a flick of one hand.

The woman exploded into action, throwing herself at the talisman in Basel's hand. "Give it to me! It's mine!"

He deftly sidestepped, and the intruder tripped and fell facedown on Tzigone's cot. Her muffled oath was both pungent and familiar. Basel had heard it from Tzigone, and from her mother before her.

His heart skipped a beat. "Who are you?" he breathed.

She sat up and tossed a pinch of powder into the air over her head. The sparkling bits caught and hung in the air, then melted together to form a thin, shimmering sheet. This floated down, molded itself to her, and disappeared— leaving a very different woman in her place.

Her features were not as delicate as Basel remembered

them, and time had dimmed her eyes and blurred the lines of her face.

Basel stared in disbelief at the faded image of a woman he'd thought long dead. Although he'd mourned her for over a dozen years, his heart did not respond to her with joy.

"Keturah?" he said, not quite believing it.

"That's what we wanted them to think, wasn't it?"

Memory flooded back. "Of course! You're Keturah's friend, the lady who helped her escape a near capture!"

"Friend, yes," the woman said. Her lips twitched into a brief and bitter smile. "Lady, no."

An old story came back to him. Shortly after her marriage to Dhamari, Keturah had traveled to Basel's home city of Halar in the company of an Exchelsor merchant band. One of the hired swords had laid rough hands on her—and lost them up to the elbows to her defensive magic. Her indignation grew when the caravan master explained that the mercenary had mistaken her for the camp doxie. A few words with the woman convinced Keturah that the "doxie" had not chosen this life. She had insisted that the woman be released in her care, and she had given her employment in her tower, and quietly trained the woman's magical gifts.

"A courtesan can still be a lady, regardless of the circumstances of her birth or her profession," Basel pointed out.

"Courtesan!" she scoffed. "That's still putting it too high! My mother could claim that title. She was a wizard's mistress. Guess what that makes me?"

"Illegitimate or not, if you know your father's name and lineage, you are guaranteed certain rights and a wizard's training."

"Oh, I know the name, but he was married into a powerful family and didn't wish to embarrass them. So I was sent away. "I was handed over to a merchant's company as a sort of movable entertainment."

The enormity of this revelation stunned Basel into silence.

Any words that came to mind only trivialized such betrayal.

After a moment Sinestra shrugged. "An old tale, badly told. Whatever you're going to do to me, get on with it."

"All I require from you is an explanation. Why did you come here looking for Keturah's talisman?"

"I didn't. I came looking for your apprentice."

Basel studied the woman. She was already reverting to her enchanted appearance: her hair was darkening to black, and her skin was no longer sallow but golden and smooth. He had worked on such cloaking spells before. "If I'm not mistaken, the spell you wear is Keturah's."

"I don't have that much talent," she agreed. "It's a permanent spell. Nothing will touch it but the powder Keturah gave me, and you can bet I don't use that very often! The medallion was mine, though, in a manner of speaking. I bought it for Keturah. She was a good friend and a generous mistress. I kept every coin she gave me toward the day when I could repay her."

Something in her tone set off warnings in Basel's mind. "Why did you think that would be necessary?"

Sinestra's face—now fully reverted to its young and beautiful form—twisted with frustration. "I can't tell you."

"I see," mused Basel. "Perhaps you can tell me what you wanted with Keturah's talisman?"

"There are many kinds of slavery," she said shortly. "Some cages have golden bars, but at the end of the day there's little difference between gold and iron. How well do you know my husband?"

"Not very."

"Count yourself lucky. With this talisman, maybe I could win free of his prying eyes. It would be wonderful to have an hour or two to call entirely my own."

"Or perhaps to reinvent yourself and start a new life elsewhere, as you have done before."

"Perhaps," she said noncommittally.

"You assumed that Tzigone would have this talisman?"

"Why would I do that?" she asked, her arched brows

pulled down in genuine puzzlement. "After Keturah's capture, her effects were taken to Dhamari Exchelsor. I planned to steal it from him, and I hired Tzigone—" She broke off abruptly, and bit her lip in obvious consternation.

"Take ease. I already know that Tzigone's methods lie slightly south of legal. Go on. You hired a thief to get the talisman for you."

"What do you take me for? I've known several different prisons, and I won't be responsible for sending anyone else there," she said grimly. "I hired Tzigone to train me, so I could go after it myself."

Basel nodded, satisfied. This woman had risked her life for Keturah. She was exactly the sort of friend and ally Tzigone needed. "But obviously, Dhamari Exchelsor did not have the talisman. He returned it to Keturah's daughter."

Puzzlement furrowed Sinestra's face, then gave way to stunned enlightenment. "Mother of Mystra," she whispered. "That's why I was drawn to Tzigone. From the moment we met, she felt like an old friend. She hasn't got half her mother's beauty, but they've got the same laugh, the same contrary streak." Her eyes widened in sudden panic. "You said that Dhamari gave her the talisman? He knows about her?"

Basel was beginning to have a very bad feeling about this. "She is with him even now."

The woman leaped from the cot and seized Basel's tunic with both hands. "Get her away from him!"

He marked the rising note of hysteria in her voice. Tamping down his own growing panic, he kept his voice low and soothing. "Tell me."

"I truly can't." She released his tunic. A brief, silent struggle twisted her beautiful face, then her jaw firmed with resolve. "I can't tell you, but you can see for yourself. Go to Keturah's tower and into Dhamari's workroom. You'll understand why—"

Sinestra's voice broke off abruptly. A shudder ran through her, and her eyes rolled up until the whites showed. She fell to the floor in a paroxysm of violent spasms, her spine arching so painfully that Basel heard the snapping of bone. Her agony was mercifully brief. Even as Basel dropped to his knees beside her, she went limp and still.

The wizard cursed softly. Many of his colleagues ensorcelled their servants against revealing secrets. Apparently someone had been more thorough than most. Even the little that Sinestra had said was enough to condemn her to death.

Basel reached out a gentle hand to close the brave woman's eyes. At his touch, she melted into mist, and then faded away. Yet another precaution, he noted grimly. Without a body to test, it was exceedingly difficult to trace the origin of the killing spell.

He rose abruptly. This mystery would have to wait in favor of more urgent matters.

There were no magical gates between his tower and Keturah's, for he wanted no path that another wizard might follow. Basel had not ridden for years, but he quickly claimed his fastest horse and made short work of the road to Keturah's tower. The gatekeeper informed him that Dhamari was not at residence. Basel had little trouble convincing the servant into letting him in regardless; in fact, he noted a hopeful gleam in the man's eyes.

Basel hurried up the stairs to Dhamari's potion room. It was larger than most wizards' studies, but at first glance nothing seemed amiss. The room was also unusually tidy for a wizard's lair, with rows of vials and vessels and pots lined up with fastidious care. A collection of butterflies was mounted against one wall, neatly pinned to a large sheet of cork. Basel sniffed with mild scorn. Not the sort of trophy most men might boast of!

Yet something about the display drew his eyes—a sense, perhaps, that something about this hobby was profoundly amiss. Basel walked along the vast cork wall, studying the collection carefully. At first the butterflies' colors were dazzling, with all the gem-like hues of a Halruaan garden. Then came butterflies he had never seen, enormous creatures armed with stingers or mosquitolike snouts or wicked taloned feet, clad in deep greens and vivid scarlet and orange that brought to mind a jungle's flowers. Next came butterflies the color of barren rock and desert sand. Snow moths, delicate as moonlight. Bats! Most were the tiny chameleon bats that wheeled about the sky at twilight. They were mounted against bright swatches of silk that tested and preserved their ability to change color.

His gaze fell upon the next creatures pinned against the cork, carefully preserved and neatly labeled. His breath hissed out on an outraged oath. There hung a fairy dragon, its bright wings carefully spread, tiny fangs bared in a final, defiant snarl. Next to it was a mummified sprite, a tiny winged lady displayed with the same precise detachment Dhamari had used in collecting insects. Basel's throat clenched as he remembered the exercises Keturah taught her apprentices. Butterflies and bats were among the easiest creatures to summon. Even Dhamari had been able to call them.

"Dhamari called them," he murmured. Obviously, Keturah's former apprentice had not abandoned his desire to master his mistress's special art. Starting with the small denizens of Keturah's garden, he had gone farther and farther afield. Where, Basel wondered, would such a quest stop?

He strode over to the shelves and began to search for an answer. One sweep of his hand knocked aside the neat rows of pots and vials. Hidden behind was a wooden box, nearly half full of tiny vials. As Basel selected a vial from the box, his eye fell upon an identical vial lying empty on the shelf. A decanter of wine stood beside it, dusty from long disuse and tightly stoppered. An identifying rune marked each vial—the same rune that had been engraved onto the potions Basel's wife had taken during their brief and tragic union—potions that would ensure the birth of a jordani child.

Basel snatched up the wine bottle and rushed through the words of a transportation spell. He would retrieve his horse later—this could not wait.

Back in his own tower in the city of Halar, a good day's ride from Dhamari's workroom, Basel hurried over to his potion scale. The traditional two-armed balance sat before a screen of white silk. Each arm ended in rounded vial of clear crystal, which would glow with intense light when a certain spell was cast upon it. Basel poured the jordaini potion into one of these globes, the wine into the other. With a quick, impatient gesture he set the globes aglow.

A pair of complex patterns began to dance on the white curtain, an arcane design made of colors and runes and intricate black lines. Basel spoke a second command word and watched as the distinctive gold colors of the wine faded away. As he suspected, the remaining marks were similar to those cast by the jordaini potion.

Similar, but different. Dhamari had dosed this wine with the jordaini potion—and with something more.

Basel placed a third crystal pot in the crux of the scale and began to chant softly. The pattern for the wine potion began to shift as the unknown substance drained away. When the wine-derived pattern was identical to that of the jordaini potion, he cast the light spell upon the third vial. A green, jagged mark flashed upon the white silk, identifying the added ingredient. Basel caught his breath.

"Son of a rabid jackal," he said softly as the whole of Dhamari's plan came clear.

Basel did not make such potions, nor did any reputable mage in Halruaa, but he knew of such things. This was the signature mark of a dangerous herb, one used by shamans in darker times and more primitive cultures to gain control of monsters that could not be called by normal magic.

This, then, was the legacy Dhamari wished to pass along! He wanted Keturah's magic, altered and transferred to a child he could claim and control, a child who could do for him what he could not do himself.

Rage rose in Basel with white heat.

The wizard reversed his spell of transportation and returned to Dhamari's workroom. He methodically searched the library, where he found a surprising trove of material on Crinti history, drow lore, and legends of the Unseelie folk.

"Rather exciting reading for a fellow who collects butterflies," Basel muttered. "Let's see what else he's been up to."

Basel found the wizard's spell inventory and carefully checked it against the missing scrolls, books, and potions. The list itself was appalling. The arsenal Dhamari carried on his "little journey" with Tzigone terrified Basel to the core.

He raced from the tower, stopping briefly at the gate to hand the servant a heavy bag of coin. "Go to the harbor. Find a boat bound for distant lands, and buy passage."

"I am bound to service here," the man began.

"Yes, I have a good idea how Dhamari binds his servants. Speak to no one of what you have seen in this place, and you should be safe enough for the next tenday or so."

The gatekeeper nodded cautiously. "After that, my lord?"

"No law or spell can bind you to a dead man," Basel said bluntly.

The man's eyes widened, then turned luminous with gratitude. "Mystra speed you, my lord!"

Basel echoed that prayer as he returned to his Halarahh tower to order his skyship readied. He knew he could not track Tzigone—her uncanny resistance to magic had kept him from following her on the days she decided to slip away from her duties—but he would damn well find Dhamari.

And his old friend Procopio Septus was just the man to tell him how.

Procopio Septus stared at his new game table, committing the landscape to memory, contemplating the possibilities presented by gully and cliff and cave.

He had played wargames for years, reenacting famous battles and learning from the triumphs and mistakes of past wizard-lords, but this table depicted a sensitive part of the eastern border, *as it now was*. The army threading its way through mountain passes had been lured by his bargain with the Mulhorandi wizard. Procopio was the only wizard in Halruaa aware of the coming conflict.

A tiny figure, a warrior mounted on a winged horse, separated itself from the battle. It flew high above the table and buzzed around Procopio's head. Irritated, he swatted at the malfunctioning toy.

He barely connected, but the impact sizzled through him like a miniature bolt of lighting. Procopio snatched his hand away and stared with disbelief at the rapidly growing figure. In moments, a full-sized horse pranced on his Calimshan carpet. It folded room-spanning wings in a sweep that set the chandelier swaying and swept hundreds of tiny figures off the backfield.

The winged horse was a dappled bay, but its coloring was unlike anything Procopio had ever seen. Its coat was mottled brown and moss green, and the mane that hung nearly to its hoofs was the shade of mountain pines. The wings were feathered in soft shades of green and brown. It was the strangest steed he had ever seen, yet it suited the female mounted on its back.

She was a forest elf, with the coppery skin and amber eyes common to the folk of the Mhair. Her hair was long and braided, and a deep jade green in hue. Simply clad in a tunic and boots, she bore little resemblance to the elaborated coiffed and gowned magehound Procopio had glimpsed twice or thrice. Procopio was no expert on the ages of elves, but this female seemed to have aged the equivalent or two or even three human decades. Her skin looked thin and delicate. Tiny lines collected near the corners of her catlike eyes, and the hollows beneath her cheekbones were deep and shadowed. Even so, how many green-haired elves could there be in Halruaa?

Procopio greeted her by name. "This is a most unexpected pleasure. Would you care for a refreshment? Wine? Perhaps a bucket of oats?"

Kiva swung down from the horse and smacked its flank. The winged creature broke into a canter, taking perhaps four steps before it began rapidly diminishing in size and rising in the air. It shrank to the size of a bee and disappeared.

Never had it occurred to Procopio that someone might breach his tower's defenses through the gaming tables' magic. He was both chagrined and impressed. "I would pay well for a copy of that spell and the name of the wizard who developed it," the wizard observed.

The elf woman smirked. "If I sold it, I wouldn't bet a wooden skie against the man's chances of surviving the new moon."

Procopio grunted. "Let us move to the matter at hand. Iago, my former counselor, affirms that you purchased him from a band of Crinti raiders. You have an alliance with the Crinti, or at least some sort of dealings with them."

"And you have a particular fascination with the shadow amazons," Kiva countered. "More importantly, you have shown yourself willing to trade information for information. Your comment about activities beyond the eastern wall led to some interesting possibilities. What else can you give me?"

"What do you want?" Procopio asked bluntly.

Kiva blinked, as if unaccustomed to such directness from a Halruaan wizard. "Many things. Perhaps foremost, the destruction of the Cabal."

It was Procopio's turn to be astonished. "How might that be accomplished?"

"Help me remove Zalathorm from power, and I will show you."

No answer could have pleased him more. On the other hand, it seemed too convenient that his purpose and the elf's dovetailed so perfectly.

He painted a disapproving scowl on his face. "Let's assume that I wished to pursue such a foolish and treasonous course. The only incentive large enough would be Zalathorm's crown. What reason would you have to support me?"

"None in the world." She shrugged. "I don't care whose arse warms Halruaa's throne. You have something I want, and Zalathorm does not."

"What is that?" he asked warily.

"You know the Crinti," she said, gesturing to one of his older tables. "Once they were useful to me, but they have become too numerous, too bold. They are coming into the Nath by the scores through the caves and mountain passes."

"Why should that concern me?"

"This activity might well draw eyes eastward. If your fellow wizards learn of the coming Mulhorandi invasion, you lose the opportunity to predict a threat that Zalathorm did not perceive. Help me with the Crinti, and you serve yourself."

Procopio carefully hid his elation. To do battle against Crinti warriors! He had dreamed of such battles hundreds of times. He had planned strategies and tested the results. This opportunity was one he had desired for a very long time! Yet he kept his voice level, his face skeptical. "What, precisely, would you like me to do?"

"You are the lord mayor of this city. Surely you have some militia under your command. Claim your great powers of divination have perceived a threat from the Crinti, and argue that because of your studies, you are better prepared to counter this threat than any other man. I will tell you where many of their camps and caves are hidden. You will win fame for this victory, and when you predict the coming of Mulhorandi troops, people will take notice."

"A compelling argument," Procopio conceded. "And if the militia requires some substantiation?"

"Two of your former jordaini travel the Nath. Report to the king your concern for these young men, the troubling visions you have received. I will use my influence with the Crinti to have the jordaini captured. Send a scouting party to 'rescue' them. When they return to the king's city spouting tales of Crinti atrocities, you will appear to be a true prophet."

"Agreed," Procopio said promptly, "but I warn you, I have studied every possible variation of battle strategy in the northern hills. Your Crinti cannot trick me, and you had better not attempt to betray me."

"Why would I?" she countered. "You wish to prove yourself in battle, I wish to see the Crinti banished. You wish to replace Zalathorm, and you will need the chaos I have proven myself capable of providing. And I wish to dance on Zalathorm's grave."

Never had Procopio heard words infused with such venom or seen such hatred as that shining in Kiva's eyes. "Perhaps I have reason to trust you, after all."

"Test me and see!"

The elf woman planted her feet wide and squeezed her amber eyes closed. Procopio quickly cast a small spell of divination to probe her motives.

Instantly he was engulfed by an icy storm of emotion, a glacier of resolve. So intense was Kiva's passion for vengeance that Procopio experienced it as a physical blow. A violent chill shuddered through him, and he stumbled back on legs suddenly stiff and numb.

"Why?" he managed.

"As long as you're satisfied with my sincerity, why should you care?" The elf woman threw her arms out wide and began to spin like a child at play. Her feet lifted from the floor. She continued to whirl as she took flight, diminishing and rising as quickly as the winged horse had done. In moments she was gone—a tiny tempest that had struck and moved on.

Kiva stepped out of the whirling spell into the bleak terrain of the northlands. She continued to spin, however, laughing and circling in a giddy little dance. This was too delightful! A wizard-lord stood willing and eager to bring forces to the Nath! The Crinti would crush them like ants beneath an ox's hooves! Not incidentally, Procopio's foray would drain the king's city of its defenses.

She had told Procopio the truth—in a manner of speaking. Yes, Zalathorm would fall, but not yet, not this way. Warriors' blood would flow in this invasion. Only the blood of wizards could quench Kiva's wrath.

Procopio's kingly ambitions would have to wait. For now, let Zalathorm sit his throne, his eyes fixed upon his troubled borders. Perhaps then he would not realize that the true danger lay in his own land, in the very heart of Halruaa.

CHAPTER TWENTY

Andris watched as Kiva strode into the camp, nodding to the watchful Crinti but coming directly to his side. "We are leaving," she said abruptly.

He rose slowly from his place by the campfire. "Everyone?"

"We two. I want to be beneath the trees of the Mhair before highsun."

She chanted an incantation and reached out her hand to him. As soon as he touched her fingers, they were both swallowed in a whirling haze of soft white light. Andris expected a whistle of wind, a sense of motion. There was nothing but the light, and a quiet so intense that the beating of his own heart sounded like crashing surf.

The light deepened, turning the golden green of sunlight filtered through a forest canopy, and the white silence unfolded into the lush cacophony of the jungle. Birds chuckled and called in the branches overhead. Frogs belched in nearby shallows. Insects whined and hummed. In the distance, a snarl spoke of a jungle cat's unsuccessful hunt. Lying beneath the complex clatter was the soft, pulsing song of the forest, never before audible to his ears.

This, Andris suspected, was what an elf heard—the voice of life, and of magic! As his hearing adjusted to its normal level of sensitivity, the song faded. He felt like a blind man, granted a moment of tantalizing sight, then plunged back into oblivious darkness.

"You look disappointed," an amused Kiva said. "Magical travel didn't live up to expectations?"

Andris had no desire to explain. "I am not unhappy to leave the Nath and the Crinti camp. But why return to the Mhair?"

Kiva cupped her hands to her lips and let out a high, ringing cry. Sweet and musical enough to be mistaken as birdsong, the call was not exceptionally loud. Yet Andris got the impression that it soared though the forest on quiet wings. A message had been sent.

They settled down in the lower branches of a flowering tree, keeping a watchful eye on the forest around them. Suddenly Kiva dropped from her branch, and lifted one hand in greeting to the elves who emerged from the deep green shadows. Andris shook his head in astonishment. He had not seen or heard their approach.

He climbed down and walked to Kiva's side. The elves were familiar—all had fought with them at the Lady's Mirror—but there was no welcome in their eyes. At their head was Nadage, the battle leader Kiva had turned into a raider.

"You are no longer clan, Kiva," the elf said solemnly. "This forest is closed to you. Walk beneath other trees, or die."

Kiva bowed her head in acceptance of this sentence. "If you will join me, I will walk beneath the trees of Akhlaur's Swamp."

An expression of utter disbelief flashed across the elf's copper face. "Is it your life task to destroy what remains of the Mhair elves?"

"The laraken is gone. Elves can walk the swamp in safety."

"Even so, walk among the crystal ghosts of our family, our friends? You ask too much."

"Too much?" She spoke the words softly, but gave them weight and emphasis. "What price would be too high to see the wizard Akhlaur destroyed?"

"He was human. Why are you so certain he still lives?"

Kiva shrugged. "Alive, dead. It matters not. Akhlaur was a necromancer, a wizard who deals in the mysteries of life and death. I know that he prepared a lich spell—I saw him do it. When his body dies, his evil may well live on. If that comes to pass, where can any elf walk in safety?"

Indecision washed over the elf leader's face. "You have led us false before. How can we trust you in this?"

"That is precisely my point," Kiva argued. "Would you accept word of Akhlaur's death from my lips? Or would your Reverie finally know peace if you scattered his bones with your own hands? Go with me to the swamp. I will defeat him, and bring him to you."

Cibrone, the shaman, threw up her small hands in disgust. "How could you defeat a wizard who destroyed hundreds of elves?"

Kiva took a small book from her pack. Andris recognized it as the spellbook he had taken from the Jordaini College. Her face was somber as she held it up. "This holds Akhlaur's secrets. Your touch senses magic, Cibrone. Test the truth of my claim."

The shaman reached out with hesitant fingers and touched the delicate, yellowed leather binding. Her face paled as an unexpected truth came to her. She snatched her hand away from the grim book, then smoothed her fingers over it in a small, sad caress.

"Filora," she said in broken tones. "My sister."

Chagrin washed over Kiva's face—real or feigned, Andris could not say. "I did not know this, Cibrone. But I can see that you, at least, understand me. You know what things the necromancer has done. Sooner or later, Akhlaur will win free of his prison. He has already learned how to send one of his monsters through the floodgate. Did you know that the laraken escaped into the world of water? That Akhlaur can take from the laraken all the magic the monster steals? Can you imagine how quickly his power will grow?

"Akhlaur must be stopped," Kiva asserted. "Here. Now. For two hundred years I have studied his magic. I know how he can be defeated, and I believe I can do it if we move with all haste. If I fail, what loss to you? You will not mourn me overmuch."

The elves considered, debating the matter in their eloquent silent speech.

"We will go," Nadage said at last. "This evil must be stopped. Yet know this, Kiva: If you spill innocent blood again or endanger the People needlessly, you will never leave the swamp."

"So be it. Prepare your warriors, and bring the undine with you."

This took the elf leader by surprise. "Why?"

"Akhlaur's tower is deep under water. The undine can retrieve the treasures from it—things I will need to follow Akhlaur and subdue him."

"I will ask her," Nadage said hesitantly, "but I will not ask her to follow you into the world of water."

"Nor would I! She is a creature of magic. The laraken dwells there and would be her death."

Nadage nodded, and the elves disappeared into the trees. Kiva and Andris waited throughout that day and most of the next before the band reappeared with the undine—a slender, white-skinned maiden with raven hair and a beautiful, ageless face. Small, delicate white wings framed her shoulders, shaped like those of a deep-diving bird. Andris barely recognized the scalded, suffering creature they had taken from the waters of the Lady's Mirror. Seeing her now, he understood why pilgrims who glimpsed her face believed they were granted a vision of the goddess.

However, as the long march to the swamp went on, the undine's beauty faded. The elves moved swiftly, covering more ground that Andris would have thought possible. He considered himself strong and fit, but he had difficulty keeping the pace. It was brutally hard on the undine, who appeared thinner and more fragile every time Andris looked at her.

When they entered the Swamp of Akhlaur, a pall settled upon the spirits of the elves. The air was as dank as an open grave. As they made their way through moss-draped trees, long filaments brushed at them like lifeless fingers. Each crystal ghost the elves passed was an occasion for mourning. Kiva urged them on, and after a while they took to singing their keening laments in time to their step, like a mournful marching song.

Andris, too, was forced to confront his dead. On the second day into the swamp, they reached the site of the battle with the laraken.

The jungle was already reclaiming the battlefield. Foliage scarred by the fireball battle between Kiva and Tzigone had healed and grown. Flowering vines entwined the naked rib cage of the lion-centaur who had died protecting his elf mistress. Andris was grateful that he did not have to gaze upon the actual bones of his comrades. Lacking tools for burial, they had weighted down the bodies and dropped them into a deep pool nearby.

A wave of odor slammed into him—a stench so foul that it made Andris dizzy with nausea. It was familiar, but for a moment Andris could not identify it.

"Kilmaruu," he murmured, remembering the battle in the swamp and the rank scent of long-drowned men.

Andris reached in his bag for the pot of pungent ointment he'd prepared for that battle. He smeared a quick dab under his nose to help block the smell. Tossing it to Kiva, he pulled his sword and dropped into a battle-ready stance. Behind him, the elves followed suit.

A rotting, swollen corpse blundered through the foliage. Its puffy hand drew back and hurled something brown and wet at Andris. His sword leaped up to bat it away, easily cutting through the spongy missile. Two halves of a vampire leech—each the size of his fist—writhed at his feet.

A shudder ran through Andris. The leeches were as voracious as their namesakes, and nearly impossible to dislodge. If the leech had hit a living target, it would have sucked enough blood to fill a wine bottle before they could cut it off.

The undead creature came on, pulling a sword from a rusty scabbard. Andris stepped in and blocked the attack. The "sword" snapped in two as easily as a dried reed. It was no warrior's weapon, but a thin, hollow tube.

Andris darted a gaze to the corpse's chest. A groan escaped him as he noted the stab wound to the heart, almost obscured by the pale, puffy flesh around it. This had been Dranth, a jordaini student who had left the college with a "debilitating illness"—as spurious a claim as the one that added Andris to Kiva's ranks. Dranth had died in the swamp, slain by a giant stirge. The weapon in Dranth's undead hand was that which had dealt his deathblow: a stirge's snout.

There was no intelligence in the dead eyes, nothing at all of Dranth. That made Andris's task somewhat easier. With three quick strokes, he beheaded the walking corpse and ran his sword through the already-shattered heart.

Dranth was dead, Andris reminded himself as he stooped to wipe the foul pus from his sword.

A whimper of inarticulate terror came from behind him. Andris glanced back at the undine. The watermaid managed to stand upright only because Cibrone linked a supporting arm around her waist. Both females stared at the beheaded zombie with revulsion and sorrow. Andris knew enough of elves to realize their great respect for the afterlife. The notion of an animated corpse was abhorrent to them.

A ragged, gurgling wail rose from a vine-shrouded copse of trees. The jordain spun away and stalked toward the new threat, bent on destroying the animated bodies of his former comrades.

◉

Themo arrived at the travel hut two days late, flushed with sun and excitement and ready for adventure. Any doubts Matteo might have had about his decision to meddle in Themo's life dissolved at the sight of the big man's grin. He leaped from his horse and swept Matteo up into a bone-crushing embrace.

"What did you say to old Ferris to get him to turn me loose?"

Matteo managed a faint smile. "Wouldn't you rather know what we're hunting?"

Themo listened intently, nodding and offering an occasional suggestion. His spirits were high as the three jordaini rode out, following the Crinti trail deeper into the hills, expecting ambush with every bush and cave they passed. Trail sign was plentiful, but never once did they see their prey.

"Not much sport to this," Themo complained after a few hours.

Matteo and Iago exchanged glances. "Perhaps his sword is sharper than his mind," the small jordain said sarcastically.

"During my time with Procopio Septus, I often joined the wizard in games of war," Matteo began, deftly cutting off Themo's indignant response. "He had a wondrous table, a raised map shaped much like this wild land. With it were hundreds of tiny figures that moved and fought. He commanded them to enact battles so we could observe the field from above, as a god might, and better understand how the battle played out. Sometimes we would play the same battle again and again with variations to learn what worked and what did not."

A wistful smile crossed the big man's face. "That would be worth seeing!"

"It was enlightening, certainly. One strategy concerned an airborne wizard—one of the deadliest of foes. We jordaini know to increase chances of success by keeping the wizards on the ground. So do the Crinti. They generally keep to the caves or the deep woods. But this path is not sheltered, and it leads to increasingly open ground. This is not typical Crinti behavior."

"None of us are wizards," reasoned Themo.

"True enough, but strategies that prove successful are not abandoned lightly. The Crinti would not take such a path without a purpose." Matteo paused and looked toward the western sky. Only a crimson rim was visible above the hills. "Because this is the Nath, we have additional concerns."

Like the voice of an actor taking a cue, the wail of a dark fairy rose from the hills. "The Crinti fear the Unseelie folk, yet they are leading us deeper and deeper into haunted lands."

Iago shot a furtive glance toward the sound. "Maybe the shadow amazons are like quail, pretending to have a wounded wing and luring danger away from the nest."

"Or perhaps the Crinti are not leading us away from something but toward it."

"An ambush, most likely," Themo muttered, studying his surroundings with new interest.

Matteo considered this a logical assumption. The Crinti trail led through a winding, narrow pass, past small dark caves and tumbled piles of rock. They emerged from the passage unscathed into a large clearing—and the strangest place he had ever beheld.

"By lord and lady," he whispered. He slid down from his horse.

Large, conical mounds rose from the ground, covered with green moss. Some of the hills barely rose to Matteo's shoulder, but most were at least twice the height of a man.

The air seemed different in the clearing. Just beyond the pass, the sky had held the brilliant clear sapphire common to a summer sunset, and the few small clouds that clung to the mountaintops were gold and crimson and purple. Here all was gray mist and land-bound clouds. Much of the Nath was either scrubby forest or barren waste, but here the ground and the hills were covered with lush, light green moss, such as might be found only in the deepest forest. Matteo had the uncanny feeling that the rugged pass had led them not into a sheltered clearing but into another world.

"Never have I seen so enchanted a place," he murmured in awe.

"Enchanted!" Themo sent him a sour look. "You've been spending too much time around wizards."

The big man's face was unnaturally pale, and he shifted his weight from one foot to another, looking fully as spooked as the skittish horses.

Iago placed a hand on his shoulder. "That's what I told him, Themo." He sent Matteo an apologetic look, his eyes cutting quickly to Themo and back. Matteo, understanding, gave a slight nod. Themo was fond of gossip, and a diversion was definitely in order. "Did you know that Matteo spends every spare hour with the girl who called the laraken?"

This bit of scandal completely engaged Themo's attention, and some of the ruddy color returned to his face. "Have you gone moon-mad? A wizard's apprentice? Though I suppose she's pretty enough," he reminisced, "especially if you're partial to big dark eyes."

Matteo was no longer listening. He walked up to one of the mounds and placed a hand upon it. "Feel this."

The other jordaini gingerly followed suit. The conical hills hummed with energy—even the magic-resistant jordaini could feel it! The moss-covered rock felt insubstantial, not quite solid.

"The veils are thin here," Iago said in a troubled voice as he scrubbed his hand on one thigh, as if to remove the disturbing tingle. "That's why we hear the Unseelie song."

"Could the fairies come through?" Themo demanded.

"They are said to do so, from time to time, but only one or two manage to emerge. Apparently the passage is difficult, possible only at certain times and places."

"So there's no chance of an army of them pouring out of

these things?" Themo persisted, nodding toward conical hills.

"Not unless they are summoned," Matteo soothed him, "and there is little fear of that. Who would do such a thing? Who *could?*"

Iago's eyes settled on something, and widened. "Don't we have a proverb about not asking questions unless you truly want an answer?"

Matteo followed the line of his gaze. Tzigone stood at entrance to the pass. Her blue robe was travel-grimed and kilted up into her belt for ease of movement. Her dark eyes were enormous in a pale and furious face.

"Behind you!" she shouted, pointing.

He turned and was not surprised to see the shadows at the far side of the clearing stir and take shape. The form they took turned his blood to ice.

Thin as wraiths and dark as drow, the dark fairies regarded the intruders with eyes of a strangely glowing black. They were no taller than children. They moved with ethereal grace, darting between the hollow hills so swiftly the eye could not follow them.

Matteo swallowed hard and drew his weapons. As he did so, the creatures disappeared. He heard a faint sound like that of wind, but the impression was gone so quickly that Matteo did not understand the truth of it until he saw the glowing eyes emerge from behind a closer hillock. The Unseelie folk did not move through magic—at least, not as he understood it. They were just that quick.

"Don't let them out," Tzigone yelled. "Hold them here in the valley!"

Matteo shot an incredulous look back at her. "Anything else?"

She was already off and running. "Make it up as you go along. I'll be back as soon as I kill a certain rat-bastard wizard!"

Tzigone's voice faded, as did the clatter of her boots against the rough stone. The fairies likewise vanished, and in an eyeblink their feral eyes peered out from the edges of a different, closer mound. The Unseelie song began, a chilling, unearthly melody that bounded from mound to mound, everywhere and nowhere.

"Mother of Mystra," Themo swore softly, the battle light flickering uncertainly in his dark eyes. "How in hell can we fight this?"

Matteo drew his sword and strode toward the nearest hillock. "As best we can."

Tzigone raced down the passage and launched herself at Dhamari like a human arrow. They went down together, rolling painfully over the rocky ground. He was too surprised to offer much resistance, and she quickly pinned him.

"You tricked me," she hissed, fisting her hands in his tunic and giving him a furious shake. The movement spilled a length of silver chain from its hiding place beneath his tunic. From it hung a medallion—her mother's talisman!

Tzigone lunged for it. Her fingers tingled as a familiar magic spilled from the token, the watchful guardian magic she remembered from her earliest days. With a vicious tug, she broke the chain and thrust the talisman—the *real* talisman—into the cuff of her boot.

For the first time she noticed the cold, malicious light in the wizard's eyes. "You tricked me," she said again, this time in wonder as she began to comprehend the scope of Dhamari's betrayal. "You told me I was casting a spell of warding and banishment, but it was really a summoning! I *called* those things!"

"An accident," the wizard protested. "As I told you, this magic is beyond me."

"So you gave it to a green apprentice!"

A contrite expression washed over his face. "Let me up, and I will give you the scroll for the reversal spell."

"Well, that was easy," she said sarcastically, "and probably worth the effort it took." She gave the wizard another shake. "I know you can cast metal transmutation—I've seen you studying the scroll! Change my dagger to iron. *Do it!*" she shouted when Dhamari hesitated.

The wizard's lips formed a grim line, but he nodded agreement. Tzigone let him up and showed him the silver knife that Basel had bought for her.

"Iron," she reminded him. "And by wind and word, you'd better be right behind me to do the same for the jordaini's weapons."

Dhamari glanced over his shoulder. His guards—those who had not already fled back down the pass—formed a solid wall behind him. "You heard her," the captain said gruffly.

The wizard took the knife and cast the spell. When the task was done, he gazed with dismay at the dull, heavy weapon. "Consider," he pleaded, "you cannot win against such creatures."

Tzigone snatched the iron knife from him and raced to Matteo's aid. As she burst into the clearing, a little cry of dismay escaped her. Her friend was not faring well.

The Unseelie warriors were swift and silent, taxing the jordaini with their speed, toying with them with their wicked little knives. All three men bled from many tiny wounds, but they could not lay a blade on their darting foes. Iron weapons would help, but Tzigone couldn't hold them off alone. She glanced back over her shoulder. Dhamari Exchelsor swayed uncertainly at the edge of the clearing.

"Metal transmutation!" she shouted. The wizard caught her eye and quickly went into the second casting. When the spell was cast, his eyes rolled back and he slumped to the ground—to Tzigone's eye, just a little too gracefully.

"Idiot," Tzigone muttered. Dhamari's cowardly ploy might excuse him from fighting, but it also kept him from defending himself.

"Get him out of here," she told the men who'd followed Dhamari to the clearing. Their faces proclaimed that they'd be happy to watch the wizard die where he fell. Tzigone's gaze swept over them. "Move him, or deal with me."

She didn't have time to wonder at the fear that crossed their faces, then the shame. "As you say, lady," murmured the leader.

Tzigone was already running. She moved directly into the path of one of the dark folk—the largest one she'd seen among them. The creature stopped before her, no more than a breath away, repelled and weakened by the iron she carried.

Tzigone lifted the knife in a gesture of menace, then brought her knee up hard. The fairie's black eyes blazed with what she hoped was pain.

"*Lady*," she repeated derisively. "I don't think so."

Her iron knife swept in.

She yanked it free and whirled to take stock of the battlefield. Matteo had tossed aside his now-iron sword—too heavy, she guessed—but he fought with daggers alongside his two friends. They stood in a triangle formation, back to back to back, moving in concert as they faced their peculiar foe. The Unseelie folk were still preternaturally fast, but the iron weapons seemed to sap their strength as surely as the laraken drained magic.

Just as Tzigone began to hope the battle had turned, the big jordain stumbled and fell. The Unseelie song swelled in triumph as the dark fairies rushed in.

She darted forward to take the fallen man's place. A fairy knife leaped from nowhere to nick her thigh. She kicked at her attacker and met nothing but air. Seeing the futility of solitary battle, she fell into position with Matteo and Iago and dropped into the rhythm of battle.

"Get back, Tzigone," Matteo panted out as he deflected one darting attack after another. "You're not trained for this."

"Who is?"

He darted her a quick, exasperated look. "Just go!"

"I called them," she responded grimly.

Matteo could not have argued even if he'd wanted to. As the iron weapons slowed the dark fairies' movements, their numbers became more apparent. Dhamari's spell of summoning had let more than a score of the fey monsters slip through the veil.

Suddenly the weird music stopped, and the Unseelie attackers drew back. They milled uncertainly about. Tzigone's heart leaped with sudden hope, but Mateo let out a heartfelt, barnyard epithet.

Her head whipped toward him. "What?"

Matteo backhanded a streak of blood off his forehead. "I've seen this formation," he said, "but not in battle."

Even as he spoke, the dark fairies began to circle. Their song erupted in a keening, triumphant frenzy. Like small, fey wolves, they closed in for the kill.

CHAPTER TWENTY-ONE

A brilliant light poured into the clearing, sending the dark fairies whisking off into sudden, eye-searing flight. Matteo shielded his eyes with one hand and glanced toward the source. His shoulders rose and fell in relief as he recognized Basel Indoulur's ship. The battle over, he dropped to both knees at Themo's side.

At first glance it appeared that the big jordain's wounds were not so bad—spiteful, superficial cuts such as he himself had sustained. The dull, haunted look in his friend's eyes suggested otherwise.

Crimson silk rustled as Basel dropped to one knee beside him. "How can I help?"

"The Unseelie folk can mark a mortal like a vampire," Matteo said. "Themo needs to be healed and cleansed, or he may never be more than you see him now. Have you a priest with you?"

The wizard shook his head. "We'll take him to the nearest temple." As he spoke, his gaze shifted to the edge of the clearing, when Tzigone stood with her chin tilted stubbornly high, nearly toe to toe with a very irate Iago. The jordain appeared to be railing at Tzigone, blaming her for what happened. For once the girl held her tongue. Matteo, knowing her quirky sense of honor, understood that she already felt the weight of her miscast spell.

Basel quickly placed himself between the angry jordain and his apprentice. "Board *Avariel*, Tzigone," he said calmly. "Get the others."

Iago spat. "I will not travel the same ship as that witch!"

"You're not invited to," Basel said coolly. "Take the mercenaries and ride to the nearest town. Or stay here and face those creatures again, as you prefer."

The jordain stalked off and held quick, angry speech with Dhamari's men. After a moment the mercenary captain came over to Basel, dragging Dhamari by the collar of his tunic. "Can you take one more? He can't ride in this condition, and every man here would rather kill him than tend him."

Basel gave a curt nod. Two of the men carried the wizard ungently up the long plank that led to the deck of the hovering ship.

Matteo hoisted Themo over one shoulder and carried him up the plank, unsure whether to stay or rejoin the other fighters. The skyship began to rise before he had time to disembark, settling the matter. He settled down beside Themo's cot. One of Basel's men brought him water and linen, and he busied himself cleaning and bandaging the jordain's many small wounds.

After a few minutes, Tzigone peered around the corner of the small cabin. She took in Themo, who by now was swathed nearly as thoroughly as a Mulhorandi mummy. Distress and guilt filled her expressive eyes.

"Don't take this on yourself," Matteo said, gesturing to Themo. "It is not your doing."

"That skinny jordain doesn't agree." She passed a hand over her face, leaving streaks of dirt and blood. "Neither do I."

Matteo beckoned her over. She sank down on the edge of the cot and submitted to his ministrations. When all her cuts had been tended, he sat down beside her and drew her into his arms.

Tzigone leaned her head against his shoulder. Words poured from her, tumbling over each other. Matteo listened without interruption as she told him about her meeting with Dhamari and her decision to travel into the country-side with him and learn what spells she could. "He said the summoning was accidental," she concluded.

"Do you believe him?"

She rose from the cot and began to pace. "I don't know. Did you find Kiva?"

"I found one of her companions."

She glanced at his bleak face. "Your turn."

Matteo told her about his encounters with Andris and the Crinti. He told her about the jordaini purification rite but did not pass along Iago's speculations about Kiva's motives. He mentioned that Ferris Grail owned the ice-house where Tzigone had been taken.

"Andris's treachery breaks my heart, but this sets me utterly adrift. Can I trust the jordaini order, the guardians of Halruaa?"

"Maybe they think that opposing you is part of keeping Halruaa safe."

Matteo considered this, especially in light of King Zalathorm's explanation of the mysterious power that pro-tected the "heart of Halruaa." Perhaps this "heart" was the jordaini order. Perhaps in deviating from its strict rule, in exploring its secrets, he was doing harm where he meant only good.

He sent a helpless look at his friend. "I don't know what to do anymore."

She sat down beside him. "You know, I'm starting to see some sense in the jordain's creed. You're the only person I know who tells the truth. In a way, that's really stupid, but it's also why you're the only person I really trust. You have a healthy respect for magic but you've learned how to do without it. I've seen wizards who can't hit a chamber pot without casting a spell. Well, I haven't literally *seen* that, but you get my point. You really *are* a guardian of Halruaa. That's worth doing. I've traveled. Halruaa isn't perfect, but it's the best place I've been."

Matteo took her hand. "When did you become so wise?"

She grinned and batted her eyes in a parody of flirtation. "I've always been wise. It's just that I'm so gorgeous, men don't seem to notice my other gifts."

They shared a muted chuckle. "So, what's next?" she asked.

"If the queen is to be believed, war is next," Matteo said quietly.

Tzigone looked dubious. "From all I've heard, the queen is as crazy as a moon moth."

"Yet there may be some significance in the fact that it was Kiva who brought Beatrix to Halarahh."

"So you think the queen and Kiva are allies?"

"It seems unlikely. Zalathorm is a powerful diviner. He has foreseen every major threat to the land for over three-quarters of a century."

She thought this over. "Let's find out if the queen really does know something. Since she's got so many devices around, no one would think much of another one."

"I don't think much of that, myself," Matteo said. "Planting a scrying device means using a magical item, which is forbidden to the jordain."

"It's not forbidden for a wizard's apprentice," she argued.

"Having someone use magic on your behalf is the same thing," Matteo countered.

"On your behalf? Listen to the man! Whose idea was this, anyway?"

"It's foolhardy, illegal, and very likely suicidal," he said heatedly, counting off these points on his fingers. "So obviously the idea was yours."

For some reason, this amused Tzigone. "So where do you go next?"

He glanced at the sleeping jordain. "I'll see Themo to the temple for healing, then I should report to the palace."

"But?" she demanded, picking up the hesitation in his voice.

"Perhaps I should bring news of this attack to Procopio Septus."

"Old Snow Hawk? Why?"

"He has spent a considerable amount of time studying the Crinti. He will wish to advise the king."

Tzigone agreed, not so much because she approved of Matteo's plan but because it suited her purpose. If Matteo wasn't at the palace, he wasn't likely to catch her there.

Experience had taught her to be wary of anything or anyone whose life Kiva touched. It was time to get a look at Queen Beatrix for herself.

Dhamari Exchelsor groaned and lifted one hand to his aching temples. He remembered the twice-cast spell, but that simple overexertion couldn't account for his throbbing head, or for the egg-sized lump he felt just under his hairline. Then he remembered—his own men had carried him aboard Basel Indoulur's skyship and thrown him into this wooden bunk. His own men!

His eyes focused and set upon Basel Indoulur's face. The wizard leaned against the closed door of the small cabin, his arms folded and his black eyes mild. "So you're awake. How are you feeling?"

"I'm feeling very unimpressed by your hospitality," the wizard grunted, delicately probing his throbbing head with his fingertips.

His "host" spread his pudgy hands in a "what can I do?" gesture. "Your men are a spirited lot. Pity I couldn't have brought them aboard my skyship." Basel smiled at the relieved expression this brought to Dhamari's face, but it was not a pleasant smile. "If you wish, I will happily return you to their tender care."

"Without bothering to land the skyship, no doubt," Dhamari retorted.

The conjurer lifted one eyebrow. "I had not thought of that, but I'm most grateful for the suggestion." He abruptly pushed himself off the door and all vestiges of civility disappeared from his face. "Know this: If you ever approach Tzigone again, if you so much as speak to her, I'll take you up on that suggestion!" He slammed out of the room.

Dhamari made a rude gesture at the closed door, then took a small moonstone globe from a hidden pocket inside his robe. He turned his back to the door and hunched over the globe, muttering the spells that would summon his elf partner.

The globe swirled with copper and green lights, which quickly settled down to form Kiva's beautiful but aging visage. Dhamari painted a look of contrition on his face. "As we agreed, I taught Keturah's girl the summoning spell. She . . . she can cast it."

Molten fury crept into the elf's eyes as she read the truth in his hesitation. "Did she?"

"I'm afraid so. I told her it was a spell of banishment in order to trick her into learning it. But no harm was done! There was a battle, and the dark fairies fled back into their hills."

"There was a battle," Kiva repeated with dangerous calm. "Between whom?"

"Three men in jordaini garb—but it was the wizard with his skyship who frightened the fey folk off."

Kiva let out a long, wavering breath. Dhamari had seen less furious exhalations emanating from a red dragon. He suppressed a smile.

"You idiot!" she raged. "It's too soon! You may have ruined all! At least tell me that the ship belonged to Procopio Septus."

Dhamari ducked his head as if to dodge a blow. "Basel Indoulur."

The elf woman shrieked, long and shrill. "He will carry this news back to the king's city! Lord Procopio will believe I betrayed him!"

The wizard tucked that information away for future use. "What can I do to amend?"

Kiva regarded him with loathing. "You can die slowly and painfully."

"You need me!" he wailed.

"I needed your spell. Tzigone can cast it."

"We made an alliance. I swore to you by wizard-word oath!"

"So you will keep silent, or die!" Kiva raged. "I swore no such oath, but those I did speak, I repudiate. I repudiate you! You are nothing but a hindrance to me. There is nothing between us. Do you understand?"

Dhamari understood full well. There was nothing between them. He had hindered Kiva's cause. When he was questioned by magehounds—and he would be—they would confirm this. He had what he wanted, and now he would dance without paying the piper.

A false tear slipped down his cheek. "You loved me, once."

The elf's face fell slack with astonishment, then her laughter rang out, harsh and derisive. She made a sharp gesture with both hands and slammed them together before her face. The moonstone globe shattered in Dhamari's hands.

The light from the magic sphere died abruptly. Shards of moonstone spilled from the wizard's hands and rained over his lap. He turned his hands palm up and inspected them. As he anticipated, they were unharmed.

After all, the shattered moonstone was his own doing— he had coaxed Kiva's fury from her. That was a foolish thing to do, but he was well and thoroughly protected from himself.

Dhamari lifted a heavy medallion from a hidden compartment in his sleeve. The magic in the talisman still hummed strong and true, but the medallion itself had been turned to iron. It was much heavier now—so heavy that it had fallen out of the cuff of Tzigone's boot to land, unnoticed, on the rough stone passage.

❧

Tzigone had slipped into the queen's palace once before, but the sight of the vast workroom was just as overwhelming the second time around. The light of a gibbous moon floated in through a high window. Creatures of metal and leather and canvas stood waiting, their mooncast shadows entwined as if in furtive conversation.

A chill wind washed over Tzigone's skin. Recognizing the touch of powerful magic, she dived for cover under a workbench.

The moonlight seemed to intensify, broadening into a whirling cone of white light. This set down like a summer wind tunnel. A slim, green figure stepped from the light. Tzigone bit her lip to keep from crying out when she recognized Kiva.

One of the clockwork figures turned toward the intruder. It was not a machine, but a woman. The silvery dress and white-and-silver wig had lent her a metallic, unreal aspect, and she'd stood so still that Tzigone hadn't realized she was a living being.

Kiva dipped into an ironic bow. "Greetings, Beatrix."

So this was the queen. Tzigone quietly reached for the magical device—a bottle carved into the likeness of a bearded sage with a smoking pipe and a mischievous, mildly salacious grin. She thumbed off the cork so that the next words spoken might be captured within.

Kiva's gaze swept the workroom. "You made many more creatures than this. Where are the others?"

"Gone," said Beatrix vaguely.

"Were they taken from you?"

"Yes. By the mists."

The elf frowned, then nodded. "Actually, that's all the better! It saves me the trouble of taking them away. I never thought you could make this many."

Beatrix turned away, apparently not interested in the elf's opinion. Tzigone watched as Kiva went through the words and gestures of a spell. The rest of the clockwork creatures faded away, and Kiva followed them in a whirl of white light.

Tzigone stuffed the cork back into place. She stayed beneath the table and waited for the queen to leave, but the woman seemed content to stare at the window, long after the moon had risen out of view. When Beatrix finally drifted away, Tzigone scooted through the palace to Matteo's room.

He was asleep. She pounced on him, seizing the pillow on either side of his head and giving it a good shake.

The world suddenly turned upside down. Tzigone hit the floor hard, face down. A knee pressed into her back. A strong hand fisted in her hair and turned her head so that one cheek was pressed into the carpet. Another hand pressed a knife to the vein in her throat.

From the corner of her eye, she saw Matteo's face shift from grim, ambushed warrior to its familiar, brotherly exasperation.

"And I thought *dwarves* woke up grouchy," she commented. "I've found that the best thing to do with dwarves is tire them out and leave while they're still sleeping. Want to hear the details?"

Matteo sighed and let her up. "This had better be important."

She took the cork from her magic mouth bottle and let the damning words spill out.

"What will you do with this?" she asked.

"The only thing I can do," he said heavily. "The truth must be told, and we must trust in Mystra that it will work to the good of Halruaa."

Matteo went to Zalathorm's council chamber first thing that morning. Many of Halruaa's elders were already in attendance, including Basel Indoulur and Procopio Septus. When the king's gaze fell on Matteo, he motioned him forward. The wizard-lords parted to let him pass.

"I have received your report, and spoken with Lord

Basel," Zalathorm said in a voice that carried throughout the hall. "You have something more to add?"

"Several things, your majesty. I believe that the elf woman Kiva is raising an army against Halruaa."

The king's lips took a dubious twist. "An army of what? Unseelie folk?"

"Crinti, among others"

"Lord Procopio assures me that there are a few raiders, easily dealt with."

Matteo sent an apologetic nod toward the hawk-faced wizard. "If there were just a few raiders, why would Kiva go to such lengths to provide a means of containing them?" He told them of Dhamari's spell and the dark fairies Tzigone had inadvertently summoned. "It seems to me that Kiva has prepared one brush fire as a back burn against another. Once the Crinti have served their purpose, summoning the Unseelie folk would drive the shadow amazons back over the mountains. Why else would Kiva place Crinti encampments among the most haunted hills?"

Zalathorm nodded. "Lord Procopio?"

The diviner's face was livid and tight-lipped. "It is possible, my lord," he admitted. "It is a reasonable strategy."

"What say you, Dhamari?"

Matteo caught his breath. Dharmari was here, in the king's council chamber? He followed the path of many eyes as they turned upon the self-conscious wizard.

"The young jordain's suspicions are not without foundation," Dhamari began. "Many years ago, Kiva and I were apprentices together. We joined in a miscast spell that summoned an imp. Matteo knew of this. Naturally, he might wonder if the association between Kiva and me continued. Lord Basel will attest that this is not so, by the word of Azuth's inquisitors."

"Basel?" the king asked, turning to the flamboyant conjurer.

The wizard confirmed this with a curt nod. "He was tested."

"The spell that inadvertently summoned the dark folk was adapted from a banishing," Dhamari continued. "I haven't the talent to cast it, so I could not know precisely what it would do, but I will swear by wizard-word oath that the casting of this spell was not intended to aid the traitor Kiva!"

The king listened to this recitation with an inscrutable face. "You defend yourself well," he said. "Now, Matteo. You said that the Crinti were merely the start of Kiva's army. Say on."

"Kiva almost certainly commanded the raid upon the Lady's Mirror. She also has access to the gate to the Plane of Water. If she commands Crinti and wild elves, who knows what other forces she may have."

"This is preposterous!" sputtered one of the wizard-lords who awaited the king's attention. "Throughout King Zalathorm's reign, he has never failed to predict a threat!"

A murmur of assent went through the chamber, but the king lifted a hand to silence it. "Halruaa remains at peace through the vigilance of all her wizard-lords and their jordaini. If there is a threat, let us work to perceive it."

The keen focus of the king's eyes slipped into haze, as if he were studying something far away. After a few moments he shook his head, frowning deeply. "There is a subtle veil over the recent past and the near future, one I cannot pierce and the likes of which I have never encountered. This is a matter for the full council."

Zalathorm motioned to a courtier, who slipped from the room and returned with a large amber sphere. As soon as Zalathorm's fingertips brushed the globe, a similar golden light touched the hand of each wizard present. Every member of Halruaa's Council of Elders wore a golden ring set with a tiny amber globe, so that Zalathorm could communicate with all his wizards at once.

"Lords and ladies, your presence is required immediately in the king's council chamber," he said somberly. "Come by the swiftest magic available to you."

The courtiers in the room hurried for the doors, not wishing to be trampled by wizards who wished to prove themselves swifter than their fellows.

"There is more, Your Majesty," Matteo said, "best spoken in private."

"It will wait," Zalathorm told him. The members of the Council of Elders began to fill the chamber.

When the room was full nearly to bursting, the king described Matteo's concerns and the strange film he himself felt over the future. At his command, glowing green runes appeared in the air. "This is a spell of divination. We will chant it as one. Perhaps together we can see where one man cannot."

Matteo's gaze shifted to Procopio Septus. The glare he threw at Matteo was pure venom.

The rhythm for the casting had begun. Zalathorm took up a staff and marked a steady beat against the floor. The sound resounded through the room, growing steadily louder as the wizards silently read the words of the spell.

Chanting filled the room, and the green-glowing runes grew steadily brighter. The colors shifted into a rainbow, which slowly spread out like a tapestry of light. Woven upon it in threads of magic was the image of a massive force gathering at the foothills of the mountains.

The chanting died away, engulfed by the horrified gasps that swept the room.

"Halruaa is about to be invaded!" one of the wizards blurted.

"Not so." Matteo stepped forward and pointed to the shimmering tapestry. "This peak is Jhiridial, in the eastern wall. Note the sun: It rises *behind* the mountains."

"Lady Mystra," Zalathorm swore softly, understanding Matteo's point. "Those troops are not on the *far* side of the mountain wall! They stand upon Halruaa herself!"

Matteo nodded. "The invasion has already begun."

CHAPTER TWENTY-TWO

Fury washed through Procopio's blood like molten steel. He stood before the king in what should have been the defining moment of his life. Thanks to that accursed Matteo, all his plans and dreams were slipping through his fingers like water!

Yet he might still salvage something of this. "Your Majesty, I will lead a skyship fleet into the Nath to repel the Crinti, then meet your army at the eastern wall."

Zalathorm nodded. "Good. If the Crinti are as numerous as Matteo fears, they could move in from behind and pin our forces."

Procopio shot a look at the troublesome jordain. "I request that Matteo accompany me. While he was in my service, we devised many strategies for just such an invasion."

It was a subtle way of taking for himself a bit of the credit for Matteo's early warning. Better still, it hinted that he had divined a threat that Zalathorm had missed. It wasn't quite what he'd hoped for, but he would work with it.

"You are obviously well prepared," Zalathorm noted, gazing at Procopio with eyes that saw far too much. "I will lead the attack on the approaching Mulhorandi army. The rest of you, summon whatever forces you command, and follow."

Good, thought Procopio. Two battles. Zalathorm will win one, and I, the other.

Matteo was not yet finished. "Your Majesty, there is another threat. I hesitate to speak of it in open council."

"This is no time for delicacy!" snapped Zalathorm. "As you yourself have observed, the safety of Halruaa comes before all other considerations. Speak!"

With obvious reluctance, Matteo told of Kiva's intrusion into the queen's chambers, of the many clockwork creatures she took with her. "I fear these creatures are nearby. The magic required to transport such large items any distance is immense. Kiva employed a spell of diffusion, a powerful battle spell that can scatter an army by sending its members to several nearby places."

Zalathorm's eyes narrowed. "You heard this spell? How did you happen to be in the queen's chambers when this occurred?"

"I was not. This device was."

He showed the king the magic mouth bottle, then pulled the cork. Procopio suppressed a snort of laughter when he recognized the carved visage of one of the northland's great wizards. It was said that the Old Sage cast a long shadow, but all the way to Halruaa?

The echo of Kiva's elven soprano filled the room with magic-rich chant, and Procopio forgot everything else. When the spell was complete, Matteo replaced the cork.

The king's face was grim. "Very well. The city must be fortified and secured. The battle wizard Lhamadas will command the city militia."

"There is yet another threat," Matteo said in a heartsick voice. "One within the palace itself."

He pulled the cork again. The voice of Queen Beatrix answered Kiva's questions. The entire Council of Elders heard Kiva commending Beatrix for a job well done.

For many moments, profound silence ruled the council chamber. "If I could have spared you this, sire," Matteo said softly, "I would have done it."

The king met his gaze. "You did your duty, jordain. I will do mine."

Procopio stepped forward to seize the moment, and, Mystra willing, the throne itself. "Your Majesty, none can deny that Beatrix is guilty of high treason. By law, the sentence is death, to be carried out immediately."

For the first time, Matteo saw the weight of long years in Zalathorm's eyes. His heart ached for the king, and for the strange, sad woman whom Zalathorm loved.

"Every Halruaan is entitled to magical examination," the wizard-king said coldly. "Surely the queen has the same rights as a fisherwoman!"

Before Procopio could protest, Matteo stepped forward. "The king is caught between two necessities. How can he defend both his queen and his country? Let this matter rest until our borders are secure."

"Halruaan justice is swift," Procopio reminded him.

"If it is too swift, it may not be justice at all," Matteo retorted.

A murmur of agreement moved through the room. "I suggest a compromise," said a tall, flame-haired woman. "The queen must be imprisoned until the invasion is repelled and this other matter given proper attention."

Zalathorm nodded slowly. "That is fair. Take her to the palace towers and place around her spells of binding. That is all. Now go—all of you know what must be done. May Mystra grant us strength."

In a quiet voice, one that barely reached the ears of the jordain at his side, the king whispered, "May Keturah forgive me."

Matteo started at the familiar name. His gaze leaped to Zalathorm's face, and read confirmation in the king's sad brown eyes.

There was no time for questions. He bowed to his king,

then turned away to follow Procopio's quick, staccato retreat.

In the very heart of Akhlaur's Swamp, the undine lay panting on the edge of the deep pool, her black tresses hanging lank about her too-pale face. Gems lay in bright heaps beside her, treasures from the sunken tower.

These riches were hard won. Strange magic lurked in the waters of Akhlaur's swamp, power sufficient to raise Andris's slain comrades into zombie guardians. The undine had apparently run into other guardians. Her arms were a map of angry red welts, and a thin tentacle, still twitching, tangled in her hair.

Andris picked it out carefully, self-consciously. His own fingers were nearly as translucent as this remnant of a jelly-fish. "A man-of-war," he said. "The poison will kill a man. I don't know how much damage it will deal a creature of water and air."

"Enough," Nadage said sternly. "The undine must rest until tomorrow."

"One more try," Kiva insisted. She described to the undine the gem that must be retrieved, its possible location within the tower. "This will open the floodgate. I swear it! Find it, and the plunder of Akhlaur's tower will be complete."

The elves exchanged glances. "It is for the undine to say."

The exhausted sprite nodded and dived deep. Time passed, and the shadows of night began to creep over the swamp. Finally one of the elves gasped and pointed.

A limp form floated amid a swath of black lilies. Andris dived in and pulled the undine to shore. The elf shaman bent over the fey creature, then shook her head. "She lives, but not for long."

Kiva stooped and jerked the bag from the dying creature's belt. She tugged open the string and spilled the contents onto her open palm. A large, perfect emerald caught the last rays of the dying day. A smile of satisfaction crossed the elf's face, and her eyes went utterly cold.

Chanting a spell, she dropped to her knees. She placed a tiny vial on the undine's chest and then fisted both hands in the delicate white feathers that framed the creature's shoulders. With a quick, vicious tug she wrenched them free.

The undine's entire body buckled in a spasm of agony, and she was gone. Nothing remained of her but the feathers in Kiva's hands and the glowing vial on the shore.

The elves stood in shocked horror. Kiva ignored them and tipped the vial to her lips. The glowing liquid disappeared, as wings sprouted from Kiva's shoulders. Andris had never seen such a spell, but it was not difficult to understand what Kiva had done. She had stolen the undine's life-force, and, at least for a time, the ability of the creature to live in the water.

Elven steel hissed free, and every blade pointed at Kiva's heart. She spat out a trigger word, and instantly the weapons flamed red with heat. With startled cries, the elves dropped their blades to sizzle and steam where they fell. They thrust their burned hands into the cooling water.

Kiva turned to Andris. "Kill them."

Andris shook his head.

"What of the Cabal?" she taunted him. "What price is too large to pay to see it destroyed?"

"This one," he said softly.

Kiva's hand came up and spat blue fire. Lighting flared into the water, skittering across the surface to sizzle into the elves' already burned hands. Before Andris could stop her, before he could speak a single word of protest, their companions lay dead.

"No price too large," she said firmly.

Dhamari Exchelsor sat in his tower window, watching the brightly painted *Avariel* sail northward in the company of a dozen other skyships. Of course Basel would go northward, despite his long-standing feud with Procopio Septus, for Tzigone would wish to fight at her jordain's side. If Basel were not so obliging, Dhamari imagined that Tzigone would find another way.

The streets below resounded with the clash of the queen's clockwork army. Their numbers were most impressive. Mechanical warriors emerged from root cellars and privies, stables and guest chambers and gardens, attacking anyone in their path. According to Dhamari's spells of inquiry, small skirmishes were everywhere. He watched as two metal gnolls—hideous beastmen with heads resembling desert dingoes—clattered down the street, tossing a shrieking child between them like a toy. Dhamari's guards took off in pursuit, leaving his tower unprotected.

No matter. The wizard watched them go, fondling a small coin that would transport him to Tzigone's side as soon as the deadly spell was cast and the dark fairies summoned.

And call them she would. Kiva had made certain of that, whether she knew it or not.

Procopio had witnessed such battles a hundred times, played out in miniature. Why then, was he so unprepared for the slaughter?

As Kiva had forewarned, small bands of Crinti had taken position on the mountains, choosing perches higher than the skyships could climb. They were too firmly entrenched to give the airborne wizards a clear target or even a sense of their numbers, which, as Matteo had suggested, were greater than Kiva had admitted. In a broad valley below, a band of mercenaries under the command of the jordain Iago fought in bloody melee against the gray warriors.

Most of the skyships dipped low into the valley. The fighting was too close for wizardly spells to be effective, so the warriors on board slid down ropes to join in the battle. Some of the more daring Crinti climbed the ropes to take the fight onto the ships.

Procopio had sent small bands up into the mountains to flush out the other Crinti, most of them to positions he had "divined." Among these men was Matteo. Procopio had intended to keep the jordain at his side, but Matteo left, sliding down a rope and dropping several feet to the ground. He stopped long enough to check the bag strapped to his back, then took off at a run. With a disgusted sniff, Procopio left the jordain to his fate and turned his attention to the battle at hand.

He gave the order to his helmsman to take the skyship higher, above the stench of death and the cries of dying men. After all, he was accustomed to watching such battles from above.

Matteo sprinted up a mountain path, running along a stream that seemed too swift and strong for this terrain, this season. From the skyship, he noted that its origin was a spring in the middle of a small clearing, very like the stream in the Swamp of Akhlaur that had sustained the laraken for two centuries. Several Crinti warriors guarded this spring, firming Matteo's suspicions.

Surely this was where Kiva had moved the floodgate.

He ran toward the deadly site, not entirely certain what he would do when he got there or what he might meet. His only thought was that the gate must be closed. He only hoped he would live long enough to mark the site for Basel Indoulur. The wizard would have to do the rest.

Far to the west, beside the pool that guarded Akhlaur's treasure with monsters and magic, Kiva faced down the furious, ghostly jordain. She forced herself to keep her voice calm and soothing, addressing the human as she might an angry dog.

"Keep your goal in mind. You know the price others have paid for the power Halruaan wizards wield. Did you think this wrong could be easily undone?"

Andris gestured to the slain elves. "They did not have to die."

"Yes, they did," the elf told him, "and so must I."

She smiled into his stunned face. "Did you think I meant to rule in the wizards' stead? There is nothing left for me in this world but vengeance. I will die with my blade in Akhlaur's heart and be content."

"But the task is not completed!"

"No, but my part is almost finished. It is your task to hold the floodgate until I can slip through into the Plane of Water. When the gate closes, you will know that I have succeeded, and you will know that I am dead."

Andris accepted this with a nod. "And the Cabal?"

"To destroy that, one must destroy Zalathorm himself."

Andris's face turned an even more ghostly shade. "I can't do that."

"No," she agreed, "but you will not need to. I already have. Zalathorm is a dead man—he is just too stupid to know it. But no more words. I have only borrowed the undine's strength. It will soon fade."

She extended her hand to him. After a moment's hesitation, he took it. Together they stepped back into the whirling white magic that led to the floodgate. Neither of them looked back.

Matteo burst into the clearing with a fierce battle cry, his sword raised high.

Two Crinti warriors ran to meet him. A third Crinti, a tall, almost stocky woman, held her place by the spring.

Three swords met in a single clash. "Mine," growled the taller Crinti as she heaved her blade free. She sidestepped Matteo's lunge and shouldered her comrade out of the way. "You, Whizzra! Get *reinforcements*."

She spat the word out through a sneer. Apparently she thought two Crinti were more than sufficient for a single human. Matteo planned to prove her wrong.

He spun back toward the elfblood, bringing his sword around in a sweeping, waist-level cut. It was a difficult attack to defend, but the Crinti brought her sword down in a brutal smash that knocked Matteo's blade low.

Matteo leaned in over the weapons and locked one hand on the nape of her neck. While she was still off balance, he hooked one foot behind her ankle and threw himself back, letting his weight bring them both down.

The Crinti was quick, but she could not get her balance or bring her sword back into play. She landed hard on Matteo—surprising him with her solid weight—and then drew back her fist for a short arm punch to his throat.

Matteo, trained in hand-to-hand combat since early boyhood, caught her wrist and gave it a deft twist. In three quick moves he had her pinned face down, hands behind her back.

He tugged off the leather thong that bound back his hair and quickly secured her hands. All the while, he kept an eye on the second Crinti, who watched with her fists on her hips and a smile of dark amusement on her lips.

"Yours, Shanair?" she sneered.

"Take him!" the downed woman shrieked. "But the trophy for this kill is mine!"

"No, Shanair," said a familiar voice. "This trophy is mine."

Matteo lifted his eyes to the ghostly face of his boyhood friend. He shifted his weight off the struggling Crinti and reached for his fallen sword, rising slowly, never taking his eyes from this new and deadly foe.

Shanair rolled away and jumped to her feet. She leaped

again, bringing her knees up high and tight to her chest and swinging her bound hand under them. Stalking over to the other Crinti, she held out her hands. The woman smirked and pulled a knife from a wrist sheath. She snapped the leather thong with a quick slice, then turned the knife point-inward to return it to its place.

But Shanair kicked out viciously, knocking the warrior's knife hand up high. She pivoted on her lower foot and kicked out again, catching the woman on her lower forearm and driving her hand, and the knife it held, directly into her face.

The brutality of the attack sickened Matteo. "Sister fighting sister, brother against brother," he murmured as he and Andris fell into a fighting crouch. "How have we come to this?"

"Do you intend to fight, or talk me to death?"

Andris came toward Matteo with a shallow, testing blow. Matteo's sword flashed forward and slapped it aside.

"No one has to die here."

"Only Halruaa. Only her wizards, her laws, her lies!"

"I can't accept that," Matteo said, batting aside a couple of quick blows. "Whatever ills Halruaa suffers, she won't die this day."

"She already has," Andris said, with a small, strange smile Matteo could not begin to read. "She is just too stupid and stubborn to admit it."

In a skyship above the clearing, Tzigone leaned far out over the railing and watched the battle. Farrah Noor, unnerved by this daring, stood behind Tzigone with a two-fisted grip on her tunic. Tzigone gently brushed away the girl's well-meaning grasp and turned to Basel. "I'm going down there."

The wizard shook his head. "This ship can't get in close enough. I'd have to let you down in the valley, where the fighting is too intense. Even if you could fight your way clear, you'd never get up the mountain in time to help."

Tzigone was not listening. Her eyes roamed the ship for a solution. "The wind-dancer sail. I could hold it and jump. It will slow my fall."

"So would a feather-fall spell," Basel retorted, "and with far more accuracy and safety."

Tzigone lifted one eyebrow. The wizard threw up his hands. "All right, there *is* a way to get you down."

Basil hurried to his cabin and returned with a small scroll. Tzigone memorized the simple spell and vaulted over the rail, chanting as she fell. The spell took hold suddenly, and it seemed as if the air had become as thick as cream. She drifted easily down, running even before both boots touched stone. Spurring her on was the sound of swords clashing and pounding in furious battle.

She caught sight of the formidable gray warrior who stood over the mouth of a spring, watching the two men battle and awaiting Matteo's death with eager eyes. A soft cry escaped Tzigone. The gray woman glanced in her direction. Tzigone dived behind a jagged pile of rocks. After a moment, the Crinti turned her attention back to the two men.

Tzigone peered between two rocks, not at all certain of the battle's outcome. Matteo and Andris were both superbly fit and trained. They fought together as skillfully as dance partners, as attuned to each other's movements as source and shadow. Tzigone sensed that the bonds connecting them were strong. Andris seemed to be fighting to sunder them. No less desperately did Matteo battle to keep his friend from slipping away.

Tzigone clung to the rock as if to hope itself. "Let him go, Matteo," she whispered.

So intent was she on the battle that she did not notice the approach of the Crinti. Suddenly a score of them slipped into the clearing and formed a ring around the fighters.

Tzigone's heart plummeted to her boots. The Crinti would not let Matteo leave this place whether he won or lost. There was nothing she could do for him but watch him die.

Or was there?

Dhamari claimed the song of the Unseelie folk was enough to put the Crinti to flight. She hoped he spoke the truth.

Tzigone edged away from the valley and scuttled up a rocky wall to the top of a small cliff so that her song might dance between the mountains and confound her hiding place. Her perch gave her a view of Matteo's battle, as well as the larger conflict in the valley below.

She glanced at the main battlefield. Three of the skyships lay in smoking ruins on the valley floor. The bodies of the slain were so numerous that the remaining fighters could barely move among them. It seemed to her that most of the survivors were Crinti. A few magical missiles fell from the airborne skyships now that the fighting was not so close, but most of the wizards were still hesitant to fire upon Halruaans who might yet be alive.

Still more Crinti emerged from the caves and passes, converging upon the dying army. She could make them flee. All she had to do was cast the spell and pray she still had the strength to banish the dark fairies once the deed was done.

Tzigone crouched down and began to sing the spell. All around her, the mountains echoed as Unseelie voices echoed her song. The Crinti in the valley below began to flee, but the circle that formed around the two jordaini held firm.

"Loyal, but not very smart," said a voice at her elbow. "The gate is thinnest there."

Tzigone whirled to face Dhamari Exchelsor, and her voice hitched in surprise. "Keep singing," he admonished her, "but hold off on the final gestures. Your friend's life depends upon it."

The wizard rose. Light poured from him like a lighthouse beacon. "Crinti!" he called in an unexpectedly clear, ringing voice.

The shadow amazons turned toward this new threat. "Behind you," he said, sweeping one hand in a dramatic gesture.

Tzigone, still singing, following the direction. A shimmering veil was taking shape in the clearing. Beyond it, going back and back into some unfathomable depth, crouched a sea of shadowy forms with glowing black eyes. Dhamari took her arm and pulled her toward the veil.

"Let the jordain go, and we will hold back the dark fairies," Dhamari said as he and Tzigone moved to within a pace of the veil. "Kill him, and we will release them." As if to illustrate the point, he seized Tzigone's outstretched hand and held it close to the veil.

"Tzigone, don't!" Matteo pleaded, speaking between ringing blows. "No good can come from an alliance with evil!"

Dhamari threw his weight against her, pushing her forward so that her hand touched the veil in the final spell gesture.

Magic pulsed through her. Tzigone's vision went dark. Against the blackness she glimpsed a vivid, agonized image of herself, her body nearly as transparent as the crystal ghosts in Akhlaur's swamp. Her bones glowed blue, and the blood in her veins was black ice.

The moment passed as her natural defenses slammed back into place, but the damage was done. The veil began to become more translucent. The song of the Unseelie folk grew louder, triumphant, a chorus of evil punctuated by the percussion of the jordaini's swords. The Crinti fled, disappearing into the mountains like gray smoke. From the corner of her eye, Tzigone noticed a copper and jade elf, moving toward the spring with the stealth of a hunting cat.

The spring!

Magic rose from the water, tingling over Tzigone's sensitive skin like the bubbles from sparkling wine. Understanding came to her in a sudden, horrified instant.

Kiva had returned to the floodgate.

What her purpose was, Tzigone could not say, but one thing she knew: If the elf woman had her way, Matteo would die and Halruaa with him. Desperate but determined, Tzigone kept singing, but this time her song spoke of banishment, of dark enchantments broken and gates closed. Her voice rose over the Unseelie song like the battle cry of an unlikely paladin, and the two spells struggled for supremacy like the two battling jordaini.

Magic built in power, shaking the mountains and sending rocks tumbling down into the valley. Dhamari tried to pull away, but Tzigone held him firm. When the veil opened, she threw herself into it, dragging the wizard behind.

Her song twined with the magic spilling from the Unseelie court—a meeting of fire and oil. An explosion shook the mountains and tossed aside the only two people left standing in the clearing.

CHAPTER TWENTY-THREE

Akhlaur stood by the coral obelisk, gazing past the glowing structure to the invisible gate beyond. By his reckoning, the moon would rise full over Halruaa. It was a time of power, when spells were more puissant and hungers ran dark and deep.

A rumble of distant magic echoed through the water. Akhlaur threw back his head and inhaled deeply, like a sailor testing the wind for a coming storm. His senses, made preternaturally acute by his years in the Plane of Water, perceived the whirl of a distant, rapidly descending waterspout. Exhilaration rose in him like long-forgotten lust.

The spinning magic came to him with unerring instincts. Bubbles spun off and dissipated, revealing a small, slender elf woman. She dropped to one knee and held out both palms, one resting upon another. In her top hand she cradled an enormous, perfect emerald, a gem worth the fortunes of a dozen kings—and the lives of a hundred elves.

His lips thinned in puzzlement as he regarded the creature kneeling before him. This was not what he had expected. The elf woman had every reason for vengeance, but she did him proper homage, and she offered him not a weapon but the long-desired key to his freedom.

"What is this, little elf?" he demanded.

Kiva raised her amber eyes to his. "The land is in disarray, Lord Akhlaur. The Lady's Mirror has been plundered, the Crinti invade the northlands in large numbers, and the Unseelie folk have found a way to pass through their hollow hills. Armies of the Mulhorandi march on the eastern borders. Even the queen turns against her people, unleashing metal monsters upon them."

Akhlaur bit back a chuckle of delight. "All this is very interesting, of course, but what has it to do with me?"

The elf still held the gem out. "I can take us both back to Halruaa. The need is great, my lord. The land will be destroyed, and all in it." As she spoke, her tone changed to gloating, and the light of madness touched her catlike eyes.

The necromancer was beginning to see the light of day. "And who better to urge this destruction along than your old master."

"Will you come with me?"

Akhlaur studied her. "What will you do with this chaos? Revel in it, like some moon-mad Azuthan dancing amid wild magic? Or is there a shape and purpose to your actions?"

"There is, my lord," she said firmly. "I want to break the Cabal."

The years slipped away. Akhlaur remembered the creation of that great artifact, the friends who had shared in its shaping—and the betrayals that had led to his exile. Hatred washed through him in great waves. He let none of it enter his voice or show in his face.

"Ah, yes. An interesting experiment, that, but long past its usefulness. Tell me, little elf, who holds the heart of Halruaa?"

This time there was no mistaking the feline glint in her eyes and smile. "Your old friend Zalathorm rules as wizardking."

This time Akhlaur could not hold back the crow of laughter. This was too rich! Zalathorm lived and ruled, and by the power of the Cabal!

"He is considered to be the most powerful wizard in the land."

"We shall see about that," the necromancer said, reaching for the emerald in Kiva's hand. "Take me to the battle at once."

Matteo rubbed the grit from his eyes and rose slowly from the ground. Instinctively he extended a hand to Andris, who was also stumbling back into consciousness. They clung together, wavering unsteadily as they struggled to remember where they were and how they came to be here.

Memory returned to Andris's eyes, and with it came a bitter chill. He wrenched free of Matteo's grasp and made his way unsteadily over to the spring. He dropped to one knee beside it. After a moment his shoulders slumped, and his head dropped to his chest.

Silence shrouded the mountains. After the tumult of battle and magic, the quiet was eerie. Even the clamor from the valley below had faded to a murmur of steel and voice. Matteo looked about for Tzigone. The veil was gone, and the song of the dark fairies silenced. Tentatively he placed his palm up as if to touch the place where the veil had hung, and where his friend had disappeared. Nothing remained of the dark fairies or the girl who had banished them.

"Why, Tzigone?" he murmured.

From long habit, he turned to Andris for answers. The jordain still knelt at the mouth of the stream. No more water flowed. The spring was gone.

The floodgate was closed.

Beginning to understand, Matteo felt for the strap that tied a bag to his back. The bag was gone, and with it the magical devices that Basel had given him, the ones Matteo would have cast into the spring so Basel could trigger a powerful implosion. They had not been certain this could close the floodgate. Now they knew.

He shook his head, hardly believing Tzigone's skill and nerve. She'd managed to cut the straps on his bag while he was fighting, while she was spellcasting, and to weave Basel's spell into her own. The result was an explosion that not only shattered the portal to the Unseelie realm but also slammed shut the tiny gate to the Plane of Water.

Once more, Tzigone had thwarted Kiva's plans, but this time it had cost her her life.

Because rage was easier than grief, Matteo snatched up his sword and stalked over to Andris. He thrust the blade firmly beneath Andris's chin and forced the traitor's head up. "Where is Kiva?" he demanded.

"She is dead." Andris looked up, and his ghostly hazel eyes held Matteo's implacable stare without wavering. Translucent blood dripped from the blade to mingle with the dying spring. "Kiva entered the Plane of Water to confront and destroy Akhlaur. Whether she succeeds or fails matters not. The gate is closed, and her fate is sealed with it."

Matteo took less comfort from this than he had expected to. This long-sought victory could not assuage the yawning void Tzigone had left behind. But neither the victory nor the loss released him from his duty. He slowly edged the sword away from Andris's throat.

"You will swear to this?"

"Send to Azuth's temple for their most powerful magehounds. I will submit to their inquisition, as I submit to you as prisoner."

"Just like that."

"Just like that," Andris said wearily. "My part in this is finished."

Matteo let him rise, but he kept his sword out and ready as they walked down the mountain, to the battles that lay ahead. Kiva might be dead, but Matteo suspected she was far from finished.

Avariel skirted the eastern mountains, moving swiftly toward the invading forces. Andris had been secured in a cabin below, and Basel Indoulur and Matteo stood in numb silence at the skyship's prow, staring with unseeing eyes at the forbidding terrain below them. They were nearly to the battlefield before the wizard put words to the loss they both felt.

"At least she took Dhamari with her."

"Yes." Matteo attempted a smile. "I wonder whom he has most reason to fear: Tzigone or the Unseelie folk."

"Indeed."

Again they fell silent. Matteo stared at the ground, forced himself to focus on the task at hand. The invading army was coming into view now. A host of dark-clad soldiers, looking distinctly antlike from this vantage, swarmed through the Halruaan militia. The Halruaans, distinctive in their sea-green uniforms, went down like trod-upon grass.

"Too few," Matteo muttered.

"And too close," the wizard added, his round face furrowed with distress. "I know of no battle spell that will sort through a hand-to-hand melee."

"What is needed are more troops." An odd quirk of memory came to Matteo: Tzigone holding a string of odiferous mushrooms, dressed as a street urchin so that she could seek out mischief to lighten the mundane shopping task assigned her.

"The fagoila mushrooms that Tzigone recently purchased—do you keep the spores aboard ship?"

Basel's eyes focused, then hardened. "Indeed I do, and I have prepared the instant army spell. A good thought, but there is no sign of rain."

"Strew the spores anyway, and then take *Avariel* above the clouds."

While the ship's mate relayed the orders to the crew, Basel took his place at the helm. Eyes closed, lips moving in a spellcasting frenzy, he clenched both hands around the magic-storing rod that gave the ship lift and momentum.

The skyship began a rapid ascent. Two minor wizards dumped small bags of pungent powder over the rail while the sailors others busied themselves with rope and sail, struggling to maintain the ship against quickening and capricious winds.

It was a dangerous gambit, and everyone aboard knew it. The skyship was not meant for such heights, and Basel stretched both its mundane frame and its magic to the edges of endurance. If they crossed that line, the ship would break up and plummet to the ground like an arrow-shot swam.

The deck pitched and shuddered as Matteo hurried along, hanging on to the rail for support as he showed the skysailors how to seed the clouds with handfuls of sand from the ballast bags. Bereft of this weight, the skyship rose still higher. Swirling winds caught the ship and shook it like an angry dog. Matteo clutched the rail and leaned far out, gazing at clouds below them. To his relief, they were beginning to roil and darken.

"It's working," Matteo shouted above the rising gale. "We've got to get back down, and fast."

Basel nodded curtly and said something to the bosun, who snatched up a glowing horn, raised it to his lips, and shouted a single word:

"*Brace!*"

As the magical warning resounded over the ship, Matteo dropped to the deck and wrapped his arms around a bolted-down barrel. The skysailors, their feet kept in place by the horn's magic, frantically lowered the sails.

Avariel plummeted though the clouds, spinning slowly as it passed through the grumbling gray mist. Canvas flapped thunderously as the sailors struggled to lower and bind the sails. Their efforts were hampered by churning hail. Bits of ice formed in the seeded clouds, kept airborne by the roiling winds until they were too heavy to hold.

Light broke over the ship as they dropped beneath the cloud bank. The storm began almost immediately. Hail pelted *Avariel* on its way to the battleground beneath, melting as it went. As soon as the droplets touched the ground, Basel's spell took effect.

Armed men, garbed in the pale blue-green of Halruaa's militia, sprang from the ground like mushrooms after a summer rain. Shouts of renewed purpose burst from the beleaguered troops. The dark-clad invaders, suddenly outnumbered and outfought, were pressed back toward their comrades.

Basel nodded with satisfaction. "A small step, but a good one." He reached out to touch the glowing scrying globe mounted near the helm. The light within parted to reveal the caller as King Zalathorm himself.

The face in the globe was almost unrecognizable as the mild man who presided over endless councils. This man had a warrior's fierce eyes and wore battle robes of ancient design, so brightly colored as to be barbaric.

"Well done, Basel! If you've more ideas like that, speak quickly."

"That was not my plan, but Matteo's."

A moment of struggle passed over the king's face and was gone. "Where is the jordain?"

"Aboard *Avariel*, sire." Basel gestured, and Matteo stepped into the king's line of vision.

The king gave a curt nod. "Send him to me. If his conscience requires dispensation from the use of a transportation spell, tell him that he is not the only one who made hard choices for the good of Halruaa. Basel, I release you from your vows of silence."

The king's visage disappeared from the globe. Matteo turned questioning eyes to the conjurer.

Basel was fumbling in his spellbag for the needed components and did not meet the jordain's eyes. "I'd keep you with me if I could, my son, but the king has need of your counsel. Come to me after the battle, and we will talk."

He closed his eyes and began to chant a spell of teleportation. Matteo stepped into the path of a small, crimson
wind tunnel that spilled from Basel's hands. Instantly he
was whisked away into a white, soundless world, but the
wizard's words—and the possibilities they offered—
followed him into the void.

Procopio clenched the rail of *Starsnake,* his personal
skyship and the command ship of the Halarahh militia. He
gazed at the battle below and sought furiously for something that could turn the battle and ensure Halruaa's victory and his own.

It was not going well. Several legions should have
marched north from Halarahh. Apparently the queen's
metal army had kept them too busily employed. Basel
Indoulur's mushroom army had evened the score somewhat, but such warriors never lasted long enough. Too
many warriors had died in the Nath. Three skyships lay in
smoking ruins amid the foothills, and at least a score of wizards had fallen with them. Even so, Procopio's campaign
was considered a victory, and his ship flew nearly at the
head of Zalathorm's fleet.

Like a flight of vengeful dragons, the Halruaan ships
soared toward the invaders. They maintained a careful
wedge formation to keep a path clear for spells hurled by
wizards on every ship. Fireballs and lightning bolts flew
like fireworks at a festival—and fizzled out just as harmlessly. The invaders had come well prepared for conven-
tional battle magic.

Unfortunately for Procopio, he had spent years studying
just such conventions. Something different was needed,
something unexpected!

A high, ringing note soared from a nearby skyship—a
metallic clarion call signaling the climax of a mighty spell.
On and on the music went, until Procopio clapped his hands

to his ears. To the east, two of the highest mountains, still snowcapped even in summer, began to shudder. The ice caps shattered like a goblet broken by a single high, pure note. Snow thundered down the mountains, engulfing the latest wave of Mulhorandi invaders and burying the pass.

But the Mulhorandi were far from finished. Clouds began to rise from the spray of snow and mist, taking the form of a man. A titanic figure etched in blue and white and gray took shape, its feet deep in the snow and its massive fists thrusting high into the sky. In its hand was an ice-colored dagger as long as a ship's mast.

The weapon slashed down, tearing through a skyship's sails and plunging into the deck. The sound of splintering wood disappeared in a sharp explosion as the magical rod that powered the ship snapped free. The skyship listed to port and began a spiraling descent.

"Storm elemental," Procopio muttered, recognizing an obscure Mulhorandi spell.

Other cloud forms began to rise, tapping the power of the avalanche. On one of the giants, Procopio saw a familiar face—that of Ameer Tukephremo, the Mulhorandi wizard who had sold him the cloaking spells in exchange for the promise of Halruaan magic.

A tremor of uncertainty shivered through the diviner. Procopio had not considered the possibility that the Mulhorandi might actually enter the land. That they had certainly done. Was it possible that they might even prevail? That he might not only lose a throne but also his homeland?

For a moment the wizard debated his course. He could confess all that he had done, let the other Halruaan wizards know what secrets and advantages their opponents had. Procopio had studied Mulhorandi magic for many years, and the wizards could use this knowledge against the invaders.

Or he could use it to promote his own cause?

In the end, the choice was simple. Procopio began the

chant of a cloud-form spell, creating a monster that could challenge any two of the Mulhorandi giants. The sight of his own visage on that godlike frame thrilled him, and he laughed aloud as he willed his elemental double into battle against Ameer Tukephremo.

The sky giants met like two opposing storms. Procopio's wielded a sword taller than a mountain pine. Ameer's curving scimitar flashed against the sky like a new moon.

As the diviner watched the battle, he reached for another spell sequence. He summoned a fireball and then a spell that would place it, greatly enlarged, in the hands of his cloudy avatar.

Light from the magic missile flowed through the insubstantial form, lending it the fire and brilliance of sunset clouds. The titanic image of Procopio hurled the fireball, which tore through the Mulhorandi's cloud form like a javelin. The elemental staggered back, already beginning to dissipate, the edges of its body peeling off into wisps of cloud. Procopio followed with a lightning-sword spell. His elemental's blade took on a jagged edge and a livid blue hue. Procopio willed the elemental to slash again and again at the cloudy form of his enemy and partner.

At last the gigantic image of Ameer faded away. Procopio held the spell, and for a long moment his storm elemental stood in the sky like an avenging god, holding aloft the lightning sword as if daring the other cloud forms to pass.

None of the elementals took his challenge. They dissipated as the Mulhorandi wizards retreated, putting their energies to other, less risky spells. Procopio released the cloud form and stooped to pick up the small book that fell from the empty air to land on the deck near his feet. Without sparing it more than a glance, he thrust it into the enchanted bag that would send it to his library. He knew what the book was and what its return meant. This was the spellbook that Ameer Tukephremo had risked so much to win. Its return to Procopio signaled the wizard's death.

Procopio sank onto a bench, exhausted by the casting,

but his face wore a smile. Halruaa would not soon forget the image of a titanic Procopio, standing triumphant against all challengers. He might not have done all the things he had planned, but his triumphs might prove to be enough.

Kiva rose and clenched her fist around the emerald, deeply aware of the hundred souls that cried out for release. The elf woman felt their pain as if from a very great distance. Her own pain had been lost to her long ago, her heart encased in something far harder than green stone.

The necromancer's cold fingers closed around hers, and the magic she had labored over for nearly two hundred years caught them and swept them away.

They flew through the liquid magic as if they had been sucked into a rising waterspout. Up they went, caught in a vastly powerful spell that thrust them across the worlds and through the gate. Like an arrow suddenly loosed from a bow, they hurtled up through the thin and empty air. The gate slammed shut behind them with booming finality.

The sheer power of the spell reverberated through Kiva's bones and exploded into white-hot pain. All light and sound and sensation simply, suddenly, stopped.

Later—Kiva had no way of knowing exactly how much later—the world slowly came back to life. She eased her eyes open, listened as the ringing in her ears faded away. As her senses slowly reawakened, she realized that the ground beneath her was soft and yielding.

She struggled into a sitting position and looked wildly around. Instead of the rocky clearing where the spring had leaked water from the almost-closed gate, she reclined on an enormous carpet that, in turn, undulated gently on a cloud.

The necromancer sat cross-legged, studying her with something approaching respect. "I did not expect so powerful a spell. You have worked hard, little elf, and grown further in Art than I had anticipated. Later, you will show me this spell."

She would deal with "later" when it came. Perhaps by then she would be able to learn what magic had gathered around the gate and thrust them so powerfully out of the watery plane.

"The battle?" Akhlaur prompted.

Gathering herself, she directed him to the point of invasion. They arrived just in time to see the giant cloud forms grappling in the sky, to witness the victory of a storm elemental with close-cropped curls and a face like a hawk's.

"Ingenious," Akhlaur murmured. "I admire a man who studies the magic of his enemies."

The Mulhorandi forces still outnumbered the Halruaan fighters on the ground. A wave of dark-clad infantry swept forward, and a tremble of anticipation ran through the waiting cavalry.

"The Halruaan army will be destroyed," Kiva said.

"Not necessarily. A water elemental might stem the tide—a truly gigantic creature that could crush the cavalry underfoot."

Kiva swept a hand over the barren plain. "There is no water in sight, my lord."

"No?" He smirked. "You have forgotten your lessons, little elf. Man is made of flesh and blood—endlessly mutable flesh and blood. What is the primary component of all this flesh and blood?"

She nodded, suddenly understanding. "Water! Of course!"

Akhlaur lifted his webbed hands and began to chant. A gray cloud grew overhead, grumbling and quivering. There was a sudden explosion, and a torrent of rain rose *up* into the cloud.

The warriors directly under the spell cloud immediately dissolved into desiccated bone. Others fell in withered heaps of bone-wrapped skin. Like the ripples cast by an enormous stone, the wave of devastation spread. The army of the Mulhorandi fell by the hundreds, the thousands. The fluids that gave them life flowed upward into the waiting cloud.

As swiftly as thought, the cloud began to take shape. Legs as thick as a wizard's tower descended and slammed into the ground. Shards of bone flew like grapeshot as dozens of skeletons shattered from the impact. The cloud creature turned and began to stalk through the ranks of the invaders.

The Mulhorandi wizards hurled spell after spell at the water elemental. It trampled them or snatched them up and swallowed them. Drowning men swirled through the fluids of their slain comrades, frantically beating at the magical "skin" of the strange elemental.

"There you have it," Akhlaur said with satisfaction. "The elemental will finish the Mulhorandi, then turn upon the Halruaans. I will be most interested to see what Zalathorm employs against this monster."

Matteo stood at King Zalathorm's side, staring aghast at the gruesome elemental. "Who in the Nine bloody Hells summoned that?"

"No one I know can do such a thing!" the king said. "But at least it is fighting for us."

"At the moment, yes. If the tide turns, so to speak, we must be ready."

Even as he spoke, the elemental turned ponderously around and began to pace toward the Halruaan line.

Matteo swore under his breath. "What is the largest creature you could hope to summon?"

"The largest land creature is a roc," Zalathorm said, naming an eaglelike monster large enough to carry an elephant in its talons, "but the nearest dwells in the deserts of Calimshan."

The jordain thought fast. "Can you do a spell of fire permutation?"

"Of course."

"Contact every wizard in the air and on the ground. On my count have them release the largest fireball spells they know directly at the elemental. You will cast the permutation."

"The spell will transmute *one* fire," the king reminded him.

"One fire," Matteo agreed. "Capture the fireballs as they converge into a single flame."

The king snorted. "You have a high opinion of my powers, and my wizards' aim."

"This requires good timing," Matteo admitted, "and stray fireballs will diminish the size of the elemental."

The king nodded and touched a hand to the Globe of Elders. He gave the order, and Matteo began the count. On his mark, fireballs flashed from every skyship, from flying steeds and from wizards yet on the ground. They soared toward the elemental from every direction. When Matteo dropped his hand, the king shouted a single word.

Airborne fire converged into a flaming roc. A wave of heat swept over the valley as the firebird seized the water elemental in its talons and winged away. Both creatures diminished in a geyser of steam—a land-bound comet that flamed orange and purple against the sunset sky.

Zalathorm let out a triumphant whoop. "The fire roc's taking it away!"

"We haven't enough weapons to waste one so promising. Command the firebird to drop the elemental on the Mulhorandi cavalry."

The king shot a quick, astonished look at Matteo, then nodded. "Tell me when." He began the spell and held it until the jordain gave the signal.

Powerful magic, once unleashed, was not easily recalled. The fiery roc let out a ringing squawk of protest, but it changed the direction of its flight and winged back, captive to the call of Halruaa's wizard-king. The roc dropped the elemental and dissipated into the sky like festival fireworks.

The elemental tumbled end over end, looking from this distance like a man falling out of a skyship. Though the elemental had much diminished in size, it was still nearly the length of a full-grown dragon.

The liquid monster hit and shattered like a broken water skin. Men and horses went down screaming under the impact, and water mingled with blood flowed over the barren plain. The hoofs of panicked equines quickly churned the ground to mud.

Matteo was sickened by the death that had come at his bidding, but he gave his report. "The elemental appears to have taken out nearly a third of the cavalry."

"Send in the foot soldiers," the king commanded. The order was relayed, and the sound of horns winded across the plain. Halruaan troops raced in on both sides, pinning the larger numbers down. Some of the mounted Mulhorandi tried to flee, but their horses floundered in the mud.

Even so, men on foot were at a great disadvantage over mounted fighters. After the first wild rush, the battle began to turn once again to the invaders.

"What is your counsel, jordain?" demanded Zalathorm.

Matteo grimaced. "You are not going to like it."

"I haven't liked any of this," the king retorted, "but if you say it's for the good of Halruaa, I'll believe you. And may Mystra save us all."

Akhlaur applauded, his long, webbed hands rasping together. "Excellently done! I wouldn't have credited Zalathorm with that particular spell. His forces on the ground are not faring so well, though."

"He will lose," Kiva said with satisfaction.

"Not yet, and not here."

A clatter filled the air. Thousands of skeletons created by the necromancer's first attack rose from the ground. An army of skeletons clattered toward their former comrades, inexorable as a plague of locusts. They swept over the struggling cavalry, dragged the Mulhorandi down from their horses, tearing man and beast apart.

"No spell should have but a single purpose," Akhlaur said. "Water from the living, warriors from the dead. There is a certain elegance to this, don't you think?"

Below them, streams of colored light poured from the wizard-king's skyship. They flowed over the battlefield like delicate, glowing ribbons, entwining the undead soldiers and releasing them from their battle lust.

"*Grant them rest and respect*," Akhlaur murmured with scorn. Kiva remembered hearing Zalathorm speak these very words long ago, and her lips twisted in a sneer that matched the necromancer's.

Zalathorm might have released the skeletons, but their work was done. The battered remnants of the Mulhorandi troops turned and fled toward the northern passes, in full retreat.

Halruaan horns sounded the call to attack, but there were few left to join in the pursuit.

The battlefield was carpeted with dead. The living staggered about, too dazed to realize that the battle was won. Groans and shrieks of the wounded and dying filled the air.

Then a single triumphant roar rose from the battlefield, a ringing wordless shout of victory that soared like a phoenix from a fire. Like a spark, it caught and flamed.

Singly and in pairs, standing tall or leaning on comrades for support, the surviving Halruaans raised their fists and their swords and screamed their triumph to the skies.

"So once again, Halruaans have secured their homeland from outside threats," Kiva said. "Once again, the cycle comes around."

The necromancer turned his gaze to her. "You are generous today, little elf. First you bring me the key to my freedom, then you present me with this fine entertainment, and now you offer a puzzle?"

"It is not a puzzle to those who watch the turning wheel of history. Halruaa has often faced dangers from without. Strong leaders rise to face them. Thus did Zalathorm rise to power, and many years has he held the throne."

Akhlaur nodded, beginning to understand. "Other wizards performed well today. The one who called the storm elemental seems rather impressive."

"Don't be too impressed," Kiva retorted. "That one is no fox, but a rogue hen raiding its own hen house. He knew of the coming Mulhorandi attack, and of shields that kept other Halruaan wizards from seeing the troops massing on their border."

"So he perceived this coming threat, where Zalathorm did not. A clever ploy!"

The elf grimaced. "It could have done even better. I had hoped this battle would discredit Zalathorm more thoroughly. It might have, had you not intervened on his behalf, but most Halruaans will believe that the king summoned the water elemental as well as the fire roc. The necromancers in his court will be quick to take credit for the skeletal army. It will be difficult to displace so powerful a hero."

"You fail to see the salient point."

"Indeed, I do! I intended to weaken Zalathorm, giving ambitious wizards enough hope of replacing him to set them upon each other! I planned to light a spark that would blaze into another wizardwar!"

"So you have. Think, little elf, and tell me the most important point."

After a moment, Kiva nodded slowly. "Despite what anyone else might think, Zalathorm knows he did not cast that spell."

"Well done. Knowing Zalathorm as you and I do, what do you suppose he will do next?"

The elf's eyes caught flame. "He will not rest until he

knows who *did* cast it. Once he knows, he will come after you!"

Akhlaur gazed out over the carnage. "This was a most diverting entertainment, little elf, but I think you and I can arrange a better one."

CHAPTER TWENTY-FOUR

The celebration began the day after the battle. Music filled the city, and proud displays of magic took place on every corner. When night fell, fireworks exploded overhead, many of them forming into the silhouette of a giant bird. The image of the fiery roc was everywhere—embroidered on banners, tattooed on the arms of warriors, in beds of flame-colored flowers that appeared overnight. Zalathorm was a hero, and the firebird the proud new symbol of the wizard-king's might.

Yet whispers against the king swept quietly through the land, along with word of the queen's arrest and coming trial. Many had died fighting her clockwork creatures. Questions passed from mouth to mouth about how the king could have overlooked this danger in his very palace. For that matter, people then asked, how could the king fail to foresee the Mulhorandi invaders?

Despite these doubts, all Halarahh gathered that night in the vast public square to honor their heroes. High among them stood Procopio Septus, who had sent the Crinti into retreat, and beat back the cloud avatars of the Mulhorandi. This was not a Halruaan spell, and the people of Halarahh were pleased and proud that their lord mayor was vigilant enough to learn the magic of their enemies.

When it was Procopio's turn to come before

the king, Zalathorm enumerated the wizard's accomplishments and asked what reward he desired. Procopio spoke clearly, his voice soaring through the enhancement spells that carried the ceremony throughout the city. "I ask only that I might continue to serve the land as a master of divination, my king, as you yourself have done these many long years."

The people erupted into cheers and huzzahs. Farther down the line of battle heroes, Basel Indoulur observed this with a faint, guarded smile, and Matteo with a face carefully schooled to reveal nothing. On the surface of things, the lord mayor's request was admirably humble, but the challenge was not deeply buried.

"So the seed is planted," Basel murmured. "Did you by chance mark the seeming familiarity between Procopio's storm elemental and his windy opponent?"

"It occurred to me that they were acquainted," Matteo responded. "In general, Lord Procopio was exceedingly well prepared. He studied the battle tactics of the Crinti, and he has an astonishing grasp of Mulhorandi magic."

"Yes, I noticed that as well," Basel said. "He bears watching. Halruaa borders have been secured, but I suspect that Halruaa has more to fear from her own wizards."

The applause for Procopio finally died, and the king's herald called the next name. When Basel's turn came, he inclined his head toward Matteo. "You see my request before you, sire. I petition for the jordain's service."

King Zalathorm's gaze shifted from the wizard to Matteo and then back. "I am afraid I cannot grant that request, old friend. But I will found a school for conjuration in your home city, as you have long requested."

Matteo's throat tightened. Did the king truly value straight and honest speech, or did he have in mind some sort of reprisal for Matteo's part against the queen's arrest?

The king regarded Matteo somberly. "And you, jordain. Will you enter my service, as reward for your part in this battle?"

"It is not quite the punishment I expected, sire," he said softly, speaking below the reach of the enhancement spells, "but neither is it my idea of a reward."

Zalathorm's lips twitched in an ironic little smile. "Well, then, you understand the task ahead far better than most." Lifting his voice, he proclaimed, "So shall it be. The jordain Matteo shall be known as the king's counselor."

He gestured to the herald, signaling the next interview. Matteo and Basel bowed and walked from the dais.

The conjurer sent Matteo a rueful smile. "The king will have need of good counsel in the days to come. I expect you will be quite busy."

"What of you, my lord?"

Basel took a deep breath and let it out on a sigh. "I will study the lore of the Unseelie folk. If there is a way to bring Tzigone out of that place, I will find it."

A small flicker of hope flared in Matteo's heart. "You will call me if I can do anything to help?"

"You will be the first to know. Expect to hear from me soon, for there are things between us that must be said. Mystra's blessing upon you, my son."

This address was often used between a man of Basel's years and one of Matteo's. Perhaps it meant nothing. Perhaps everything. It was one more thing that a jordain could not know.

"Mystra's blessing," he echoed softly.

After the festivities were over, Matteo went to his new chambers in the king's quarter. To his surprise, Zalathorm awaited him, sprawled wearily in one of the chairs that Cassia, Matteo's predecessor, had scattered cozily about the room.

"I have need of your counsel, jordain," the king said, his voice faint and scratchy from overuse.

Matteo nodded, waiting for him to continue.

"Before we discuss this matter, a question. Near battle's end, before the skeletons arose, you were about to give me advice that you thought I would not like to hear."

"There is no need for it now," Matteo said, frowning. "For that matter, there was no need for it then! You saw what was needed and took action without waiting for my counsel. It is grim work to raise skeleton warriors, and all Halruaa is grateful that you took this task upon yourself."

"Did you observe me cast that spell?"

The jordain hesitated. "No, but none of your necromancers have come forth to take credit for it, so I assume it was a prepared spell, unleashed from some magical device."

Zalathorm did not offer comment on this observation. "This celebration will last a tenday. After that, the queen will come to trial. If she is condemned, she will be executed under the light of a gibbous moon. You have twenty days to prove her innocence."

With great difficulty, Matteo kept his face impassive. "Forgive me my presumption, sire, but I know what it is to lose a loved one. The two best friends I ever knew are lost to me, and I cannot yet accept the reality of it."

"What would you do to save those friends?"

Matteo envisioned the veil between the worlds, and the glowing eyes of the dark fairies beyond. "If I could, I would follow them through hell."

"I thought as much. That is why I give you a seemingly impossible task."

He blew out a long breath. "We heard Kiva commend the queen for creating a clockwork army. What could negate this?"

"There are other circumstances, surely, that will sway the council's decision."

"I will not color the facts to save the queen," Matteo said quietly.

The king nodded as if he had expected this. "You hold the good of Halruaa foremost in your heart. That is why I require your services. Nonetheless, keep in mind that even an honest man can convince himself of a dubious truth, and the most zealous of paladins may learn to his horror that his holy end does not justify his every bloody mean."

"I will remember this, sire. In all candor, however, I do not understand your point."

Zalathorm rose and looked deep into the young jordain's eyes. "I have learned many things since the battle's end. I cannot yet tell you how this knowledge came to me. This much I can say: Queen Beatrix was once known as Keturah, the woman your friend Tzigone sought so desperately. No one alive knows this but me, not even the queen herself. So tell me now, jordain, what will you do now?"

The ground shifted under Matteo's feet, and his head hummed like a swarm of captive bees. He swallowed hard. "The same, sire."

"And if I tell you that Keturah could open that door for you, so that you could march into hell after your friend? Would you be tempted to save them both at any cost, or would you cling to truth even then?"

"Even then," he said in an anguished whisper.

The king nodded slowly. "Well, perhaps you have a chance at success. You have twenty days."

Zalathorm turned and strode swiftly away, no longer able to meet the young man's burning eyes. He understood all too well the pain written there.

Keturah's daughter. He closed his eyes and brought to mind the image of the girl with the shorn brown locks and impish grin whom he had seen at Basel Indoulur's side. It was she who had brought the magic mouth device into the queen's workroom, thus getting the evidence that would condemn her own mother for treason. Would she have done this, had she known? Or would she cling to principle as firmly as did Matteo?

With a sigh, Zalathorm made his way down a hidden stairwell into the deepest and most secret part of the palace. As he walked, he cast a powerful magical disguise over himself. He never approached this hidden chamber without this disguise, though it had been many years since he'd worn this face outside the palace. The lines of necromancers who stood like sentries outside the door knew him only by his assumed face and nodded to him as he passed.

Zalathorm shut and warded the door, then turned to the enormous gem that floated precisely in the center of the room. It was vaguely star-shaped, redder than garnet, with hundreds of smooth, glittering sides. Light pulsed within its heart.

The king bowed his head before the sentient gem, more in apology than supplication, and whispered, "The Heart of Halruaa seeks your counsel."

THREE OF THE MOST POPULAR
FORGOTTEN REALMS
AUTHORS TELL THE STORY
OF FAERÛN'S GREATEST KINGDOM
—AND ITS GREATEST KING.

The Cormyr Saga

CORMYR: A NOVEL
Ed Greenwood & Jeff Grubb
A plot to poison King Azoun IV brings the kingdom to
the brink of disaster.

BEYOND THE HIGH ROAD
Troy Denning
With the threat from within at an end, Cormyr faces an even
greater threat from the barbaric Stonelands, and a princess
begins to understand what it means to rule a kingdom.

DEATH OF THE DRAGON
Ed Greenwood & Troy Denning
Plague, madness, and war sweep through Cormyr and the people
look to their king for salvation. Only the mighty Azoun has any
chance to defeat the horror that will change Cormyr forever.